Praise for

THE QUEEN OF TUESDAY

"An impossibly daring premise for a novel—an act of almost Lucy-level audaciousness . . . Exceptionally well told . . . [Darin] Strauss conjures up those heady days . . . with such vibrancy that it's impossible not to hope that everything might work out after all. . . . Brilliant."
—RON CHARLES, *The Washington Post*

"[A] delight . . . You will enjoy Strauss's fictionalized life of the comedian who was calling her own shots at a time when women were expected to fade into the background. . . . This book makes you hope."
—ELISABETH EGAN, *The New York Times Book Review*

"I love this book. . . . It's a brilliant evocation of a magical time and place, and it's really fun and smart."
—BILL GOLDSTEIN, WNBC

"As in Strauss's other books, the movement here is perpetual and multi-directional; it never stops. . . . A close comparison would be to certain American filmmakers like Altman, Cassavetes, or the Safdies—always churning, developing. . . . The author asserts himself, here as elsewhere in his books, through his rigorously playful approach to language. . . . [*The Queen of Tuesday*] reads like a dream painted in bold and fearsome strokes."
—*The Boston Globe*

"'Half memoir and half make-believe,' this boisterous novel relates an imagined affair between Lucille Ball . . . and the author's grandfather. . . . The novel is a touching account of the sacrifices that Lucille makes to preserve her 'most genuine' relationship: the one 'between her and the public.'"
—*The New Yorker*

"Timeless . . . Strauss's ingenious and bittersweet fourth novel, *The Queen of Tuesday*, . . . seems to genuinely lament a love affair that never happened. It'd be a perfect '50s screen romance. But Strauss knows what time we're living in."
—*Los Angeles Times*

"Weaving fiction with family memoir, Strauss delivers a rollicking read that touches on Long Island's 1950s suburb-boom, the birth of the modern television era and a reassessment of his family's legends."
—*Newsday*

"*The Queen of Tuesday* . . . succeeds because of how seamlessly Strauss blends the familiar with the new. You'll believe the narrative about Lucille Ball even as the story ventures into flights of fancy."
—*Los Angeles Daily News*

"No one could write a better book. . . . If Darin Strauss isn't the best contemporary American novelist, he's near the top."

—*New Pop Lit*

"Engaging . . . You will enjoy this. . . . What's not to love?"

—*Bookreporter*

"Anything Darin Strauss writes is magic. I have been his fan since the beginning of time, and I will be his fan until the sun explodes."

—ELIZABETH GILBERT, author of *Eat, Pray, Love*

"With *The Queen of Tuesday,* Darin Strauss rescues history's outtakes to edit his own gorgeous Technicolor take on America in the middle of the twentieth century. . . . Bold, brassy, and bighearted!"

—COLSON WHITEHEAD, author of *The Underground Railroad*

"A great read!"

—JENNY OFFILL, author of *Weather*

"*The Queen of Tuesday* is a beautiful, cinematic story. . . . In a gorgeous imagined history of a not-long-ago world, the novelist Strauss allows us to remember our deeply held wishes to invent our lives and memories for our privately held loves. As in *The Great Gatsby,* Strauss reminds us here that ghosts unseen who remain deeply felt renew our hearts' most passionate yearnings and ambitions."

—MIN JIN LEE, author of *Pachinko*

"A home run!"

—GARY SHTEYNGART, author of *Lake Success*

"I can't wait for this one. I'm a big fan."

—JUDD APATOW

"Darin Strauss has resurrected a lost world—the grand movie that never aired, the truncated epic of what might have been between Lucille Ball and his grandfather. Part elegy, part mystery, part speculative memoir, here is a love story unlike any you've read before—spiked with Hollywood scandal and the secrets families keep across generations. Strauss is a beautiful and funny and piercing writer, and this book is a gift."

—KAREN RUSSELL, author of *Orange World and Other Stories*

"Wonderful!"

—ANDREW SEAN GREER, author of *Less*

By Darin Strauss

NOVELS
The Queen of Tuesday
More Than It Hurts You
The Real McCoy
Chang & Eng

MEMOIR
Half a Life

GRAPHIC NOVEL (WITH ADAM DALVA)
Olivia Twist: Honor Among Thieves

COMIC BOOK SERIES (WITH ADAM DALVA)
Olivia Twist

THE QUEEN *of* TUESDAY

THE
QUEEN
— of —
TUESDAY

A Novel

DARIN STRAUSS

RANDOM HOUSE
NEW YORK

2021 Random House Trade Paperback Edition

Published in the United States by Random House, an imprint and division of Penguin Random House LLC, New York.

RANDOM HOUSE and the HOUSE colophon are registered trademarks of Penguin Random House LLC.

Originally published in hardcover in the United States by Random House, an imprint and division of Penguin Random House LLC, in 2020.

LIBRARY OF CONGRESS CATALOGING-IN-PUBLICATION DATA
Names: Strauss, Darin, author.
Title: The queen of Tuesday : a novel / Darin Strauss.
Description: New York, NY : Random House, [2020]
Identifiers: LCCN 2020012804 (print) | LCCN 2020012805 (ebook) |
ISBN 9780812982572 (trade paperback : acid-free paper) |
ISBN 9780679643852 (ebook)
Subjects: LCSH: Ball, Lucille, 1911–1989—Fiction. |
GSAFD: Biographical fiction.
Classification: LCC PS3569.T692245 Q44 2020 (print) |
LCC PS3569.T692245 (ebook) | DDC 813/.54—dc23
LC record available at https://lccn.loc.gov/2020012804
LC ebook record available at https://lccn.loc.gov/2020012805

Printed in the United States of America on acid-free paper

randomhousebooks.com

2 4 6 8 9 7 5 3 1

Illustrations by Taufik Ramadhan/iStock

For Susan Kamil

Oh, the movie never ends. It goes on and on and on and on.
—JOURNEY, "DON'T STOP BELIEVIN'"

NIGHTFALL, THE BEACH AT CONEY ISLAND

A CLOUD LIFTS, AND look—here's Manhattan, tiara-bright and brash, American initiative written in glitter. It's 1949. Hundreds of cars are driving from the city to the sea. Cadillacs and Packards and wood-bodied Fords. Snaking along Stillwell Ave, they stretch a tail for miles under a Warner Bros. sky.

People are coming in the tangerine twilight to view a collapse.

Hey, that's your favorite celebrity over there. On the boardwalk, her white shoes scuffed black with sand. (If she's not famous now, just wait.) She's striding—*confidenting*—right into this party. And into the elation of this party. Banners promise or warn A NIGHT YOU'LL REMEMBER. Walking beside the actress, her husband raises his fist. She isn't really sure he's joking.

Earlier, she'd been angry enough to throw a glass; he'd smashed her compact. Your typical knock-down-drag-out. Her husband's not quite famous yet, either.

And the actress certainly will remember this night. There's a boy in suede gloves who's botching it, failing to reach her. The gloves are lemon-colored: it's a bright-colored time. Tonight, the actress will drop into trouble and watch the sparks in their upward flight. And her husband's fists will be used in earnest.

For now, the husband mopes. "It's no good you keep insulting me," he says, his accent having its way with the words. "I have to know this 'torch' expression. Can you explain 'carry a torch'?"

She says, "Just a habit men have of walking around on fire." You recognize her—a woman who's learned the score. "Burning yourself, getting singed, like that."

Another banner: A PARTY FOR THE AGES—*Elizabeth Trump & Son.*

The actress feels chilly. That's Coney Island in April for you. She's also frustratingly unseen. The actress has bumped through life knowing what it is to be ignored, even by quote loved ones. At tonight's party, she wants to be noticed by the husband she loves. But also, especially, by men she doesn't.

First she has to push her way to the boldface names at the water. It surprises her, a little, how the confident can darken a big, open beach.

Partygoers have thronged to the tide line and the first pleats of brown sand. It's like a religious ceremony where the theologics have been erased. These people are here to worship themselves. That's only natural. Americans in this little breather from history stand pretty much alone on a cindered map. Every house needs a Westinghouse. The ad style is peppy, with pep and sincerity intertwined. Relax in casual slax. Make a date with Rocket 8. Across the country: fresh purchases and attitudes, fresh beliefs. Plus, it's been sunny all year and the perfect song is always playing, at just the right volume.

The actress and her husband start down the sand.

In this moment, there is no city but New York City. The long Atlantic keeps pulse at the shore here. It's glamorous. The air's strung with laughs and the rattle of sequins, popping flashbulbs. But the actress has a problem now. Her last-chance break is *simply not happening*.

She doesn't consider taking her husband's hand. Nor has he offered it. "On important nights, you louse things up," he says. "Many times I just do not get you."

"Hey, that's *my* line. You always make me come get you."

She—or the woman she has trained herself to be—is a bit excessive when not the center of attention. The high, provoking brows; bright hair pinned and lifted off the neck.

"Don't snap your cap, sweetie," the actress continues. "When I accuse you for real, you'll know."

The kid wearing lemon-suede gloves has to run over and tell the actress about the destruction that's coming. It's his actual job tonight. But will the kid reach her? His path across the boardwalk is choked by tuxedoed waiters and linen tabletops. The actress even from this distance is a woman of sedan curves, fantastic. Legs he'd want to die between. The kid's driven by intensities he had no idea were in him.

"Good luck," the actress tells her husband. "So remember, the plan is— Hey, wait a second."

The husband piles ahead; he pretends not to hear. All around, partygoing women contemplate the beach, shoes in hand. And the actress is alone.

This is a party with a political purpose. As is the custom at such parties—the shifts of bigwigs and schemes—the biggest and most important have together made their own scrum. The actress watches her husband jostle toward these fancy people, and she—

She feels somebody's stare. On her mouth, neckline, her throat. She moves a protective hand over the dimple in her collarbone. And keeps it there. Fingers on two hard dots.

It's the kid with the lemon-suede gloves: "Miss Puente!" He comes straight up. "Martha Puente, right?"

She stops walking.

"You know, the world's never seen a destruction party before, miss." The kid gleams with the importance of any teen given a duty. He recites his statement: "Ready, Martha—may I call you Martha?— er, ready to destroy the world?"

The kid, and with good reason, keeps calling her Martha Puente. Martha Puente is not her name.

She knows what's what tonight. The man hosting this party wants to get something obliterated. The actress is here to get something made.

She isn't Martha Puente, any more than she's Diane Belmont or

Montana Hearn. With those names, she'd been trying to catch something she'd almost found.

The kid's saying, "I mean, destroy metaphorically. It's gonna be a hoot. Because . . ."

What a time to be left alone here. She's just schlepped back from Hollywood. Nightmarish trip! Los Angeles: a shuffle of faces and studio commands. Instructions about eyebrows, diction, about posture. Also about not falling for nice ethnics. She had been run through a showbiz machine that existed, far as she could tell, to conventionalize the neck length of swans for better sale to a nation of ducklings. (She'd sat through studio reprimands with parted lips and just listened.) But MGM terminated her contract last month. She'd failed as a movie star.

"Miss *Puente*?" The kid's scratching at a puberty cluster on his cheek.

The actress gives her smile of special elegance anyway. (Her beauty can still draw a gasp when she smiles, when she pouts.) But after twenty bit-part years, although still kind of young, she's also probably washed up.

Another bad break: It looks as if her husband is holding back to chat with Nanette Fabray, of all people. Goddamn him. Nanette Fa-bare-ass?! Now?

But hang on a sec.

Instead of quitting and slinking back upstate—where the cold Chautauqua always springs tears from her face—after silently admitting, It's over, I'll never achieve, and also my husband's talking to a harlot *not ten yards from me,* instead she surprises herself.

"A hoot?" she says. She often surprises herself. "Kid, parties are for single women and cheating men. When you die, you'll regret the things you did when you could've been home relaxing. Nice gloves. The name's *not* Martha Puente."

And her brazen right eyebrow rises just a little.

"The name," she says on this April night two years, six months, and four days before her triumph, "is Lucille Ball."

· · ·

MAYBE IT'S JUST an innocent little chat there across the beach with Lucille's husband and Nanette Fabray?

Looking over, she doesn't notice that the kid with the gloves's face has gone red. She'd done a few wartime "Martha Puente" spreads for *Yank* magazine, the Army publication. (The G.I.s had had fun with the centerfold, with the word *Yank* itself, General Ike's hairy-palms-and-blindness campaign.) The kid's standing here smitten, having kept that photo under his mattress all through junior high.

He doesn't know what to do. Say something to her.

"It was only that . . ." He hunts around his brain for a suave line. "It was I could see right off you're uh . . ." (Being an adolescent means running this kind of vain scavenger hunt every day.) "I guess I don't know what you mean. You're *not* Martha Puente?"

Lucille brings her hand to his shoulder.

"Kid, I'm in show business." She smiles right at him. "I don't mean a thing."

And he swallows, closing his eyes. He's trying to make the moment a keepsake, like a photo, for later use.

But Lucille barely registers the kid now as he gives her a foggy little—

That's no innocent little chat with Desi and Nanette Fabray. Male interest has made Fabray's face beautiful. The eyes, the color on her cheeks. That is *not* just a chat.

—as the kid gives her a foggy little smile.

Maybe the world wants Lucille to fight. Or maybe it's just the torch of her hair. The blunt call to arms of redheads. She appears to steady herself against a lifeguard's chair. No one so glamorous will ever die, the kid thinks. (A woman of charisma makes you content with being ignored, so long as you stand near her.)

"Well," she says. "Off to rescue my husband."

"Okay, oh," the kid says.

But like so many people, he finds himself inclining toward Lucille Ball. "Now, of course, Miss . . ." Already he is touching up the photo in his memory, taking her hand from his shoulder and placing it on his cheek, emending general kindness into personal affection.

Anyway, she is gone. "Let me get you a brick!" he calls after her. Too late.

A jazz orchestra is meanwhile corrupting the sandy night a little. The lyrics—*You may see a stranger*—are very nearly articulated by the swooning horns.

NANETTE FABRAY'S BIG eyes look to steal from each moment whatever it holds. This is why men have made her a star.

Lucille's crossing the beach toward her, high heels stabbing tiny sand holes. Nanette cries, "The darling Mrs. Arnaz!"—too late by a second. In her Juilliard voice: "Come over, Luce, don't high-hat us!"

Lucille huffs right to her husband and her nemesis (*one* of her nemeses). She has always had to carry the conjugal water, and that has made her strong.

Nanette, she thinks: Stupid bitch.

Desi does not wear a hat; even minor celebrities can sail above fashion. His scalp blazes at the part of his hair. (Lucille a half minute ago had caught the easy smile that Desi flashed Nanette.)

"Hi de ho," Lucille says, sounding distinctly unmiffed. Maybe easy smiles don't mean anything.

Nanette says, "Desi and I are talking about your TV plan, Lucille, which sounds to me like the absolute darb."

Easy smiles are not the rhythm of years. Easy smiles are nothing compared to the abiding beat of a shared life. (Lucille had missed it, but Desi, just before flashing Nanette his smile, had stroked Nanette's hand with his thumb.)

And the TV plan is a thing he is supposed to have kept secret.

"Truth is," Nanette's saying, "I've been so *gone* lately about my Tony nomination. There's been nothing else."

"Lucille," Desi says, reaching for his wife, "come here, darling." And it's this warmth of possession that makes her finally despise him.

"Ah," Lucille says. "The big Tony nom. I thought they gave that award for *theater*?" Smiling, smiling. The tip of the blade is in the intonation.

"Oh, you dizzy Dora." Nanette laughs, an uncomplicated woman. "Why, it *is* theater! The Tony? Why, that's the award I've always . . ." She stops herself.

Lucille's smile could kill daisies.

"Lucille and I, uh"—Desi jumps in—"we are only in New York for the weekend. Isn't that right, Lucille?"

"How loveable you are when you consult me, Dez." She's fists on hips now. "You should do it more."

Is Lucille being mean? Hard for Nanette to say. There is that optimistic color to Lucille's hair, her mouth, to her ten lighter-flame fingernails.

"Was that a *slight*, Lucille?" A dying hopeful note in Nanette's voice. "A crack about my Tony nomination?"

"Slight? Not at all." Lucille smiles. "I meant it to be substantial."

Nanette blinks and blinks like an offended Tinker Bell. And Desi rubs his forehead. "Now, Lucille."

Sqwauuhweee!—a surprising noise. Some beach birds are flying whoosh over the sand. *Sqwauuhweee,* wheeling around. The birds with their faces of beaked apathy kite on the wind. Gliding over this era as any other. But one of them hesitates in the sea breeze; it idles overhead like a pause in Lucille's conversation.

Nanette slaps Lucille in the face. *Smack!* Rudeness is being the first person to succumb to what you really want to do. And the birds circle overhead in a shape that expands and contracts, like a breathing constellation. A second blow comes. *Smack!*

Desi does not budge.

Lucille watches him watch Nanette move off, galumphing across the sand in her heels. (Only men would have planned a formal gala on a beach.)

Desi asks: "*Why,* Lucille?"

I can't dance, Lucille thinks, her hand to the fizz of her reddening cheek. I can't dance and I can't sing. I can *talk.* That's why.

Desi's saying: "Jesus."

"Don't bring religion into it, sweetheart," she says. "Gets you close to some famous commandments."

But she will always love her husband, and hate him, and right now she thinks, Give me back what you took from me. Give me all that you took from me.

TEN YEARS BEFORE, the press had named Lucille "Queen of B Movies." They had seized Fay Wray's crown of invisible plastic and set it on Lucille's almost-famous hair. She can name the coronation date: January 23, 1939. It took *Daily Variety* two Page 7 sentences to end Wray's brief epoch. *Ball, the contract player on Phil Baker's* Gulf Headliner, *also helmed nine low-budget program melodramas last year, including RKO's* Five Came Back. *Let's call her the new Queen of . . .* Lucille had not wanted the throne—it was shoddy, its legs were shit—yet recently, the world's unseen topplers had come to topple her. She had somehow believed they would never come to favor another woman. The new queen was Marie Windsor (*I Love My Wife But!*). So what comes after B royalty, after a B coup? Nothing, usually; or radio.

At the time, she'd still had a program called *My Madcap Bride,* CBS 880 on your AM dial. Lucille played a character named Montana Hearn. The show had bumped along all season, but they canceled that, too. And now, despite her cheek that still feels hot; despite Marie Windsor, Nanette Fabray, and the gloved kid who did not know Lucille's real name; despite her pride, her sore feet, her old wounds and many trials; despite the hundred-to-one of her mission here and even her husband's many infidelities—despite her fisted hands—Lucille's spirit rises a little on some sweet, get-started smell in the Coney wind.

She is an optimist. This is a party about buildings going up and buildings coming down. So she turns to look at the Manhattan sky-line, that dapper eyeful. It seems, blazoning up in the distance, so much more sumptuous than the New York she walked through, that hive of yells, trolleys, odors, soup kitchens, car horns, dog mess, sirens, taxis, people people people.

"Do you know *why* I was talking to her?" Desi's saying. His hand travels, slowly, down his face. "To Nanette Fabray?"

"That nice, juicy pair of Tony nominations she has flopping out her dress?"

Desi sighs. Without resentment, he reminds his wife that Nanette Fabray—and, come on, sweetie, why would you forget this—Nanette Fabray is married to Dave Tebet.

"I want to believe this plan is the best plan, Lucille," Desi says. Like everyone who has lost or nearly grabbed real success, Desi Arnaz considers himself wronged by the world.

(Dave Tebet is a big shot at NBC.)

"It is," she's saying, reaching for a smoke. "It is the best plan."

"You make it cost so much to plan with you."

She understands the caliber of her siege artillery. It is not in her nature to silence her own guns. But she does.

"Sorry," she says through the smoke of her smoke.

"Fine," Desi says. His anger just goes.

He is five-nine, seven years younger than Lucille, and what you notice is the bullish sensuality. She touches his face.

"It's the best plan, all right," she says. "'Cause it's the only plan either of us could think up."

When he smiles, she just loves him. Lucille does not have the stage yet to show viewers how it's done. To show that a couple is a performance. That you can have a quick jump from fighting to part-ners. They will make their ideas of marriage into the universal idea of marriage. As long as Desi doesn't stop to talk to a new woman.

"Here's to long shots," Desi's saying, on the move once more. "I'm going to find some big and scary wigs and do the plan."

"Wait," she says. "*Wait.*"

She wants to remind him to find her buddy Gale Gordon,

whom she has cast in the plan's supporting role. (Gordon, an actor, is supposed to walk by at the right moment and nonchalantly mention what a million-dollar idea Desi has.)

But Desi's off again. Holding back, Lucille raises a bare shoulder to her own cheek and feels the echo of the slap. Just for a moment, with nobody looking, she relaxes from the work of hiding panic and shame.

THE BIRDS ABOVE Ocean Beach see the drum-shaped premiere lights slide glamour beams along the clouds. The birds see—with a clapped paper bag sound of wings passing—a giant steel-and-glass pavilion, all a-sparkle. The birds see Ziegfeld girls, restaurateurs, a late-arriving Broadway impresario exiting his pleasure sedan. That wind picks up, goosebumping eight hundred arms. The birds see pinups, radio luminaries, heartthrob clarinetists. They see the covetous attractive charmers who take root in the soil around celebrities. (These are the career fawners—the money-takers.) They see Bing Crosby in the flesh. And Ted Mack. And Mary Martin holding Vic Damone's thick arm. They see clothes as a standard and elegant repression. They see the boardwalk as a splinter that pokes the beach in the eye.

The steel-and-glass pavilion is five acres wide and will remain so for the next hour.

"**FOR YOU, MISS BALL.**" It's the kid with the gloves. Back again and carrying two red bricks—holding one out for her. "Ready?"

Lucille's gaze takes a bounce over the sand. She's looking for Desi over by the white-linen tables that mark the limit of the party. It's where the night's top dogs have gathered.

"May I, um, let you in on a secret, Miss Ball?" the kid says.

There's Desi—stopped at the shoreline to look at the Ferris wheel. The red brick feels surprisingly heavy. The Ferris wheel is a giant iron dandelion with its fluff blown away.

"Jesus, Dez," she whispers. "Do *some*thing."

"It's, um, almost time, Miss Ball."

Desi's drawn back from the three powerful men who, drinks in hand, appear to be talking all at once. There's gray, dapper Frank Stanton, president of CBS, and Columbia Records' Edward Wallerstein. And Fred Christ Trump, the thin, balding real estate man. It's Trump's party, his beachfront, his night. All three impose their status on the landscape, their comfort. It is Stanton whom Desi will have to convince. The vibe the men give: decorated battleships, cheered at some victory anchorage, accepting ticker tape after a lifetime of service. And then there's Dez.

"Thanks, kid," Lucille says, acknowledging the brick at last.

Yesterday her manager had warned: Don't fool yourself, no chance in hell the networks play ball, better not to bother. And now, here she is, slapped, feeling marked, holding a brick for some reason.

But no one became great listening to her manager's warnings.

Right before Lucille decides to go to Desi, he strides off again. He's rejoining Nanette Fabray, who's standing alone; maybe this was a planned rendezvous.

"Would you get a load of that," Lucille says.

The kid is nervous, but he focuses on Lucille to make up for it. *She* is nervous. Her cigarette is out but still clenched between her fingers, its gray pine cone of dead tobacco. (The kid's name, not that she asked, is Philip.) He works to depatsy his presentation. Throwing back his shoulders, he sees a rescue coming.

He asks: "Want to meet my brother?" He does not add: "Because if *I*'m too young to make it with you, I'd like to know someone who does."

Lucille looks at him. No. She wants that not even a little.

"Well, kid," she says. "What kind of gloves does *he* have?" And her peripheral vision itches, right as the brother comes up. "Oh," she says.

It's not that Lucille is anti-Semitic. (1949 is not long after those Auschwitz photos; copping to anti-Semitism is about as big a setback as having a Jewish surname.) Even so, Lucille has told herself she is not attracted to Jews. Or hasn't been since Pandro Berman and Mack Gray—big men in the way she likes those who happen to be Jewish. But now she has seen the brother. And her mouth peeps open—a red gum–like pop from her lipstick.

"Oh," she says again.

The kid's brother Isidore—Izzy to his crowd, now eating a deviled egg—approaches with a blip in his stride. This gives his large body a haphazard charm.

"Well, look at this, Phil," the brother says, wiping his hands on his lapels. "You made a friend."

Maybe he's a studio executive I don't know about, Lucille hopes, fearful that he'll see the red in her cheek.

"I've seen you before," Isidore says. "But not in real life, I'm guessing." Lucille transfers the brick from one palm to another, feels the grainy weight. She shakes Isidore's hand the way a man would.

"What's real life?" she says.

"Whatever this isn't."

He seems preoccupied, as if he's also listening to a radio in a room down the hall. As she talks, Isidore looks not at her eyes but at her mouth. (The kid Phil has been thrown from the saddle of this conversation. He is as far away now as someone can be while standing here.)

She turns to hide the slapwarm cheek. "So, besides hard labor on ladies' ankles, what is this party?" She has to tilt her head back to meet his eyes.

"I'll show you a secret," Isidore says.

He's got Johnny Weissmuller shoulders, a Cary Grant chin. Wearing his hat pulled low, he's good to look at—imperfectly good. He has known stress; it's fanned in arrows across his brow. (Most of the men she knows look wrinkled only when you see their newspaper spreads crushed and tossed in the trash.)

"Oh, you've got a secret, have you?" she says.

Is she flirting? She doesn't know. This man will not be pushed over. Suddenly, Isidore is leading her to the pavilion, Coney Island's giant steel-and-glass centerpiece. Philip has been abandoned, left to his gloves and idolatry. "Come," Isidore tells her. Meanwhile, her fingers nibble at his sleeve—the only way for her to keep pace. He's going fast, and she's following.

"Come."

"STOP!"—LUCILLE WILL SAY. "Not tonight, Dez!"

Here is what will happen in about twenty minutes. Lucille will step between her husband and Isidore. "Stop!" she will cry. It will be easy to see big public scenes in Desi's attitude, to see fisticuffs; his eyes open insanely—the whites visible above and below. Fighting words will come.

"I'll chin you right now!" Desi will say.

But before this, the entire party knows that something else is about to happen.

SOMETHING IS ABOUT to happen. The shimmery Pavilion of Fun, with its thousand moon-holding windows, looks huge and dignified, even on pegs. People crunch by. Guests, waiters and captains, the crowd hustling closer, climbing stairs from the beach. It's almost time. The pavilion, like a royal at the guillotine, awaits the blade.

This is why the press has come, and politicians, celebrities, the supermen of city real estate and industry. To witness a New York relic meet its theatrical end.

And they've come also to assert their place, to shine their status. "See that, Lucille?" Isidore says.

When Fred Trump bought this entire area in one swoop, he knew everyone would *tsk-tsk*. He planned the eradication of a landmark. He also knew he could undercut the scandal by sweeping people up in a fantasy. No one knew they wanted to demolish a building until the doing it revealed the desire. (Watch City Hall get torched? *Nah*. Light the fuse yourself? *Let's make an evening of it!*) People love to get swept up. Like all myth-makers, Fred Trump takes the thing at hand and spins a fairy tale. And so: all these bricks. And a crystal palace that smacks of bygones.

Isidore and Lucille are standing at a bar set up on the sand. There's a liquor skyline on the counter: whiskey bottles, gin and scotch, champagne, amber, green, the works.

Isidore hands Lucille a glass of champagne, then gestures at her brick. "To me, my guess is, you're a seasoned clay-tosser."

"First time I've heard that one," she says smiling, nodding, frisky eyes. "No, I came to take care of something kind of difficult."

The moment is sweet. Except there is the sense that his gaze is trying to hoard all that is between them. But that man thing of not wanting to be seen doing it brings the sweetness back.

"Nothing too serious, I hope," he's saying. "I don't mean to pry."

Hmm. This human quality, the unasked question of *You okay?*, is the thing her husband hasn't shown tonight. She feels compelled to share her plan. Ever since her CBS Radio show was canceled, she and her husband—because the executives at CBS were so stubborn—have decided . . .

No. He's a stranger. Not going to share things yet. "Got a gasper?" she says.

Putting down his brick, Isidore scrabbles through his pocket. "Here's my deck"—holding out his pack of Chesterfields.

A cig is passed; looks are, too. Eyes brightened by match flame. "Thanks, kid," she says. "You know—"

Isidore jumps in. "You're married?"

(Later, she'll remember his smile here. The wolfish curve of it.)

She asks, well, is *he* not married? And he shrugs, yeah, yes, almost ten years. The exchange is quick. So, where *is* she, in that case. My wife? Well, who else—do tell; where's the little woman? After just the shortest hesitation, Isidore says, "Couldn't make it." (He doesn't mention that he proposed to his wife at Coney Island.)

"Ah." Lucille inhales, exhales, and there's glamorous smoke.

She resolves not to call this man Isidore, doesn't like the Ellis Island stamp on it.

Her brand of cigarette is Fatima—a *Madcap Bride* sponsor—but now as he bends to pick up his brick, she tastes Isidore's Chester-field.

"So, what do you like to do?" she says. "Have any talents?"

He decides to be serious. Thinks about saying, I dream I'd writ-ten *The Naked and the Dead*.

"I like to scribble, to be honest," he says.

She was looking at her cigarette, ignoring his answer. "Hey? Tell me what to name you," she says.

He is, for the first time, confused by her.

"You know," she says. "A nickname. A *nom de beach*. Some-thing."

His mind goes empty; he stalls: "Hold on . . ."

"Yes!" She laughs, charmingly, lifting a hand to soften the teas-ing. *"Hold on."* Her eyes seem washed in naughtiness. "Interesting name. If I 'hold on,' what will I find in my hand?"

Isidore can feel this all the way down. But then his face goes thoughtful. "Tonight, you'll get whatever difficult thing it was you came for, I bet," he says, then smiles again. "Though you never told me your plan to get it."

When Lucille was a kid upstate, her crush Ted Sward dropped the cloth napkin he'd used to wipe catsup off his mouth; Lucille had skedaddled across the cafeteria, snatched up the gory rag, and kept it in her bedroom—the gusto and scrapbooking of the love-struck. Feeling stirred by a napkin. Love at first sight is a dopey promise. Lucille's legs are now shaky. What is it? *You'll get whatever difficult thing it was you came for, I bet*. The wideness of the shoulders when a man stands close and takes hold of your gaze. Also he said that perfect thing.

"It's just a scheme to land a television program," she says. "Well, but a person *does* have to stand up for herself. It's true! No one else does. They just run to some other schmo who's learned to stand up straight. I hope the CBS executives—"

"They'd be idiots," he says with such joy it's impossible not to fall for him, at least a little, "not to want you."

"Well," she says. *Don't kid yourself, Lucille; no chance in hell the networks play ball.* "Everyone says they're likely to play ball," she tells him.

"Of course."

Torch flames take bows up and down the boardwalk. Isidore cannot stop looking at her.

"I know what you're thinking," Lucille says to him.

But *I* don't know what I'm thinking, he thinks. Thoughts I shouldn't be.

She says, "You're thinking my husband is right over there."

Oh. Isidore has forgotten to be aware of the husband. Isidore is aware of her elbow in his hand.

"But it's all right," she's saying. "Once in his life, Hold-on, every man is entitled to fall madly in love with a gorgeous redhead."

Jeez-o-pete, she thinks. She loves Desi, and isn't a cheater. (Where *is* Dez?) She and Hold-on look each other in the eye. But she wouldn't. Maybe Hold-on has missed the connotations. Married women flirt—but behind a guardrail. You can throw bread to them, you can buy popcorn while you watch, and then stroll to the next exhibit.

They have staggered closer to the Pavilion of Fun; Lucille nods at it.

"Get a load of that glass," she says. "Take away the glass, what would you have?"

Now here's a test, she thinks. If he says something wrong, or maybe just anything at all, the moment's frail perfection will go to pieces.

He lets his hand fall from her elbow. (*Could* Hold-on have missed the connotations?)

The orchestra has moved; it's seated here, sweating out jazz. The beseeching puffs of brass, the drum's confident, sexual *tuh-t-tomp!* The horns beg you to fall in love; the beat demonstrates how to express it.

She is an actress and can wear the mask that improves the scene. The mask might become double-sided; an actress can look, even to herself, like whatever person the scene needs her to be.

The music and wind rip at Isidore's words—". . . Wait, did you say CBS is . . . ?"—but Lucille can get enough of what she needs from the happy look on his chin and the laugh he barely keeps in check. So the perfection of the moment holds.

Hold-on squeezes her arm again.

Men do business, *fine,* she thinks. Let Desi handle it. . . .

An actor she recognizes passes. The man's tuxedo tie is undone. This party seems to be unraveling. The sound of sand tramped under formal shoes. People moving fast now, mostly in pairs. And this, she and Isidore, is her pairing.

For once, Lucille has gone silent and smiley.

Over her shoulder, Lucille sees Desi through layers of shoulders and faces. Desi is on the beach, crossing a dance floor that hasn't been used yet—what a ham he is, she thinks fondly, and wonders if he'll do a little shuffle. He is looking around for her, in his thick-necked way. The ocean smashes at the sand.

Desi is alone, Nanette Fabray nowhere in sight. Hold-on still, lovelily, has her arm.

"Well," Isidore's saying, "you can throw or not throw the brick"—looking toward the pavilion—"but that thing's coming down."

It has started to drizzle. Isidore fails to see Desi making his way to them. Isidore's attention is pulled to someone else moving through the crowd: "Let him pass!" "Mr. Trump!" The orchestra quits playing. The alto player takes the opportunity to wrist at some sweat on his forehead. Voices repeat other voices, which is how a crowd begins to realize it's a crowd: "Let him pass!" "The host, the host." And finally, at the entrance to the Pavilion of Fun, there emerges Fred Trump, balding and mustachioed. Hurrying, hurrying. He is quite thin. This moment—all of it, Lucille Ball, the pavilion, the jazz orchestra, Desi, this whole corner of sand and ocean—is his.

Even the waiters stop and watch. The cigarette girls, hair peeking out from their caps, cover their trays and wait. The man of the hour astaires up the steps. He stands at a little dais near the doorway—someone showing brisk resolve in a boring suit.

Meanwhile, Desi is coming quick. He has seen Lucille, the closeness, the man's fingers on her.

Fred Trump, beginning his speech, raises a brick.

"Gentlemen!" he says, and the fat microphone crackles. He is ignoring the light rain. "Thank you for coming. And ladies. Can't forget them, they're too expensive." General laughter, except for Lucille. No, that's what we are, she thinks, in this year of our grace 1949: expensive adornments, investments, showpieces. Forming the thought even as she orders herself to smile. Because men are where you sink your youth and hopes—with all their sturdiness, caution, their slowness to engage. They're hard to motivate. Oxen. She'd like to broadcast something that gets this across. But also funny. How to make a man do what you want—and even when he sees your stratagem, and even if you give him the consolation prize of thinking you're a fool, you've still got what you want.

"We are here for an occasion," Fred Trump says. After twenty-five years in construction, he has taken on the right-angled solidity of buildings. He has that air of self-reliance: a fifty-year-old structure, small with the sun on the façade, that would be surprisingly tough to knock down.

"Let's hear it for this wonderful beach," he's saying, "and the workingman's sanctuary that it will become!" Thin applause.

Trump is no magician of talk. Unlike his aide-de-camp, Joe Herzfeld, who can take any topic and hocus-pocus it so the listener smiles and even *oohs* his amazement. When a plainspoken guy like Fred Trump reaches in the hat, no entertainment comes out twitching its whiskers.

Isidore, meanwhile, edges even nearer to Lucille. What would it be like to feel her hands on my body? And she is wondering the same.

"Lucille!" This is Desi's yelling voice. *"Lucille!"* A seeable muscle jolts in Desi's neck.

Trump's saying, "I must thank Mayor O'Dwyer"—tapping the brick at his hip—"Governor Dewey, Senator Wagner, Councilor Lieuvain . . ."

Trump is looking around for his man Joe. As Vespasian had Josephus in Rome, as Pharaoh had Joseph in Canaan, Fred Trump has Joe Herzfeld in Brooklyn. This is how Jews (men like Isidore's father) got ahead in real estate: the trust that an at-hand Israelite might transfer a bit of those ancient desert smarts.

"Who's your friend, Lucille?" Desi cries now—he has come up very close. His sealskin-black eyebrows are twinkled with rain.

Lucille in astonishment turns to him, appealing. "Dez."

"Who's your friend who has his hand on your elbow?"

"*Shh!*" Lucille says, meaning it's obviously nothing. But of course this is why you don't leave the side of your wife to flirt with another woman.

The noise has gotten a few people to turn, but not many: It so happens Fred Trump is finding his voice.

"To build new things, you have to break with old things," Trump says, and fingers at his pencil mustache. "And building a new thing is why we are here. For tonight's wonderf—"

"You're not going to make one of your scenes, Desi."

Desi stares with hot eyes at Lucille. Isidore, he won't acknowledge. Desi is bouncing with excitement.

"You seem like an actor, mister"—he addresses Isidore at last, still not troubling himself to move eyes from his wife. "Are you? I don't know you, see."

"People claim I lack a feeling of artistic taste—recently said to be uncouth by the quote 'newspaperman' Meyer Berger," Fred Trump says.

"Not in show business," Isidore tells Desi *sotto voce*. His throat feels two sizes smaller. He swallows. "Real estate."

"A bricklayer, too, eh?" says Desi. "A Property Man?" He chin-gestures at Trump. "You lay bricks and call it art. Like him."

"Nope. Wrong. I'm not like him."

Desi rounds his thick shoulders to Isidore; the taunt is in his face. "What *are* you like, then?"

Fred Trump senses a slight commotion and speaks louder:

"Meyer Berger has never built anything himself. And so he does not understand great places never come easy, never. Let's say, for one famous example, that vital building project, the pyramids of Egypt—at least *we* never exploited the sweat of men against their will for our important projects."

"Stop! Not tonight, Dez!" Lucille says and sends a hand to her husband's wrist.

But Desi is bull-rushing at Isidore. "I'll chin you right now!"

"*Shh!*"

Isidore—nose-to-nose with Desi—feels the sweat ride down his back. Which wakes him deliciously up. Here, the only two men in the world.

THE REST OF the assemblage have lifted their bricks on cue. "Okay," Trump's saying, looking at his pocket watch. "At the stroke of the hour!"

"What do you suppose will happen," Isidore says, "if you come any closer?"

"I say two birds of a feather all smell the same," Desi says. "You are just talk and a second-rate suit like all these real estate clowns."

"All right, guests!" Trump's saying, just as Desi moves into Isidore, chest-first. "It's nearly midnight!"

Isidore has braced his whole body in opposition to Desi. Their bodies wrench and twang as they collide and collide.

Trump: "Bricks ready!"

Lucille pokes her own body between them. This should be on television, too. The sudden changes in mood, and now her absurd— if you stepped back from it—slapstick move. It is not easy to perform such a poke with nonchalance (fingers, wrist, elbow sandwiched amid jackets and hot breath). But with one turn, you could make it comedy, that sunny feel of no-one-can-really-get-hurt.

"Plan," Lucille says through her teeth. "The *plan,* Dez."

Immediately, Desi backs away. His demeanor suddenly is nonplussed. "Okay, Lucille. Have it your way." Even his hair is nonplussed. For him, sociability is only that which interrupts periods of brawling.

Isidore just stands there, breathing hard. He doesn't know this man—not the way you would know a character on a program. How could he?

"Ten," Trump's saying. "Nine."

Desi ignores this as he grins. "Here's to long shots, Lucille."

"To long shots, Dez."

It appears nobody—except maybe a cigarette girl, a couple waiters, and some real estate boobs looking over their shoulders—has seen the shoving match. Lucille is thankful for that, at least; this is a private humiliation. But as an actress, she almost misses the end of the story, the nice working out of the plot.

"Sorry, Hold-on"—the curtain-drop of her voice. "I'm a partner act."

"FIVE!" TRUMP'S SAYING. And everyone can sense it. The excitement. Every city-dweller crowded out by buildings is looking to see one come down. "Four, three . . . !" And here is the Pavilion of Fun—everything perfectly gleaming—the evening now purposefully about some lustrous thing.

"Now!"

A nervous moment. Uncertainty. The sound of the ocean. And then, a first brick is daringly thrown. One pane shatters. But now— *tck-dsssh!*—brick follows brick—*tck-dsssh! tck-dsssh! tck-dsssh!*—and the Pavilion of Fun spits all its glass.

"That's it!"

"Throw!"

And Isidore is in a trance, a cat by a rainy window.

"Smash it!"

Hold-on? he thinks. How wonderful! He does not know which movies he has seen Lucille in, but he knows he's seen her somewhere in black-and-white. Another minute, and I would've slugged him, Isidore lies to himself.

Isidore almost has the sense that his touch gave Lucille her color, that he is part of the glamour.

Here's that (tardy) applause and the kernel-pop of flashbulbs. A fancy building that lacks its windows is a queen standing with her teeth out.

Partygoers' faces shine bone white, the outlines and differences blurred as the camera immortalizes them as a crowd.

And Isidore waits before deciding what to do.

Okay, he's got to act now, or it never will happen.

CHAPTER TWO

I THINK MY GRANDFATHER *was the person, other than my parents, whom I loved the most. My first memory is playing with a big balloon, that silvery, shining, crinkly helium kind you buy from a street vendor. It was a gift my grandfather had given to me. My dad and I were visiting him and a woman in Manhattan, a woman I didn't know. She was not my grandmother. My grandmother was alive, then; she lived alone, not far from us in Long Island. But this was someone else— a brassy woman with dyed red hair who held my grandfather's hand.*

*T*HE WOMAN IS on the run from forty, but middle age, evidently, has quit the chase.

Thirty-nine years old and she looks good. But does that help? It does not help, much.

How do you take defeat—the defeat of a life's ambition? Say you're a woman who's kept loyal to a studio, and that studio balled up your career and tossed it in the commode. And it's a world for men. And say you've been around a bit. How, in this world for men, does such a woman crab together a living?

Lucille's sitting at a drugstore counter in Buffalo, New York, eating a butterscotch ice cream, and she wonders.

How firmly those Coney Island TV execs had recited their expected lines! No, sorry, Mrs. Arnaz, just not for us. Okay then, fellas, but this is *not* goodbye; I promise *we'll show you*. . . . Yes, but pretty or not, she's aware even now of the lines like tiny shark gills around her eyes.

A radio's going at the top of its lungs—*da-doo-da-dada,* Les Brown and His Band of Renown. On Symphony Sid's nationally broadcast *After-Hours Swing Session.* Playing Birdland or maybe the Royal Roost. *Da-doo-da-dada.*

Desi's at her side, talking. "Tonight went good. Went *well.*" Dez's a grammarian when anxious.

"Mmm?"

Lucille's personal movie, her life film, sure doesn't seem like a Capra. It seems like a Douglas Sirk, soggy plotline and all.

"Come now, Red," Desi's saying. "You don't think we made everybody feel fine?"

Symphony Sid (she thinks): a particularly New York specimen, one of those Jewish men goofy for Black People Music.

Jewish men.

Hold-on had sauntered up to her again at the end of the Coney Island night—after she'd thought they'd said goodbye. And it had been lovely. On the beach near the city in the rain. That encounter had been just a trifle, however. Just something to make Desi jealous, she thinks, almost convincingly. The man's strongly coiling black hair—thick, brilliantined. And his nose, its hourglass-shaped bridge. Certainly foreign, stirringly familiar. A Jew, all right. Tall and handsome, if memory could be trusted, and thrilling.

Not because he in any way was unusual; because he wasn't. Sometimes a woman just needed something different. A nice guy, human and refreshing and normal. But also trickily witty around the eyes. Hold-on looked to her like a man who ruffled life on the head.

And a whole year has rolled by.

Ah, enough inappropriate memory! "Sure, sweetie," Lucille hears herself say.

"Well, Red, so then our plan might finally work." Desi swallows. But his smile is a guest who's forgotten to leave. "Will it?"

Lucille's face tightens a little.

"Why is ice cream so much better in places like this?" she says, kind of sharply.

"Buffalo." He nods and narrows his eyes in disbelief. *"Buffalo."*

THE PLAN, THE plan, the stupid plan.

Months back, CBS, which hadn't wanted to sacrifice any of its radio properties, had been interested in repurposing Lucille's failed *My Madcap Bride* for TV. Maybe, that was the rumor, anyway. TV, the mongrel new medium. Well—count her in. Even that flickering appliance beats unemployment.

But, of course, a problem. *Bride*'s husband had been played by Richard Denning (blond hair, Gerber cheeks, middling charisma). Lucille liked Denning. She'd also planned to replace him. Not that Lucille, at that career moment, had much power to issue ultimatums. But working with her husband was the only chance she'd have to dust off her marriage, get it back on its feet. The Arnazes were often apart, frosty, and thwarted. Desi'd cheat to his heart's content were Lucille to go off and film a show without him. She thought up a scheme, then, to have him at her side all the time. But CBS didn't think the public could—hell, CBS execs *themselves* didn't—accept a redhead married to a Cuban.

That forced the Arnazes to prove that Middle America would buy what they were selling. *If we can show you that crowd accepts it, then you must* . . . So, under the aegis of their new company, Desilu Productions (meaning, as Lucille saw it, she and Desi are the saps forking out the entire $20,000 for what amounts to a public audition), the Arnazes now tour what remains of the dying vaudeville theaters, covering the seaboard with pratfalls and puns. Also a bunch of the Midwest. Save the career *and* the marriage, that's her thinking. Even the accountant says the tour will bankrupt them.

In this reckless and quip-filled junket, tonight's performance was stop No. 4. Sixty-plus shows a month. Two a day, six on weekends. The loaded-cello routine. "Cuban Pete/Sally Sweet." Domestic resentment turned into a somersault or a smile. All of it arguing: I'm white and he's Latin, but see how you people don't care? The only thing that transcends race, creed, and color? The happy performance of a difficult marriage. What can top that? (The accountant disagrees.)

Forearms heavy on the counter now, Desi licks his mouth. It's the look of someone who isn't used to being pensive. "Buffalo," he says. "Christ." He shakes his head. Narrows his eyes. The exaggerated gesture shows his esteem for thinkers and doubters. For the people whose depth, he suspects, replaces the optimism and constancy he takes for granted in himself.

"Look, we're, er," Desi says. "We're bound to . . ." Maybe narrowed eyes are a kind of blinking red light, a warning that someone's brain is in over its head.

I'm being cruel; he's my *husband,* Lucille thinks.

"You're right, lover," she says. "We made the audience feel fine."

Desi brightens. "Oh?"

The applause from the cheap radio speaker sounds like paper crinkling. "You know, he discovered Doris Day," Lucille says. After Coney, she'd pined after Hold-on for a few weeks, then hardly ever.

Da-doo-da-dada. Kind of an annoying melody—childish. Lucille knows Les Brown, or at least she did, and Symphony Sid, too, that reefer-smoking hophead, and she knows everybody, and here she is. In Buffalo. Not far from Jamestown.

"Who discovered Doris?" Desi asks, but in a sighing voice.

I'm talking about Les Brown, Lucille would say if she weren't so tired. Les *Brown* discovered Doris Day. It's one A.M. A ceiling fan kneads the muggy air overhead. And thoughts of Hold-on sneak in.

If you are a New Yorker, your dial is set right close to the mighty eighty, WJZ, broadcasting at 770. Or nationwide on the ABC Radio Network.

Lucille looks to the soda jockey. A kid in a nincompoop's white paper hat who can't lift his shy eyes to return her gaze. Rubbing the counter, probably his thousandth swipe. Kid's kept the place open just for us, Lucille thinks. Buffalo stardom, one more pissant triumph. The ceiling fan's twisting cigarette smoke about its blades in white wisp tassels.

Desi yawns and keeps yawning. "I don't know, I don't know . . ."

A red-winged blackbird lands on the windowsill, barely visible out there in the dark. Lucille, hating birds, looks away.

Sit back and relax in the most fabulous city in the country. From Manhattan. This is! Symphony Sid!

No bird is going to be a bad omen tonight. Lucille slaps the counter, extravagantly casual. "Come on, Dez," she says, "you old dust mop."

When she winks, the other eye charmingly squints.

"We knocked 'em dead, Dez. We'll knock 'em dead tomorrow, too, and we'll be in Chicago by Memorial Day."

"There you are!" Desi slaps the counter, too. "That's the stuff."

"Gonna be the high pillows. You and me."

"The *plan,*" he says. And she says, "The plan."

Together: "is working."

Sure, okay. Yet anybody who saw Lucille now would say that principal photography has officially wrapped on her fame and success.

IF YOU WANT to know a person, learn what she keeps herself from remembering.

Images from her cutting-room floor: A steam train taking young Lucille from Michigan to Buffalo after her father's funeral—that long, traumatic trip, those tears, geese that flashed up beside the rails. She was three and a half years old. Would Daddy be coming back home, too? No, dear—never. And then her aunt opened the kitchen window and a blackbird flew in. It crashed and broke a mirror. The next morning, Lucille's mom, DeDe, said Lucille would live on her own with her great-grandmother for a while. What sticks in memory is the crashing blackbird—and that small, old-fashioned locomotive, No. 4, clanking, stumbling down from Selston, Michigan. Its screech and its smoke; its wheels and their thrusting forearms; geese flickering in the raw afternoon.

Jamestown, New York, where Lucille was miscast as a normal child, is about seventy miles from Buffalo. The cold and green stage on which she grew up—and from which she cut and ran.

Drop another coin in the slot, see another memory flicker and play.

Lucille Ball, 1918, now living with DeDe's second husband's parents. (It's complicated. DeDe Ball, widowed at twenty-three, had relinquished her two children to her own grandparents, then to her sister, *then* to Lucille's step-grandparents, the Petersons.) One day, six- or seven-year-old Lucille was hiding in Mrs. Peterson's closet. Five unnoticed hours. Lucille transformed that tiny space— mothball smells and candlelight—into a theater. This was Jamestown to her: isolation, self-reliance, a non-home she lived in. And she, tiny, blond, and father-mourning.

Inside that makeshift theater, clothespin dolls were her costars—dolls more real, and charismatic, than kids she knew. You go over here, and *you* there, now all of you repeat after me. That was the start.

"Lucille, how special you are," DeDe said, opening the closet door, applauding. "My love!" (DeDe had returned, in a way—visiting occasionally, looking more or less alive.) The mother had the prototype model of the daughter's quill-feather eyebrows; their noses were almost touching now. "My sweetest." (DeDe never believed she could be a mother, but really she did love me, Lucille always thought. Time would prove DeDe right.)

Two hours after the closet, DeDe sat next to her second husband and sniffed at Lucille: "Well, look, it's the half-pint Sarah Bernhardt—or, rather, it very much is *not.*" Smoke from her bitter nostrils. This, a reaction to her husband's having clapped enthusiastically. "Watch out everyone, here passes the *thespian* of Jamestown Elementary."

DeDe laughed and Lucille's step-grandfather laughed and this meant Lucille laughed, too, though she didn't feel like laughing. "Go and play with your little dolls now, kiddo." And five weeks later, DeDe was gone again. . . .

Jump ahead now, again to 1950, back at that Buffalo drugstore with Desi; Lucille feels sick, and she is sure it's the fault of all these memories. (It isn't.)

DeDe and her second husband, Ed Peterson, had gone off to Detroit without Lucille or her brother. DeDe and Ed were seeking "respectable jobs in the skilled or semiskilled industries." And so, at the Weideman Cigar Co. of Michigan, for a while there, DeDe very nearly got a— Okay, well, next she inquired at the Krolik garment factory and almost, or just about— But, see, *then* DeDe did find partial employment, at least a couple days at— DeDe ended up taking classes in "domestic science and household arts." This was at the Lansing Young Women's Christian Association's vocational school: old-crone teachers, parchment diploma, good luck to you.

When Lucille was nine, DeDe finally returned to Jamestown for good. And daughter looked up at mother and new father.

Lucille said, "DeDe, will you and Ed stay and be my parents?" Ed Peterson eyed her, and not a thing in the man smiled.

IT'S 1:30 A.M. now, in Buffalo, and Lucille has left that drugstore counter; she's walking arm in arm with Desi. The screen of every storefront's window is playing its late show of the moon. Lucille notices just one stranger halfway down the long, dark street, in front of a lunch stand, lurking—maybe a fan, maybe a drunk, could be both—and when this man sees her, he begins waving frantically, without a sound. She's glad to have the manly shield of a husband between her and this person. She leans against Desi as they cruise smoothly to the hotel.

Desi's all right. This is how she'd patched things up with him after dancing with Hold-on: Desi had said, "Did you know that Jewish guy?" She'd answered, "It's not like we drank out of the same bottle." Then Desi'd snorted, closed his eyes, opened his eyes, smiled at her, and that had been that.

The hotel doorman has Bill Holden's manly glossed hair, neat even at this hour. But he doesn't have Holden's shoulders or dimply chin. We all have one or another thing. Only the Bill Holdens of the world have them all.

Lucille and Desi open the door to room 258, the suite, such as it is. Their longtime maid, Clara, is there. "Mr. Arnaz!" Clara says, her plump, milky face clotted with worry. "I told them you were out, but they insisted."

"'S'okay!" Desi says. His hand thrusts out to receive the newspapermen—all three of them—who now cross the drawing room.

"Miss Ball," one wearing a blue suit says. "Give us a quote!" the second says: "You certainly made us wait all night."

All of them men, she thinks. Men, men, men. Are there no real-life Lois Lanes? She can feel their eyes on her body.

This is what it means to be a beautiful, famous woman. Or famous enough for the press to come out in Buffalo. Not that the fame was ever much. Even before its current fade-out. And perhaps the beauty, too, now. She can feel eyes prod her face, prod her skin, the exposed real estate under her throat. Her breasts. It is not friendly. She can feel eyes prod her hips and her thighs; it's too forward. And even if she doesn't want the attention, she's cursing the scratchy crinkles around her own eyes—those little autographs signed by years. Do other actresses feel what she feels? This staring, these invasions? I hope I look all right. Ugh, the hungry insistent searching eyes of men.

It half-reminds her of some other time, some other night, some other man, very young, who looked at her like that. What was that kid's name?

"How's it feel to be back home, Miss Ball?"

The reporters appear lumpy compared to Desi; undercooked.

"She's not *from* Buffalo," one says. "Don't tell me *you* call Jamestown *Buffalo,* Harry."

And now, implausibly, two of them start talking to each other as if she and her husband weren't there:

"Ah, it's all the same once you get west of Syracuse."

"A coffee-and-doughnut hole like Jamestown, though?"

"Fair enough. A dump if ever there was one."

The third reporter catches Lucille's attention. "You know," he tells her, "there *is* the Buffalo Audubon Center. Might be fun for you. The mornings are nice and cool here."

"Boys," she says. *"Boys."*

Why do they treat me as if fame works retroactively? she wonders. Why would it change where I was born? Do they think I don't know it here?

She goes to bat now for a place she's always putting down.

"Here's the thing about Jamestown," she says. "You ever try to enjoy some crowded, dirty California beach after seeing how pretty Lake Chautauqua looks in August?"

"Well," Desi says. " 'S nice, but Jamestown's not the Playa del Este, now, is it?"

His voice still surprises her after all these years. How it loses its characteristic tightness when easing into Spanish.

"Cuba, gentlemen," he says. "Cuba."

"Bet the Chiquita banana girls down there are nothing compared to Miss Ball," says reporter No. 1 in the blue suit. His voice is a vocal leer.

Desi has numerous ways he might answer this: *Hey, my mother is Cuban,* for one. *My mother is no banana girl.*

"Ah," Desi says, giving himself a small, calming breather.

One of the things he's good at is frightening the type of men who could use a good fright. Does he curl his hands into fists now?

"Ah," he says. "Gentlemen."

And with effort that only Lucille notices, Desi smiles his widest: his big-timey smile that would light up a million cathode-ray tubes behind a million screens, if only given the chance.

"I may be Cuban Pete," he says, "but you've got something there, fellows: She *is* Sally Sweet." A meeting with the press was not a time for fists.

In his smile there are just top teeth, a dimple nuzzled in one cheek. And his wink shows charm, and material comfort, and striving itself. The reporters nod like a troop of baboons.

Where had these reporters kept hidden these pads they're now scribbling in? "Oh come now," Lucille says, "my hubby's just getting sentimental about me, fellows."

Normally she'd be up for this banter. She's a bit ill now, though. Tired and sort of nauseated, and she wants to speed these men toward the moment they'll bow out of the room and her life.

She senses Desi sensing her restlessness. A twitch in the hand he's rested on her back. So she feels the first rattles of her own smile coming on. Even though sleep's begun to pull at her eyes and brain.

Because ambition isn't a targeted dreaming; you can't knock down *any* one enthusiasm without knocking down the whole pile of matchsticks.

"Boys?" she says. "If you want another quote, the secret to looking this good? Live honestly, eat slowly, and lie about your age."

There's also an inescapability to her delivering what Desi wants—the appeal of sacrificing her mood to his.

"Yup," reporter No. 1 is saying. "You lovebirds love each other."

She keeps up her smile. Soon enough, this tour will be at an end, in the big final show in New York City.

Phil. Phil! That was the name of the young kid with those gloves on that beach. With the prodding eyes. Hold-on's brother. Turns out, it was lovely to want to kiss someone else, to remind yourself life can still surprise you. Or had there been more to it than that?

AS ISIDORE WOKE one morning from an uneasy dream, he found himself transformed in his bed into a monstrous adulterer. And with a bruised face. Or, a would-be adulterer. *Am* I, though? What happened to me? he wondered. It was no dream.

Ow, he thought, my cheek—and the memories returned with force. He'd been out on Coney Island eight hours before.

This is what happened: Isidore had watched Lucille leave him; later, he'd hurried to her a second time. Then he actually stole a kiss. A single kiss. And got punched for it—all of which occurred after we cut away. . . .

On a brain-sized movie screen, he was reliving it all in his bed, eyes closed.

His own light silver hand combed through Lucille's dark silver hair. Memories playing in opulent black-and-white. A gloss on her opened lips, raindrops across her collar, shimmer and flash.

"You and I got interrupted, Lucille," is what he'd walked up and said, that second time. "And we'd been having such a lovely conversation, too."

He'd known the husband would reappear. But Lucille stared

into his face—smiling cheeks, thrilled eyes. And the ensuing pause in banter, a little nook of intimacy, was a break in the hard weather of such knowledge. "Some Enchanted Evening" played again. The choppy noise of a horn section, a drummer going *slap* with his brushes. Then Isidore had said, "Hey, we can relive the times we almost had," and led her by the hand. But with Desi's arrival, that pause, that nook, caved in. . . .

Afterward, Isidore slunk back home and into this bed with Harriet. Her sleeping face looked slackly kind. He lay touching the warmth of her and in the guilt of resting in that warmth. They had been married about ten years. But he'd scarcely thought of Harriet the night before, even though they'd gotten engaged there.

"Mmnf," she said now, waking, "ugnfff"—worming her body to full length.

Somehow, with a look, Harriet always detected every bad thing Isidore'd ever done, every fib, every evasion. Would she know?

He spent last night's homeward drive inventing a breezy explanation: Ah, Harriet, boring party, you missed nothing, I just stood (he would say) listening to that Fred Trump guy, *alone,* then I tripped, and my cheek, and, oh you know me . . .

But now Harriet slithered from bed, escaping on considerate tiptoes. Thinks I'm asleep, he told himself. On his bed table, his to-do list—an artifact of some extinct age, the doting-husband period, where he'd worked on what he now believed shouldn't be work. Or maybe he could convince himself he believed that.

Sounds from the kitchen reached the bedroom, smells, the sputter and salt-tickle of bacon, some ear and nose identifications of home.

Get up, he told himself.

Approaching the kitchen, Isidore had a sense, or a hope. In the hall mirror, he avoided the bruise under his eye. Or maybe what he had was a fear.

When he looked at Harriet, maybe it'd be like turning to a page of a beloved novel after you'd lost the ability to read. Hard as you try, the old text would hold no meaning.

He lost nerve at the door, turned from where his family was, imagined going back upstairs, outside, away to Mexico.

What you seek in vain for, half your life, one day you come upon suddenly, your family at dinner. You seek it like a dream, and as you find it you become its prey. He'd read that once, Emerson or Thoreau, and hadn't understood then.

"Hello!" he cried, entering.

His wife crossed the floor—Harriet passing the window, its stripy light.

Nobody acknowledged him. In his robe, his pad-about slippers, carrying a folded *Herald Trib*. A whorl of bacon smoke rose in the sunbeam like a blue thought bubble.

Bernie, Isidore's dark-eyed son, sat eating cereal. He was eight. The kitchen radio played staticky classical. Haydn? Bernie's younger brother, Arthur, stood near a second woman at the table.

"Hello," Isidore tried again.

The scene felt eerie as Pompeii. It was all just the way he'd left it, frozen; none of the reticent particulars spoke of last night's cataclysm.

But did his wife seem to him a stranger? That was the question.

Stuff about Harriet people noticed (pick a card, any card): She had her mother's slightly pointed nose. Out in the world, she was kind and inhibited and always last to take a sip of anything. Or to be offered one.

"Smells good," he said now.

Yes, Harriet lived in a locked crate of shyness; her vivacity did come out to wag its tail, but only when she was with Isidore and the kids.

He took a seat now and leaned his elbows on the table. It felt poignant to see his backyard in the window. His home, his family.

A different Harriet fact was more relevant this morning: Very occasionally and unpredictably, she could fall into anger through the littlest of holes.

". . . no, don't thank me, Bernie," she was saying now, her robe cinched. "Thank the lady who cooked it." She gestured to the second woman here. This was "Aunt" Mary, an African American of the family's employ.

Mary sat holding out a forkful of egg to the younger boy. White privilege had spread its apron wide and now Mary was here, cooking and cleaning and living with the Strauss family, five, sometimes six days a week. Mary was the only person in the room not wearing pajamas and/or a robe.

"There you go, a big boy today," said Mary to Arthur. "Yum."

Isidore watched his wife walk to the oven, the skirt of her robe not lifting at all. He realized her walk had a short, practical, thud cadence.

"Daddy!"

"Hello." Isidore looked straight ahead while he talked. "Everybody. Hello."

Harriet came to place before him a breakfast but didn't say hi or quit the run of her conversation:

"Mary, you're always so diplomatic, but can't you agree, I don't want to pressure you, but, I mean, it's difficult when somebody close to you lets you down, isn't it?"

"That certainly is the case, Mrs. Harriet. Hello, Mr. Isidore."

"Hi there, Mary"—and next, quiet. Whatever troubles he'd had in the past, he always entered this family tableau with a calm sense of his own vigor. Difficulties receded, then.

Harriet made a noise like *nnnh*. She said, "It's just upsetting."

Isidore's head shot up. Upsetting? Somebody close to her? Fred Trump's party had *teemed* with photographers. The newspaper! His picture, leaning in to kiss Lucille, on some page near the middle. Or maybe a snapshot of him getting slugged? Probably Harriet saw it already.

He opened the *Herald Trib* discreetly, without looking down.

"You're really welcome to disagree, Mary," Harriet accused. On the counter, a copy of *her* paper, the *Daily Mirror,* lay perilously open. Yes, she was definitely talking about his wrongdoing. In front of him. As a kind of torture.

Harriet stood with her back to the counter, patting her dark hair. Her thin waist. And the newspaper in Isidore's hands sounded like rustled leaves. He was shaking.

"You know how it is, Mary," Harriet said, "when you're mad at someone in your family."

She wasn't looking at Mary as she talked; she lay her gaze on Isidore.

Isidore whipped past five pages, six, *whooth!* And, right there in his ear, the knowledge of good and evil was broadcasting its staticky program.

Slow down, he told himself. Could it be that Miss Lucille Ball herself, wherever she was, now acted suspicious and lovelorn, too? Seven, eight pages, no smooch pic yet, *whooth whooth*.

"Well?" Harriet said. "Well, Isidore?"

He raised his eyes to Harriet. She faced him full on. *Ulp!* Panic. Her dark brows. She knew, she definitely knew. I don't want my marriage to end, he thought. Her eyes bright under her widow's peak. It *did* feel like torture, just sitting here. Isidore was the type never to manhandle life and in fact preferred not to leave any fingerprints on its lapels. But what if I lost my world, my family, this house with that nice backyard—

"*So?* Come on," Harriet said. And with contented, smiling nosiness, added, "How was the party?"

She went to him, touched the side of his face. "I was lonely and waiting for you," she said.

He coughed out relief—a breathy, laughish *humf!* Saved.

They hadn't had sex before they married. Ever. But she'd let him—and that's how Isidore thought at the time, she "let" him—do almost everything else.

"Wait," he said now, chewing a forkful, his mind curling like a dog around this domestic table. Saved. But he realized what it meant that Harriet had reached her hand to him—heartbreaking!

"So, uh, what were you talking about?" he said. "With Mary just now?"

"My mother. I mean, who else could make me so—*hold on.* What happened? Your eye looks like I don't know what."

"This?" he said. (Hold-on!

Harriet wasn't turning out to
wifely concern in her face; she *was* g
dren and even kind of a beauty and I l
Spouses now and then just find themselves
situations. That's all.

"It's nothing," he said.

Hold-on. Last night, on that beach, he'd stepped
out of the cool serene drowning waters of his marriage.

He managed to say, "I banged myself" right as Harri
"You got a little bruise, looks like."

Her face, so exposed smiling its compassion, made him sad.

"Oh, Har," he said. "Your mother shouldn't make you so angry."
And he looked meaningfully at the boys. The good family man.

"Daddy's eye is a black eye," said Arthur.

Isidore thought—as he was saying, "fine, I'm fine"; as he tapped
the ache high on his cheek and added, "thanks for breakfast"—he
thought about something he'd read in Proust.

"*Is* it a black eye, Daddy?"

And the look on Harriet's face with its pointy nose asked, "Is
there something you're not telling me, Isidore?"

The prospect of infidelity is the key to marriage, Proust wrote.
Is it so surprising a builder from Long Island read Proust? That's me,
he often said. That's who I am. He'd once wanted, against his father's wishes, to become a writer. (Every first-generation Jewish
family had one such. Isidore's penniless cousin Harold worked
spearing up trash in the street while quoting Spinoza.) Proust wrote
that the possibility of the spouse cheating is a necessary spark. An
awareness that betrayal is possible. The thing that keeps couples
together. Nonsense. The ignorant marriage presumptions of an unmarried man. It would lock anger in and make for a lasting doubt,
a barrier to closeness; cheating would bring down a life, Isidore
thought. I'm a moral person, besides. And so I can't do this. Obviously I can't.

"I tripped, actually," he said. "I, well, I took a tumble on a slick

the collar of his

uch." Her charac-
your spouse's vir-

king if everyone
ouse. Bernie said
mental life. And

ew it was unrea-
ed between him
rotecting them.

Sigh.) And he touched the achy skin.
be unfamiliar, of course. That
reat. The mother of my chil-
ve her and she loves me.
n very different mental
or a moment
t said,

Why won't you tell me you love me, Harriet? he yelled inside his head.

In the first blush of marriage, Isidore had been surprised by what he could only call—and he still got embarrassed thinking of it—his wife's sexual ravenousness.

"Time," she was saying now, "for my shower." She winked at him. "Sorry about your eye. Love you. Stop acting so strangely." He reached for Harriet as she walked away. Don't leave me with my memories, he thought. Or my wants.

Isidore knew he had been kidding himself. Harriet was never going to be unfamiliar to him. (Her hand slid from his.) His typical self-control went; *he* was now the stranger to himself.

What had I been *thinking,* trying to kiss a starlet—a beautiful, glamorous, fun, wonderful redheaded starlet who was someplace in the world right now, living her own life, having her own morning. What would she be saying this instant?

"Daddy?" Arthur was holding up a fork-spear of breakfast, pointing it. "Why are you laughing?"

Listen here, Dezdee [or whatever her husband's name is], *certainly I did* not *enjoy the kiss from that handsome man last night.*

"What is so funny, Daddy?"

No, señora, the husband says. *You cannot hide love, Lucille.*

What could Isidore now tell his son? That he had fallen back into one life and was grabbing at the other as it passed overhead?

He saw—projected in his memory, but with her décolletage flushed via the reshoots of desire—Lucille's flirty smile, the lips pulling to the side. *Of course it's something we can do again, Hold-on. Don't deny it was glamorous.*

I would never deny that, madam.

His sons did not know a strange woman was thundering through their father's mind, whooshing with abandon through the doors Isidore tried to shut. Bernie looked at his father with a dimple that said *I am living the best day ever.* He said, "Do you know what today is, Daddy? Parade!"

ISIDORE WAS SERIOUS about being a Jew, if—like many Jews in Long Island—he wasn't too observant. Or too specific about faith. Or even certain about much Judaica, including the language used to express it. He considered himself a Jew. And that was that.

With his father years before, Isidore visited an Orthodox synagogue in deepest Brooklyn, though the old man hadn't been Orthodox. (Isidore's father's father *had* been, however, back there on the steppes of history.) Isidore felt claustrophobic in that sweat-smelling Williamsburg chapel, his nose, his worldly nostrils, aching for the air of the rational world, the world of modernity and science, of assimilation and leniency. He was generous to his own mind. He called himself an intellectual. He'd received (he told himself) the wisdom of the great books. And yet it'd been hard to follow these old irrelevant Orthodox men arguing about the *oldest* book, whether original sin didn't exist because God created the inclination to evil, and that this inclination lives within everybody, right next to our inclination to goodness, which means that free will is just an obedience test. The logic was exacting. The men bobbed to God as they argued. That was when Isidore decided he'd read the Bible, on his own terms. He'd compose his own prayers.

But now, all this time later (holding his son Bernie's hand out on Great Neck's Northern Boulevard amid the paraders juddering up the traffic-free street), he remembered having thought spitefully that these had been old men who would never be tested by temptation. It had been a young man's thought. He was not that young man anymore.

He had considered himself a moral person; he'd maybe—secretly—thought himself *better* than his colleagues. The particulars of this betterness were not specific or spoken, even to himself. (How many builders had read Melville and Emerson and Dante and got the lessons therein?)

But how could he know exactly what was moral and good and *still have done*—?

And still want to!

Isidore tried to right the frown on his face. Not that he'd ever been perfect. Even before this, he'd stand next to a beautiful woman on the elevator, imagine having sex with her, and then guiltily call his wife to profess his love.

This was different. *In the middle of the path of our life, I went astray from the straight road and found myself in a wilderness where the right course was lost.*

The famous words came back, but to what end?

IN SOME WAYS, Great Neck was like old Brooklyn's antonym. It was built to be an equation: candidly rural Americana + elegance + young secular Jewish families, minus ethnic markings or any unsightliness. Isidore watched his neighbors who had come to cheer the parade. That was how it went every week. A haughty advance of local podunk athletes each Sunday. And the Property Value Fairy would show up, too, looking for any hatted or gray heads; with her magic fairy wand, she'd poof into oblivion the buttoned-up, the pale, the otherwise unvivacious. The old, for example; the visibly immigrant. And in their place, she'd produce these carefreely sundaying Long Islanders.

In Great Neck, you didn't see Hasids, with their fur halos for hats, their wigs, their curlicue children. Here, you saw dogs on leashes. You saw chipmunks. (Chipmunks who stood and rubbed their claws like Dickens's famous miser Fagin, but still.) This was the story line Property Men were trying to shape and push. Property Men like Isidore. Or those less ambivalent about it than Isidore. Here, Jewish women shone with (department store) haute couture, a darker-complected copy of Manhattan WASPs.

All around now, wives smiled at their husbands—why, it was smiles everywhere—children smiled with lifted faces like wondrous dentifrice advertisements. *Brusha, brusha brusha.* But do none of these happy children, wives, or husbands struggle with the grave problem of the penis and the vagina, or a heart that sinks and leaps and pulls the brain with it? Isidore couldn't restrain his crazy thoughts now.

A Property Man! Having lacked chutzpah to tell his father, *No, I'm not going into the family business. I'm a writer.* That was Isidore. With his middle brother, Norman, he had some of Great Neck, had some of Baldwin, some of Syosset; some of Long Island City he had, too.

"Look, Daddy!" Bernie yipped and tugged Isidore's hand. "Charlie Conerly, leading the parade!" An eight-year-old, sweating with enthusiasm.

"Fantastic," Isidore said.

He imagined a smiling ideal of attentive fatherhood, of amused concentration, and he impersonated that. (In fact, Charlie Conerly, the New York Football Giants' quarterback, was *not* here, marching down Northern Boulevard in Great Neck's weekly parade of high school players.) "I think it's maybe someone just has the same number on his jersey, Bernard."

"Do you know Mommy says for a snack I can eat fudge?" The boy's cheeks above his smile glowed. "Do-o you want a fudge snack, too, Dad?"

"Grown men don't generally have fudge snacks. Grown men don't generally have *snacks*." He surprised himself by what he said next. Also by the surprisingly bitter laugh that he fired from his nostrils.

"Grown men"—*pfff*—"aren't generally allowed to enjoy many things."

Those in-house despots, the penis and the vagina . . .

Ah, who had I been to feel bewildered disappointment in Harriet for having had bedroom wants like mine, only a little more intense? he thought. "How do you like them apples?" is what she'd said, so many years back, after having surprised him with their first kiss. (Over the years Harriet's passion faded, and his did too. And here they were.)

"Nine is pretty grown, for a kid," Bernie said now. The parade had tapered to its last few marchers in the sun.

To have a love affair, to live the beautiful cliché, the stuff of movies and books! To any sophisticated person, to a woman like Lucille, the kiss would be nothing. But then—he felt his cheeks go hot—let me be unsophisticated!

Even after the band had started that final time into "Some Enchanted Evening," Isidore's hope had stood on wobbly legs. But, after a moment, those wobbly legs were on a dance floor with a beautiful starlet. What a night. The soft nude arms of women. All those men whose hair shined and didn't budge. The dancers like clocktower figurines in synched courses, swayed, spun, swayed more. Rehearsed competence. Whispering, flushed skin, skirts that fanned out with every swish. There were shadows everywhere, too; one shadow even reached out courageously to stroke Lucille's face. Do something bold, Isidore had thought.

But the husband showed. Desi stomped over from the beach. Fists up and ready. Isidore kept on. Lucille was lifting her chin slowly—what Isidore said to make her laugh will remain between them—and he was in a mood to blow up his life, to sway in place, to feel the ashes of who he'd been rain down. If I stop, I will regret it always. Time mercifully licked its thumb and waited before turning the page. And Isidore took Lucille's shoulders—gripped them—and kissed her. This is when Isidore saw his father, Jacob Strauss, who in his draconian black tie looked at his son in condemnation, quit it, quit it, you have a family. What? Lucille was saying after the kiss. What? Wait. She had been married for almost ten years and this was the first time she had cheated. It's not cheating, Isidore had answered, it's living.

Then Desi had been upon him.

". . . And *I'm* almost nine," Bernie was saying now. "And *that's* grown, Dad. Dad?"

Isidore smiled, looked. But Bernie didn't smile—the boy stared at his father, his head at an angle, his lip hung in puzzlement.

CHAPTER THREE

*O*NCE, AN ADVANCED *Comp professor at Tufts had spotted a very green talent pulsing around one of my memoir pieces. Every few weeks, I'd exhume that paper—my eyes inching across the corpse of it, like a pair of slugs. Why had that piece stood out? (My eyes, for all their slurping over the pages, could never determine.) A later effort—"The Twins"; second runner-up, Undergraduate Writing Prize—the department called "an energetic third-place fiction" but "in the final analysis, too in love with concepts." (It would take a decade to admit that this hadn't been disguised approval.) I hadn't done much, and what little I had done wasn't good. But I doubted those two bits of evidence. This was the positive doubt that comes with ambition: the reach for the small fluttering thing suspended between solid certainties.*

My ambition came to me from my grandfather. A very particular ambition, for literary achievement.

*N*EVER IN MY life did I imagine I would become a heart-breaker, he tells himself.

"There *is* a place, actually, come to think of it," Lucille says. An intense blush of desire colors her throat. "My dressing room," she says, huskily. "My dressing room. That's where we can go, Hold-on."

It's late and warm on Fifty-first and Broadway. And Lucille Ball isn't looking around to see, at this moment of her star-rise, if anyone recognizes her.

This whole thing is such a shock that Isidore won't allow himself to ask *why.* (No one does recognize her.)

No, I'm not cut out to be a heartbreaker, Isidore thinks.

A heart *mender,* possibly. He'd known who he was. A heart tape-and-gluer. The sort of man women look to when they need to be made whole. But now—with his wife waiting for him a half block away—Isidore feels Lucille take the first step toward where Harriet stands under the marquee, hazardously downtown. He spins the actress by the shoulders ("Perhaps we should, ah, find another route?"), and he catches her hand, and they're walking, *phew,* away from his wife.

Harriet! Harriet who is going to—who surely *has* to—turn around and see them soon.

A fire engine passes, the second in the last minute; a red giant rejoicing with its blushing and jubilant light all a-spin.

"Let's go, Lucille." Walking has never felt so much like running.

Through the theater's side entrance, backstage now. A red-lit passageway, otherwise dark post-show, and quiet. Columns everywhere. They're on an illicit footpath leading from Juliet's yonder window; or, they're Elizabeth Bennet and Mr. Darcy out hurrying together at Longbourn. . . .

Lucille speeding ahead has a performer's meticulous grace. In the past few minutes, some burden has released its grip on her. The show's crew has finished up and skedaddled, and, already, forty-five minutes after curtain, it's serene. Even Isidore, who's never set foot backstage, can sense it's not usually this peaceful. He bumps against something—hard. Doesn't care. Bruisable hip, table in shadows, this passageway a maze of darkened spike corners, and he is happy.

Her dressing room at last, and here on the door is MISS LUCILLE BALL, script inside a sparkly cardboard star. ("Miss": The sign, too, has forgotten her marriage.)

Isidore notices a backstage worker loitering under a red bulb, and then Lucille sees him too; she releases Isidore's hand. Her husband could be anyplace, everyplace.

Lucille is breathing in a way that may or may not be nerves. That backstage worker has gone, at least.

Isidore swallows. This is the moment.

It's not just that he's worried about his wife and her husband; it's that Lucille might back out. Or—

Or:

That the plump woman Isidore saw a few minutes ago—an employee of Lucille's?—might nudge her head in, through the doorway, peeking around for her boss.

Which actually does happen.

A real face now under the framed black-and-white faces of performers on the wall. This is Clara, the Arnazes' maid. Looking in to see why Lucille's taken such an age.

Lucille pulls Isidore—*Hide!*—behind one of those columns. Her perfume lights up his nose: Chanel No. 5, that unnatural composition of jasmine and soused flowers. Standing so close, her delicate breathing, the exquisite pulse ticking in her throat.

They wait—petrified, trying not to laugh.

The moment stretches, and Isidore, giggling despite himself, is reminded of old times with Harriet, years ago, when they were courting: all those contented balcony nights in Brandt's Flatbush movie palace. How do you like them apples?

Now Lucille leans away from him and says in a whisper: "This is not something I do." Whatever it is they're doing. "Really, I don't."

And yet. Her smile may be subdued, but it is still there.

Her very large, eloquent eyes add a footnote: *I've spent a long time being in love with a man who does this kind of thing.* And then her head lowers, and her crinkled forehead adds something like: *So that is why I'm doing this. Although I do feel surprised to be enjoying it.*

"Well," Isidore whispers. "Who *does* do this kind of thing?"

He laughs softly and checks to see that Clara has gone. "Rogues, that's who. Scoundrels."

Lucille's head goes back in surprise, but she catches the spirit. "Vamps," she says.

Laughing. "Scamps."

"Tramps."

"Not lamps, though?"

"Villains."

"Ne'er-do-wells."

She's recovered her performance voice, that cigarette sound, those rasping lifts. "Floozies," she says.

"Lovers," he says, taken by glamour.

And there's something else Lucille has recovered: her rapturous expression. "Lovers," she says.

CUT TO: Five days before. Isidore had his brother and next-door neighbor Norman's family in his living room, everyone frittering away the morning, newspapers and coloring books and coffee, four children, two wives, the lady of the house at the piano, the adults' easeful cigarette smoke up to the ceiling, the children quiet after having been chastised—you *know* not to run in the living room while Harriet's playing—as

Isidore sat contemplating his wife and, in the black sprinkle of piano notes, told himself that she was the mother of his children, talented, kind, and pretty even with her pointed nose, and he should be all right with all that. *I doubt I'll ever have the chance to see* her *again, anyway,* Isidore thought. And then he came across a paid notice, a surprising agony column, in *The New York Sun:*

Lucille Ball. Two Nights. The Havana-Madrid Theater. Showcasing Her Husb—

And the duality of his feelings returned. He hadn't seen or talked to her. And when you pull an illicit trigger, there's a kickback; it changes the forensics of who you are.

"Iz?" Harriet said.

He just looked, blinking. *Can't deny Harriet's been a good wife. And when our moods are matched, she's wonderful to talk with, gossip and secrets, not big secrets,* he told himself. *Not* the *big secret.* "Uh, don't stop playing, Har," he said.

"Okay," she said. She was shy even in front of her brother-in-law's family.

"You sounded wonderful," he said.

Pull an illicit trigger? Idiot! Boaster! His burning cheeks mocked him: How did I *pull any trigger? Who's to say the woman even remembers? Jesus, to suffer so, for nothing but a kiss!*

He closed his eyes. *Twenty-four hours a day, seven days a week, the assembly lines of sin roll out ever more heartbreak into the world. How angry he was now!*

Norman was asking, "What's shakin', Iz? Did they run something bad, the newspaper?" He was sitting on the couch opposite his brother. "Again with Auschwitz pictures? Is it corpses?"

Before waiting for an answer, Norman said to the room (his favorite conversation partner being an abstract congregation of ears): "They should leave off showing those, it's been long enough."

Norman's wife agreed. "Do we need gruesomeness on a Sunday?"

Isidore would've needed to hail from Krypton to flip the newspaper pages fast as he wanted. "Mmm," he said.

His mind was a drawer of sharp and perilous things. He had worked hard to control himself, to keep the drawer closed; don't let the blades and soft lips and regrets come spilling out.

Say something now. "I don't think we need gruesomeness," Isidore said, lifting his chin.

And he had managed it! He'd gotten pretty happy again, he thought—even these past fourteen months, after the kiss-emotions had settled—with wife and family. He'd been happy. Pretty happy.

What was so wrong with Harriet? Long ago, she'd improvised bawdy variations to "Boogie Woogie Bugle Boy" on the piano they'd bought that afternoon. ("Izzy was a famous cranny-prodder from out Brooklyn way/He had a child-gettin' style that no one else could play. . . .") Sometimes it bothered him that his friends and even his brothers didn't know shy Harriet had this silken, feisty side to her. They likely caught in the thin face, the black hair, and stately brows only a touching sort of home ec allure.

Lucille Ball. The advertisement read. *Two Nights. The Havana-Madrid Theater.*

This miracle made him furious.

It made everything seem as if he'd dreamed it and kept dreaming it. And there is no morality in a dream. No morality and no free will. You just do what the dream tells you to.

Showcasing Her Husband and—

Harriet was smiling at him, and he smiled back. Her flat mouth always had to make up for a lot with its intense red lipstick. And Isidore's friends and even his brothers were not privy to the gleam in her wide dark eyes, the sometime look of friskiness and appetite.

Not that he'd seen that appetite look much lately himself.

Isidore had been taught to believe—by popular music, movies, books, even many of the serious books he read; by the most sophisticated people he knew; in fact, by society itself—that love was its own reward. That a perfect love equaled a higher morality. Forbidden love most definitely included. (Not that people talked like this; it was simply and generally understood by cultured people.) *Fools give you reasons / wise men never try / some enchanted evening / when you find your true love.* Et cetera. *Was it Victor Laszlo or were there others in between? Or aren't you the kind that tells?* Yes, even Norman (who was not just Isidore's brother but business partner) cheated. Maybe, by remembering that, Isidore could sustain his sense of a principled self. He must have loved Lucille.

Harriet, meanwhile, seemed no longer to care if they ever had sex again.

Lucille Ball. Two Nights—a touch of defeat in the words. As in a great book, when you read some familiar insight and feel that you already knew it and might've written it yourself had you only articulated it. That very feeling, times a hundred.

"We should go and do something fun this week, Har," Isidore said.

It was a beautiful morning. Isidore was turned to his wife with the blatant eyes of the guilty. Sunshine lay across the floor, a golden light.

"Iz," Harriet said, "you're so pale. Everything okay?"

"Am I?" he asked. In the realm of morality, *should* can fall short of *did*. "I'm fine," he said.

"Okay," Harriet said.

The moment Harriet saw Isidore noticing her worried look, she blanked her own face. Isidore didn't care now. He was, as he sat here, moving away.

"These papers, they suppose it's their job to educate you," Norman was saying, "even on a Sunday. But on Sunday—"

"I *meant*," Isidore butted in, "let's you and me go into the city later this week, Har."

Bernie ran past Isidore's ankles, chasing Arthur, who wore a movie Indian's feathered headdress. This was not a disastrous family.

Harriet cocked her head and thought a second. "You mean besides the thing on the first of the month?"

Swallowing, Isidore was still moving away. He could see all that had been with him on the other shore, but could he make the jump and get back to what he'd had?

"Yes," he said. Did he *want* to get back to what he'd had?

Inside the newspaper, in the black-and-white allusions that went beyond his family, beyond Great Neck, Long Island, a different life was crooking a come-hither finger at him. And he went toward it.

"In fact, there's a theater thing I think we should go to," he said.

"Well, I'm jealous," said Matilda, Norman's wife, who sat near Isidore.

"BUT HARRIET WOULD never forgive," Norman whispered a little later in Isidore's driveway.

"Tell me," Norman added. "Dad saw?"

"It was nothing," Isidore said. "All right, she'd half-murder me, Harriet. But I can't forgive *myself*, is the thing."

"Uh-huh."

"I mean it."

Isidore craning his neck to look up Norfolk Road saw his father hadn't arrived yet. Harriet and the children were still in the house. He and Norman were going to pick up bagels for their father's weekend visit. Harriet would not forgive. But Isidore also knew she might act as if she had. And he couldn't abide living with that guilt.

"If Dad saw, we're talking about *Dad,*" Norman said. "All the standard rules shouldn't reply." He was the middle brother who acted like the oldest and almost smug about his dullness of mind.

But Norman was right. Their father wasn't the type to avoid saying something. Yet after the kiss, the old man had stayed quiet.

"A position you put him in, Iz." Norman was scratching at the perfect, tan yarmulke of baldness on the back of his head. "A father, to have to see that."

"Oh, please," said Isidore, opening the door to his Packard. "Coming from you."

"What about Phil," Norman said. He eased into the passenger seat. "Philly saw?"

When Isidore had kissed Lucille, he'd felt surprised at how close to relief it had felt. But somewhere in there, he'd definitely been ashamed, hadn't he, maybe he had, he definitely had been, right?

"You've done worse in your marriage, Norm," said Isidore coolly.

Together, Isidore and Norman had recently founded a business— NORMIDOR REALTY CORP.—that built almost the entire four-street development in which they both suddenly lived. (NOR-MIDOR's matter-of-fact slogan: "Building middle-class housing.")

"Your wife isn't my wife," Norman said, winding his wrist-watch. "You're not me."

"Ah. Thank you, Edward R. Murrow."

Norman gave a nasty chuckle. *"This I believe."*

In NORMIDOR's skyrise office near the Brooklyn promenade; at the horse track in Belmont or with foremen on muddy construc-tion sites; at the Boro Park Deli and in Temple Beth El, where twice a year everybody burned candles and opened scarcely under-stood prayer books for their dead—*everywhere* it was agreed that Isidore and Norman Strauss had each inherited half the qualities of their shrewd, moralizing father. These guys are like those twins Eng and Kang, people said. Norman has the stomach for business, they said. Isidore? Carries himself like a poet, wants to build affordable housing for working people, but does he care about profit? Now, if you could mix Iz and his brains with Norman and his appetites! I mean, that Norman is nothing but stomach. Ah, you don't know what you're talking about, Izzy's all right, let's go eat. . . .

"Anyway, she'll never find out," Isidore begged.

Maybe he could change the way he did business to be someone worthy of Lucille, someone who shined. Maybe he was looking at being a builder all wrong.

"If this is what in Long Island they call a bagel, it's for sure not Brooklyn," their father complained later that day as he sat in Isidore's kitchen.

Will Dad say something about Lucille to me? Isidore had won-dered. I'll never see her again, he thought. How will I live with that?

. . .

AFTER A CURSORY dinner in Manhattan, he and Harriet went to the theater. The Havana-Madrid on Fifty-first Street. He'd thought all week that maybe it would merely be an enjoyable night at a show. Or that being there with his wife would break the spell. "There" was the Lucille-Desi revue, a two-hour production, skits about marriage and music, which had now just about reached its rollicking finale. Drum-accompanied hip shaking, a hole in the stage narrowly avoided: a vaudeville show.

"It's funny, right?" he whispered to his wife next to him in the dark. He would like to hear her tell him Lucille was dazzling. Even a second-rate recompense fills your pockets with something. (A merely joyful husband-and-wife night out seemed impossible now. That husband, transmogrified, had gone.)

"Right?" he asked. "Right?" The show approached its big finish.

THE TRAVELING LUCILLE-DESI revue's big finish stood on three pillars of funniness:

1) The physicality of it had to look impossible; 2) the leads could reveal no effort in doing the impossible; 3) Lucille, in the midst of the impossible, needed to throw in some of her own uncanny, comic quirks. That was the conceptual basis of it, anyway.

Now, if you removed just one pillar, it'd be *whump,* instant stage death. It was time to test the concept.

Lucille's previous gag ("That's what I said: Dizzy Arnazzy. But anyhow, I want a job with your orchestra . . .") flopped and went, a very protracted two seconds ago.

The audience sat here, balanced between laughs. There was a quiet—even a nervous—attention. It was hot and still, and Desi and Lucille lingered for the longest short while.

Lucille saw Desi, at the back of his collar, sweat; she felt herself sweat from her armpits. This was worrisome. Cuban Pete, Sally

Sweet: their crucial, improvised bit of circling each other and tumbling. No recusing oneself. But in Columbus it hadn't gone right, nor in Hudson. Nor in Duluth; in Mt. Lakota, he'd tripped, or she had.

A stoplight kind of a moment, everybody waiting for the signal that'll set the evening rolling again.

"Can you do this—you're panting so?" Desi asked in a whisper. (Not that she had another choice.)

"Shh," she said.

They'd finished the bit with the xylophone; she'd just chucked her fedora behind the wagon wheel and her tear-away baggy pants getup the Rube Goldberg cello had already yielded, from its hidden compartment, the footrest, the flowers, the toilet plunger. But Lucille's breathing was—well, she was huffing. A lot. And they had another joke to tell. And there was only quiet from the audience.

At last, she took Desi's hand in her sweaty own. She began her stage yell: "I'm"—*huff huff*—"Sally Sweet!" (More like Sally Flop Sweat.)

The audience basically just realized that, somehow, she'd managed to switch her buffoon-wear for this sequined gown, this feathered hat; that she was beautiful; that Cuban Pete was suavely dancing Sally Sweet right toward a giant hole set up at center stage; and, worse, that Pete was gazing too distractedly at Sally—and Sally was too engrossed by reading the book in her free hand—to notice that they were heading straight for the imminent fall that'd surely kill them both.

"I'm Cuban Pete, and"—Desi's singing voice ran syrup-thick, although it did thin, a bit, when he had to stretch a high note over a consonant—"I hurry like Arthur Murray. I come from Havana and there's always *mañana . . .*"

Lucille's turn now. But . . . *huff huff.* What was the story with her breathing?

"I'm Queen of Delancey Street!" Lucille almost coughed.

Still, she was, even while she read the book and huffed, singing loudly. "When I start to dance"—she began to move—"everything goes chick-chicky *boom!*" The drum-timed pendulant of her hips. "Chick-chicky *boom!*"

ISIDORE SAT POTTED out there in Row 2, Seat 5. Those sexual hip explosions were for him a delicious anguish. Each *boom* after the *chick-chicky*s made pain.

Up on that stage, Cuban Pete ("I place my hand on your hip and . . .") was twirling Sally Sweet right at the perilous hole—in fact, already, they were smack-dab in danger.

Her foot arced out above the drop, and she tootled out her own comic *"Eeugh!"*—an idiosyncratic Lucille noise, a gag, a soon-to-be trademark, a signal to the audience, a signal to Desi, telling everyone that she'd been whirled into danger. But she kept dancing. Sally Sweet evidently remained (except for that dramatically inexplicable and inexplicably hilarious *Eeugh!*) unaware of the threat.

Earlier today, right up till curtain time, Lucille had been distant, pale, cross with her husband. It had annoyed Desi. "Enough!" he had said.

"Can't a girl get the jitters?" she had answered. "You know, New York, the big one, the night we've been—"

"Sure, 'course you can." He waved her off. "Just not to your stage partner and husband. Forget this. I'm off to get the papers."

But once Desi left her dressing room, he didn't visit the newsstand. He kept to his own wing of backstage, napping, playing the radio, where he heard something that floored him. (Was that the right word in this impossible language? Floored? Why not walled or ceilinged him? *Este país es comemierda.*) What the radio brought was news, but not just. *Personal* news. He greeted the hard surprise of it with some favorite behaviors: smoking, pacing, and—when the maid, Clara, arrived—giving a woman a good razzing. He started in on the way Clara dressed—the maid outfit. *¿Soy yo quien te hace mirar de esta manera? ¿No serías feo si no fueras nuestra doncella?*

"Oh, Mr. Arnaz," Clara said.

"Another cigarette, please," he said. "That a new hairstyle you got on?"

Clara was twenty-six, nearly and plumply genderless, and she didn't know how to answer a man like Desi, so she just smiled. There was something unreachable in him, and not just for Clara: some special Arnaz languor you'd never mistake for boredom. Like most gifted entertainers, he gave the sense of looking at you with all he had, but with Dez, you felt, too, that there was a mirror at your back or in your eyes—and this mirror was the reason he'd aimed his powerful notice in your direction in the first place. To see how he looked reflected in it.

"I actually *need* a hair appointment, Mr. Arnaz," Clara said. "And as we're in New York, maybe Miss Ball could give me a name."

"Now why would you do that?" he said, absently, his mind on the bad news he'd gotten from the radio. "You don't need to change anything."

Desi was personable. He had learned, chapter and verse, all the social manners and strategies; still, he would remind you of a me-chanic who was pretty okay up front with the customers but who wanted to slip out back and tinker with the dream car he was always fixing up. The dream car was himself. Anybody could sense this. The question was whether you were intrigued by this unreachabil-ity or resented it.

After he heard the radio item, at showtime, he went to fetch Lucille. Maybe I should break the story to her. She deserves to know.

But as he'd knocked on her dressing room, he'd decided against telling. Why risk bothering the show? And maybe it's the kind of news best shared alone. . . .

Now, onstage, another "Chick-chicky *boom!*" But with the added danger over the hole.

The actual jump had come.

There was no alternative now. Desi and Lucille knew—though for some reason, she huffed like an old lady—there was no more delaying.

The act of leaping in the nick of time. Some of it came out of those years of shared intimate bodily knowledge, but mostly, it was the result of plain old stage practice. *Chick-ch*—the spark of rehearsed movement. It can light over differences; it can buzz the world into one shared current. Lucille and Desi were now—*icky boo*—at the hole; their toes wiggled into the deep nothing below. Up to this point, the show hadn't gone great. Not terribly, but not great.

(The crowd—*"Ooh!"*—began to react; Izzy closed his eyes. Then couldn't *not* open them.)

Together, Lucille and Desi leaped—up they went over the hole, they were singing even, such grace and harmony, as synched as a deer and its reflection over a pond, she in mid-leap able to glance at the audience; goodness, would you just look at all those stone-idol faces, row after row, it's a bit drafty up over this thing, wait a second, who's that there, up near the front, is, is that . . . ? *And I'm Sall*—she and Desi cleared the open hatch, but Lucille was off course now, and her heel came down mid-rotation onto some unexpected thing. A fleck of wood off the Rube Goldberg cello. A banana peel. Who knows what. She didn't gasp; she winced. She even twisted a little. Desi followed, or, he didn't exactly follow. He just sort of predicted the activity, greeting the move with a corresponding twist. A responsiveness close to ESP. They were onto the next turn in this singing dance. And the audience kept laughing. Safety. But there was still something missing from the act.

And why was she breathing like this?

All the same, the revue tonight had debuted its new name. *The Desi Arnaz and Lucille Ball Revue* was now *I Love Lucy*.

"SO, I ENJOYED IT," Harriet said. "Their marriage is like our marriage, except for the trapdoors in the carpet; or maybe we've got them, too. Just kidding."

She walked holding her pocketbook to her chest so firmly it gave her shoulder a tilt, a posture of self-repression. It was as if her public shyness were creeping in to their private dealings.

"*You* liked it," she sort of asked.

Isidore was determined not to sacrifice the pleasure he felt. Lucille, her vital flash; don't tell *me* that was just the spotlight.

"I did, I did enjoy it," he told her. "I *did*. Did you? You did, right?"

He hadn't thought of the hole thing to be a metaphor until Harriet brought it up. Who cares? Wasn't Lucille a radiant humdinger? Wonderful, superb. And yet somehow it all made him feel an atom or two of disappointment as well.

"The woman does have something, sure," Harriet said, squeezing his hand.

If I'd never met *her,* Harriet's familiarity and niceness would've been enough. I want Harriet to be happy, he thought. I do!

Even the great books have it wrong. It's not that you marry a Karenin and then you meet a Vronsky. Marriage transforms every spouse, makes us all both. You fall for a Vronsky and end, Isidore thought, with a Karenin. (This kind of insight made up for missing the point of the trapdoor thing, right?)

Isidore looked and looked at the proscenium curtain. On that stage, in the spotlight, the applause she'd gotten—Lucille would never make that marital journey in his head from shiny to dull. She wouldn't have the chance. How unfair to Harriet.

But how sad to leave now. Lucille had vanished into some backstage El Dorado of glamour, of hiddenness, while he was pretty much exactly where he'd been, down here by the cheap seats; he'd joined the collective bovine schlep toward the exits.

"I'm not in a go-home mood, I don't think," he said.

"What? Really?" Harriet held her handbag in one hand and let go of him to fish out her umbrella (just in case) with the other.

She'd had a tough time when they moved to Long Island. She'd had to pick up the big shaggy plant of her Brooklyn life and hump it all the way out to Great Neck.

"A drink somewhere?" he said. Drinks were her soft spot. The first weekend of every month—or, as they referred to it officially,

The Thing on the First of the Month—Isidore and Harriet had been coming to Manhattan for drinks and/or dinner. It'd seemed a nice recent change. And it had never seemed pathetic to him before.

He was now as nervous as he'd ever been, and as giddy; he knew what he had to do.

AN ACTRESS IS a kind of Baskin-Robbins franchise of smiles.

Every movie actress in 1950 needed the soggy-eyed, mournful smile. And the shut-lipped smile, the *make-love-to-me*—another requisite, right behind being "leggy." Some varieties were particular to certain women. Lucille's smile came in six flavors.

Bette Davis smiled in eight flavors, damn her. (And Bette wasn't even a smiler.) Kate Hepburn could pull twelve.

After tiny to big parts in more than seventy movies, Lucille had found her trademark: the *I-know-something-you-don't* comical smile. Teeth showing. Eyeballs up and looking to the side. (This was a Harpo Marx deal. But nobody realized this, and wouldn't for five years, when she'd graciously invite that mop-headed genius and has-been to appear on TV.) More than her unequally thick lips, Lucille's giant moon eyes decided all her smile flavors.

At this moment, she was working the simple-gratitude smile. "Roses?" she said to her fans. "How sweet. Thank you."

She laid the flowers aside immediately for her maid, Clara, who would get them later. But it was true: Lucille loved roses, she loved the autographs and the post-show jostle, and her fans she loved most of all.

A knot of admirers stood before her in the corridor.

"No, Miss Ball, thank *you*," a female fan said now. People Lucille talked to often felt their cheeks go hot. "For, well, for, um—?" she asked. "You two aren't *really* married?"

Desi laughed.

When celebrity is in attendance, a gathering of normals sucks in its gut.

"I am lucky," Desi said into the undifferentiated white faces of these undifferentiated white people. "Because she married me." This worked. The fans' chuckles arrived gratefully.

Desi was able to cast a sentence out there like a twist of wire and feathers and know the fish would come swimming toward it. That winning skill of born celebrities. Even with his unwieldy voice, his limited wit. Didn't matter. He'd lure in the human fish.

"Certainly, I'll sign that," said Lucille, reaching for some straw-hatted biddy's autograph book.

"Make it out to M-A-R-T-H . . ."

For the rest of Martha's life, she would say, "Lucille Ball? Met her. She's just like one of us." Not so, however.

Lucille held Martha's pen gently, redly. Nails red enough to look cheerful about something. She *wasn't* one of them. She wasn't a stand-in. She had an extra vividness.

Or she could have. Now she was still breathing hard. It had Lucille a tad worried. She was able to feel her own face, tired and wheezy, amid all these covetous mouths and covetous faces.

After signing two more autographs, she rubbed her arms.

"Tired, Dez. I'm *tired*."

She spoke as if her fans weren't there, which was confirmation. "What say we make a clean squeak and go to the hotel?"

Desi knew it was just about time to reveal the news. "Sure, honey," he said.

HARRIET WATCHED ISIDORE fail to leave the theater. His hands behind his back, he dawdled.

"Something in your shoe, Iz?"

"Huh?" he said. "Oh. Ha."

She and Isidore took two steps before having to stop. Momentarily held up in a cloud of audience chatter. "Are *you* tired, dear?" he asked, loudly, over the din.

"Tired?"

Harriet worked to hide any hardness from Isidore; she didn't often give herself the right. Her voice, even when she felt grumpish, might sound borrowed from the polite lady down the street who offered relationship advice. Maybe because Harriet didn't like this about herself, she also worked to hide any softness. "If you want to get a drink, we can," she said now.

Isidore brightened.

He said, "Where do you want to wait for me?"

"What?"

"Sorry. The john. Have to use the john." He was already moving. "Stomach upset." Even pushing a chair out of the way. "Meet you out under the marquee? Ten minutes," he said. "Fifteen."

ISIDORE SHOULDERED PAST the concession booth, past the ladies' room, the men's, looking, looking for a backstage door, still looking. "Please," he said into the departing crowd, the sourness of exhaled smoke, the mothball musk of wool coats, of furs. "May I get through?"

How many little suicides had he committed since Thanksgiving? "Please." How many times had he killed who he had become that night on Coney Island? "Please let me pass."

A mustachioed concierge, sharply dressed, tartly compassionate, told him the stage door was *that* way. But the truth, boss, is, I don't suppose you'll be able to get in.

"Okay, then, I'll just, er," Isidore said. But he would make sure he got in.

Hey, bub, take a powder—(this from a separate concierge)—no backstage visitors, got it?

Meanwhile, just out of Isidore's eyeshot: Lucille.

She was just now getting to her feet in the backstage hallway, with a fur stole draped around her.

"Sure, Red, you are tired," said Desi, smoothing the fur. "You will feel better" is all the news he told her.

Lucille looked back with the sacrificial glance of the con-demned. "In all my years, Dez, have you ever known me to be tired after a standing ovation?"

"I have a hunch why," said Desi, "take my arm"—who, secret be told, didn't care for his wife's playing Joan of Arc at the stake of an autograph line. Or playing Bette Davis playing Joan of Arc.

Her reaction to the news might be complicated. She was child-less at thirty-nine, and for all her ambition, it hasn't been easy. Maybe he should tell her only after they hit the air of West Fifty-first.

"I'm sure Clara will come in a minute; Robert'll find her," Desi was saying. "But it's going to be a good evening, I promise you."

"What are you on about now, you crazy Cuban? Oh, you never listen to me, I swear. I'm *tired*."

"Ha, yes, I know. You'll see."

Desi tried to look jolly. He believed he knew Lucille enough to predict her actions—though he wasn't one to bother trying, really, to know somebody else, let alone a somebody as full of multitudes as was his wife—but he was surprised anyway at his own helpless-ness to forecast the sort of thing she would say upon learning that Walter Winchell had broadcast to the world a crucial and secret detail about their lives, a secret that her doctor had kept even from her. She was pregnant. *The hospital leaked it to Winchell before they told me and you,* he'd say. *But, anyway, darling—we're going to have a baby!* He wouldn't linger on the fact that the listeners of ABC Radio knew before she did.

"Where the devil is Clara?" Lucille said.

"*Fine,*" Desi said and went to fetch the maid himself.

A glowing red exit sign watched Lucille stand there; it anato-mized her head into elements of pink, red-pink, and shadow. And she gave a stylishly imperious nod to the few autograph seekers there. *Thank you,* her face told them, *but no. Don't.*

The sort of background people whose jobs Lucille never would get a handle on—spotlighters, riggers, etc.—came and went, in-quiring about her comfort. Desi returned, lugging things the maid normally would. Lucille's purse, flowers. And it was Desi who opened the exit to the street—"I'll go try again to find Clara, okay?"—but it was Lucille who first saw what was out there in the alley just off Fifty-first Street.

She seemed at first not to know him. Lucille blinked at the man with her lusterless blue stare until memory showed in her eyes: a school of bright fish darting straight for the surface.

Good God.

It was the man from the Coney Island party, taking off his hat. "Lucille," Hold-on/Isidore said.

He looked calmly unsurprised and suddenly very close and in front of her. Hello.

Lucille found herself in a brief fantasy, and in this fantasy, Desi storms off and divorces her, and she doesn't necessarily accept Isidore/Hold-on's courtship, not fully or at first, but she does, in spite of herself, begin to allow the man to take her out on the town, and, yes, she's unmarried and disgraced publicly, but somehow she holds up all right, and the guy's a good snuggler. All this in a milli-second.

She said, "Hold-on, is it?"

"I'm hoping it still is."

Meanwhile, Desi *was* ten yards off, fifteen now, and failing, for the moment, to notice Isidore; Desi's attention in that bustling place was taken by somebody else walking up to his side—Robert. Robert was their occasional New York chauffeur and even more occasional New York houseboy. And Desi would see Isidore if he'd just turn.

A long while ago, going back to Desi's birth and right up till he turned sixteen—which was when President Batista snatched up all Arnaz property and on balance just kind of poked the family in the eye—Desi's father had been the mayor of Santiago de Cuba, which is a way of saying that Desi, or Desiderio Alberto Arnaz y de Acha III, had been accustomed for many years not only to wealth (having been heir to a San Simeon–sized home, three ranches, and a vaca-tion address on a private island in Santiago Bay) but accustomed to poverty also, because his Miami refugee days had plunked him down in a boardinghouse and shuffled his mornings from odd job (busboy) to odd job (doorman). And so here was the final result of those two lived pasts, the prosperity and the austerity: a sort of relaxation of the spirit. That's all. A relaxation among the working-class people of his life. In handing his care over to Robert and Clara, Desi felt comfortable. Most old-money rich Americans wouldn't, probably; neither would the nouveau, the egalitarian of heart. But Desi acted neither rudely to "the help," nor overly polite (over-politeness being another kind of disrespect, a more delicate form of rudeness), and this made his hired caretakers more fond of him than they were of Lucille—or of anyone else they were paid to serve.

Desi had stopped, and Robert had come right beside him. The chauffeur didn't look at his boss, but down the block at Isidore— fearfully.

"Mr. Arnaz, I can't find Clara."

But even as he talked, Robert's eyes stayed on the strange man who stood there next to Lucille holding a fedora to his chest. Robert submitted to curiosity and imagination. Well, I'd like to take a nice long dip in her blue eyes myself, Robert thought.

Lucille's face—now looking at Isidore—was unreadable. Isidore stood wondering at its mysteries, and Desi showed up at his side.

"It's you, huh?" Desi said.

Desi's expression was wild. Pleasurable anger. Gratifying, meaty anger. I should've dragged this *maricón* back where he came from, library or pawnbroker's, down in Brooklyn, off to Palestine.

"Yes, me," Isidore said. "I think I owe you one."

Desi faced Isidore; Isidore faced Desi.

Isidore didn't want too much. Just a little enjoyable time with a glamorous woman. A slippery tail of time, just once, grabbed and held.

"If you're trying to upset me, friend," Desi said.

He had a flared look; Isidore tried to match it. What if I come back to Harriet with a black eye again?

Desi said, "This time I take a swing, I won't miss."

"You didn't miss last time," Isidore said. He could feel his heart twist on its cords and vines.

In the middle of the path of our life, I went astray from the straight road and found myself in a wilderness where the right course was lost.

WHERE IS MY husband, Harriet thought.

Out under the marquee, just around the corner from that husband, with walkers flowing by—and she getting bumped and jostled like a marble in a funnel—Harriet couldn't quit looking at her diamond-salted watch. There was a chilly breeze, and she kept tensing her shoulders. What in the world could be taking so long? Maybe a long line. These words a way to disavow, to convince herself that this was her only question.

Isidore found himself skulking alone back to where he guessed his wife might be.

He was tensing his own shoulders against the wind. Jesus; so damn *cold*. Lucille was gone. And he'd never be a heartbreaker, he thought. Yet he found himself falling for her.

This idea was interrupted: that panicked fire engine, its repeating yowl.

A minute or so ago, Lucille had said, "Just wait a second, Desi." Or something like that. "Don't do anything rash." And then she and her husband were gone.

Isidore tried to piece it together, on this street where taxis and hansom cabs kept rolling past.

Lucille's husband's expression, its raw fury—*that,* and then everything had gone chaotic. I'd been in front of the husband; Lucille had said, "Just wait," and then—? Okay, some woman who seemed to work for them had rushed over. Clacking heels. This woman had been in a state. "*There* you are!" She'd worked to catch the husband's eye, to convey some message. "What is it?" Lucille had said. The husband had answered in Spanish. *"Tengo que decirte algo."* Isidore didn't understand; maybe Lucille did. The husband unclenched himself. And then the entire Lucille-Desi crowd up and left—and Isidore ended up being the guy looking at fire engines and cabs and wondering what happened.

"Falling for"—what can that even mean? All this should be said with enough caveats to overflow his pockets. Anyway, she was gone.

Shmendrik! An actress talks to you, next thing you're climbing streetlamps and dancing with parking meters. And, there down the street, there's Harriet. That's your truth. Facing the other way, kind of dopily, at the end of the block.

Anybody else looking at Harriet would have seen a handsome if stiff woman, fur coat and pointed nose and anxious posture, waiting. What did Isidore see?

Arguments, laughs, that one crack in the playroom wall he has yet to seal up. Countless reminders of countless events. He slowed. The inscrutable emotion that sparked a very pretty glow to Harriet's face that time, right before she asked Isidore how did he like them apples. Shoving his hands in his pockets now, Isidore sighed. Back in 1938 or '39, he'd thought that Harriet's having opened her coat to him at Brandt's Flatbush theater was the only real happiness that ever surprised him or ever would.

"Hey—Hold-on! Hold-on!"

AND NOW HE can feel Lucille's presence in the shadows. Her dressing room is dark. "Not much of a hideaway," she says to him.

Isidore's shyly smiling. He's barely here. This backstage moment is not real life. This backstage moment is literature and cinema, is the American songbook, is boffo footage, reaction shots and shadows, is delicious agony in frames that flicker; it's all the dreams of romantic deceit to be found in the modern savoir faire.

Minutes ago, she'd called to Isidore on Seventh Avenue, just up from Fiftieth—"Come back, come back!"—and explained that she'd sent Desi off by asking him to let her go to the powder room. Same excuse as Isidore's, pretty much. He took her hand. His own wife had been sixty yards away, maybe fifty, how much longer will she wait, she must even now be looking for him.

The shared lie and rush gave the added heart-jolt of communion—an intimate, exhilarating secret.

"Well, I never doubted it," Isidore had said. This had been untrue, but he believed anyway. "I never doubted you'd come."

He'd forgotten about the dimple of her collarbone. Hello, dimple, hello!

"I should go back to my husband," she said already, not seeming to realize she'd gentled Isidore's hand downward. "It was nice to see you again. But I really came, if I can say this, I really came just to apologize. And now I should, um, I really *should*—"

She stopped talking.

She stood so close, anyway, out there on Seventh Avenue. Her hand still in his. I am Hold-on. She's christened me.

"But I can't," he'd said. Miraculous that he could hear his own voice over the whamming in his chest. "I can't accept your apology."

His heart was a sledgehammer on a trampoline.

"But, God, you're a kick," she said. They might as well have been—it was as if she wanted to be—dance partners, chest touching chest.

Never had Isidore been described as a kick. But he wasn't Isidore just now. He asked, "What say we go somewhere?"

The hard little slash of her laughter. She said, "My *my*, Hold-on." He watched her cheek flush its affection. "Hold *on*, Hold-on."

Isidore's question beckoned—*what say we go?*—a substitute feature suddenly playing at the cinema. Her hand felt like it softened in his. My movie-star girlfriend.

And the laugh on her face changed—she tilted her head.

"I was feeling very tired, Hold-on." Her mouth, her eyes, gorgeous with pleasure and nerves. "Now I'm not."

"You were nice to me on the beach that night," she said. "We danced. I don't know." A Lucille scaled down now by shyness, into a particularized woman.

"There *is* a place, come to think of it, Hold-on." An intense bright desire had passed into Lucille's throat. "My dressing room," she'd whispered. "My dressing room." The words had come from deep in her. "My dressing room."

And now here they are.

(It's a cozy place once Lucille snaps on the lights: sunflowers, framed photos, a chocolate sampler on the table. Domesticity. Lucille is always seeking a home.)

She comes to Isidore now; he holds her at her arms.

"A simpering, whimpering child again, Hold-on." For a moment, Isidore doesn't know she's quoting.

"Rodgers and Hart," he says at length.

"*They* knew."

She ashtrays her Fatima (Isidore must let her arms go), and he watches the blue smoke climb and curl. "Hold-on," she says. "If you were to try, I'd like it."

A wife, material comfort, a slice of pie after dinner. If these are all you get, what is the point of being born into this adventurous century?

The head of a match scrapes inside his chest, flashes. The lovely feel of her. He has entered the next room of his desire.

And so Isidore's lips do try; they try her soft and perfumed neck. They try the line of her jaw.

They try her lips, slippy and sweet.

He doesn't think about the husband and whether the guy's looking for Lucille, even now. Her hands float along his face and shiver the skin. He doesn't think of his wife or all that had been the foundation of who he was. If reckless abandon is in the cards—

"Now," Lucille says. "Do what I want you to."

—let's abandon ourselves to recklessness.

ACT TWO

"A stray canary had fluttered into her house and mine."
—*Vladimir Nabokov*

—SET PIECE—

Tennessee.

Sundown. The curtain of day is falling, and the dead won't shut up.

It is 1864, wartime. On the banks of the Mississippi, across from Fort Pillow, we see a Union soldier named Meriday Edgefield argue with ghosts.

Forty men, thirteen of them wounded, lie on the windswept scrub that is Chickasaw Bluff. Everyone's been killed. Everyone. They'll kill us, too, soon as they find us, the men around Edgefield are saying.

Edgefield doesn't listen to these wounded; he is listening to the already dead. You have to take command, the dead say. You must lead.

Me?

Edgefield is not used to ghost logic, ghost arguments. He holds the rank of private. Never has he led anyone—never.

Red is spilled all across the horizon; the long white neck of the sky has only just been slit.

A CinemaScope view now of the land between the fort and these hiding survivors, a wide shot from a helicopter. The camera pans the entire distance from river to bluff—a flood plain, scattered with dead and wounded soldiers.

Cut to Meriday Edgefield's dark-complected face, thoughtful in close-up . . .

—*Opening of* The March of the Tenth, *a film treatment by Isidore Strauss, with Lucille Ball; handwritten on Beverly Hills Hotel letterhead*

CHAPTER FOUR

M Y GRANDFATHER AND I *had talked literature at long, haphazard intervals. He'd slipped me* The Jungle Book, *Thanksgiving 1985; at high school graduation, I showed him my senior essay,* "Gatsby: *How to Endure a Bigoted Work," 1992. He was a real estate man who admitted he'd wanted—once, long ago—to be a novelist; I confided my identical hope. We rarely discussed it. But this near-secret commonality, a tough little garden, flourished even under such irregular watering.*

And now I learned he had done it! It turned out that, furtively, when he was a young man, he had done it. Or, almost. And with someone famous.

*F*OUR, THREE, TWO—*BEEP*. Go, go!

The natural thing is to respond. But you can't. You can't just turn your face to the wind of applause.

The soundstage as Lucille crosses it feels awfully big. Red camera lights blink like alien eyes.

Call it, this blinking red evening, her *last* last chance.

This is not the pilot episode. There had *been* a pilot episode—she and Desi filmed it back in March. The pilot episode did not air. The pilot episode had been terrible. . . .

An audience wants you to be happy, and that goes into your blood and makes you happy. But turning your face to applause is not acting. Turning to applause is acting's opposite. But maybe huge stardom—the phosphorescent super-prominence she's after—involves more than acting. More, and less. (Though nobody knows yet if TV can bring that intensity of stardom.)

Lucille would swear this is beyond the last chance for her.

Her image is going to be sent out via unfathomable technology—or maybe it *is* fathomable, but in the way prayer is fathomable—and aimed at the montage of between New York and Los Angeles, where adults are judged too prissy to see a married couple in their marriage bed; the farm towns, sure, but mainly the hopeful and somehow still rural-in-feel urban centers of greater America, your Lansings, your Cheyennes, your Tulsas, pale towns—thataway, past Piscataway—where, to hear Lucille tell it, neighbors provide a real community (it's the sense of many hands giving you a boost), which can be lovely until in one way or another you distinguish yourself. And then the many hands slide up and seize your throat.

The first line of aired *I Love Lucy* dialogue—"You didn't get that dish clean, you know"—isn't spoken by Lucille Ball. "There's a schmutz still."

"Nuh-uh, Ethel. That's *not* schmutz," Lucille, as Lucy, responds. (No, she can't show that the applause makes her happy.) "That's a floral decoration!" Her character is doing housewifely work in the kitchen.

"You sure, Lucy?"

"Positive, Ethel"—pointing to the mark on the plate. "Can't you see? Flowers in a pattern of [pause] gravy." A specially calibrated comic beat. "Okay, fine. Schmutz."

The audience's laughter: respectful, obedient, we'll give you this one. The other speaker is a heavy-haired actress named Vivian Vance—tonight and forever Ethel Mertz.

The script wants Lucille to come off as miserable here, a housewife scrubbing at a greasy life. But why would her character be cleaning the dinner dishes midafternoon—and accompanied by a friend? Not important. (Let Lucy scrub; *Lucille,* on the other hand, hasn't cleaned a thing in at least seven years. Ricardo isn't Ball.)

AGAIN, THIS IS not the pilot episode. Lucille during the pilot episode had been four months pregnant and caught in some choppy physical seas. Swollen ankles, belly; painful swollen walk—she'd been asked to hide the evidence, couldn't. Bad nausea, too. In the pilot, the Ricardos had no comical neighbors. No Ethel, no Fred. More, it was overtheatrical and sluggish; it lacked a second act. (But it did have thrilling comic eruptions.) CBS shopped the pilot to the big advertising agencies; in the space the Mertzes would later fill, the pilot had singing, the numbers "The Continental" and "Babalu," it had Pepito the Spanish Clown. Not one agency wanted it. Still, after the Arnazes agreed to an insultingly small salary (in exchange for their getting one hundred percent ownership of *I*

Love Lucy's film prints and negatives, which anyway seemed pie-in-the-sky), CBS *had* managed to get Philip Morris tobacco to take a flier on Lucille. One condition, though: CBS had to agree not to broadcast the awful pilot, ever.

The upshot is they're now filming Episode No. 2. Which will air as Episode No. 1. Or will if it's any good.

So, the last, last chance. And Lucille delivers her line.

"ETHEL, YOU WANTED to ask me something about you and Fred?"

Vivian/Ethel: "Oh, right! About Wednesday evening." That half-decibel-too-loud 1950s TV voice, if a bit mumbled.

Well, if Vivian Vance doesn't want to be here, fine. I mean, if Vivian Vance fails to see the appeal of television. But jeez-o-pete, Lucille thinks, don't just *mumble* it in. It's odd—crass and superficial—to need to be the most famous person in the world. I know that, Lucille thinks.

Lucille has her hair tied with a kerchief that comes to top knots like puppy ears. And the dialogue leaving her mouth tastes a little stale and expository.

"Isn't that your big night, Ethel?" she says.

Can the audience even follow the story line? (In the pilot episode, there had been some voice-over: *"In Manhattan, you'd find Ricky and Lucy Ricardo. Ricky Ricardo you know— the famous bandleader. And Lucy is a renowned, um, well—her hair is very bright. And she's married to him. . . ."* But the writers have dropped that announcer, that explanation, for this second try.)

Now Vivian/Ethel is saying: "Yes, Wednesday's our wedding anniversary."

"Yours and Fred's?"

"No, mine and Gary Cooper's."

Laughter even less enthusiastic. Nobody likes dialogue that exists just to tell the viewers who is with whom.

Vivian/Ethel: "I was wondering if you could help plan something for it?"

"What are you thinking?"

(Without that narrator, how will this audience know who Ricky is? Lucille worries this script might be hopeless.)

Still, for this episode, there are things she and Desi have made certain of. This time, shoot in a theater that's closer to movie studio than to radio set. Have water-cooled lights, three cameras, constant dolly movement. And a live audience for a filmed show. (All firsts.) Yes, they learned from the pilot episode, but you can't rig the calendar. *Streetcar* with Brando, armistice negotiations at Kaesong, Judy Garland at the Palace—Lucille has found herself in a rainy news season; it won't stop drizzling headlines. Which is to say the time feels kind of event-drenched, and how can a *never-quite-was* become umbrella enough to shield America from the downpour?

Ethel: "Fred and I have been together since I was a girl, and I promised myself that at least once in my life I would visit a fun nightspot with him."

"Who would deny you that?" Lucy says.

She puts the soiled pot down without having scrubbed it, nor does she sweat. A performer can exemplify the audience, but a star shouldn't change herself too much. Screw the collective average— even when the collective average is what's meant to be portrayed. Average is no path to veneration. Would-be idols forget that.

"Why, a fun nightspot is your due," Lucy's telling Ethel.

Mary Pickford and Jean Harlow put silly ideas into our brains about what matters, Lucille thinks. Of course it's cockamamie to want that much celebrity. All the same . . .

Lucy: "Okay, tell me your plan."

Ethel: "We march in and say to our husbands, 'I know what let's do. A fun night out.' You back me up. Then Ricky hops to his feet to say, 'Wonderful—'"

"Ricky hops to his feet?"

"Of course."

"Of course *not*," Lucy says. "Ricky hates fun nights out."

"But he works in a fun nightspot."

Lucille has Lucy answer with her trusty pout-smile. "Exactly."

Every other television show Lucille can name is broadcast live from New York. But she's more comfortable in L.A. What a hassle executives gave them! *Do it from California when the whole damn country's on the East Coast?* "Well, we can record it in L.A. and ship it to New York," Desi answered. And Philip Morris, too: *Wouldn't recording a show mean the sound quality will be crap?* "All right—so we do it as film." Then CBS weighed in. *Is that even feasible? The cost!* Lucille: "I learned doing *Hey Diddle Diddle,* I need to hear the laughs. And I'm not moving back to New York."

And so here she stands now. Filming; acting; L.A. That is, she tries to appear a harried housewife people believe in *while being a star they desire.* She's in an apron, a modest kitchen, and full glamour makeup. (The room is only three-walled, as if there has been a shift in the accepted disposition of things.) Doors that won't shut, windows that can't open. And because wardrobe changes cause a lag, Lucille wears two layers of clothes. She's flanked by gaffers working the light-dim machine; a "script girl" stands in a booth ten feet over the stage. And each set and everything in it has been painted various shades of gray, is built from tobacco profits. Audience cigarette smoke looks like pencil lines in the glare. You try ignoring all activity. You turn down the flame of charisma just enough and still get the audience to boil like water.

Lucille feels her hands go slick.

"No, guess what I think, Ethel?" Lucy's saying. "You *should* have a special night out."

Why am I nervous? Wasn't I the star of *The Big Street*? Lucille thinks. But—what's the plot of this show now? Not enough, maybe?

There's also something else that causes her nervousness.

This is all very strange. Her ambition has never eased off before. But now there's a serpent in the garden, a thought. What is so great about veneration? Who needs to put forth superhuman effort? For what?

Could the way out of unnameable discontents be found someplace other than in this show—in something already there in her brain? Yes, maybe. Anyway, she's been thinking about him since makeup. About the relaxing normality of him.

TWO HOURS EARLIER, she'd sat in a chair by a mirror, and a man brushed color onto her cheeks. "Whaddya know?" the man had said. His name was Hal Brade. He dressed all in black like a Greenwich Village Prospero. "Whaddya see?"

And she told Brade, "You're going to make me a knockout if it kills us both."

How much would any man understand about mirrors? For Lucille, a mirror was a thing you approached lightly, then dug out a few purse-articles of faith to begin a 1950s woman's liturgy.

She'd heard Brade had worked with Jean Harlow on *Red-Headed Woman*.

"Oh, *Red-Headed Woman* was before my time," he said.

"I was hoping." Lucille patted her 'do. "For obvious reasons."

"Though wasn't she some dancer, though."

"With those legs?"

"A dancer from the calves up," Brade said.

"With those *arms*?"

Brade pulled back her bangs—"That's the type of thing, I assume, your hair, you're adjusting the color yourself?"—lifting the forehead, opening the face.

She gave him her grimacy look of *Was Hollywood built in a day?*

"I can see immediately, the camera has always loved you, though. Tonight will be a giant success." He smiled. "I have a feeling we're going to be old friends right off."

"*Giant,* you think?" she was checking out her face at various slants. "You know, the Apaches were right about the camera," she said.

"Takes your soul?"

"Worth trading for a bottle of whiskey."

This was her program; there were examples to be set. A star of her own show cannot simply be *friends* with a makeup jock. Unless she can be. Maybe I just like Jews, she thought.

She allowed herself an inward chuckle. Jews. Like Pandro Berman, but people thought that had been because—well, let people think what they want. Berman ran the studio, but he was good, she thought. In the Desi vein, just not as handsome; sweeter to deal with. Ah, there was Hold-on, too. Nice and handsome, in that kink-haired way. Strong nostrils. What is love at first sight? Lust? Yes, lust—but not only. And love at first sight is not, lord knows, friendship. (Mack Gray had been a Jew, too, turned out. How long since I saw him—old Maxie Greenberg? Probably all of them communists. Well, I was a communist, too, for a time, she thought.) Friendship was too thin and runny a word for love at first sight. But love at first sight shares things with friendship. She thought, it's kind of like when you meet another gal and think, *This stranger and I will definitely be friends.* Or like me and this makeup guy. Something trivial might start it. Some joke one of you tells. Someone has a handbag you like, any little thing. Sudden friendship happens, often between women—just takes you. But sudden romantic attachments? Well, there was that fella and me. Hold-on. Although the first time with Desi, too, it took me, she thought. At the RKO commissary. Desi had walked in; Maureen O'Hara said, "I hear he's a real lady-killer," and Lucille said, "Well, he's about to meet his next victim." And that was that. But what *is* love at first sight? An immediate belief in soul-similarity, soul-unison. This was all just a dim sense she had; she wouldn't put it quite this way. Words didn't get at it, anyhow. It was a kind of hunch of the body. Like with Ted Sward when he dropped the seventh-grade napkin. Or like kissing Hold-on, the desire to initiate the kiss—a hunch of the body that didn't involve *just* the body.

"I do my best—Hal, is it?" She was leaning toward the mirror to ink-in the line of her cleavage with shadow.

"Hal Brade, yes," the makeup man said. "Is Miss Ball happy though?"

Hold-on, a different kisser than Desi, kissing my neck, my ear. His warm cheek, that thorny hint of bristles. She told herself not to think about her suspicion that love at first sight had gotten her here, geographically speaking. Had she forced CBS to do the show in L.A. partly to get far away from the temptation of that guy?

Well, let's not be overly dramatic, Lucille thought. She was not so delusional—so actressy—that she couldn't acknowledge there were other reasons. More pressing reasons. She and Desi owned a roomy and cherished ranch in California. And New York is where she'd failed, and so to her, it stood for failure. (She'd never say that aloud.) Plus, some skies may change but some rains just keep squalling. Which is to say, had Lucille not wangled it so she and Desi could work together near home, her marriage would have been all downed trees and power lines, flooded streets. Because, offered distance and opportunity, Desi would cheat up a storm. The TV show was meant to be a kind of hurricane cellar. ("Who'm I going to believe, Dez," she'd said, "you or my eyes?" Joking even then about his behavior.) And after so many years of having given up on being parents, Lucille and Desi now had a nine-week-old daughter. Lucie Désirée Arnaz. Their ambition and now the child had formed the scaffolding of their love.

Maybe a woman can love two people?

NOW, HOURS LATER, the character Lucy is trying to lift her neighbors' unhappy romance a little, while the person Lucille stands before microphones and two hundred spectators, and, oh yes, possible millions at home, thinking, don't squint in the lights, and facing three fearsome archangels, black and humpbacked: the 35 mm cameras that prowl the stage.

Lucy is scheming up an intrigue: It's marriage as genial trickery. The story line scrapes ahead, barely.

"Marriage *should* include some nightlife," Lucy/Lucille says. "But ever since 'I do,' there's too much 'we *don't.*'"

Maybe the show is not a storm cellar. Maybe my marriage is

already dead, she's thinking. Maybe what the show is is an under-taker, dressing up the corpse, giving it a dignity it didn't possess in life. Desi is almost seven years younger than Lucille: hard on any couple. But on a Hollywood couple? Yet as Desi and she left the ranch this morning, they passed a broken fence, and he said, "Ha! Remember?" and she said, "I was thinking of that, too." And just last week, Desi went down to the basement on me, did it the French way, she thinks. But why have I put myself in that position, to never age, if I can help it; why did I choose a young skirt-chaser for a husband?

And so thoughts of Isidore come again, surprising, buoying, the whispering serpent in her ear.

THERE'D BEEN A surprising wickedness to Hold-on's mouth in her Broadway dressing room that time. She remembered the fun as he'd unzipped her, goodbye to dress, goodbye to brassiere. She'd had a mind to stop and to voice some prudence, but her hips, on their own, had carried toward him. . . . Now Ethel and Lucy are ap-proaching their TV husbands under TV lights. They left the three-walled kitchen to try to "catch more flies with honey than with vinegar" in the three-walled den—female sensuality as nothing more than a means to something nonsensual, as a trick to get Ricky and Fred to take them dancing. Lucy sits on Ricky's lap. Fred sits on Ethel's lap. The audience laughs. And her hips really had pressed into Hold-on. And Hold-on had scooped Lucille's breast into his mouth. In lowering his own head, he'd needed to crouch a little, which somehow had enhanced the tall mannishness of him. Hot breath, cold room, the slight tickle of teeth on the most responsive skin. *Stay like that, Hold-on,* she told him. She rested her backside against a table; on the table was Isidore's wide-brimmed hat. The entirety of her body, cocked like a handgun. His blue tailored suit. One of his hands clasped strongly on Lucille's hip. He lifted his memorizing eyes to her body. No smile, standing fully clothed, even his tie done up, the coat playing tight on his shoulders—and she felt her breastbone go chilly. The top of her dress now at her midriff. She reached behind her and put on Isidore's hat. Prop comedy. She'd added the hat to feel less naked when subtracting her clothes. Isidore didn't laugh but looked as if he were on fire. The practical mathematics of nudity. She bent and gyrated on one spot, trying to push down her underwear. Isidore with both hands grabbed her dress, a whispery noise—*shoosh*. I feel the open air on me down there, she'd thought. She'd thrashed her melting hips into his fingers. The TV audience keeps laughing now. TV's Fred and Ricky don't want to take TV's Lucy and Ethel to the Copa—the characters say they want to go to the fights, alone—and it's turned into a four-person argument. Ricky pleads Fred's case and Lucy pleads Ethel's case, friends as defense counsel. "If you're going to act that way, then Ethel wants out of this marriage!" Lucy says, which makes Ethel shriek: "No I don't!" [Laughter.] Lucy says: "Regardless, Ethel and I will find men who *will* take us," and Ricky says: "In that case, me and Fred will find some ladies to entertain *us*!" Then in the kitchen away from their husbands, Lucy says: "Ethel, I'll bet we know a couple men who are handsome and unattached." [A funny little pause.] "A couple men who are unattached?" [A pause that's funnier because it's long.] "A couple men." [A pause that's funniest because it's short.] "Boy and his G.I. Joe doll?"

And Lucille doesn't even hear herself, as Lucy, earn the audience's laugh; she's off to the next gag, and preoccupied anyway. But the tone of the evening is changing, warming. Hold-on, in pulling off his necktie, had chucked it onto the floor. Now his hands were on Lucille's backside. He bent again, he licked her breast. The throb of her body. Small acts in quick succession: the lifting of one of her legs as she eased onto the table; the struggle for his zipper; two of his fingers skimming into the center of the throb. And the sort of gulping feeling of this in her, of her taking his fingers in. And that torpedoing boom of her nerve endings, and that wonderful liquid warmth. A quick gaspy breath. Her heart a paddleball going on a crazy elastic *thwap thwap thwap*—she was so wet, her legs were quivering. Reaching through the teeth of his fly, into his boxers. Ah, that slurpy sound of him going in. She had a sense of *finally*. And that melting candle feeling there. Her nose against his sweaty neck. She always gasped when a man pushed into her. Already, the table banged an ache into Lucille's hip. She felt Isidore filling all that space—but why had she thought "*finally*"? How silly. The waterspout inside her had begun to spill. She started to breathe really fast. The black coiling fuzz on his chest. She gripped his hair, or thought she had; she'd gotten light-headed. I feel my body curling inward, she thought. Her muscles tightened. *"Finally" what,* though? She began to feel tiny mouths sucking inside her thighs, and sensed, too, the end coming from some ways off—the candle now heating like a furnace, that *more more more* sensation, the awareness of your body below the waist, the whole length of it, even that hair was tingling, and the invisible fingers running along her head.

—And after that, Hold-on wanted me to call him, she thinks. Then I had my baby.

On the show, the characters of Lucy and Ethel have disguised themselves as homely bumpkins. They trick their husbands into taking less-attractive women to the fights. That is to say, unwittingly taking *them,* their own wives, in ugly hick disguise, and, okay, maybe the script doesn't make lots of sense. It doesn't matter, Lucille realizes. This world has its own rules, its own ordering logic. Arrivals that surprise, departures, kicks in the narrative teeth. As long as it's funny.

The middle camera rides closer; microphones lower at Lucille.

"Oh, relax, Ethel," Lucy says, mocking Ethel's doubt. "Wait till you hear the plan to end all plans."

The distraction of Isidore, the serpent of the thought, withdraws.

Lucy: "Lemme tell you how we trick 'em."

She whispers the idea into Ethel's ear. Ethel makes a face. The laughter stretches, and it's loud. Louder even than in the barnstorming tour. Maybe it's thanks to those cameras; maybe it's bound up with them—with the audience's knowledge that they're aiding in something their neighbors will see.

"Hello, hello, hello," Lucy says, hidden behind a closed door and knocking. "Might you go by 'a name a' Ricky?"

And when Desi as Ricky answers, Lucille as Lucy pops into frame wearing a tatty, black hillbilly wig. Eyes comically wide, slouchy, her front teeth painted black. Now in a loose, deep voice, her accent is from nowhere yet spells rural stupidity. Hello hello hello, pronounced: 'a-lo, 'lo 'lo. And yet her prettiness is evident too—italicized, even, by a low-collared, roomy, lumberjack-ish shirt.

"We be huntin' down a pair a' buckaroos, name a' Ric-arr-doo-ie and Mertz?" She is carrying an actual moonshine jar, marked xxx; nothing is subtle here. "Be you the buckaroos?"

Lucille's commitment to the part is absolute. "Let's smooch!" Already Lucy is chasing a frightened Ricky around the living room of pasteboard and furniture painted gray for the cameras.

Desi obviously is a good comic actor, acting quite well; Vivian Vance obviously is, too, as is William Frawley as Fred. Not Lucille. Lucille has fully relaxed into—has converted to flesh—these gags. She is not acting, obviously or otherwise; she's giving all. The difference between talent and genius, right there.

"We be your paramours for the evening, Señor Ric-arr-doo-ie!"

She's never felt this easy, this wanton, at-home, funny, this herself. No one on television has. Never in real life has she felt it, either.

Why? What makes tonight different from all other nights?

Pride seems to squeeze the back of her neck; the chin makes its way up a few more stairs of glamour. Under the kliegs, Lucille's eyes go bright with fire.

"I'm going to smooch this slickster over here," Lucy says. "And tha' one you can have your way with, Mommy."

Ricky, whimpering: "Uh, oops, there. You must have me mixed

up with someone else. We're expecting two cousins of Isabelle Smith."

"That's us'n!" Lucy says. "I'm Sue-Ann, 'n' right here's my mom, Sue-Ann the first."

An entire televisual medium attaining its potential—a woman attaining *her* potential by scooping up all the jacks of her past. Supporting movie actress, put-upon wife, showgirl, B-movie queen, small-town kid, glamour-puss, it's all there, to help the world believe in a shaky new enterprise.

"Come on! Gimme a peck, dagnabbit."

It's half theater, half film, and that's probably the secret. Broadway's flagrant stagecraft, plus the winning glitz of Hollywood. Early TV has been an embarrassment of homogenized radio gags and maudlin romances. *I Love Lucy* is in its way total art: the outlandish hijinks, real-seeming marriage, no condescension, and what's still noticeable is how unaffected it is. And the laughs come easy now.

It seems so easily replicable—the key that disappears the lock.

"Well, break into some soft-shoe hoofin', señor," Lucy says, "if a song-and-dance man you be."

"Dance?" Ricky says. "I couldn't."

(But, no. This comedy isn't easily replicable.)

"Then let's kiss."

[*He starts tap-dancing manically.*]

Next, a minimum of stage business with Ricky's guitar; who knew a guitar was there? "Okay ma'am, how 'bout 'Begin the Beguine'?"

"Yes!" she says. "After."

The audience is panting heavily, all laughed out, ready to sit or fetch at her next command.

But it's more than the audience. Lucille feels a wobble and jump of the lower belly.

It's like what a woman feels when, having checked her reflection in a limousine's dark window, she can sense, without really seeing anything definite behind the reflection, that there are people sitting inside the car; and, though the people aren't visible—she can't really discern their figures—the woman knows they're there, and it changes the way she sees herself; being watched invisibly gives her image in the glass significance. The concealed figures behind the studio audience are the home viewers.

This has the strangest effect on her. A sense of unfamiliar millions thinking her more than she is, and so soon. It's a thrill she'd never had making movies, and it's very odd that it's also kind of terrifying.

Lucille does remember to recite the next line: "Let's smooch, smoochie, smoochie, here, smoochie, smoochie."

Her image will replace her forever, that's what's terrifying. She wags her head to concentrate, to stop herself from thinking.

Ricky, saying: "I— I would like to take a bathroom break, please."

And, like that, she's about to lose the character. The way Desi/Ricky said it, that uncharacteristic comic falter in his voice, it's subverted and usurped her timing. Has the director noticed; will he stop filming? Because she can't laugh. Laughs will break the scene. Which will ruin everything. Stopping, resetting, a kind of death for audience morale. And if she loses the audience she will lose the feeling, the bright magnification feeling. And that feeling may be all that keeps her tethered to her ambitions.

Ricky: "Hey, Fred? Join me."

Fred: "What's wrong, pal? Can't, uh, do your business in there by yourself?"

Lucille tries not to break. This is the devil's last stand.

Because the question for Lucille Ball, entertainer, has always been: What does she have to offer? What, exactly, is her talent?

After DeDe had come back from Michigan, she'd squeezed young Lucille's hand through two-comedies-plus-a-feature at the Shepherd-Meadows Movie Palace, where silent, monochromatic men flouted danger by sallying into a threat tranquilly, obliviously, hilariously: a narcoleptic on roller skates pirouetting at some canyon's edge (tourists shouting, pointing, fainting), or, in the next reel, a hiker deciding to rest and dawdle in the very spot, at the very moment, that a collapsing barn fell *whomp* into its collapse. But there was more. Right as that skater flung out into the great startling void (and as young Lucille gobbled up her popcorn), a lucky twirl brought safe passage under his wheels. Or gosh if that hiker—who just happened to've positioned himself exactly under the barn's open window—that hiker didn't fail to notice as everything around him came to crash and smoke. And she knew (audiences always knew) our hero would end up unhurt. This happy knowledge is like everyone you've ever wronged turning the other cheek. But now—in Lucille's klieg-lit, adult here and now—what does she have in her performer's tool bag? Who is she? (On the dolly nearest her, the big camera is pulling back. She feels her heart go panicked.) Who can she be? Lucille Ball had dangled from a comical telephone pole in *The Fuller Brush Girl,* but she is no Harold Lloyd. Lucille Ball looked sexy in *Thousands Cheer,* but she is no Lana Turner. Lucille Ball danced the soft-shoe in *Meet the People,* but she is no Ginger Rogers. Lucille Ball acted with assurance and passion in *Five Came Back,* but she is no Katharine Hepburn. Or Bette Davis. Or Olivia de Havilland. . . . Lucille Ball was handy with a joke in *Stage Door,* but she is no Groucho Marx. Lucille Ball hula'd her hips in *Dance, Girl, Dance,* but she is no Carmen Miranda. Lucille Ball held a tune in *Hey Diddle Diddle,* but is she an Ethel Merman? No, she is not an Ethel Merman. Can Lucille swim? Not really; not like Esther Williams. Lucille Ball was forgettable in *Too Many Girls, Chatterbox, Winterset,* forgettable in *Don't Tell the Wife.* Lucille Ball was forgettable in *So and Sew, Nana, Fugitive Lady, Carnival,* and *Panama Lady.* Lucille Ball was forgettable in *Jealousy, Roman Scandals, Dummy Ache, Lured,* and *A Girl, a Guy, and a Gob.* She'd been pretty good in *The Big Street.* (If Lucille's heart has gone terrified now, facing this live studio audience, it's because she—like that camera on its dolly—feels herself backing away from this comic moment, withdrawing; she feels wholly Lucille and has lost all of Lucy. It's awful.) But what if she could be something utterly new? Maybe? If she could glide through the middle-class experience like that skater on that canyon's edge. Wouldn't that be wonderful? If she were to sail unaffected past the steep bluffs of ego and unrelatability—isn't there a chance the world might be flattered and fall in with her and transform itself into a heap of blessings? Maybe it's good she hasn't lost the baby weight. Maybe she can be the audience, only funnier and a little prettier. Perry Como isn't, Sid Caesar isn't, Ed Sullivan isn't them; urbane, distant, Jewish Milton Berle isn't able to unite with them in their entirety, in partnership, a giant comedy-family, all shared affinities. It strikes her: She can conquer the world with realness. Maybe that's what she's been doing tonight, up till now. Yes, the studio audience felt it and she felt it.

"No, you're serious?" the character Fred Mertz is saying to the character Ricky Ricardo.

"Those two *stinkers* over there?" Ricky's saying. "That's Lucy and Ethel."

Fred: "Nah. Not really?"

The director is no longer calling the shots from a control room; he is perceptible here, in front of the soundstage, and now turns at Lucille.

"You're right, Rick ol' pal!" Fred's saying. "How do we get our revenge?"

In fact, the director came to lurk among the actors and the crew, but he has gone still; Lucille feels caught in the focus of his flustered face. He keeps staring at her. There are looks that are slaps, they sort of ring in the air between.

Meanwhile Ricky tells Fred his plan:

". . . turn the ol' tables, Fred. Show 'em the same lovey-dovey interest they been showing us!"

The director had seen Lucille lose the character. That's why he's come down. Now his face is reckless in its scheming. He is about to cut the momentum, the scene, the whole shoot and all that comes with it. He likely feels he has to.

The actor playing Fred is oblivious to the problem.

"Let's go show 'em who's boss," Fred is saying.

Lucille senses Vivian Vance giving her an *Are you okay?* look.

Vivian has one of those rare mouths where (when the lens is off her) the hydraulics of the frown just keep going.

Ricky and Fred approach their wives, and a camera follows. The director starts to lift his "cut the action" palm, a signal in prospect.

Ricky: "Oh, girls . . ."

There can be an inescapable road to disaster; there may instead come a moment when things cannot help but find rescue. Lucille smiles.

Lucy: "Oh, 'ello, Mister Ricky!"

The director stays his hand. Lucille has gotten Lucy back.

Some physically comic effects: She comes after Ricky, her elbows up and bent, hunting, the arms making a circle. It's funny. This improvised shtick describes pure sexual hunger.

"I'm hopin' to catch a little pony," Lucy is saying. "Cowgirl style!"

And the audience laughs. And Lucille's TV career isn't killed in its crib.

"Aw." Lucy is happy-pouting, realizing her prey is on to her. "Ricky! You knew!" The audience hasn't really stopped laughing.

It's time for the plot to turn away from the world of freedom and risk—to end its flirtation with madness, its repudiation of normality. And so the TV husband hugs his TV bride. (The actual husband and wife, of course, must therefore hug, too.) Lucille and Desi, Lucy and Ricky. With this program, there's a pleasant glaze of self-referential complexity that the audience doesn't give special thought to. But they sense it. *This feels kind of real, the husband-and-wife couple we're watching?* And now, a musical prompt. Even after the jokes shut down, the audience continues its laugh, and this goes straight into cheering. In fact, it's avalanchine, a huge crush barreling down on them. The loudest Lucille's ever won. And you think her brain, just for one second—while she stands in all this undreamed noise and while commanding that bright and flabbergasted theater—you actually think her brain has gone to thoughts of Hold-on? Why, that's nothing but a scurrilous rumor! (Ah, Hold-on. The cute jut of his ears. His fingers callused and warm.)

Desi has taken Lucille's hand and curtsied her into this applause. Yes, yes, folks, we love you right back.

At the edge of vision—in the plunge of their double bow— Lucille sees a dark, wet lock of Desi's usually disciplined hair slip free of the pompadour.

She drops her husband's hand with purpose: Take that, you always-cheating shit.

"Ladies and gentlemen, one more time: Lucille Ball and Desi Arnaz!"

She can feel Desi's oblivious smile on her cheek but doesn't turn.

(All our forgiveness has a far margin of grace. Lucille's is the door of her ranch. Last summer, a few weeks after Hold-on, she got home early from the wrap party for Ginger Rogers's *Storm Warning*. And it was the old familiar bit: husband caught out, boxers down; wife gone pale at the doorframe; some young lady, her posterior in the air, diving into the pillow to hide her face. Lucille had been enraged, but first she'd felt frightened by him and so, when her rage did come, it came with real force. Why the hell'm I afraid of my husband in my own house? Humiliating images. Legs, sheets. The Cheshire smile of Desi's belly skin where his undershirt didn't quite reach his waistband. Worse was the rough, grabby argument that followed. The few thumb-size shadows that later ran along Lucille's wrist and, when she peeled up her sleeve, along her forearm. That's why she'd been afraid of her husband in her own house. Jesus Christ, I was pregnant, Lucille thinks now. Compare that to Isidore, who far as Lucille can tell is the guy at the end of the evening who pauses to befriend dogs and kids while other grown-ups find their coats. And Hold-on is waiting for me to call him. But the new child, but the career . . .)

The theme song has finished. The ovation hasn't. Lucille sees the director shrug and smile and shake his head. Up in that booth, the script girl stands to cheer. Lucille is thrilled. The name Lucille Ball in recent years has made—what? Well, it's made nothing much. Just the gossip pages and their slapdash, smudgeable dishonesties. Or maybe they weren't dishonesties.

Desi is saying: "Sweetie, we did it." The cheers are loud. Still, she doesn't turn to him.

Near the front row, Lucille watches as two women jump in the aisle and keep jumping: enthusiasm they can express only with their bodies.

The director shouts at the crowd. "Watch it again, Tuesday, nine P.M., when the show airs! We love Lucy!" the director says. He's hopped in front of the Arnazes. "We love Lucille!"

Lucille closes her eyes. Her fantasy has quit humming 'round her head; it's now loose into the world.

"This is true!" Desi half-shouts to be heard. "We all love you!"

She doesn't turn.

"That is truth, Lucille," he says.

She doesn't turn.

"Sweetie?" Desi asks.

She does not turn.

What she does is sigh. I wasn't cheating if he cheated first, Lucille thinks. First and often.

She feels her loneliness like a prop she's dragged across the soundstages of her life. My loneliness belongs to Desi, she thinks. The guilt I refuse to lug around is his, too.

The cameras continue shooting. Nobody thought to tell their operators to stop, anyhow this ovation feels film-worthy.

"Thank you," Lucille addresses everyone. Her throat looks puffed out with pride. "Thank you all."

The cameramen already see it: This isn't the movies; this is not heroicizing cinema. TV is intimacy. Right there inside the home, free from the proscenium arch. But TV is also lamp-lighting and microphones and this artifice lends importance to it. TV is hybrid. Lucille Ball understands. On the small screen Desi boasts a Rushmore chin and princely hair; but Lucille's got the smile of the girl you should've kissed.

She turns to Desi, finally. Handsome Desi, his brows raised, smiling, we did it, baby, we beat 'em.

Lucille says to him what she hoped he'd say to her: "Of course we beat 'em." And to the crowd, "Oh, your appreciation means so much."

Desi reaches for Lucille; she lets him catch her palm. His big, strong hand. Ah, Desi. Lucille can't help herself. He is her husband and the father of her child and she loves him.

She sets a kiss on his cheek. Theatrical, but heartfelt. And Desi spins her and dips her, tango-wise. In the crowd, some woman laughs, and this warm, recorded guffaw will never really fade. Which is to say it will eternally clang and rattle through television's first ever laugh track, a recording used on programs that don't have *I Love Lucy*'s confidence for live filming.

Desi keeps his nose in her hair. "You were amazing"—right into her ear.

"It just came." She closes her eyes. "It just came."

And now Lucille pulls from Desi. She gives a last gesture to to-night's crowd. Wide-open eyes, pouted lips, a baffled finger thrust into her own cheek. This quirky confusion, Lucy's newest profes-sional gesture, soon to be one more Lucille trademark.

Then: offstage. In the wings, an executive from Philip Morris: "Excellent! Have a smoke, kid!"

Sure, why not a cigarette? It's the start of her life.

The first episode of *I Love Lucy* won't air until Tuesday, October 15, 1951, at nine P.M.

On that night, Lucille will be flying across the country and miss the broadcast and it won't matter. By October 15, 1951, at 9:30 P.M., her professional faces and comic gestures and that lady's re-corded guffaw and everything else from tonight's episode will take in all the diamonds spread across the land, that sparkling mesh out Lucille's airplane window.

But everybody knows that already.

CHAPTER FIVE

*I*N MY GRANDFATHER'S *hospital room, I found two Styro-
foam cups, two white sugars cubed on the tray, a coating of
disease everywhere. "Was I asleep?" my grandfather said. "I'm glad you're
here. I think I can fit you in between my four-thirty and my five."*

"Funny, but it's after six," I said.

"Oh," he said, "a time Nazi." Yet there was a strain.

*A curtain separated his bed and someone else's. My mother had said he
had something for me; he—concave and depressed—looked in no position
to hold something valuable. "I'm fine," my grandfather said. "Talk to me.
How's work? Sorry I didn't neaten up."*

*I had never known Poppa Izzy as anything like a young man, but even
I was surprised by how ruined his handsome face was. "I'm very glad to see
you, and I'm fine," he said. "Don't look at me that way."*

*To speak with anything like candor, he and I would have had to voice
our undisclosed fears, life, death. "Talk to me," he said. "I happen to be
interested in you." His hand fell* thwap *on the bed. The woman he now
lived with—his very longtime girlfriend—didn't like leaving him alone in
the hospital, but she was old, too, and couldn't always be there. I remembered what my mom had said, and so I had something to ask Poppa Izzy.*

*"Yes, I do," he answered my blurted question. "I do have something.
Thanks for reminding me." Now he was shy and smiling. "I do. For you.
For you, I do."*

*F*ROM DR. PITSKER he hears the acting is marvelous. From Essie Newburgh he hears the writing is marvelous. From Norman, it's the *star*—the star is marvelous. Marvelous in humor, in sex appeal; in everything. Isidore believes them all. He believes his dentist, secretary, his brother—but he won't check. He won't snap on the TV set. (His wife hasn't mentioned *Lucy,* thank goodness.)

Isidore is trying otherwise to busy himself.

With Norman he's been putting up homes in Brooklyn—the Housing Act of 1949 offered developers like him great incentives. He's busy with his family, too. With dark-haired, confident, athletic Bernie, the firstborn who seems almost ready to take care of himself and never to cry. And with Arthur, who, a few years behind Bernie, is blond, more sensitive, and—to his father's repressed disappointment—a tad duller, sitting as he often does with one elbow resting on the sofa cushion, looking off at nothing. And Isidore has occupied himself, too, with being a husband. That has been harder.

Busy Isidore's brain finds itself not busy enough. He'd done the terrible wonderful surprising inevitable thing he'd done with Lucille. An act that forged its own excuses. A moral man being immoral—is this even a possible path?

About a year after the Havana-Madrid, the constant news about Lucille made the secret feel like an itch. One morning, Isidore burst into his brother's office as their secretary handed Norman some mail.

"What's the rush, Iz?" Norman said. "Something up?"

Isidore tried to sound blithe. *That's all for now, Miss Newburgh. Bye. Thank you.* And Norman watched Miss Newburgh go. Specifically, the vertical line—distinct even through her skirt—that hemisected her departing behind.

At length, Norman said, "Something about her you didn't want to talk in front of?"

"Well—"

So many thoughts knocked against each other and made sparks in Isidore's brain:

When Lucille calls me, I'll say no. Having to move out, to pay for two residences, leaving the kids . . . He also didn't want to see himself as immoral, to admit failure, to have to tell his father.

"Hey, listen." Isidore spoke extra quietly. "I heard the television program you and Miss Newburgh were discussing. Norman, that was *her.*"

Often, in his imagination, he approached Lucille Ball with declarative sentences. Straight, bold announcements of fact.

"Iz"—Norman just blinking. "You lost me. *Who* was what now?"

Isidore wasn't ready to admit to having had sexual intercourse with Lucille Ball. But he missed her, and talking would bring the kind of frizzle he needed.

"Remember I told you about Fred Trump's party, Norm?" He'd practiced this line, and now chewed it off and spit it out bit by bit. "How I kissed a beautiful actress? In front of Dad?"

"*What?*"

"I did. I did that."

Norman sat considering Isidore with his fist over his mouth. Isidore wasn't sure *how* he would feel about Norman's inevitable smile and congratulations.

(*Look here, Lucille, I love you, you know*—a perfectly good declarative sentence.)

Norman said nothing. His eyebrows went up and looked like

snapped sticks. All this reached Isidore as a mark of something like his brother's respect.

"Norm," he whispered, knowing that sharing this was irrational behavior, but the frizzle wasn't rational.

"I kissed Lucille Ball," he said. "That was who."

The frizzle didn't want to go away; its goal was to shine as a bruised eye shines before the world with its message of *This is a wound*.

Norman finally laughed. "*You?* Be serious. Come on."

So—not respect.

"Give it up, Iz. I think"—*snort*—"I'd remember."

Isidore shrugged. Resentfulness squeezed out all other feeling and turned into the kind of jealousy that spears the chest and goes all the way in.

AFTER TALKING TO Norman, he has kept his reminiscence private, visiting it with a kind of wonder, this secret that brings pride and feels problematic and that he refers to, in his head, as *my concern*. In the way that a father who's raised an unexpectedly brilliant child—suspiciously handsomer and cleverer and stronger than the father had ever been—might say of his patrimony: "Well, that's *my* concern."

Afterward, I'd hailed her a cab—so reckless, being on the street together—and watched her leave, he thinks. I'd given her my telephone number. And then I schlumped off to find Harriet and made my explanations. And she believed me. Harriet believed me. (I *must* love her, though the time together had been so short. Love Lucille, that is.)

"But," his wife had said with shy rapidity, "did you get hurt or something? You were so long back there in the theater." And he'd realized Harriet was offering an excuse. Like a Rapunzel letting down her forgiveness to him, so that he might climb the golden offering.

Harriet was the same attractive wife, with the same wide eyes, unchanged, though he half-expected her to have a bloody lip or a bruised eye or some other stain of his cruelty. He hadn't wanted to cheat. (When she calls, I'll just have to tell her *no*.) Honestly, he hadn't meant to do more than come watch a show. That's the horrible thing. Lust is a slave driver. Lust is the Mr. Hyde we all forget—until Hyde's wretched rearrival. We all forget we have it in us. And yet! Blissful slavery!

I gave her my number—but didn't ask for hers. Idiot! he thought. What if she doesn't call?

And after Norman, he thought he wouldn't talk about it to anyone else. But he did—once.

ISIDORE'S FATHER IN a short-sleeve button-down had pretty much commanded him: "Walk with me to the bedroom to speak to your flesh and blood."

This had been before that Havana-Madrid evening—a couple Thanksgivings ago, in fact, at Jacob's house in Boro Park. (At this point, Isidore thought he'd never get to do with Lucille the things they would later do in that dressing room.)

A second time—"Isidore, come!"—Jacob pretty much decreed that Isidore excuse himself from his wife and children in the living room and join him for a confab. "Let's go."

1949–50: That autumn had been full, lies had been told there. Jacob had seen Isidore at Trump's party—had seen Isidore the first time he'd kissed Lucille.

"Me and you?" Isidore said. "Now?"

"Somebody better? Come to my bedroom."

Once alone with his father, Isidore began the chat by talking work, even though he kind of knew his father wanted to discuss something else.

"Okay, I called up that *shadkhen* from Moses's office," Isidore was saying.

(Yiddish he spoke only when in the presence of his father, whose own English had remained unleavened.)

Robert Moses, city construction coordinator, planned to get insurance companies to invest, without interest, in moderate-rental housing. Jacob believed there was no way this would happen. Isidore believed differently—and that's why he and Norman had been constructing affordable homes for G.I. Bill grads.

"Numbers, though?"

"Yes," Isidore said.

"Yes? What yes? You want maybe to share them?" Jacob said.

"Almost thirty-seven hundred families, the guy said," Isidore told his father. "Also, they may have Liberty National."

Jacob sounded his astonishment with a whistle. He sat on his bed, snaking a thick red tie through his collar.

There was also something called the Mitchell-Lama bill, another plan to goose moderate-income building: the city loaning up to ninety-five percent of project costs to a few lucky housing companies, the state handing out big tax-abatements, the feds ponying up government-subsidized land.

"Probably won't happen till next election, though."

"Ah, okay, you see." Jacob wasn't able to keep satisfaction from his voice. "I knew it wouldn't go perfect. I'm sorry," he gloated.

White chest hair squiggled through the open buttons of the old man's shirt.

The overall feeling you got from Jacob's big new house (or, his second wife's big new house): *A polite hush is better than a conversation, and family is to be slipcovered against.*

"And, Dad, the state—"

"Enough." Jacob held up a hand. "Governor Dewey is not what I asked you in to talk. Months I've held my tongue. Months. You know what I'm going to say, correct?"

"No," Isidore lied. He felt, at almost thirty-nine, sixteen again.

"Come on, Mr. Smart Head," Jacob said. "Mr. Brain."

The hush of two men who knew each other intensely—and intensely didn't. Jacob was doing his cuff links.

Maybe you only reach adulthood when your parents turn over the keys to their maturity. When they say, after their lessons and advice, their little road tests: Take it out of the garage; it's yours now. I can't drive it anymore. But once you come back, they frown over the nicks in the fender, the dinged panels, the passage of time and accident.

"It's a *shandeh*," Jacob said at last: a sin. "Stay at home. You won't wear out your shoes. You follow me?"

Isidore was going to say, *You think I haven't thought about sin?* A mere kiss—is that a sin? Isidore wondered. Is it? It's not as if I'll ever get to do more with her. . . .

"Dad," he found himself whispering. "My wife is in the living room. My children. My *mother-in-law*. Okay?"

Jacob was small but forceful, intimidating. But it takes just tiny changes—earlobe hair, a wavy forehead vein—to dim some of the power of a man's face.

"Would you think I was in the wrong," Jacob said, "if I tell Harriet what I saw?"

Isidore snapped to, felt the crisis of the moment and his father's heavy gaze on him. Oh, Dad! Jacob Strauss, born Stromolofsky, had been the only Jew in Yustingrad—to hear the old man tell it, maybe the only Jew in Russia—to have broken horses for the Cossacks. That's the kind of rider, the kind of brave young boy. Ramshackle stables at the edge of a Russian tableland. A long stretch of green and straw—and at dinnertime, six or seven Cossacks sitting on hay bales, looking up at some surprise. What surprise? A little Jew, ten, eleven tops, chin pitched high, shoulders back. I'll show you Russians how to ride this fucking horse. The Cossacks jostled to their feet—*Ha!*—wiping supper grease on their pants. Go home, little Yid. Make tracks. This horse will break your Semitic ass. Nearby: an untamed reddish-brown Arabian trotter, its hooves stamping dirt, its terrible glorious nostrils. Just looking at the stallion's flanks seemed to press a bruise on Jacob's scrawny legs. One of you godforsaken pricks lift my Semitic ass onto this horse already. And the men looked at one another. The origins of the first warrior Cossacks are uncertain. The People of the Prairies: self-governing and Jew-hating Tartars, loyal only to the czar. This was happening at the foot of the bluish Ural Mountains, on the Great Steppe. The horse's large black eyes were lighted purple by the sunset. Here and there, you could see smoke from the prairie catch like cotton in the trees.

Three years later, a friend among these Cossacks would warn Jacob about the imminent pogrom—the Jew slaughter they were planning. *My brothers-in-arms will smear the dirt with your people.* From there, it was the same old immigrant tale. Jacob's parents (*Oh, Jake-leh, how we love you, our youngest son; take care of yourself*) fled Yust-ingrad, walking down the Siemiatycze-Bialystok Road and right out of this story. Jacob, at fourteen, didn't follow. He sailed alone to New York. Illusions lifted him in their fist and carried him to America. And then they let go.

He had no English or money. And the older brother who had already been living in Brooklyn, the one who was supposed to meet him—Nathan, called Nitsky—got the date wrong. So the young, impoverished infidel had to find his own way, illiterate in Christian America, to the Migrant Relief Organization. Then to a swarming collective apartment, a job in a hat factory; to owning, after twelve years, a rival hat factory; then to employing that dead-beat brother of his (Nitsky, who *had* known, it turned out, the cor-rect date of his brother's arrival). Finally, during the Depression, enterprising Jacob became a *giltbal haluwá,* a lender, no shame in that; in impossibly short order, Jacob splashed his money all over. On foreclosed buildings in Brooklyn mostly, some steals in Man-hattan, 554 Broadway, 126 Joralemon, then a few office towers. He had left all the madness behind. The crazy pervasive Hasidim and the crazy forgotten Mitnaggedim, all the blood hatreds of old Na-berezhnaya Street. And the questions of theodicy that vanish in that new place when God is either so good or no good to you. Point A, as they said here, to Point B. That seventeenth-century stable on the Polish border—with the horse whose eye looked like sunset—to Jacob's seventeen-story cash cow in Tin Pan Alley. He returned to religion, as so many Jews do, in old age. That ancient hedge, the old stories, the papyrus dreams of an enduring people. How else can a proud man with a big chest deal with the fact of his own dwindling? Either he'd persist or his people would.

And still, years later, in this house fragrant with Thanksgiving, it was Jacob's son Isidore who hoped that the old *macher* might actually tell him something hopeful now, something that perched in the soul and sang the tune. But Jacob's advice was his own life. Which couldn't be lived now anyway, because of all the things the whole generation of men like the old man had done.

"Dad, I don't know. I'm sad, but I don't regret it. Anyway, you wouldn't tell Harriet. Not really."

The old man tapped his forehead with his finger. "If I let her know what I saw," Jacob said, a stern kindness, "maybe you would stop your dreaming, finally. You might in your life open your eyes."

Isidore's hands whipped upward.

"Jesus, are you . . . I mean, even discussing it now is, is—"

Jacob mocked: " 'Jesus,' he says. *Jesus?* Who's he?" Jacob attracted the eye; when he lowered his face, it was a silencing rebuke. Even the old man's baldness seemed the result of powerful thought: the hair having slipped down the sides of the head, the brain pushing up on the skull like a fist stretching a balloon.

"But when your mother was alive," Jacob said, "do you think I ever would kiss—"

"No. *No.*"

Jacob didn't look up at his son, until he did.

"I owned, as you know, a factory by the time I was twenty-six. And *you,*" he said. "You're given a nice career with your father, it's not enough. You get a nice family—not enough."

Isidore now had *his* turn to point his head floorward: the pose of contrition. Even *this* was about Isidore not having wanted to be a builder.

Contrition was something he knew his father required and that he himself maybe even felt.

"The past year, I—" Isidore began.

He wanted to be sorry. But the beach birds swinging around overhead, the brick that felt heavy in the palm, and Trump's shattering cathedral of glass: It was all, still, so vivid! His chosen picture of himself.

He let in a silence. Or, more specifically, he was asking, in silence, *with* silence, for help. This wasn't apology. It was solicitation. *Please, Dad. What do I do?*

The old man had *wanted* to be asked for guidance. That was why he'd summoned his son to this room. But Jacob—having *been* asked, more or less—now just said, "Fine, fine."

He rubbed his eyes. "Isidore, you've got this Maimonides streak, only it's all cockeyed. A person is allowed to enjoy and not feel guilty about everything." The old man glanced with longing at the slipcover on the sofa. "For, okay, one example, it's all right for a man to enjoy his money. A good livelihood is a cure for lots of ills."

"Oh?" Isidore said. He hadn't expected to laugh. "A bunch of great men say no: Gandhi, et cetera. Your friend Jesus."

"Not *my* friend," Jacob said. "So in this example, you're Jesus? You're Gandhi?" He snorted. "You do something wrong, enjoy it, move on. You don't want to do it again, don't. After the wedding, it's late to have regrets."

"That's it?" Isidore said. "That's the advice?"

"I'm trying to be a father here, Mr. Jesus."

"This is trying?"

"This," Jacob said, "is me trying."

LATER, AT THE Thanksgiving table, Isidore thought that he'd spent his adult life as a hill that asked to be leveled. But now I want to be a mountain.

Harriet was making some nice dinner conversation about Great Neck—sweet of her; she hated Great Neck. "It's like Manhattan," she often said when they were alone, "but without the tall buildings and wit." This in somebody else would've been resentment, or comedy, but from Harriet, the words came in a sort of a baffled quiet. He felt both gratitude and dissatisfied. Don't blame her. If love goes, there's an uncertainty, and if you weren't careful, dislike tumbled into it.

Isidore made a show of leaning to peck her cheek, which was an absorbent little place, a parched acre thirsty for the watering of his kiss.

Isidore's father had invited Harriet's mother tonight. And here his mother-in-law was, slighting Isidore, slyly, by bragging about her own son Melvy. And to Isidore's left, his young brother Phil just talked baseball. Finished off by the Yanks in four. Shame the Whiz Kids put up such little fight! Isidore didn't want to talk baseball, didn't want his emotion for Lucille merely to fizzle.

"Phil," he said, as if waking. "I was remembering that party. You remember the one?"

And Phil turned. The smile, the thrilled eyes—he remembered; the arrow had struck him severely, too. "And now look at her!" Phil said, as if it'd been on his mind, too. "The biggest star in the world!"

NOW, ISIDORE'S LUCILLE has for months been the biggest star (*His* Lucille? Ha!), and he allows himself to think of running off with her only once a week, as a kind of gift—a reward for making it six days without giving serious consideration to leaving his world. A gift to replace the gift he really wanted, the gift he'd never open.

Ah, Hold-on, Lucille had said, *if you were to try, I'd like it.* And my hat on her head, and nothing on her body.

Yet he rarely has time to wallow. His brother and business partner Norman won't let him.

"Hey," Norman says, "you never told me, all right?" Doubt sharpening his voice: *Enough of this shit. We have work to focus on.* And so Isidore invented a reason to focus on work.

NEW YORK HERALD TRIBUNE

JANUARY 30, 1952, REAL ESTATE SECTION

BUILDERS MAKE
HEADWAY
IN L.I. PROJECT

Harry L. Osias, builder, started construction on the Meridian, an apartment building for seventy-eight families . . .

[Fifth paragraph of fourteen:]

. . . Successes in other Westbury developments were announced. Isidore and Norman Strauss report selling ninety-one dwellings in the past month. . . .

At first, Isidore tries to find satisfaction in making something real, something that would help people and would leave a mark in the world. Whatever other craziness gunks up his life, that would be tangible, and good.

But it didn't feel like enough.

THE NEW YORK TIMES

MARCH 11, 1952, REAL ESTATE SECTION

TRACTS IN GREAT NECK, L.I. CHOSEN
BY BUILDERS FOR NEW HOME GROUPS

[Fourth paragraph of twelve:]

. . . Other developers, Isidore and Norman Strauss, builders of University Gardens, L.I., reported the completion and sale of twenty dwellings this weekend. . . .

By federally insuring mortgages, early fifties legislation—along with the interest–free loans—called Property Men like a siren to empty suburban fields. This encouraged builders to slap together single-family homes, tract houses with low-shingled brows. (In Levittown, in Roslyn, in the rudely named Hicksville.) So maybe Isidore can be bold and make something epic of himself here. Building Long Island. The way Lucille built television. There must be famous builders, glamorous Property Men. Look at Fred Trump. Or maybe don't.

The government's intention—"to secure a homeowning workforce in affordable housing accessible to major centers of employment"— was actually, if unintentionally, pretty much an uppercut thrown right at the brittle chin of "urban renewal." It urged the middle class of New York City to abandon middle-class New York City. Isidore saw this. But he also saw, in his imagination, and more than once, some stoic war veteran, his eyes shimmering, closing on a new, affordable house; coming from the train to the comfort of a lighted window upstairs.

LONG ISLAND NEWSDAY

MARCH 27, 1952

L.I. CONSTRUCTION CONTINUES BRISK AS BUILDERS PLAN MORE HOMES IN L.I. PROJECT

[Third paragraph of twelve:]

Builders Isidore and Norman Strauss have purchased for development fifty-four acres of farmland. . . .

A working man's quarter-acre *can* seem immense, if only to him. Sitting on grass—his grass—with his kids, a warm night, the stars overhead also his to contemplate. Pretending, at least subconsciously, that his ancestors had not arrived from a ghetto in the Pale but were the proud issue of some never-existed America/Ashkenaz amalgam. Clipped lawns and barbecue and kinky hair. There was so much that Isidore used to feel were among life's most solemn, *fullest* rewards. And now? Had Technicolor love screened its Hollywood footage for him just long enough to keep day-to-day life from ever again seeming tolerable?

HARRY TRUMAN'S FAIR DEAL—everyone has a chance to live a better life! Especially in New York, where Mayor Impellitteri and even Governor Dewey promise homes for anyone. It's hard to say whether principles of fairness have actually been advanced. This troubles Isidore. That predominantly black areas are blocked off from predominantly white areas, that New York is a drivable chessboard, light squares, dark squares. He *is* troubled. In theory. But what does he do about it?

I *will* stand against Norman and sell to a black family—after we really get established, he tells himself, with just about believable conviction.

At night, he reads history and hopes to do something more creative and comes across a squib about the 38th United States Colored Infantry Regiment and thinks, if someone were to tell this patriotic story, the brave black soldier's life, it might help things. And be glamorous enough to be worthy of her.

NEW YORK HERALD TRIBUNE
APRIL 6, 1952, REAL ESTATE SECTION

LUXURY-TYPE HOUSES ON L.I.

Strauss Concern Starts Construction of
Final Thirty Dwellings in 175-Family
Development at University Gardens

Thirty dwellings will be erected in the 106-acre village of University Gardens in Great Neck, L.I., to complete a 175-family community, it was announced yesterday by Isidore and Norman Strauss, builders.

LONG ISLAND NEWSDAY

JULY 13, 1952

L.I.ERS FIND
PLACE IN THE SUN

Vacation Starts Early for Some
Local Families

[photo feature; caption for photo on bottom left of page]
Traditional deck snack of bouillon and sandwiches is
served to Mr. and Mrs. Isidore Strauss of Great Neck
on their return trip from Latin America aboard the
SS Homeric. After all, would you bother to watch
your waistline on such a jaunt?

YES, ISIDORE AND Harriet have found their own way into the newspaper, and merely for going on a summer cruise—where they
sprawl and bake themselves across chaise longues, spend three hours
in Panama, and slice up the Atlantic without thinking much about
being in water. Isidore had suggested, and taken, this trip in a state
of unspoken apology. And supplication. "Yes, Harriet, I'm having a
great time—you?" His kids are back on shore, at summer camp. His
guilt seems always (like his wife) with him. For weeks Isidore—
when he remembers to try and shake off his obsession—has been
extra-attentive. Caress, shame, irritability, ambivalence, even jealousy take turns in a kind of offbeat rhythm. But right now he's
brooding in bed. With his chest to Harriet's back, her wearied exhalation the only sound. "Hey," she says, turning over, not asleep
after all. Every once in a while, a panic crashes into her eyes. "You're
having fun, right?"

"Yes, I'm having a nice time—you?"

In the morning they pass a man and his wife, the guy touching
his sweaty hairpiece under the sun. I'm just like him, Isidore thinks.
We all are. Wigs, a girdle, some pancake makeup. A beard over a

weak chin. The body and its faults, the body and its vain wishes: Being an adult means you have secrets you cover.

"Me?" he says. "Having fun, yes."

She holds out her hand to his cheek. That seems to be her thing now—reaching for his face. Did she always do this? He can't recall if it's new.

Marriage once seemed easy. He used to tell single friends. He knows Harriet still believes in that feeling. She may sense it going, but she believes. It wasn't even that he'd felt the marriage decline. No, the marriage had always been all right. Once, at a Madison Square Garden Knicks game, Isidore had been quite enjoying his seats until a friend who worked there sidled up and offered him a courtside ticket. That was kind of what it was like having sex with a famous redhead comedienne. Or maybe better to describe it as like a snowy field that didn't know it was cold; but then the first rays of warmth came.

Maybe I'm crazy, he thinks. Maybe one is lucky just to have tickets to the game, wherever one sits.

"It *is* fun, isn't it?" Harriet's saying now, the reel and splash of a Wednesday evening. "On the boat."

Figure out something nice to say, he tells himself. There's a big band in the ship's dining room. The menu is crown roast or creamed chipped beef on bread, with baked potatoes and green bean casserole, and a surprising reserve has seized Harriet and Isidore both. Well, she's often shy. Maybe it's that. Now he's tilting a lighter to her cigarette. The intense red of her lipstick. They had talked for a while about "that little white hotel" in the Catskills they'd gone to just before Bernie was born, the really fancy molding the place had. But now that's done. The music gets louder. And Isidore leans nearer and has to sort of shout. "You're such a fun person, Har!" He hasn't planned on this, but it feels important now that he stop behaving prosaically. "No, no, I mean it! It's so lovely, really lovely, just to spend time alone! I—do love you!" He feels his mouth crimp with a yearning to say more. Something that will erase what is unerasable. And there is in Harriet's eyes a look of luminous craving. She needs him to go on. "I mean!" he says. "Sometimes I—forget how funny you are! When it's just you and me, I mean. You're really a very humorous person!"

If his wife has been truly funny it hasn't occurred to him before—and he's never imagined he fell in love with her for her humor. But now he's convinced that what he's saying is true. She does joke around, sometimes. And all of a sudden, the pleasure of a secret disclosed has come over them both. Isidore thinks this is the first genuine thing he's said in a long while. It has the thrill of a furtive but real intimacy. When it's just the two of them, she *can* be funny. Yes! Now and then.

Harriet's look intensifies and then restores itself. "Oh, *right,*" she says. "Like *I* was the one who had them laughing that time at Kutsher's resort." Maybe what he's said has been off base. But she's felt that intimate thrill, too. Hasn't she? Finally, appreciativeness or fond disbelief lifts her eyebrows.

"Isn't it hot in here?" she says. "It's loud and stuffy, and I want another cigarette. You feel like going out for a smoke?"

He pats his jacket pocket. "Left my pack in the cabin." And he doesn't smoke her brand, anyway.

"Oh, well." Her voice, her appealing voice, often so shy, takes on some added charm: She sounds a bit frisky. "Come watch me have a cig," she says.

And it's a nice moment, out on the deck. The sun, before setting, rolls through the white of the clouds. Isidore lights Harriet's cigarette.

"Listen, I don't want you to—you seem kind of . . . Wait." She tilts her head. "It wasn't the molding."

"What?" he says. Then, smiling, "No, it wasn't the molding."

"The ceiling. It was the *ceiling* at that white hotel, how it was decorated."

"Yes," he says. "I think it was."

She pauses a second, her pointy nose pointing up as she blows a vertical rush of smoke. "You didn't correct me," she says.

He flushes, too red, too much for the situation. "I just wanted, you know, the Golden Rule—no one likes to be corrected," he says. "Wouldn't be nice."

She stubs out her cigarette on the railing. "Remind me to ask you not to be so nice, then."

This is the silken, feisty side to her. Isidore's trying to feel moved and also doesn't want to feel moved.

"Ooh, I know one, Iz. What do you do if the boat gets sick?" Dramatically, she raises another cigarette to her lips, and he lights it.

"Take it to the doc," she says. "Get it?"

He shades his face with a hand to look at her. "Good one," he says.

Harriet tells jokes the rest of the evening. She tells a joke the next morning. One's about a widemouthed frog, and she makes faces and everything. "One day, a, er, what is it? A widemouthed frog decides to take a walk." And Isidore eases back in bed, surprised that she is actually telling it.

Another: "You know that little bump when the ship pulls into port?" She's holding his arm as they walk the deck. "That's *pier* pressure."

Harriet's jokes never go all the way up. She gets them onto the elevator, but whatever button she pushes, they rarely make it out of the basement. Bless her for trying.

Another: "Do you want to go Dutch?" Harriet says this at dinner because the meals are already paid for. Trying, trying.

"I don't look good in pointy wood shoes," he says, working at it—working to tunnel into the missing fineness of something, the skeleton of what he felt with Lucille: that unresurrectable shell.

"It's not the clogs as much as the flat caps," Harriet says, sounding cheery.

Would he smile back?

Isidore again looks up at the lowering rags and pinks of the sky. But it's not like the solace of a sundown lasts. Or even is a solace that means anything, Isidore thinks. It's just sun, it's just cloud. It's just God's concealment that makes us fill these empty things with meaning. It's just the same hand in yours for decades. It's not glamour.

I Love Lucy is a time machine. Every week it takes him back: newspaper photos inadvertently flipped to, recounted jokes inadvertently overheard. Other passengers talk, as people do, of popular culture. "It's the worst part of the cruise, missing that program!" How can the mental scab form?

"Have you ever seen a funnier woman? And that husband, with his accent!"

Whatever expression hearing this has brought to Isidore's face now must resemble a look of husbandly love. Harriet meets his eyes with appreciation. "Thank you for suggesting this cruise," she says nuzzling closer.

He goes back to telling her: "It *is* fun here." And: "Try the bouillon" or "Try the shuffleboard."

Post-Lucille, when Isidore had first seen his wife naked again, he'd been surprised by his own oddly prudish reaction. He dropped his gaze. As if his innocence—so decimated by wrongdoing—had returned in a surge. Like an overreactive immune system. Attacking everything. He's carried this quirk of priggery to this cruise. What's funny is, after Lucille, he'd remembered Harriet's recent passion as having been kind of pale; but now, out on the water, in the July heat, atop the starched white bedding, there is a feverish, sunstroked quality to her, as there had been in the newlywed years. "Come here," he mumbles and gasps now. Emotion makes the words hard to get out. "Oh, oh," says Harriet, as he kisses her cheeks, her eyes, her neck, he squeezes her arms, too hard, her shoulders, buttocks, hair, his hand to her mouth finally presses on her startled gasp to stifle the sound. Forgive me. Forgive me. I do love you, he thinks.

But that is only his body.

LIKE MANY PEOPLE whose bad behavior forces them into *further* bad behavior, Isidore has come to feel annoyance at the person he's sinned against. This is gross, and he knows it, and that makes him feel even lower. Still, though—annoyance. At Harriet. She should, in bed, detect on his body the contours of someone else. The physiological effects would've been obvious to her, he thinks. If she loved me. The change in the taste of his sweat has escaped her, also the new way he comports himself under the sheets. "What," she hasn't asked, "is *that* new thing you're doing?" As a wife, she's remained oblivious. She can't spot the cause of Isidore's brief, unexpected incandescences. She can't spot the cause of her own new and frequent downheartedness. She can't spot that her requests that he do chores, and even the timbre of her "Hello, Strauss residence, who's calling?" really annoy him now.

Not that she always takes his bad behavior.

"JUST SAY WHAT the hell it is that's bothering you, Isidore."

This is one of those infrequent occasions when, through the littlest of spaces, her anger has geysered right up.

"Nothing," he says. "I'm sorry."

The kids are just home from camp, and Harriet makes that sound she sometimes does, *mnnh*—that stifled noise that looks for escape.

August has kicked in gently for New York, humanely, without its usual roaring ambush. The family is visiting some empty farmland he will soon develop. They're walking over grass now to find a spot for a picnic. That summer cruise, followed by this trip into the soft warm orbit of his family—maybe that's the blessing Isidore's been hoping for? The surgical cut that will slice away guilt and desire.

But he'd snapped at Harriet about how long it took the family to get on the road, or something, really just an excuse to snap. To release the pressure that's always there.

Now Bernie cuts in, "Mommy and Daddy are fighting," with odd jokiness—his little voice trying out the big challenge of derision. Actual parental arguments are so rare. The boy walks alongside now, tight socks, blue shorts, watching. It's like a bullfight.

"No, no, no," Harriet says. "We're *not*."

Isidore risks taking her free hand—the other holds Arthur's—

and that contact is what breaks the spell. It surprises, rare as it must be, the breath from her.

Harriet says: "Okay, well." The anger wipes off her face.

"I'm sorry," he says. Harriet can't stay mad, no matter how hard she tries, and that's a blessing, he thinks.

But why haven't you called? Why, why, why, Lucille?

The grass reaches mid-shin and makes a very silky noise as they walk through it and everything Isidore says has the flavor of a lie. Even what may be true. "It's overcast, but nice out." He points to the clouds. "I mean, not too hot." And then he decides to kiss Harriet. And Lucille Ball rests on everything.

She'd asked me for my phone number! So, why . . . ?

Isidore ends up not kissing his wife, after all. Don't be *too* nice to her. That's how you avoid getting caught. Also, don't hesitate when you talk—ever. Isidore stops walking: "Maybe here's good enough, guys?" From Long Island, it would take fifty-five nonstop hours to drive to Los Angeles.

"These roast beef sandwiches are delicious," he says. "Look, I was a first-class heel, sweetie. Sorry again."

The trip back to Great Neck, through a fresh fall of rain, is unmemorable. Mind if I turn the radio down? I think we need gasoline. Hey, we made good time. Didn't we, though.

CHAPTER SIX

*I*N MY GRANDFATHER'S *hospital room, at his request, I
found myself pawing through a briefcase that sat under a
Burberry coat on a chair across from the bed.*

"Found it?" he said. "I think this will be something you can use."

I pulled out a manila folder filled with papers. "No one knows that exists," Poppa Izzy said. "Did you ever hear I knew Lucille Ball?"

*A*MAN PAUSES, CHIN up, vigorous hands on vigorous hips, smiling. His biggest spur is an unchecked masculinity. And spread around him are his ambitions, a tangled majesty of cables and microphones and fawners—and all of it calls for his presence, while the generators hum. He isn't supposed to be in California today. He isn't supposed to be here, and this will end up an important fact.

Feet spread wide, dark eyes alert; he is happy in his anger. "You all know just enough to be stupid!" He says it with a smile.

"What'd we screw up, Desi?" This is Jess Szilárd, the producer, who sits opposite him. "I don't see a problem."

Were Desi Arnaz now to leave this set that serves as his television home, he might find his wife doing something in his real home—something that would make him angry enough to kill.

He says: "Jess, why do you think"—the last word pronounced as *"thin"* in the manner America loves already—"we have succeeded so far?"

Seven months after the first episode, Desi has taken to saying he is—and who'll contradict him?—the best executive now in television. Maybe the best ever. It's a fledgling industry, why not? All across America, cathode tubes have lost their minds over his wife and made her their idol. But that's her genius. Desi goes about it differently. Across yellow pads he scratches mad diagrams, blueprints, administrative charts; with real flair, he makes compound lists of who's failed at x, y, and who's failed at z. He names businesses to develop or purchase, he draws buildings to erect, their flags tight squares in the wind. Preparation is the coin he hoards. He shows his jottings to big-shot friends and reports back. *See that, Szilárd? Bill Holden thinks it's genius.* (Many of these big shots can more accurately be called Lucille's friends.) Desi will chuckle, shake his head, and act out mock wonder: *Just admit no one thought there'd even be a Cuban Louis B. Mayer.* (He brings Cuba with him everywhere.) *Treat me nice, gents; I'll be a one-man industry. I'll make extras stars and writers directors.*

To his left, some gaffer now walks out of the stage-set kitchen; Desi knows the fake door will shut with a clang, then rattle, then creak as it swings back open—the way it always does. Desi's never spoken to this gaffer and couldn't guess his title; he doesn't have the terms for his studio's everywhere wires and monitors. At the moment about fifty strangers in his employ bustle around, yelling, jotting notes, rearranging the fake furnishings, and drinking coffee from Dixie cups; he's happy in his nameless kingdom where at every step some new unknown delivers his wants and needs.

Clang, rattle, creak.

"Well, I don't know, there are lots of reasons we've succeeded, Dez," Szilárd is saying. It's afternoon, but it seems no particular time in this tall, windowless hangar—this somehow touching, flimsy, cut-up replica of a home. ("Your wife is why we succeed," Szilárd knows *not* to say.)

Szilárd brings a hand over his own neck, as if that was where his pride were leaking from. This droop of the head isn't a cowardly retreat from Desi's high, steady egotism; it's a nonviolent resistance. In the past, this worked. On most days some tiny redress would occur when, as on some unseeable incline, the littlest bit of force did trickle from Desi to him.

Not today.

"Correct, Jess," Desi says. "You *don't* know. You don't fucking know." What he is upbraiding Szilárd for, Desi couldn't say.

"I can't do everything," Desi snorts, tapping his foot. Angry? He looks splendid, ecstatic.

This week had debuted the thirtieth episode, "Lucy Does a TV Commercial." More people had watched it than they had anything in the history of the world, and that's the truth.

A Western Union messenger just this morning pressed the parchmenty sheet from Nielsen into Desi's hand. The news was very good. *Very.* Almost seventy percent of homes that contained a television—or, by another measure, almost nine of every ten viewers who'd actually been *watching* TV at that hour of that night—tuned in.

And none of this addresses the fact that if Desi left here now, he'd find Lucille in a compromising spot.

"Let us have," he's saying, "a peek-see at the script pages."

But Desi's actually looking up at the script girl in her booth. She is hazardously pretty. He says, "Slide me a copy, someone"—and keeps eyeing the girl.

Desi, even to himself, universalizes his particular offenses. People enjoy skinny pale blond script girls with big breasts, girls who work for them. Which is to say, *he* isn't confusingly weak-willed and amoral; *people* are. People feel their mouths foam when looking at a young Southern belle who works on their TV show; is it a crime for people to do that? He smiles at his philosophy of human nature. But how come *this* belle is not coming down here now? It's not just Szilárd; the writers also take Desi in with half-lowered faces, loving him, hating him. The warmth of his smile roars its confidence at you. (What's the point of warmth if it doesn't scare up a little envy?)

One thing about those *Lucy*-viewing homes. Nielsen measures them in the tens of millions, and this doesn't even count all the TV-less Americans who descend on neighbors' living rooms to watch.

"This episode's story has to be sharper," Desi says. He lights a cigarette, blows a perfect smoke ring. The Johnny Hartman single "Wheel of Fortune" plays on some radio, bright horn blasts, syrupy violins, low volume.

"Jess, you ever see an episode of *anything* that starts by not showing you who's talking?"

"Only show I ever saw do it is *Young Mr. Bobbin*."

"Correct," Desi says.

"And *The Gallery of Madame Liu-Tsong*."

"Correct."

"And where are those programs now, you mean?"

"Correct."

Szilárd is the first to open and start reading the dialogue-heavy script, whose voices now harmonize in his brain with Hartman's violins and horns.

"No, see," Desi says, frowning into the pages.

The shadow of his hand stops across the very first joke. "See, no, unacceptable." As he speaks, his eyes darken; in his face's intensifying color, the pupils go deeply black. He shakes his head: I am a boss more sinned against than sinning.

Desi likes this particular staff, or the idea of this particular staff—or at least having *a* staff. Now with staff around, he ad-libs; the conversation drifts on whatever smoke-ring of thought rises from his lips. CBS are a bunch of ankle-biters. They demanded I learn about amortization, well I never heard of it, he tells the staff. And so now, it's all gravy for me—by two episodes in, all the costs were paid for. I'm going to sell fucking *I Love Lucy* pajamas and dinner sets, you watch. Desi looks overhead again; what is that script girl *doing* up there? Desi has gotten very rich very fast, and there are things he desires and people to take revenge on. Fuckin' *I Love Lucy* pajamas—at a huge profit! Desi knows Szilárd and the writers have heard at least some of this before. The success, though! Huge! An example: New York City's municipal reservoir-pumping station reports visible pressure drops at *Lucy*'s commercial breaks. The city's water commissioner, his incredulous fingernail tapping the gauge, sees Lucille Ball steer the largest city in the world to the toilet. (Where *is* Lucille now, anyway?)

"Okay, this first scene"—Desi thumbing through the script pages on the table—"how long is it?"

Brooklyn-born Szilárd wears what looks like a wardrobe-closet cravat. His outlandish mid-Atlantic accent gives his voice a poignantly fancy elocution; that's the voice he uses to tell Desi: "This is a rough draft. The script is not due till tomorrow, Dez."

This is the response Desi has been looking for.

"Lazy attitude!" he says. I know these people, he thinks, even if I don't actually know each of them very well.

He takes out a pen and with swooping bravado lines out, willy-nilly, an entire page. "Lazy!" I know what work they are capable of and what work they are capable of avoiding.

Carol Pugh—of the four writers on *Lucy*, the only woman—gasps. And silence falls like dust—coats the table with its grainy foreboding. Szilárd likes to say his work schedule gives him everything but the pleasure of spending time in the heart of his life.

Desi lays down the script. "I am Desi Arnaz." His eyes light up with absolute joy. "I am nobody's fool, least of all yours."

This is a lift of a quote that he knows, that everyone knows—it's from *All About Eve*. Desi, the king bee, is also their meal ticket and their second lead, and his favorite gesture these past few weeks is to give them the honey of his wisdom. He lifts his chin now and approximates the look of some passionately eternal bust of George Washington—the intensity, force, the quality of being *seen*. Success drives his staff to love him, or at least to gobble up whatever honey he puts on offer. Nobody minds that he'd stolen the *All About Eve* line. He's a slightly talented young aristocrat-turned-refugee. A Miami busboy who overcame unfair history and racism to win at life and can you say for certain you'd behave better than he? (Can you really?)

Compassion is another unit of power. He tells himself to be lenient with everyone, tomorrow. So he reminds them that their contract requires that they hand in—*do any of you deny it?*—the script by today if asked to.

"I want you to make this week's program even bigger, even better, is that so bad?" he says in his purl of an accent.

On his way out, he slaps one of the three cameras as if they're his loyal pets, which in a way they are. And without guilt, he smiles and winks up at the girl in the booth, in case she happens to be looking down. All the women he doesn't deny himself. He never, ever feels guilt, though he'd swear to himself he does. What he sometimes actually does feel is regret—specifically, the hangdog remorse of getting caught at something, *if* he gets caught. He hates getting caught. In getting caught, he feels wronged—wronged by the world and (here's what tastes enough like penitence for the moral distinction to slip past him) wronged by himself. Why do *people* do the kinds of things that make them get caught? he wonders with philosophical sadness—the same way he would wonder why it feels worse to walk in accidentally on someone using the toilet than it does to be the person whose shit is disturbed?

Starting this week, a sign in the window at Marshall Field's, Chicago's most famous department store: WE LOVE LUCY, TOO, WHICH IS WHY WE'RE CLOSING TUESDAY NIGHTS. So who fucking cares about guilt?

Desi bounces on his toes and walks as if he were trying to bump his forehead on the clouds. Crossing the parking lot, he feels transported to some other land of wealth, imagines a prairie wind and himself wearing a bolo tie. Oil field gushers he pictures at his back, jetting up their Texas tea. A different mogul in appearance, and, he thinks, maybe *that* guy would spend his afternoon imagining life as me!

And still Desi has no idea about the sticky surprise that awaits him.

"DO IT OR don't, Iz, but quit moaning," is pretty much the last thing said on the phone call. This is the second or third time they've discussed this.

"But."

"You want to call her, there must be ways to find the number," Norman says. "You don't want to call, then stop complaining to me about it."

But Isidore, seated at his kitchen table, fiddling with the lazy Susan, wants to keep on. "Isn't it strange, though, that—"

But now Harriet enters the kitchen. Isidore had thought she was out food shopping.

Oh, Christ.

"All right, goodbye." Isidore's already moving the receiver from his face. "Thanks."

Before he hangs up, Isidore hears Norman say: "Welcome to the crooked path, big brother."

A quick slam down of the receiver. A quick, markedly pleasant smile at Harriet. Markedly pleasant has become everyday mode with her, no matter what. But she doesn't smile back at him now. Who was that on the line? Oh, just, you know, work call with Norman. And next it's the typical busted-husband reaction—falling into the claws of panic.

"Why," she says, "did you ring off so fast?"

"Getting bored talking business. You came in. I didn't want to be rude to you. My ear was getting sweaty."

"Business? You were asking something about your father."

Isidore hopes Norman won't be dumb enough to call back and ask *why'd you hang up on me?* Okay, Isidore, let's see what kind of fiction writer you would've been, he thinks. Maybe don't come up with three separate excuses this time.

"Dad sold his Plainview property at a nice profit."

Harriet's gone to open the fridge and now bends into it. The top of her has disappeared into the appliance. *A nice profit* was a good line, Isidore thinks.

"Really?" she says, standing straight. "You seem"—and emerges carrying an uncooked pot roast to the counter—"not to be telling the truth."

"Why?" he asks this wife he'd been sharing a life with for years. "How long were you listening?"

"You tell me why. You got off so quickly, Iz. I don't know. You sound nervous."

His heart jolts and tugs, but his panic isn't manifested in a tied tongue. "I can't imagine," he says smoothly. The panic manifests as an urge to giggle.

With one hand, she opens the oven, and—as Isidore asks, "Do you need help with that?"—she puts in the pot roast. Find me out! he thinks. The tickling impulse to ruin it all was whispering in his ear. You end it for me! Make everything easy!

Harriet brings her hands to her waist, and, in thinking it over, she appears to be holding back from something.

"Well," she says. "Why is it your father always does seem to make you nervous? Didn't I say not to bring him out of retirement and involve him in Long Island?"

"You're right!" The giggle emerges. "I shouldn't have involved him!" Relief!

But then, the laugh goes. The years once made Isidore and Harriet nearly indivisible. Had the situation changed before Lucille or because of her? And could it be that Harriet didn't feel it?

He's hit by a real fondness for his wife, for her obliviousness, for his luck. Harriet has joined a full and diverse cast of millions. It's the age-old drama of a woman wronged by her husband and yet faithful in her ignorance. "You're right! I shouldn't have!" he repeats.

THE SCENE IS tropical now. Frogs fill the air with an angry noise; the sound one hundred frogs make together is weird and strident, like page after page being torn from an old hardcover. A hundred frogs at least. Of course, there might be no frogs in here at all. Not actual frogs. That's this crazy business we're in, Lucille tells herself. The reality of anything can unravel. . . .

She hadn't met the handsome John Archer until after *Lucy* had been airing for four months.

Her friend Ann Sothern had been filming a pilot (*Private Secretary*) at the old Hollywood General Services Studio; Lucille arrived to offer a pep talk—see, TV's just like the movies, Ann; a set is a set is a set! The world will be yours, kid!

Ann had been filming on Stage 2. On Stage *1*, director Wallace Grissell, B-movie regular John Archer, and the Esskay Pictures Corporation (this was before the federal tax lien) were slapping together

A Yank in Indo-China—in which a tiny budget, a Pacific Theater WWII set, and some Technicolor once more grinned the lipsticked grin and hiked up the skirt at the indifferent public. (*It's somebody else's battle,* read the breathless poster, *but it's a Yank's gal they're shooting at . . . and he's shooting back!* It didn't mention the frogs.)

In the General Services commissary, at the lunch break, Archer swaggered up to Lucille. She didn't know him. He bobbed his head, a kind of synopsis of a bow. "Ah, the woman who gives men like me hope!"

Lucille tilted her face at this. "Not sure that's a compliment."

And with a relaxed, sort of cozy movement, he sat down across from her. "Give me time," he said.

She smiled. He smiled.

Right off they spotted each other as champions of resolve, maybe lucky, maybe unlucky, mostly intent that luck not have a say. Like the soldier he was playing, Archer was tall, lean, a confident man in uniform.

After one coffee, Ann Sothern excused herself and returned to the set—time for the afternoon "Martini Shots," what they call a day's last bit of shooting. Before Lucille could join her, Archer said, "Lucy, I'll get you an éclair."

Lucille squirmed, and bells went off in her mind.

"No," she said. "You got this thing wrong. *Lucy* lives in a one-bedroom apartment in New York and scrubs dishes." She raised her nose a little higher. "My name is Lucille, and I have a beautiful California ranch. With my husband."

Archer just sat elbows on the table, rapt, pinching his lips between his hands. Looking at her. His hair was thick and wavy; his careful part looked ax-chopped in the grain of his curls. Some men have a birthmark, a beard, a memorably loud voice. John Archer had that part, hewn right into the cowlicks.

"The cream filling's delicious. Try one," he said. "*E-clare.* Fun to say too. Say it."

And Lucille's brain just kind of stopped.

When they got to his dressing room, she wished she hadn't

come alone. He stared at her too long with his light and crinkly eyes, and with that detachment and near impudence you see when a guy thinks he's cut out for Hollywood. What was she doing? Maybe part of it was just how much she hated being by herself. She held—wrapped in a cloth napkin—a runny, boring, deflated éclair. *E-clare.*

Maybe Archer sensed her doubt. "Thank you for coming. As I said, if you're willing, I'd ask your career advice here." The dressing room was quite small. "Hey, apologies for the 'Lucy' slipup before."

Archer's wrists were sinuous and elegant; his shirt cuffs were perfect tight hoops, as if the suit had been darned around them.

"You don't want my advice, and you know it," Lucille said, serious-browed until she smiled.

Lucille was right. He wasn't, in fact, asking for assistance; the manful tone made that clear. (Me, *need help from a* woman? said his 1950s smirk.) The one professional gene that all born actors share— along with clever facial muscles—is a lunatic's optimism. He didn't need anyone; success would come with this film, finally, for sure.

"And don't bother about the 'Lucy' thing," she said. "I've been getting that."

"Hey, it's a problem to have, first of all."

He looked at her out of those crinkly, dangerous, domineering eyes. Then Archer aimed a finger pistol at her, because he had no second of all. Bang. It'd been better when he had only been looking.

ISIDORE FOLLOWS AS his wife leads two guests into their house, right into the den, the circle of general comfort. These friends haven't seen the home before. They rubberneck, take in the cherrywood, the mirror and its cold iron frame, the unequivocal leather. Everything is dustless. Everything is spanky new. This place talks (Isidore knows) in a clear silent voice, and what it says is: *fancy.* Maybe even a little celebrity shine right here in Great Neck?

The couch once faced a glossy black piano. Now it faces the television screen.

"This *house!*" says the woman. Her name is Mona Feinman. She is Harriet's good friend.

Isidore, taking his seat, watches Harriet's face go scrunched with pleasure. "How much time do we have?" says the other guest, Gary Feinman. He's Mona's husband and *Isidore's* good friend.

"Oh, it won't be long now."

Both Feinmans still stand, their shoulders pulled straight, as if on the threshold of something illicit.

A hint of small talk and yet everyone has to wait until the exact appointed time. I'm good, Gary; you? Oh Harriet, the drinks are perfect. I'm glad, Mo, and you know that's a *fantastic* dress. . . .

Just stalling. The Feinmans came over tonight for only one reason.

There is a pleasing completeness to Mona. She is what she is, confidently. A smile on a handsome face, pert, just a little fleshy. But Isidore isn't attracted to her. Mona he sees as *the* housewife among Harriet's friends—the woman most housewifely in spirit. She is now leaning to the bowl of almonds. Mona has full-looking smooth skin under her jaw, and maybe this is why Isidore thinks he receives signals of sexual compliance off her full frame. Harriet, too, is a housewife, but not only. She can play Gershwin on the piano. Harriet holds opinions about what she reads, is politically aware, has lately been trying to tell jokes and be funny. As for Mona? She's bending her stout figure at the moment. Her bosom swells from beneath her blouse, and Isidore has no trouble receiving the signals. But she appears not to have interests, or much of a mental life. Or maybe that's unfair.

"We going to watch, or sit letting me bore each of you?" Gary says, the ice in his Tom Collins rattling pleasantly.

"It doesn't start for a bit."

Mona and Gary don't have a television of their own. "I can't wait," Mona says.

"*I* can't believe you've never seen it."

"She's wonderful, I hear."

And Isidore has to look down, biting his mouth and causing enough pain to kill his sad, wild grin—

"How's the Hicksville project?" asks Gary. Isidore lifts his face, a smile that says, *Oh, you know, it's business. Going okay.*

Gary is a garmento, selling bridal. Gary has struggled. Isidore tries on his humblest look. "Units are moving, Gary," he says. "I guess they're moving."

"This guy," says Gary, shaking his head.

It could be that, tonight, Isidore's humble look hasn't conveyed much humility. It could be that his humblest look—when Lucille is already sort of here in this room, her expansive vitality, that warmth and humor—is no longer humble. Could it be Isidore has become a celebrity of the mind? (*Hold-on.*)

"How's about you? Business good?" Harriet says. This is the wrong question to ask Gary, and Harriet seems to realize it immediately.

"Ah, bridal's bridle. Dress the gal up," Gary says, "before she walks to the gallows."

And none of this matters to Isidore, who is thinking, thinking.

"Funny, I don't think Isidore's actually ever watched, either," Harriet says. "It still doesn't start for a few min—"

Isidore—"Oh, let's turn it on already"—skims across the floor to the set.

When Harriet had invited the Feinmans from Brooklyn to watch *Lucy,* Isidore had said, "Here? *Lucille?* You did?" And then a blast of heat, felt down in his socks, whooshed right up to his throat. I hope my armpits don't stain this shirt, he thought.

But maybe he and the evening will be calm. His tongue has gone dry like a leaf in the oven.

"Yeah, yes," Isidore says now. "I haven't watched, ever." It's been almost two years since he saw his love.

To sit beside Harriet, as Lucille will be in that box with her singing husband? He's been dreading and craving this. A thousand times he's told himself that he'll never, likely, meet her again. But maybe it's all right. It may be an enjoyable proxy. . . .

Gary's on his feet—"No, Harriet, I got it. Sit, sit"—fixing himself a Pimm's cup.

Strike one against Gary Feinman's looks: his height, what little there is of it. Strike two: his suit. It's obvious he can't—as Isidore can—be fastidious over thread count, seam integrity, the value of negligible difference. Gary has had his jacket brushed and dry-cleaned within an inch of its life. It has a kind of poverty gleam. But above his collar, Gary is finely handsome. His dark eyes jump left, right, on the pulse of a thought. "Oh, is that what I *think* it is?" he says now as the screen goes dark following a station announcement. "This means the program's about to start?"

It is; it does. First the string-and-brass theme—those marching, happy *daa-daa-daaa*s. Next the counter melody, which consists of two jumping beans (*ta-tum te-tum*) hopping right into the ear. And the screen goes light. The title calligraphy curves like a woman's delicious body. Isidore—to do *something*—analyzes his fingers. He can hardly wait. The black-and-white version of the unforgotten, never forgotten, ever present face. Let the first joke come. There's a dot of grime under his left pinkie nail. With the first gag, he'll be able, without causing suspicion, to look as if his tears are from laughter.

The camera shows us: Lucy flipping a pancake. She is beautiful, Isidore thinks; she is funny, she is charismatic, on Tuesdays she is *the* woman in America.

"Do you think Lucille's *that* great?" Isidore asks everyone, no one, himself. He rubs his mouth where she had bitten him. "I mean, really? Do you think?"

"She's wonderful," Mona says. Lucille on the screen looks not leeched of color—more like *expressed in pure silver*. "I can already tell," Mona says.

Pan in on Harriet; she's smiling hard. "Isidore and I saw her, you know. On Broadway, not very long ago. Did I tell you? Quite beautiful."

Gary nods and dreams: "That Latin fellow—very lucky."

There have been few words spoken in Isidore's adult life that feel as much like a vindication. Lucille/Lucy is talking to Ethel, the eternal friend. . . .

Isidore stands. *Very lucky.* He can't help having stood: all that energy.

["I made Ricky a promise," Lucille/Lucy is saying.]

Isidore's walking, then stops behind Harriet's chair. The Feinmans are too entranced to notice. But Harriet turns and looks. *Iz, Iz, what are you doing?*

It's hard to tell with her sitting down, but Harriet is three inches shorter than Lucille.

Isidore bends and awkwardly embraces Harriet. She tilts her head and he kisses her and kisses her, forehead, eyelids, mouth.

["Oh, brother," says black-and-white Ethel.]

Harriet only begins to kiss Isidore back—but now she pushes him off; there is *company* here. Her eyes blink, then narrow, considering him.

The Feinmans are blushing for them.

Once upon a time, Isidore had imagined, without having quite known he was doing so, an alternate future for him and Harriet. A crazier life. As if some alp of emotion would one day appear, only to be scaled—new heights of bliss or maybe even giant, bracing fights. But neither happened.

Harriet, now embarrassed, thrilled, perplexed, says, trying to keep her composure: "What's, uh, what's gotten into you?"

Isidore answers with pointing and shrugging, no, don't worry about me, don't worry, just going to the kitchen. A silver satin pillow and swooping calligraphy is what's gotten into me. . . .

Joy, pain, horniness, misery, all of it. Why did I think I could withstand this? The cracked mug of his night: No matter how much humor *I Love Lucy* will pour into it, the joy's leaked out.

Alone now, he leans back on that little kitchen counter next to his fridge. He's breathing like one of those hamsters in a pet store cage—the scared little guys whose hearts you see ticking in their chests.

Televised laughter filters in now through the closed door. Isidore sighs. He shuts the kitchen lights; he's not sure why.

Sometimes, thinking about Lucille spreads a feeling like warm butter over his insides. But she hasn't phoned. There is no future with Lucille. No gooey warmth now.

Near his face, a mosquito bounces on its air trampoline. Isidore's been too guilty or afraid to try figuring out how to reach Lucille himself. If that's even possible.

The physical stuff hadn't been exactly perfect, in fact it didn't, uh—*no, don't think of that!*—his memory jumps—he remembers it smelled a little chalky in there, remembers the photographs, Bette Davis, Humphrey Bogart in black-and-white, remembers Lucille's cold blue stare, and, okay, it hadn't been exactly *perfect,* but it'd started out truly great (*the snips of her teeth on my neck; the desktop's edge biting into my palms; my erection that would outlast Stonehenge*).

Out in the other room, *I Love Lucy* gives way to another show, *It's News to Me,* and this passing feels like the fall of Athens. . . . —okay, it didn't stay truly great for long (*Nervous about missing the moment I was too, was too . . . I tried to count backward, by sevens. I recited—Ralph Branca, Preacher Roe—baseball lineups. Ninety-three. Ninety-one. Er, eighty-something. Roy Campanella, Carl Erskine. I tried thinking of General Eisenhower, which didn't help as much as you'd think; Stonehenge sank to grief*). Ignorance is what kindles love with someone new.

There's a kind of reverential not-knowing. So, how can an everyday intimate, with her blemishes and odor details, compete with a mystery? And how can a guy stay in love with the person whose every detail he knows? And how can a guy not?

Isidore groans, unzips his pants in his kitchen, and—is it wrong to hope for some peace?—spits into his hand.

AND A WEEK later, here's Lucille, come back to the Hollywood General Services Studio, *A Yank in Indo-China,* that soundstage air torn by frog sounds.

It's a sweaty temperature in here. She, almost without being aware of why, has come a second time, at the invitation of John Archer.

Perhaps the heat's meant to mimic the Mekong. The director, Wallace Grissell, smiles at Lucille. "I do a lot of takes, which is just my approach." He winks, genius to genius. "Perfectionism, you know."

Lucille has to smile back. Her increased celebrity, seven months in, is an onerous splendidness. (She'd immediately left Archer's dressing room last week, just after downing that washed-out balloon of an éclair, with nothing unchaste having happened, yet.)

A Yank in Indo-China is obviously—despite the boost that her presence brings—going to be crap. Archer must be aware. Why'd he invite her? Most performers are insecure, secretly. But some are not.

She's stopped allowing herself to fret about infidelity in the almost two years since she and Hold-on had, had— She wouldn't phone up a nonfamous man, that seems a risk, a transgression, a—

It is hard to think; the damn croaking! There's a Hollywood idea of a jungle mist to the air here, which honestly helps the gray in Lucille's blue eyes. Small mercies.

Last week, right before she'd left Archer's dressing room, Lucille had caught her own reflection—and Archer's—in the makeup mirror. Two actors, framed by a TV screenish square. They'd both stood watching the glass, her lashes lashing; to herself, at least, she'd looked pathetically eager. No, I can't do this, she'd thought.

And yet here she is, on set, to see John Archer.

Moreover, she understands the effect of her presence. Fame of her almost planetary magnitude is a kind of gravity. Grissell, wearing his thin-brimmed fedora, yells "Cut!" now and looks not at his actors or cameraman. He looks at *her*.

"Sorry, Miss Ball," Grissell says. Sorry for what?

Every day thousands upon thousands write to her, send poems, photographs, some propose marriage, give flowers. A few have offered their children for adoption. It feels sometimes like a foot pressing against her windpipe. When people write about her, it is said that she is worshipped, but "worship" gives the wrong idea.

A clapper loader walks past Lucille holding a magazine of film, head down, his mouth pursed. Too nervous even to take a peek?

"I'm that bad?" she says.

She mimes smelling her underarm, *har de har har,* and the entire crew bursts into laughter. The director, the screenwriter, the star. They stop to laugh.

It's not the kind of worship you see in a church. "Idolization" is a better term. A kind of civic kinship with a favored patron, maybe close to what the Greeks knew. Athena for Athens, Poseidon for Corinth, Lucille for America. Someone's very existence felt as a sort of communal bond. Admiring her is close to a national duty. But she isn't feared as a goddess. She may as well be the wife of the general public.

"Hey," Archer says approaching Lucille. "Sorry, give me one minute, doll"—padding right past her, gone to chat with the screenwriter over some detail.

Oh, *really?* she thinks.

"People copy me," Lucille had been saying just the night before. It'd been on the gray couch of her TV set; she'd sat feet-up on the gray table. (To meet the contrast demands of the camera, everything—players' wardrobes, "books" in shelves around the apartment, flowers on the mantel, all of it—was stripped of color.) As she sat there last night, everyone had gone home, even her husband. The only person with Lucille had been Hal Brade, the makeup man.

"I could wear, I don't know, a man's suit," she'd said, "with a shirtfront sticking out the zipper. I could dye my hair chartreuse. And still, a flock of housewives would look like hell in trying to be like me. I could chop it all off."

"You suggesting I get my garden shears?" Hal said. His banter seemed forced, his voice pinched with nerves.

Lucille was always the last person here, and she often coerced Hal into being the second-to-last. When the cameras were off, the gray of this place could steal into your head. But she liked to go around returning scrap paper to the closet, collecting pencils. She

was a pencil hoarder, a paper re-user. She told herself this had nothing to do with the snowcapped memories of Jamestown, where the
locals in shaggy Depression suits hiked the streets all day because
where else would they go; the locals who hunted squirrels and pi-
geons to eat or to sell, the locals who carried valises full of can
openers or melting chocolate bars or yards of twine they'd found.

"On the other hand, isn't that the very end?" Hal was saying.
"People copying you?"

He'd become a trusted friend to Lucille. But for her, the truth
was too complicated to answer *yes* honestly.

"Yes," she said. "I suppose in a way."

It *was* fun, and a thrill, and flattering—she loved her fans, but it
was a bit disheartening; had the people souls of their own?—and
somehow a little disappointing, as if to say, "*This* is what it feels like
to attain your dreams?"

"You gonna meet John Archer tomorrow?" Hal said, his banter-
ing tone dropped.

"How'd you hear about *that*?"

"Somewhere around the seventh time you mentioned it."

"Listen," she said. "I was going to see Ann Sothern, is how we
met."

"Great. What's tomorrow's excuse?"

He slid his hands to his kneecaps: the *I'm going to level with you*
position. "Aren't there public figures who—" He waited to be interrupted but wasn't. She said nothing.

"Lucille, people with a public platform whose—position
shouldn't be—that is, maybe the risk isn't . . ."

The back of Lucille's head inched toward the wall behind her, as
if Brade's meaning hit her brain as a pushing thumb.

"I'm going there to lend encouragement to a new friend," she
said. After a second, she said, "Desi and I are fine."

"Look, you and *I* are new friends," he said. "The press. They
would—"

She lowered her brow to glare her big eyes at him, a long, steady,
unrelenting look, leave it, leave it alone.

"Desi has done well by you," Hal said—and tardily added, "business-wise."

"How dare you," she wanted to say. I have to be the one to worry. I am unhappy, Desi carries on, and I have to be the one, she thought. Desi has done *well* by me? This impudent makeup man!

—Desi gets furious if I talk to another man, while look how he acts, showgirls, secretaries I'll bet, whatever he wants and I never despite any of my suspicions ever did a damn thing wrong, but only just tried to make him jealous, a little, only just harmless games, pretending to have a crush on someone when I didn't, or not answering the phone if I thought it was him calling, to make him a tiny bit—not even *jealous,* just involved. It was only just innocent games, at least at first, and then it turns out that the whole time I was playing these innocent little, er, this sort of little harmless *scheming* that normal wives do, while, in fact, he's been actually whoring around! Well, I did burst in that time screaming my stupid head off about him still liking Betty Grable, when there was nothing between them—though looking at it *now,* who can say?—and I came in and yelled in front of his mother, and he said that should've tipped him off to not marry me, but I think he secretly liked that I wasn't like his sainted Mama who took so much terrible humiliation from *his* father. But I take it myself, I take it and take it, Lucille thought.

Oh, you chump! She remembers the handwritten cards she left on his pillow when he'd first gone from her to do a show or two in Cleveland. *Don't worry darling—if you're as conscientious as I am, we have nothing to fear. Yours always, LB.* What a sap! she thought. Because after that show, he didn't come home for three days.

"Look," Hal Brade was saying, "I owe it to you to be telling you this."

Do you know what it's like to be out with your husband, or at that time fiancé, in Ciro's or the Tailspin Club and the waiter delivers a note from another woman and you're sitting right there? Lucille nearly asked this of Hal Brade. ("I don't *like* to make you angry," the makeup man was saying now.) Jesus! she thought. That story in

Collier's after our wedding. *The interview procedure runs as follows: this reporter begins chatting with Miss Lucille Ball and then Mr. Desi Arnaz enters and Miss Ball leaves. It is not that she is so rude as to leave in person, merely in spirit. . . . Miss Ball looks at Mr. Arnaz as if he were something that has floated down from above, on a cloud.* But what happens when the person you love in that cloud strays and strays? Desi went out on a USO tour with Bob Hope and Mickey Rooney, and those people couldn't even *look* at me after. My peers! she thought. In front of *them* he betrayed me! Not one could look me in the face!

Now Lucille started to build, with effort, a smile for Hal Brade. There's a practice to saying exactly enough, or almost enough, to uphold your dignity.

"You have no idea," she said. "You have no idea."

Simply one more woman swallowing down an injustice; if suppression were torque, Lucille could lift the Sierra Nevadas right over her head.

"Time to vamoose, Hal!" High-spirited despite herself. "They need to close the stage!"

—Even on becoming a father Desi cheated; even when the TV program began, the TV program I cast him in to keep him, he cheated. Internally, she chuckled now. Because, the thing is, if she were being honest, you had—sort of—to admire the brazen consistency. Charisma was a powerful intoxicant. And Desi got you to suppress yourself—for reasons you would never know. Self-doubt, cultural mores, love? She couldn't leave him. She loved him and was famous for loving him.

"Okay, doll," Hal Brade said. "You've convinced me. You're innocent."

Could a woman be called a cuckold?

A lot of time had passed since she'd talked to, seen, or thought about Hold-on. Not in any front-of-the-mind way, at least. He'd been shelved like the black-and-white books on the set's black-and-white bookshelf. Lucille gave almost no suggestion to herself that Isidore touched her life at all. Still, a trip to John Archer's shoot was in order.

"Thank you, Hal, for your permission," she was saying. "Now let's go."

This discussion would add to tomorrow's visit with Archer the expectancy and suspense of something right out of Hollywood.

FROM THE RICH soil of her closet, Lucille has harvested an outfit. Wing-collar shirt with Gibson Girl sleeves, a knife-pleat skirt she swirls before the mirror.

I'm impulsive, sue me, she thinks.

On this visit, John Archer seems nervous around her. It's clear Lucille has come here specifically to see him. Yet Archer looks unsure. Hesitant.

He talks to the director, watches her. He tries to focus on the faux jungle, watches her. He shoots a take, watches her.

"You're an Army *pilot*," the director is instructing him. "Imagine the way a pilot handles his parachute. . . ." (Lucille sits behind the camera, at what must be the outer edge of his vision.)

Soon the director yells cut; Lucille with her shoulders careening forward goes to Archer: "Don't you look romantic in uniform."

The most flirtatious she's been. "I hope the camera will do you justice"—as if she doesn't know cameras, their fickle magic, their strict justice. What's most coquettish is the soft, Monroe-ish way she says it. A puff of words.

How does a 1950s accomplished woman talk to a less-accomplished 1950s man?

The day's shoot is done. Now Archer sits with her, right outside the soundstage.

A bit of tension clouds the space between them. Maybe it's because they're in the observable open air. She is anxious about even a semipublic appearance with a man. She gets to her feet, pacing—even without knowing that this is the one day Desi happens to have left work early. Which might really scotch her plans.

It's a sticky afternoon. She's looking into Archer's strong, wholesome face.

"You were good today, John."

"Good in that turkey of a movie, you mean," he says.

And you know how it is when someone trashes himself in front of you:

"Oh jeez-o-pete. *You* were good," she says. I didn't come to be nursemaid to his ego. But then why *did* I come? Extras in straw hats walk past, pretending not to notice her.

"Is the film so bad?" Lucille says. "Who wrote the script?"

"I'm not sure about the guy. Samuel Newman."

"He's in television?"

"He's never *here,* is the thing," says Archer. "I think possibly television, yeah. Working on five projects."

"Well, that's what makes professionals," she says. They keep up this conversation of stale air. "Don't slight a TV man—working hard, doing the work."

With his quick eyes, Archer looks like he has more to say than he does—which may be a requirement for an actor.

"Even in a squawker like this," she adds.

You can see Archer has an impulse to stand, to kiss her.

In his gregarious, pleasant voice, he says: "Gobble gobble." He doesn't stand or kiss her, yet. The thick expressions of his face can be very handsome.

"Yes," she says, and comes to sit, "let's talk turkey." Archer watches every inch of her figure descend onto the bench.

But if she's the live audience he's playing to, Archer won't break the fourth wall—won't crash through the wide, clouded atmosphere around her.

"All righty," she says, patting her hair.

Still, they get closer; nearness transforms mood. It may just be the expression of compliance from Lucille's body, I will let you kiss me, all right *please* kiss me. Even out here. And so that wide atmosphere widens to include him and is charged. But Archer still is unsure about making his move. A mosquito—people are wrong to think there are no mosquitoes in California; and this one has a cousin in Great Neck—has flown up, and it bops on the air, infatuated by Lucille. Merely the latest admirer. She swats at it.

The aims of men and women in the 1950s can appear to be in clashing opposition. People are trained to think the man is always determining if he can—no other word for it—*take* what the woman hopes to guard. That's not true in this case. Archer shakes his wrists free of their cuffs, futzes with his hands, where jitters are most conspicuous. From opposite angles, this man and this woman both silently ask, *How little of what I want can I ask my behavior to reveal?*

This bench has been plopped down under a streetlight that burns all day. "All righty," Archer says, too. *Swat, swat* at the mosquito. Then he gives her his smile. A lascivious one; Desi would recognize it. "Glad you came," he says.

Has Lucille heard this, though?

She rises and tells Archer, well, maybe she'll see him again. *What?* He tries to catch her eye, but she won't look at him. An odd turn of events. What's the point of this hope, why do I cover myself with it each day, so stubbornly? she wonders. It's hard to talk now— her suddenly emotional throat. I do *like* the guy, she tells herself, walking across the lot. Then why has her optimism mutated in her chest, shaped (as she imagines it) like an upraised middle finger at him?

I didn't come to be nursemaid to the guy's ego.

Or is there another reason?

Lucille owns and drives—as fewer women did in the 1950s— her own car. A white Crestline Sunliner. It may have been a gift from the Ford Motor Company, she thinks. Anyway, she's driving alone now, gripping the wheel, seeing the countryside go brown as it pulls east. *Do* I like Archer?

Unhappiness has seeped into her chest—the way a chill shows up in a house. Maybe in another life I could. It's early for the sky to be going dark like this. A spiky heaviness there, in her every swallow. *Why did I go to meet him?* Any explanation for her behavior besides "I truly liked the guy's personality" would divulge something to herself she'd rather not know about herself. Even if she's partly doing it just to get back at Desi. She thinks of flipping on the wipers; it may be about to rain. *I'm just a girl from Jamestown, New York.*

And now behind the wheel of the Sunliner, Lucille has put on her sunglasses, rain or no.

Was he ever going to kiss me?

What she really wants, what she's always wanted, she tells herself, is Desi. His easy insensitivity ("Standing me up on New Year's Eve, one of a hundred examples!" she thinks) and the lies—so many of those—and the gale-force humiliations ("It's just what Ginger told me, 'Ah, you married a man so much younger, what'd you expect?'"), and, yes, the risks to her career if she left him. But, for all that, she and Desi have made it big anyway. She wipes her wet cheeks with her sleeve. Bigger than anybody thought possible for us! A white woman and a Cuban. The success of it had been clear at the relaunch party for the show. Bubbles having foamed over Lucille's glass onto her hand; her dress having made a kind of rain sound brushing against William Frawley's suit; her licking the champagne from her sweetened wrist. The right-away conviction that the show would be a hit. And Desi's touch on the pit of her spine. Well. What the problem might be is, maybe Desi found a talent for deception, for *self*-deception, in me, she thinks. I maybe want to be lied to.

Her baby, Lucie—jeez-o-pete, ten months old already; God I should really . . .—I hope she doesn't grow into a fool for men.

Sometimes an actress walks from a battle scene smiling and feeling okay—until that evening's bedtime when the bruises welt up and there's no one to complain to. That reminds Lucille of an affair. You have them, you forget them? Not the way it is for me. I'm just a girl from Jamestown. There's something she makes herself not think about.

Pulling into the drive at the Ranch—ah right, Desi isn't home yet, won't be home for hours. (But, no, he's on his way now.) Raindrops plonking on the windshield. Archer's a handsome guy with his crinkly, kind-of-awed eyes. But he's no actor, Lucille thinks. It's not that his performance revealed this. Only the screen can tell you how *that'll* turn out. It was his demeanor. Before filming, Archer'd joked: "What's there to be worried about? It's just a part." When the cameras started rolling, however, Archer took gulpy swallows. Which is fine—everyone gets nervous. But the real actors get nervous *before*. "Action" is called, and real actors go tranquil, exultant, are transformed. Those able to metamorphose *for others* have first to metamorphose *in themselves*. *That's* an actor.

Maybe I'll never see Archer again, she thinks, not knowing he is on his way here, too.

The best actors don't quite deliver memorized lines; they speak their own spontaneous thoughts that happen to have been written beforehand by someone else. That's not skill. That's not a technique, or even art, Lucille realizes. My brain just thinks exactly what the writers guessed the character would think. Only my brain thinks it more correctly, more fiercely. When the cameras go on, Lucille is the genuine thing the writers had been trying to simulate.

You know who could've been an actor? she thinks—she lets herself think, at last. But the funny thing is, she won't finish the thought, won't even think the name of the kind man who exhibits that ugly-handsome mix. Maybe she doesn't know herself what their time together has done to her. But no, she won't, not even in her head, land on the man who looks "like a Jew Gregory Peck."

IT'S TWILIGHT NOW, there's a western clarity to the blue air, and all through this arroyo, snakes sleep in the dirt. Then it happens. With stunning quickness: a surprise arrival, then another arrival. Then the dustup.

Minutes after she aims her Ford up her ranch's driveway, a tan Mayfair pulls in, behind the Crestline Sunliner. Did Desi get a new car—no, wait. Who is that? No. Lucille thinks, *Oh, no.*

Archer, slamming his door too loudly, says, "I intend to fight for you"—trying to quell the chattering of his teeth.

Lucille lowers her chin and looks at him through her lashes. "You do," she says, "and I'll kill you."

Clara, the maid, walks out next to Lucille on the porch. "Who is it?"

"It's okay," says Lucille; her tone means *go inside.* Bossiness has become one more diamond she wears, extracted from the mines of other people's servility.

"Hello," Desi says, seconds later, once *his* concise red convertible has pulled up. He crosses the front yard quickly—right to Archer. Handsome-in-a-dumb-way Archer.

Desi says, "Don't think I know you, friend."

"You don't, *friend.*"

Archer adjusts his posture as if he's got a cramp of the shoulders. And then he steps to Desi. He has to pass Lucille and won't return her look. *Please don't,* her face says—and if a face offers a message alone in the forest, does anyone hear it?

It's now Desi's turn to speak. He doesn't. Instead, he squares his jaw in the fakely confident swagger of men facing what he thought he was facing.

"Dez," Lucille pleads.

The blood thumps in her ears. And, after telling herself not to swallow, she swallows.

"This is John Archer. He knows Ann, he's a friend of Ann's," she says. "Ann Sothern."

"You're an actor?" Desi says. "You look like an actor."

Is it an insult? It's a strange insult, coming from an actor. It sounds like an insult.

"Mr. Archer is someone I've been—giving advice to," Lucille says. Perhaps the "mister" in "Mr. Archer" was too much.

"You having trouble in your career?" Desi asks.

Because, Lucille thinks, it's not untrue, what I said. Nothing *has* happened with me and Archer.

"No trouble, *friend,*" Archer says. "I'm doing a movie now, a war picture." And then, as if passing a spiky gallstone: "But I could always use some—advice."

"You'd like to get on our show?" Desi asks, in something almost like a friendly voice. Offering help to a man in a lesser position.

"If I wanted on your show," Archer says, unable to hold his tone, "I'd go through William Morris."

Desi flares—his eyes, his skin. " 'Zat right?" he says, crunching forward on the darkening drive.

And now comes more of Desi's spitting anger, sudden boorish slurs; but right off, he falters. He hears the rudeness in his own voice—because maybe he's wrong, maybe Archer *hadn't* spoken with the daring of the adulterer. Desi doesn't want to hear that particular news.

People say I fly off the handle, Desi thinks, and is that good for a mogul to do? Plus can he really see himself cuckolded? A man like me? For a half second, he looks down.

And Lucille in this little intermission does the strangest, cleverest, the best-acted thing.

She walks to Desi, stretching out an arm. A saint gesturing to farthest, unseeable heaven. She talks to herself—Come on, Lucille—as if kissing a lucky rabbit's foot. This has to be good.

She rests a hand over Desi's shoulder. Her skirt, she is aware, italicizes the surge of her hips, her tapering waist. She does not need The Method. She can act using her body, her voice, her resolve. She with happy eyes leans into her husband, auditioning: Okay, imagine you're a very dutiful bride at some altar somewhere in the sex-deprived heartland and the crowd is silently crying because they know no one besides that groom on your arm will ever see you naked. Go!

"Desi." She sighs. "*Dez*. Let's talk about something important."

He is startled. Archer is startled. Lucille is nuzzling into her husband's neck. "But, I've gotta ask," Lucille says. "Why're you arguing with our guest?" To come off as natural, the great ones match every movement of their body or voice to the intent of the story.

She scratches the back of Desi's hair.

Desi squints like a cowboy trying to see an Iroquois across the MGM prairie. His tantrum fizzled, he says, "Okay, long day," and smiles at Archer—then at his wife, whose hip he warms with a pat. "Let's give the man advice." And the look that Lucille gives him conceals both her pity and her fear about what it means that she's pulled this off.

ACT THREE

"So much of love is love of love."

—*V. S. Pritchett*

CHAPTER SEVEN

A T MY HIP, I clutched a sheaf of notes about Lucille Ball. A twenty-five-ish assistant (quiet skirt, glossy hair) walked me to the bigwig's door, then withdrew—the Cerberus to the secretary's Kharon. I also held my grandfather's film treatment. "But I said on the phone, it wasn't necessary, you coming in," the secretary said. I asked her name. "Okay, thank you, Catherine. Is it all right if I sit for a little, Catherine?"

Fine, if you want to sit, whatever. William Morris dominated the wall in chrome letters behind her head. Make sure it doesn't seem communist, read a mystery scribble written on my grandfather's notes, in a female hand. My leg wouldn't stop bouncing. This made a thin nervous sound hitting the leather couch—a conductor's baton on a lectern. Can't afford even a hint of commie sympathies now, the note read. A shiny door opened to the bigwig's office. And in front of me, there, not quite filling the doorframe: the (little) bigwig. Agent Suzanne Gluck, five foot two of rude health, mahogany brown hair cut and polished prettily, a striking face. "Hello," I said. And Suzanne Gluck swiveled that face downward at me with all the interest of a barcode scanner.

"So I'm here," I began to recite my line. It was the 1990s: Modems behind me tore up their throats yelling. Each screech like a thrown splat. "I'm here to show you something amazing. Hi," I said.

*B*ECAUSE SHE'D BEEN abandoned by her mother, even
if for a short time. Because she'd been naïve. Because
her grandfather had always been kind to her. Because she hadn't
realized times would change. Because she actually cared about poor
people. Because she's a woman. Because now times *have* changed.
Because nobody believes a woman deserves success. Because people
now cry *traitor!* at the littlest things. Because her grandfather (rest in
peace) was a fucking idiot. Because, in fact, she'd been a poor person herself once. Because having your body on crummy lighted
screens all over America means time and again you must endure
seeing your body on a crummy screen. Because that screen may as
well be the wicked mirror in a fairy tale, and your face hovers there
daring people to find the more beautiful options at the ball. Or
because universal worship is now just the preface to universal scorn.
That's why.

As if coming up with an explanation will change a thing.

"Maybe I like trouble," Lucille says over and over. She's a parrot
in an embroidered blouse—"Maybe I like it"—an unthinking voice,
an almost lullabied refrain. "I must like trouble."

Desilu Ranch is short but it sprawls. Chimneys, weather vanes,
a portico that unspools along the entire façade. Inside it, Lucille is
speaking to no one. "Why else would I make it so hard on myself?
I must like . . ."

The fear gets her under the arms. She touches the window
(needs a dusting) and waits for the strange men to arrive. Behind

her, sedate shelves of tall books she'll never read. Oh, Grandpa, why did I have to be nice to you that time?

It has all gathered force and like an avalanche come rolling down on her—all the whispering, gossip, all the slander. If you live big, you fail big.

When Desi left home an hour ago, he'd said, "Pretend you like the dog. To the men."

"What? I don't dislike Pinta."

"It worked for Nixon with Checkers," he said.

All across California, there was a drought on; the heat, however, wasn't what had sucked the color from Desi's face.

"Bring Pinta to the news conference is what I am telling you," he said. "Put her on your lap."

And then he turned to leave. "Jesus Christ"—closing the door behind him—"it's so fucking hot out." And then, gone. Away to motor off his nervous energy before the strange men came.

For most of the morning, the normally happy California has refused to smile; its face now is covered by beards of haze.

LOS ANGELES TIMES

NOVEMBER 11, 1953, PAGE 1, NON-BYLINE

REGISTERED RED IN '36: LUCILLE

Star Denies She Voted Commie, Blames Grandfather

[The body of the article was too painful to read and is not reproduced here.]

IT REMAINS AN odd thrill, in 1953, to find yourself at twenty thousand feet, beckoning with the lift and tilt of an empty glass, ah hello young stewardess, another Beaujolais, that's right. This is crazy, this is absolutely crazy, Isidore thinks.

"Oh, me?" he says in response to a predictable question. "Real estate. I'm a Property Man."

Two hundred bucks for the ticket—*more* than two hundred.

Crazy. And sixteen hours, door to door. Crazier still. TWA Flight 103, "The Golden Clipper," foie gras, salmon and caviar, even for those in tourist class. But Isidore's stomach lurches.

The passenger in the seat next to his—fat hands on the tray table, a shaving cream aroma, that's all the man was to him before this moment—has asked another question. A pushing voice, chunky legs. Like the distance separating love from lunatic need, the space between the TWA seats isn't as wide as one might hope.

"Yeah, I build homes," Isidore says. "Long Island."

"A builder! Long Island!" The man uses his hand to flatten his own slick brown plateau of hair. "*Love* the architecture out on Long Island!"

Ha ha, very funny. And then, Isidore couldn't sleep. Thwarted by the small abuses passengers inflict on one another, the border skirmishes of the elbow.

A few months ago, he'd told Harriet: "Of course, the program is narrow"—dismissing *I Love Lucy*. "I mean, life is more than spousal scheming."

Faker! But who cares now, he's got other things on his mind.

"You'll get to the studio, and she'll be at the, what's the word, it's not studio, the *soundstage,* and she'll be wearing that dress from Coney Island that showed off her back"—the plane touches runway; his imagination is taking off—"and she's not exactly ready to introduce you around, but she's happy to see you, or maybe that dress is too formal, maybe she'll have a blouse, and you'll bring a finger to the brim of your hat—*Hello, young lady*—or, even better, she just comes up and kisses you on the cheek. A quick one, but with meaning. Or she'll walk past a lot of TV people with their smiles and teeth and we'll lock eyes. And maybe you'll think it's all foolish, you know, you'll remember that you have a life at home, and the crooked path is just"—no, come on, why do you do this, even now, even now—"and, all right, maybe you'll see her and instantly it will be that same forceful thing we had, she's perfect, and you can be stoic about this and not let guilt overtake you, because you have to do this, you can do it, maybe this *is* you, maybe more than—just why won't you let yourself enjoy doing it? and, okay, maybe she'll come up and whisper something dramatic and movieish, like, 'If there really is no way that this isn't doomed, then let it be doomed. If there is *no* way that this will not be tragic, then let it be tragic. All the great stories are tragic.' "

It's one thing to aim for romance in the luxury of your imagination. Another to find yourself across the country in a just-landed airliner. His being here is preposterous—but he feels robust and happy, even cunning. Maybe he keeps telling himself he's panicked because he knows he isn't feeling panic enough.

"The Beverly Hills Hotel," Isidore says to the cabbie and falls into the back seat. "Ha!" he says. "Sounds like the start to a movie." Then softer and softer to himself, "The Beverly Hills Hotel. The Beverly Hills Hotel."

How did he get here? A quick and easy excuse: Oh, sorry, Harriet—um, last-minute business trip, yes, weird, I know. Checking out potential land to buy in Chicago, though. And, uh, Pittsburgh. "Casting a wide net?" she said. When he was a boy, he'd once told his mother, "I'm not going to the movies because I have to study with George or Lew"; his mother had said, "Well, either you're the worst fibber ever or the best."

"All right, *all right,* mac," says the cab driver now.

Out the taxi window, Los Angeles! The golden gift of the sun may still be tucked in its wrapping paper. But even in a cloudy November, it's like New York in summer. Better—it's glamour!

One of Isidore's Jewish wisdom books has the story of Rabbi Zusya of Anpol. (It had become a favorite story in Isidore's recent search for answers.) Rabbi Zusya is dying. And his disciples say, "Don't worry, you lived a good life, why do you fear?" Zusya's deathbed answer: "When I stand before the Lord's throne, if the Almighty should ask me, 'Zusya, why were you not more like Moses? Why were you not more like Solomon?' I can answer in good conscience, 'My blessed Lord, you did not grant me the greatness of soul you granted Moses. Nor the wisdom you granted Solomon.'" But Zusya realized he did not know what he would say if the Almighty simply asked Zusya, "Why were you not more like Zusya?"

"Famous spot, though," Isidore tells the cabbie now, blinking away the jet-lag burn. "You must get a lot of fares asking to go there."

Out the window, the sky has cleared; horseless cowboys meander in the smiling weather, everything bright, everything receiving a kindness from the blissful sun. All of it so familiar, the city that the entire world knows.

"Not really," says the cabbie.

Once checked in to his room, Isidore sits on the toilet, looking anywhere but the shaving mirror. Today of all days, he doesn't need another reflection—a further account of the obvious flaws. Each un-Hollywood part—his deep nostrils, his magnified eyes behind those glasses, the fuzz of his hair—feels hot and glowing.

He is supposed to wait. Waiting for her is the plan. But *how,* when time's a slug moving through glue? He rubs his face, which takes up a good second. Then what?

Out of the toilet, he turns on the television—a surprise to see a big set holding the room; he's never stayed in a hotel that's provided a TV—but watching the idiot box throws extra kindling on his anxiety. First some news program, an atomic test, some irradiated archipelago somewhere, that's no good, so now it's onto *The Larry Larkin Show.* Why, Lucille probably knows this man! Even Larry Larkin is likely intimidated by her.

"Well, hi there, network, come right on in. This is *The Larry Larkin Show.* And this portion is brought to you today by . . . Franco-American spaghetti!" Larkin's voice isn't simply or even primarily a channel through which his messages run. "America's favorite ready-to-eat spaghetti and new *Italian*-style Franco-American spaghetti . . . with meatballs!" Laughter. Larkin, like any good TV comedian, is attentive to sounds, rhythms, words dropped just behind the beat. He can assemble laughs from anything. Where do they learn that skill, these comedians? And what skill do *I* have? Maybe Isidore can answer the Almighty's question *Why were you not more like Isidore* by saying *But now I am trying,* even if he didn't want to be the kind of man who would do this to . . . No, it's not fun to go down this road right now.

Writing. I have always wanted to pursue writing. He's in Los Angeles. It's time to try writing, for her.

On the desk opposite the bed, there sleeps a pad of paper; taking up a pen, Isidore endeavors to wake it. He begins to scratch out the contours of an idea, and he scribbles the title just under the crest for THE BEVERLY HILLS HOTEL.

Will Lucille really show up?

ONE WEEK EARLIER, on very thin stock paper, Lucille had received a note from the HUAC, written in language you'd expect in a cotillion invite. *The presence of Mrs. Lucille Arnaz is formally requested.* (The HUAC: the House Un-American Activities Committee.)

Okay, when Lucille was young, or fairly young—before World War II *and* in a time when we didn't quite know about the badness of Stalin—her left-wing grandfather had blathered on and on. Do you even care about the working man—will you even sign the pledge? Yes, sure, Grandpa. . . . That was the whole kit and caboodle. And now, look, I'm the most popular American, gal or guy! Forty-five million people watched "Lucy Goes to the Factory." That episode had her on more magazine covers than Ike's inauguration. Why, J. Edgar Hoover himself sent her fan mail! What could happen?

They're doing this to *me*? she thinks.

Last week, on a dry sunny morning, a tan scarf wrapped at her neck, she was compelled to steer her Ford to the center of Los Angeles—at first, brown scrub hills flanked the road, then palm trees, and then it was all glinting downtown windows. And finally,

201 North Figueroa Street, the Department of General Services, where, tugging her dress straight, Lucille went to meet with an HUAC investigator and his suspicions.

Faltering before the entrance to the lobby. Breathe, she told herself. Swallow, kid. Looking in one of the mirrory windows, she lifted her chin, smoothed her fleshy neck, couldn't avoid the truth in the glass. Breathe. What a day to show your age.

The elevator let in a gush of hot air before its doors closed. Maybe it, too, decided to hold its breath.

"Ah, Mrs. Ricardo, I was hoping you'd come."

Someone or other said this. The usual scurry of secretaries and other insignificants—middle-aged women in starchy dresses, middle-aged men with the under chins of an uncle (or a longtime husband)—they were usually her crowd, the unseen folks out there in TV land. She wasn't going to correct the name now. Let them call me Ricardo. As long as I can leave.

HUAC told Lucille to arrive alone. (I don't do anything alone but go to the toilet, thank you, she'd thought. Still, she'd come naturally as a little girl to isolation, when her mom had left her with one relative after another.) Desi and their lawyer Herm Gottlieb had coached her, Just say nothing and don't lie. Meanwhile, she hadn't told CBS about the letter, the visit, her grandfather's communism, anything. She smiled now, tried to look unworried. Would the story leak? She needed a moment to herself. No such moment was forthcoming.

The high ceilings and bad lighting of municipal L.A. She exuded anxiety and confidence both. "Where," she asked, "do I go?"

Why me? I've been pretty good—her mind skating away. A pretty good person, even a pretty good wife. Except for a slipup. Or one-and-a-half slipups. And there was another in the cards—which probably wouldn't happen now, she thought.

Stop, she told herself. I need to concentrate.

"Mrs. Arnaz, come in, come in." Like more and more young L.A. men, the HUAC investigator was bewilderingly handsome.

Johnny Weissmuller mashed into a G-man's sport coat. Alone with the investigator in his little office now, Lucille thought *hmm*.

"Golly, a lot of the staff is excited," he said, rubbing his buzz cut. (Maybe a knack for bewildering the ladies helped with the job; well, two can play at that, she thought, and smiled. But the mirror showed a deep furrow lashed between her brows.)

The investigator stood close. His handsome face like a moon over her. "Okeydokey," he said. "Just this way. Please. In here. Would you like a Ritz cracker, Mrs. Arnaz? Water?" Sharp jaw, dark hair, delectable squint. His presentation seemed to say, *I am the kindest, most sympathetic, and least stuffy employee in the U.S. government.* And she understood that her past life, her present associations, even her down-to-earthness were under scrutiny. "No, thank you, Mister . . . ?"

"Oh, the name's Plates. James Plates Sr.," he said, and smiled at what he thought of as a joke. "Junior is due in about two months."

"Mr. Plates, this is all a misunderstanding, is all. My grandfather was a sick man, and I was devoted to him."

James A. Plates, mid-level investigator, HUAC, nodded, gentled her to a pale blue chair. "Right here." He had a squeaky voice.

Lucille introduced Plates to the mythic figures of her past: the absent father and sometimes-absent mother in Upstate New York, the grandfather she brought out to L.A. The rise from poverty, family, devotion, the almost hummable American tune. The hushed pink of sundown on the red brick houses, the breeze that smelled of cut grass, the river leaves you saw carried by the Chautauqua. She didn't mention the melancholy, the blues you felt walking down the empty shaded streets at dusk, the yearning. The insistent wordless voice telling you there is more somewhere else. When my father died, I opened the window and a bird flew in, she said. Broke stuff in the house. Then I got into theater. My grandfather made some requests, and, well . . .

That was all she had. It would have to do. "Congrats, by the way, in advance," she said. "On your family's, uh, impending birth." Plates hadn't sat and was now orbiting the room.

"Can you sign this, Mrs. Arnaz?" Handing her a pen, some paper, shrugging his ramrod shoulders. "Sorry to hear about your dad."

Dad? Oh, that he's dead? But he's been dead forever. I didn't really have a dad. "Sure thing, I can sign."

The pen sounded scratchy on the paper; the walls of her throat began to inch closer together. "Happy to. I've hated birds ever since."

"What?"

"Nothing. Happy to."

The document's signature line, Plates's desk with the framed photos, the little flag, the big phone. Everything made her want to burrow into the floor, jump out the window, get away.

"Sign in only the one place, sir?"

She looked at him with her enormous blue eyes and worked her facial magic—a shame they don't give out a Best Smile Oscar. Even with the air so dry that she couldn't sweat.

Stopping at her side, taking the pen from her trembly hand, Plates made certain Lucille saw him slide the paper in a file—made certain she saw the file—marked LUCILLE BALL-ARNAZ. SUSPECTED COMMUNIST SYMPATHIES.

"You know, Mrs. Ball, pinkoism is a scourge." Each one of us has a favorite way to show he's nobody to be trifled with. Plates pointed his ballpoint pen knifeishly.

"It's just not a good arrangement. Collectivism. Doesn't make sense for anyone," he said. "And it can damage you, of course. If you met someone at work and started to talk, or—look, association alone can be dangerous. Bad influence and like that. You understand."

This was how it worked. Threats and appeals to the American penchant for common-sense decency.

"Of course, I agree," she said. "As I mentioned, my grandfath—"

"Well. I guess you know that," he said. His heart not in it? The pen as if on its own lowered. For a while, Plates stayed watching her, as if she were a TV. And then he couldn't stop himself from gushing.

Not a problem, Mrs. Arnaz, is what I mean. (Walking in circles again.) I follow ya, ma'am.

Every time he passed the credenza, he'd pull a Ritz off an old plate, look at it, and stick it in his mouth. Was this really all there would be? Amid the steam of coffee poured from a government-issue pot, James A. Plates Sr. backed off. Yes, this was all there would be. A daze of steam. Plates had said his piece on communism, done his duty, and now he could be, merely, one more fan. Lucille began to rise, the back of her legs gone damp against the chair's vinyl.

Plates said, "This will remain confidential." His solid handshake felt callused and warm, like a summer's walk across an American backyard. "'Cleared' is what you can consider yourself, Mrs. Arnaz."

The threat had lifted, just like that. She'd stopped fretting, had an easeful couple days. And then.

And then, not long after, Walter Winchell announced on his radio program: "A beloved TV comedienne [has] commie connections." For the next twenty-four hours, Lucille let herself believe Winchell had been referring to Imogene Coca. Then came that front-page article. *Star Denies She Voted Commie, Blames Grandfather.* And worry splattered through her life, gurgling up her phone line, clotting her husband's forehead, threatening—would CBS stand by her? Philip Morris?—to drown everything.

And so now, here she is, nervously peering out the window at Chatsworth, waiting for men to come. Please let Desi get back before those vultures show, she thinks; her fingers are still touching the pane when the first strange jeep pulls in the drive.

WHEN THE GROUP of men parts, she walks between them, down the lane of faces.

There are photographers in her yard, there are klieg lights, reel-to-reel recorders, studio fixers, assistants; there are television cameras, there are radio antennae, there are jeeps that have sprouted telescopic arms and some of the first-ever microphone cannons. By the sage bush, red camera lights blink. But do the palm trees of California usually drop microphone cannons from their fronds? No; Chatsworth is reporter-haunted. "Distinguished members of the newspaper world" gawp at her; TV guys with their clear stares and hearty skin tones gawp at her, too.

CBS set up today's news conference at Desi and Lucille's home, giving them a single chance to clear her name. And now Lucille's heels can be heard poking the soil.

She's carrying Pinta—her bestest little floppy-eared friend, all yips and wriggles—as if the dog's pinned to her bosom. I'll smile, she thinks. A queasy, bad-dream tone rests over everything. Not a single face smiles back. At the end of the human lane sits her thickening husband/business partner, awaiting her with a hand spread over his mouth. His body twists half off his slack director's chair. He's eyeing Lucille flatly, steadily. Such discomfort. Is he angry at her? His face bloats from stifled pressure. One guy near the end of the row raises a camera, and like some cruel thought a flash sparks out from his head; but theatrical Desi, now smiling Desi, lifts his hand to take Lucille's, and she has seen all this already happen, in just this way, she is sure of it.

She sits. Two chairs, husband and wife, accused communist and her Cuban husband, in front of a lot of standing men.

"Shall we begin, fellas?"—Desi. Right behind him, the Arnazes' quite uncommunistic swimming pool, shimmering blue. And Lucille's dreamed this all before.

"Thank you for coming," she says. "I'm here to answer all your concerns," a line she's practiced all morning: different inflections, different tempers and humors. And now she's made good on the delivery.

Lucille has trained to expect applause. None comes.

"Now, before you ask your questions," Desi says, "my wife would like to explain something." (Perhaps he has chosen *explain* because it is part of his catchphrase.)

Lucille's next to Desi—Pinta in her lap now—and she hasn't released his grip. With the other hand, she squeezes her chair. The dream keeps playing out. As for Desi, tense leg muscles press contours in his trousers. He's quiet but far from uncommunicative—there can be a ferocity in silence.

Lucille has a different approach. Okay, she thinks. Letting go of the chair, lighting a cigarette. Showtime.

"I didn't know a thing about politics in 1936. I registered as a commie only to please Grandpa, who was, yes, I admit, a socialist in those days. Maybe I play ditzy well because I *was* ditzy."

"No one knew this stuff then," Desi says and gives her hand a further squeeze. She squeezes his back.

"Thank you, darling." On the show, this would've been a wry punch line. Something about thanks for nothing. She hates telling the reporters she had been ditzy. But she has always known how to spend her talent, and on what.

"Take it up with FDR. We called Stalin 'Uncle Joe' and loved him for a time, right?" Desi's saying. "I am crazy for my wife, and there's a reason America is, too."

"Thank you, darling," she says.

Oh, the impulse to accept Desi—Desi in full—with his boorishness, his cruelty, womanizing, temper, with his shining black hair, the surprise of his business panache, his softening gut, warm hand, and perfect memory. His good looks. His grubby, snarling, jagged self, and all the invisible phantom stuff that, once accrued, comprises the body of any marriage. Perhaps she could agree not to mind any of it. He *is* here for her now.

"Lucille's pop-pop was a wonderful guy, loveable guy—the kind of guy, he wanted everybody in the world to be happy, you know? To be happy and have more money. In 1936, it was a, a kind of a light thing." (Pronounced: *"thin,"* Desi playing up the accent, as if it's Tuesday at nine P.M.) Now, a tonal shift: "If Pop-Pop was alive today, we might have to lock him in a back room."

"Thank you, darling," she says, with a strained laugh. Then, an encore: "I want to thank my husband for everything. He loves America, as I do."

LOS ANGELES TIMES

NOVEMBER 12, 1953, PAGE 1, NON-BYLINE

LUCILLE BALL EXPLAINS 1936 COMMUNIST LINK

Lucille Ball and Desi Arnaz faced the press near the swimming pool of their Chatsworth ranch home.

They were glad the truth was out about Lucy's fleeting affair with Communist politics 17 years ago, they said.

The nation's top television star and her costarring husband were interviewed at home as the House Un-American Activities Committee revealed that she had been called in to a California field office to answer for her Communist Party membership. . . .

LUCILLE ASKS IF the reporters have any questions, and the hands creep up, and some hesitant voices too; there's none of the anarchic feel of a White House press event. "One at a time, please." Her nervous dog has jumped off her lap.

"Okay, sir—you there."

Eric Salat of Reuters is the first lemming into the water. The question is the obvious one. That doesn't make it easy to answer.

"Well," she begins. And takes a moment to blow, from the side of her mouth, a frank refractory jet of smoke. She's giving herself time to shape and voice the answer.

"Will it hurt me, you ask?" she says.

LOS ANGELES TIMES

NOVEMBER 12, 1953, PAGE 3 (CONT'D)

. . . Miss Ball, the red-haired star of TV's "I Love Lucy," said, "Will it hurt me, you ask?

No, I have more faith in the American people than to think this will hurt me. I think any time you give the American people the truth, they're with you."

Lucille insisted she knew nothing of politics in 1936 and registered as a Communist only to please her grandfather, Fred Hunt, who was a zealous Socialist.

On it goes. Lucille finishes her fifth answer, her sixth. Yet there're still more inquisitional follies.

The *Los Angeles Examiner*'s Ronald Barnett's blurted question concerns the risk of Mao in China and the possible comfort this knowledge would be to those who would . . .

Wearing a grim, newsroom scowl, Mr. Barnett stands here young, assertive, and stupid. Desi ignores him. He recites a point he'd already vetted with Herb Hubbard, of CBS's legal team. "We're lucky this happened to us in America, where *newspapermen* ask the questions. In commie countries, they shoot first and ask the questions later."

Lucille bends in her chair, picks up a random twig. The next day, in a sidebar that will run after that page-one story, the November 12 *Los Angeles Times* will report:

The story of a loving, close-knit family that humored the wishes of a doting grandfather continues to emerge from the Actress Lucille Ball's Communist Party imbroglio.

Lucille Ball's mother, Mrs. Desiree E. Ball, also registered to vote Communist in 1936, as the actress did to please "Grandpa" . . .

Two days after that:

LOS ANGELES TIMES
NOVEMBER 14, 1953, PAGE 2:

[photo caption]
Lucille Ball and Desi Arnaz, comforted by stacks of
telegrams from well-wishers, luxuriated in the privacy of their Chatsworth home yesterday, glad that
the storm was over.

[second photo caption]
Desi said they felt no resentment over their ques-
tioning by hordes of newspaper reporters since Lucille's 1936 registration as a Communist was made
public.

There is almost nothing to say about the rest of the press conference. But it *is* worth lingering over, for one reason.

"I was kicked out of Cuba because commies wanted to take
power and failed, as they fail always," Desi's saying. "Lucille Ball is
one hundred percent American."

Lucille crunches the twig in her hand. I should be happy, she
thinks. The press conference is going well. Desi has them where we
want them.

". . . I mean my wife, my favorite redhead; in fact, that's the
only thing *red* about her and even that's not legitimate!"

Laughter, brusque, male laughter. It *seems* to Lucille she's lived
through all this, exactly this, before. The childhood sadness has
crept back. Hearing herself talked about as if she's not here. Her
throat goes thick. Is she a good girl? Is she worth keeping around?
She realizes Desi has dropped her hand. It's as though her success
has been the dream and she's awakened back to those terrible days
just outside Jamestown. To the vicious catastrophe of her true life.
Her father's death, marked by a bird flapping through an open window and breaking things. Desi still defends her: "Why, you fellows
know it. She's as American as Barney Baruch and Ike Eisenhower."

She waits for it all to finish. One way or the other. Fame, beauty, money, everything goes.

The press conference is worth lingering over because it's the first time Lucille realizes this.

And I have—*what?* she asks herself. My husband, my daughter. Family. (Where is Lucie now, at this discordant hour? With Clara, the maid.) I love Desi, she thinks. And there's a *man* coming to visit me? Now? Oh my God, there is! What was I thinking?

Desi is reaching out for her hand again. "You see, do communists love each other wholesomely like this?"

He punctuates the words: one of his booming, famous laughs. His *sexy* laugh. No one thrills her to the core like Desi does—that is, she is thrilled by him in those rare moments he remembers he has a wife. She is forever his, then. Wrapping a hand around Desi, taking in a fist the still surprising bigness of him, in her mouth, feeling him grow like that. Or even when she glides her hand over his chest and reverses the dark tide of his hair. (She pushes out of mind a different emerging memory: that fight in 1942 or '43 when he'd vanished for days and she didn't know if he was ever coming home, until the third morning found him crying in the front yard, blotto, declaring love for her, petting the dog.) Or, or . . . when she lays against him, her head on the packed rise of his biceps.

Now the sun is coming through the clouds, as if the outcome of the press conference were happily settled. I should get happy, too, she thinks; my career will be over if I don't make the marriage work.

A MONTH OR so back, at the final bend of summer, in Brooklyn, Sig Mekheles's brother Abraham married off his youngest daughter.

On the way to the wedding in Brownsville, Isidore had driven through the old community with the window open. Line after line of laundry in the sun. Men in dress pants, undershirts. He passed the schmutz and relics of his old life. Women whose hair looked strong-armed back off their foreheads. He passed (in reverse) the route of his (why not say it?) escape. Stickball and churches, shadows and smells, hubcaps flashing in the sun.

Inside the wedding hall, voices overheard: ". . . and her grandfather used to wear two skullcaps, one in front and one in back." Another: "Before you know it, we'll all be lying side by side in the dirt." And people danced, fast and slow: husbands and wives, parents and children, laughs and debates, a Jewish gathering. Harriet's hand lay on Isidore's shoulder. Up, back, step-step-step, she was a prize-winning hoofer.

"Glad I got you on the dance floor," she said. "You love this song."

"Perry Como," he said, trying to pick up the spirit. "I think it's *you* who loves it."

"I knew it was one of us," she said, then half-hummed, half-sang, *"You may see a stranger . . ."*

Meanwhile, nearby on the dance floor a lovers' quarrel caught fire, a woman with carefully dyed red hair and a man whose few hairs stretched over his tan scalp. No, *you* be quiet, you can't talk to me like that. Oh, you can be a harridan sometimes, maybe I was wrong to marry you. . . . The woman in the argument happened to turn; Isidore felt caught in the spotlight of her seething face.

"What is it?" said Harriet, who evidently hadn't heard the fight. "What are you thinking about?"

"Oh," Isidore muttered, stepping back and looking down. "Uh, nothing, just my clumsy Strauss feet."

The fight, this return to Brooklyn, all of it spun the turnstiles of who Isidore was.

Now Harriet was talking about where they would spend the coming winter. "I really did have trouble with that hotel in Miami, because, you know—"

It was not fun to think he might cause her suffering.

"The Biltmore Hotel is nice for us," he said. "We have a nice time there. Why not go back?"

"Iz," Harriet said. "The room service at the Biltmore is—"

The current of the dance swung them around. Isidore saw the couple who had been fighting. Looking into the man's face, Isidore felt linked to him.

"Iz?" Harriet said.

"No, I'm all right." He found himself watching his wife's ankles swim and glisten on the screen of a tear. "Just—"

Sorry, excuse me, Isidore told Harriet, he needed the bathroom, excuse me. . . . I'm not a good man, he thought. Excuse me, please. Maybe if he thought it with enough vehemence, he'd start to feel bad about it. Last week he read a quote whose aptness hurt him: "There in his past, as in every man's, he found things he recognized as bad, and it was for this that his conscience should have tormented him; but it wasn't the recollection of these evil actions that caused him so much suffering. Not at all. It was the trivial but humiliating reminiscence of a love gone wrong." Fine! he thought now. Tolstoy figured me out. But I have a right to *live!*—the thought so lame even he heard the lameness in it.

Before you know it, we'll all be lying side by side in the dirt. Of course he knew that. (Men's room sink, tap water, splashing his cheeks.) But something was different in hearing it said aloud.

In the bathroom mirror his under eyes showed bloat, his face looked tired. He rubbed his jaw, as if it might assure him he was fine, everything looked fine. Maybe it wasn't his age. Just be honest with yourself, he thought.

Isidore found Harriet waiting for him with dance-flushed cheeks. She stood in a bright angle of party light.

"Another good song," she said.

He rubbed more at the bristle skin of his jaw. Everything was fine. "Gene Kellystein reporting for duty," he said. But the charm belonged to someone else.

"What was that, Iz?" Harriet asked. "You okay? Your voice is—"

Love has many faces and many voices. It can speak in a soft, calming way until you fall asleep. It can put a hand behind your head and yell in your ear, *Don't forget me! Call me!*

"Do you want to leave?" Harriet was saying. "Should we get out of here?"

"There's something I want to do," he said. "Don't think I'm crazy."

"Fourteen years, you're worried I think you're crazy?" Then, seeing he was serious: "Okay . . ."

"This is, I know, a little odd." Isidore felt outside himself and heavy, like some cartoon villain to whom you hand an anvil. Then you see him crashing down through floor after floor. "Bear with me," he said.

Isidore leaned in and, between his thumb and forefinger, took Harriet's chin. "Don't feel self-conscious," he said.

Say it, he thought. Say "I cheated." And stop doing this.

Harriet's face with its simple frown broke his heart. "Iz, what are you—?" But he didn't let go.

Oh, please, let there be some magnetism between me and Harriet. Let something stop me from going anywhere.

"Can I just . . ." he said, after having already lifted her face. "Can I see you in this light?"

"Um, this is very"—speaking the best she could with tipped head and chin gripped.

Isidore scrutinized her, his mouth a bit open, a jeweler entranced by a gemstone of yet-to-be-determined quality. The pointy nose, the very red mouth.

"Okay," he was saying. "Can I do one more thing?"

Harriet's eyes slid from the ceiling to show him her sidelong confusion. He moved her head side to side, gently.

"This is silly now," she said. "This is silly."

But he was spreading two fingers to the width of something in his memory. He brought those fingers, pliant as whiskers, to her collarbone, gently touching the two hard dots.

"Iz?" Harriet said. Her mouth tightened.

But already he'd let his gaze slide from her, as if his eyes had changed a channel.

"Iz?"

. . .

LATER THAT NIGHT, driving home in the dark, Isidore felt like an ant colony: so many little black questions in him, wishes and doubts, crawling every which way.

For most of the drive, Harriet was quiet. What she said had a kind of discomfited formality to it. ("You were acting so strange. Not to say it wasn't *nice* to be admired, and thank you for saying I looked pretty. But . . .")

And then it happened. A surprise even to him: He began an argument. "I'm sorry I did that weird, you know, weird thing back there. But, I don't know, you've been acting weird lately yourself. And, and I wanted just to see. Did you have—*something* you don't want to tell me?"

"Why would you say that?"

He felt bad, and wanted to feel worse, is why.

"Do you remember when we saw *The Third Man*?" he said. "And I said how could Joseph Cotten not see Harry Lime was evil?"

"I'm confused. What's the—"

"And then you said if I ever wondered why it was so important to me that I think of myself as a good person. How come I—your words—'gave such a damn.'"

"No, I don't know," she said. "What are you talking about? Yeah, I said I treat the people I love well—beyond that, who would worry about the idea of being a good person?"

"Yes!" he said. He still couldn't look at her. It's not her fault. Some people don't have a big personality. "Yes, I'm talking about why being a good person is meaningless to *you*. That's what I'm talking about."

"Don't be like that. I just mean, outside the family, I—"

"Maybe *inside* the family is where you should be concerning yourself."

He realized now he had taken Harriet on a cruise not to appease her or to throw her off the scent. Or he hadn't done it *merely* to appease her and *just* to throw her off the scent. "If we could just get away together," he'd thought then, having called the travel agent. It was clear now. He'd gone away to throw *himself* off the scent.

It's now about a month after that car ride. He has escaped from the light of family and to L.A., at least for a time. He has flown the crooked path and has come here, to the Beverly Hills Hotel, dripping with darkness.

CHAPTER EIGHT

*S*UZANNE GLUCK OF *the William Morris Agency repre-*
sented novelists. She did not represent moviemakers. In
my stupidity I hadn't known.

"What you brought me sounds like a film treatment, for one," she said.
"And it's not about Lucille Ball, am I right? You're saying it's by her.
And your grandfather. And who is he?"

"They came up with a really good story together."

She looked unsurprised, neither by my presentation nor by me. "What
is it you want?" The kindness of her tone was where the thorn hid.

"I want someone, I guess, to represent it, or—me."

Her eyes basically said whatever decision she made now would be irre-
vocable. "Represent you for what?"

For all my literary ambition. I was more or less a kid who'd never before
written anything. Suzanne Gluck sat waiting for me to tell her this. And,
in this expanse of moments, I felt like that notorious animated coyote who'd
overshot his prey. Held by the empty air beyond the canyon's edge, hanging
in space, inert for the preposterous helium instant.

"I'm not sure," I said.

Maybe that's what it meant to be a man in his early twenties. Not to
know exactly what you wanted, but to want it very badly.

"I'd like to do something for my grandfather," I said. "To get his movie
out there."

*L*AST NIGHT, SHE'D dawdled in the corridor by room 317, on the point of bringing knuckles to wood, also on the point of not. But nothing ever came of nothing. She knocked, once, and the door opened immediately.

In her head, where the light was better, Lucille had seen Hold-on as taller. Three years had touched him as a vertical crease between the eyes. Oh, good to see you. Yes, you too, you too.

That was yesterday.

And it *has* been good to see him—if strange. For months after that dressing-room night, she'd designated some thoughts as trip-wiry—land mines that would (were her brain to drive over them) blow the hell out of everything. These thoughts had involved Hold-on.

And here he stood.

Hold-on began talking right away about her TV program, how proud he was, about how he knew the pride was misplaced, but . . .

"No, I mean it." He put his hand on Lucille's shoulder to stop her headshaking protest. "You're wonderful."

"Oh?" she said—inexplicably angry. Or explicably.

"Of course," he was saying. "I see you every week, and . . ."

He stopped mid-sentence, pursed his lips, looked unsure, helped her off with her coat. She sighed. That televisual rendering of her, the "person" she fabricates for the public—that forgery, *Lucy Ricardo*—had evidently fooled him too. What a complicated disloyalty from Hold-on.

"Let me get a look at you," Hold-on was saying. He leaned back a little, hands on her shoulders.

"So," she said, feeling surprising nervousness, "do I look different?"

A gaze can feel like a sunlamp. "It's you," he said. "You've really come."

"Not as far as you have."

"On TV, you're beautiful, but the camera doesn't capture the whole of it." Ahh.

She smiled, lowered her face, she looked up at him through her lashes. Sweet guy.

I WANT TO take her outside and buy her suntan lotion, thinks Isidore. Suntan lotion? How about a diamond pendant?

A day has passed, deliciously. He's forgotten to be shy. Shades are down.

How decadent to find oneself, during working hours, in a snarled bed that isn't yours. This is joy. He's just waked from a nap. There's a glow on the curtains. And the almost occult warmth of someone else's body under blankets. The assorted naughty scents. Unbearable joy. Lucille makes a lip-popping *I'm waking too* noise.

Her skin, its intense paleness. She has a scar right at her meaty above-elbow crease. Lucille is the rainbow and its cache of gold. Few of the Lucille-besotted millions will ever know about that scar.

"Mmm," she says, after a catlike stretch of the spine.

"Keep snoozing, you want to snooze."

But beginning at her shoulder, he telemarks two fingers down the white trail of her arm.

"It's too nice to," she murmurs.

"Good."

Feeling bold, feeling unlike himself, he tugs at the sheet and he kisses her clavicle, next a rib, lips still heading south—to the soft aromatic skin above her nether hair: he gives a lick. "The most prime real estate in the world," he says into her belly. The sound of her leg moving: that hiss of sheet against sheet.

"Oh, come now." She takes between her fingers some of his wavy hair. "Maybe just in California."

"In any case"—little bombs of atomic happiness go boom all through the archipelago in his chest—"never sell."

The air is gloriously stale in here. After last night, what a morning and noon it's been. All that time and in-bed commotion. Oh, there had been a few breaks, a few lulls. There'd been shared laughs, secrets, there'd been quiet schmaltzy periods of eye-to-eye staring. Lucille went at his chest hair with inquiring fingers whenever she asked a personal question. The coziness of that. But mostly Lucille had climbed up his body and they'd gone.

He shimmies now beside her, lays his head in the declension that slopes down to her breast. Something unexpected happens. Lucille tips the two of them right through this easy moment and into a very different one. Frowning a little, and taking some of the magnificence out of her voice, she says:

"Do you know why rich and famous people get divorced so often?"

"They're immature?"

"The press would agree. Ha." In her quiet smile, amusement isn't the only thing written.

Wait, he thinks, how did we get here?

"The truth is," she says, "it's because they don't get to know each other, the two people. They think they can buy away problems. They're very busy; they pay people to handle responsibilities. They never know if the other is able to clean a dish. Every life has its problems, and they're not prepared," she says.

"Let me tell you a theory," he says, and he knows he's not the Isidore from the day before yesterday.

"I think immortals would have a one hundred percent divorce rate," he says.

"Oh?" She lifts her eyebrow in the way the incalculable citizens of TV land have seen before.

"Eventually you get to the end of people," he says. "Love means it takes longer."

His little nod says *But eventually it happens.* Does he believe this, or does he just want to sound cavalier? He doesn't know.

"You charmer," she says.

Now she reaches for a cigarette and her breasts nibble across his chest and, oh, he's ready to go again. "Saying all the sweet things," Lucille says. "Do you think you'd come to the end of me?" Playing it cool, but there is a sadness in the question. "Maybe I wouldn't get to the end of you."

"How else would you learn, for example, if I can wash a dish?" he says. "Sure, that's good. Everything on the table, that's my motto."

She leans back, her red, red hair is down and looks sexier than on TV, less bright. In person it's the color of rosé enjoyed in the early evening, lighted with the sunset; but its color also holds the shadows that live in the wineglass.

"Do all Christians have a motto?" he asks. "Jews are curious."

Her *pff* laugh is softer than Lucy Ricardo's, flappier.

"Yes," she says. "We do"—reaching her hand between his legs. "Do unto others."

She leans to give his shoulder an unexpected bite. "You're funny; I forgot that," she says. "Do you do accents? Don't answer. Hey, speaking of immortals. 'Give a protozoa a billion years and it could make Paris.' Jess Szilárd is always telling me that. Time is the key to everything," she says.

Jess Szilárd? Isidore pushes his face into her hair and breathes in. She's obviously a woman used to having her associates' names known. I don't care who Jess Szilárd is as long as he's not in bed with us, he thinks. And funny? I'm not funny; it's being with her, in this place.

Now they go into a series of improvisations on a theme, and the theme is: How can we say we want today to mean something without saying it?

"What would this episode be titled?" he asks.

No hesitation. " 'The Highlight of the Season,' " she says.

He is about to answer: " 'You've Got Some 'Splainin' to Do,' " then decides it best, even as a joke, not to bring up Ricky, er, Desi. What he says is, " 'Lucy Decides She Doesn't Want to Go to the Club Tonight After All.' "

" 'Lucy Is Not What You Thought.' "

" 'Lucy Is *Better* Than You Thought.' "

" 'You've Got Some 'Splainin' to Do,' " she says, and they both laugh. This is joy.

She says, " 'Middle-Aged Star Has the Time of Her Life.' "

"You're not middle-aged."

"Tell it to the sponsors."

"You look very young," he says. "Come now. You must know this."

"You *got* me here already, what else do you want?"

It's obviously just a joke, and yet—*what else does he want?*—he doesn't answer.

"Having the time of your life," he says. "That's nice. 'Dropping Everything.' Maybe that's what we call it."

"Or 'Sweeps Week.' "

He doesn't dare hope for much. She's only holding the reins of her life and her television show because she's holding them with her husband. Putting them down means putting down *all*.

Her lowered face says that something new is coming. "You know why I never called, after the last time, Hold-on?"

With shyness, with warmth, she tells him. It just comes out. The pregnancy that she'd learned about immediately after they'd slept together; the miscarriage in which it terminated. With despondency, she's looking at Isidore. What she leaves unsaid, but implies, is that after the miscarriage she realized she wanted to have another child, with Desi. And that she has now had that other child. What is mysterious to him: Why is she here now? It can't just be that we are so natural together, Isidore thinks; with charisma like hers, she must be natural with so many men. So why? He has never known, from the first up till this very moment, why him for her.

"I'm glad you called, though," she says.

. . .

HIS HAND HAD lingered above his office phone. And lingered. This had been ten days back. He'd placed by his phone a business card, on which, in masculine handwriting, Lucille had penciled Desilu Productions' number, Los Angeles, CIrcle-7-2099. That was crossed out. Under that was another number, in his own hand.

Isidore double-checked that his office door was shut. He gulped. He found himself telling the Desilu receptionist, "Just say it's from Hold-on." He repeated that, and then did so again, to a second person. And as he leaned all the way back—the gravity-flouting design of a 1950s office chair—he thought calling was a mistake, possibly a mistake, a definite mistake (zooming his chair back to upright), maybe not a mistake; a waste of time and money (having called five New York private eyes before finding one who had Los Angeles contacts; then paying that California P.I. to get the number where he could actually reach her, instead of the switchboard that had put him off). And when Lucille Ball answered, the thrill of her voice, his fantasy captured in a plastic earpiece, Isidore's laugh sounded like a bark. He felt a great release of pressure—the stone in his throat dissolving in a puff of air.

For Lucille, the past week and a half had been different. Even after having talked to him, she'd been certain, at first, that she would avoid seeing Isidore.

She had cured herself of the red scandal before it metastasized. (*A review of the subject's file reflects no activity that would warrant her inclusion on the Security Index*—FBI memorandum: SAC Los Angeles to Hoover, Subject: Ball, Lucille.) The HUAC *had* had a good case, if it'd wanted to make one. In 1936, sponsoring the Communist Party's candidate in her local California Assembly election, Lucille had signed a certificate: *I am registered as affiliated with the Communist Party;* the same year, she got appointed to the State Central Committee of the Communist Party of California. And so on. She'd picked up the hammer and sickle, halfheartedly, ignorantly, merely to placate her grandfather, but still. The HUAC had blacklisted many for less. This had been her boffo year, however. Lucille had made the sort of success from which you can't really get dislodged.

Lucille had gotten the call from Hold-on right before the HUAC mess and during a stretch of relative calm in her marriage. Little Lucie was around two. After a firstborn joins a house, the home-front action is filled with husbandly solicitude, husbandly kindness. Even if just for a short while.

Desi was a strict, loving dad. His charisma got expressed as a light and sometimes even frisky fatherhood. Laughs, games, tickling. And with Lucille, too. The birth of their daughter brought one of Lucille and Desi's dented reconciliations. She might have wished for a husband who went out less at night, who didn't have at the very least an eye for other women, whom she trusted more, or a little. But even in all this, Desi seemed to be getting better. He'd quit, or paused, making coarse and disrespectful scenes. He took her out dancing just after little Lucie's first birthday, and, as the photographers' cameras flashed, and as Desi smiled at her, and as the dance floor cleared for them, she said to herself, Really, why shouldn't I be happy with him?

And then, one knotty morning, she took Hold-on's surprise call. *Oh. Yes, sure, I suppose, come out to Los Angeles.* Well, the Russian and French Revolutions also broke out only as the yoke had been lifted, a bit, off those poor serfs.

I do everything late in life. Having a baby now, in my forties, for instance. Having your first affair in middle age is late, also, she thought.

An affair! And yet, after Hold-on reached out, Lucille's scruples— or professional qualms, anyhow—placed in her path one last hurdle. The HUAC investigation told her she couldn't risk it. But even the fear of being labeled un-American only put her off until after the press conference, and after the worry of the press conference. Well, I *did* tell the guy to come to L.A.; I can't just not show up. Sometimes doing the right thing, the prudent thing, was hard; she decided, therefore, to see him. She thought, I am deciding, at last, to cheat. After all the pain my husband caused me, I am entitled.

She more or less ignored the fact that, with Hold-on, she had already, once before, cheated.

Lucille bid Hold-on to wait in the hotel for a day or two until Desi would go out somewhere to give her an afternoon free. And if Desi *didn't* make plans to go out, she'd either think of something or just give up on seeing Hold-on. But she didn't worry too much about that; her husband was like the tides.

Sure enough, Desi told her he needed, during this filming hiatus—bless him, damn him—to take a trip with Gordon MacRae and Hoagy Carmichael to Las Vegas for "golf and to look into a possible business opportunity." Great, great—take your time, darling. You're not steamed, Red? No, no. Have your little fun with Hoagy. She wondered what she should tell Clara and the alternating nannies Rae and Ronny before slipping out herself. And then she realized: I don't have to tell them anything at all.

She'd found it difficult to keep news of Hold-on's visit to herself. She considered telling Vivian Vance, who with the fixity characteristic of homely actors had become a true friend—her most trusted friend, in fact. (Viv had an awful husband herself.) But Viv knew Desi and saw Desi often and depended on Desi for a paycheck. So, not her. What about Hal Brade? But Brade had acted so oddly about John Archer. And wouldn't *Hollywood Confidential* pay a year of his salary to blab something like this? Okay, there was no one she could trust. Didn't matter—she was already on her way to the Beverly Hills Hotel.

And here she is now, and has been for a day and a half.

"**WHAT DO YOU** call it if it feels like you're dreaming while you're awake," Isidore asks.

Pause.

"Hollywood."

. . .

"HE WAS HAPPY, of course, that I convinced the press I'm not a, you know, a commie," she tells him. "But he can't—he truly can't handle it when he's being treated, as he would say it, *unequally,* in relation to, you know, *me.* Even after the press conference, which went great for us, you know, really well, he was upset 'cause he thought reporters condescended. I don't remember that happening, but they *always* do, I guess, and for someone like him, here's a man who had four houses in Cuba, disguised himself as a penniless rebel, and fought to make his way here—after his whole childhood, where his mother was convincing him he's going to be the Cuban Teddy Roosevelt or something—and even before he met me, women like Betty Grable were all over him, and, oh, everything's a reaction to that. He's spoiled. Pride. Vanity. You know. And here he is, finally a star for real." She drags on her cigarette, then an exhalation of smoke that takes the hotel room sunlight. "But, it's on *my* program, his fame—he's second banana to the quote ditzy wife. And these reporters really do treat him like Carmen Miranda in chinos. It's not fair. This always happens. There was one afternoon, he's screaming at me, really screaming, you know, terrifying. *Screaming.* And I remind him it's not *my* fault that some fly-by-night treated him like a busboy, what can *I* do, and he laughs and comes back, after spending that whole evening out, he comes back with an idea for a program. The idea was *Make Room for Daddy.* He's smart, you know. He's underestimated. The accent. But maybe if he got more respect, we wouldn't produce such good television, so it's actually a blessing. Do you think I'm awful to think like that?"

"He screamed at you."

"He didn't *scream* at me." Shame and loyalty tug at her answer like opposing hooks. "He—raised his voice."

"He raises his voice with you."

"Well."

With the cheating and outbursts and recently with his drinking, Desi—his solicitous phase notwithstanding—takes Lucille's love for granted. His actions dared her to do this, to come here. Still, she'd failed to appreciate how even a seemingly innocent Desi story might come off as a denunciation. It's a surprise to have it pointed out. And to find herself defensive on his behalf.

Right, she thinks, that *was* no way for Dez to've talked to me, and ogling at Mary What's-Her-Name, last week, the script girl, right in front of my face, in front of *everybody,* but I have to admit also that I do like something about that, that Dez Arnaz goes and takes what he wants, boy, and I can't help how that makes me feel. Though Hold-on has spunk enough of his own and is kind, she thinks. I think he may be actually kind. And who needs *that* much spunk. Plus, here the guy is, smiling at me like he invented fucking.

"Enough about that old bandleader," she says. "What about you?"

"Me?" He sounds kind of exhilarated at the question. "My mother told me I was going to be the Cuban Teddy Roosevelt."

"All right, you," she says. "I like funny, already. But say something for real."

ISIDORE LIFTS HIMSELF on his elbows and braces for discussion of the inevitable Harriet.

"But what do you want me to say?" he asks.

"Tell me about, I don't know. For instance, if you hear about someone who's sick, tell me about yourself, how you see that. Are you one of those people who sympathizes with the sick woman?"

"*That's* the thing on your mind?"

"Or do you think about the husband," she says. "The guy who has to spend her time taking care of him."

"Wait, which one's sick, her or him?" he says. "Seriously, why are you asking me th—"

"'In *sickness* and in health.' What would you feel, I wonder, if the 'sickness' bill comes due."

"I would, I would be there," he promises. Stupidly, pointlessly. He'll never be asked in earnest to make that vow to Lucille. Though he is here now. Harriet has been so present in the folds of his life that he's seen her historically. Once upon a time, his wife had been the girl who answered the door to a favored suitor, leaning into the threshold Katharine Hepburn–style, jaunty and smiling a la *The Philadelphia Story,* saying, "Hello, *you.*" And young Isidore, having rushed from his father's office, this being 1938 or early '39, would perspire on the spot, breathing heavily. His collar scratchy and tight on his strong neck. He'd then cradle Harriet's elbow for block after block to Brandt's Flatbush theater, where they had to themselves the whole swooning balcony, and this meant they petted, even before the newsreels, and more than petted; Isidore threw open her fur-collared coat, unwrapped her scarf, which felt like unwrapping the package of her—*der gantser shmir*—and Harriet leaning back and sighing, and giving Isidore a sense of falling right into who she was, right into all that warmth. Who cared that his friends didn't see this side of her? She was giving him this! And still, her legs closed closed closed to him, and one evening was the evening when she quit holding those legs closed: and he took this as a profound welcome, in 1938 or early '39. She did have a personality then. Or he thought she did. And for a long time after that, she'd breathed sighs into his ears, nipped her teeth into his shoulder, until she didn't.

And now here he is in Los Angeles.

Still, the history. The countless little details, through which, in her noncelebrity way, Harriet has made him feel loved. Her surprisingly wild dance steps, her weekly or biweekly playing of the piano for him, the vacation mornings and the nighttime drives home, and more things, and of course still more, her having mothered his sons, for one; not to mention, well, the still pretty legs and the forceful, sexy, Ball-esque eyebrows of her own. And Isidore has to acknowledge that, no, he hadn't ever been gravely unhappy in his married life, but in order to experience this hotel room moment, he must tell himself that it's been less like a real joy than a blankness. It all *does* look a bit pathetic when seen from a bright hotel in Beverly Hills. But even now he can't lie enough to convince himself that, in his cozy suits and breakfast smiles—at the front door in the morning when he kisses her cheek and grabs the paper and scoots off to the station—he's been lumping around in his life without having ever been satisfied. He can't say that. Isidore has been satisfied. But the light that shined from that word— "satisfied"—has now sputtered and gone out. Celebrity sin has convinced him that his marriage, as he thinks about it from this celebrity bed, is like tilling the same crop over and again on a field of lessening returns. Lucille and Desi never had to do chores.

"How you would handle a sick spouse would depend," he's answering now, "on the spouse, I guess. With kindness and understanding, if she deserves it."

"*Ding ding ding*. Right response," Lucille says. "It's important. What kind of person you are. Caring, or the opposite."

His skiing finger is back; it takes the moguls of her ribs. Soft skin, warm. Sometimes regret is just the determination to begin acting more selfishly from now on. While guilt, on the other hand, asks you to practice self-denial. Each is a tyrant, he thinks. Each keeps working to overthrow the other—and the disputed kingdom is my brain. Oh, don't be so pompous. He moves to suck on Lucille's shoulder.

"So, your wife," she says.

His open mouth is arrested halfway to the target. "My turn now?"

"I talked about the Cuban."

"Certainly, you did." Leaning on elbows once again.

Lucille looks discomfited, the swoops and cords of her neck, the skin freckled under the collarbone. "Tell," she says.

It's a surprise, this humorous jealousy of hers. Other than in a commercial on last night's TV, Lucy Ricardo hasn't been seen at all around here.

What should Isidore say?

"She's, you know, a housewife, but . . . well, pretty. Harriet. Kind of a Jewish Joan Crawford, but more shy." He doesn't say that she has kind of a peaked nose and sexy lipstick. He doesn't say that the first word his wife's name brings to his mind is "circumspect" or that she is smart and even witty, in a low-wattage way, but that sometimes it seems her wit and her smarts have been interred deep in the ground.

"She's clever," is how he puts it, "but she doesn't get much chance to show it." And maybe that's my fault.

This is a celebrity-grade brood. Pleasurable, in a way. As if cheater's guilt is a decisive expression of the stylish adult. Except, don't think about Bernie and Arthur. Get your sons out of your head.

"Pretty?" Lucille's saying. The pause that follows comes across as comic, isn't meant to be. "*How* pretty?"

He falls back by her side, gazes at her face. She looks vulnerable on the tousled bed.

"I have something for you," he says.

IT'S AN ACT of bravery for her to read standing at the window, naked. She got up from bed, a minute ago, carrying a loose scribble of pages.

The curtains are mostly drawn. Even so. Through the rift of curtain, anyone outside still would see a sliver of Lucille. Famous shoulder, immortal hair, just a peek of the soft-limbed star. Standing there is a tiny, nude rebellion.

"It's—" Not finishing the sentence. Serious, biting her hangnail, engrossed, she is reading.

People always offer me stories, she thinks. Well, people *would* if she came into company with more of the unfamous. But Hold-on had called himself a writer, and so: She can hardly be expected to lie down with him and not read this. But is it good? Does she feel used? Does she *want* it to be good?

Okay, well, hmm. Yes, all right, see, right there. A little glimmer. Here, too. She tells herself she'd caught a hunch right off— faint, to be sure; performance wasn't Hold-on's line—a foretaste of something, a hidden specialness. There had to be. Oh, wait now, more than a glimmer here, in this paragraph. Why *else* would I feel this for him? she asks herself. In a good movie treatment, there's a tug, even in outline form, that goes into the cool white fibers of the story. (But what *do* I feel for him? she wonders.)

In 1863, Meriday Edgefield, an educated, freed black man, joins the 10th South Carolina Infantry, African Descent, a regiment of black soldiers, largely ex-slaves, who fought deep into Confederate territory . . .

"He's a Negro," she says, turning.

"Light-skinned," he says, then: "Yes."

"All right," she says, "but." Smiling, shrugging in disparagement of his naïveté.

Lucille speaks—"True, it is a good story"—her voice slow and stained with regret. It's November. Not long before, a black man named Oliver Brown sued the Board of Education that had required his daughter to schlep her classwork a daily hour when a better school stood five blocks from her house. This past December, the Tuskegee Institute declared that year the first in seventy not to see any lynchings. In January, someplace called the Highlander Folk School held a course in civil disobedience promising a new and better future to its students, including one young woman named Rosa Parks. At the window, Lucille reads now.

"How could we cast it?"

Correll and Gosden were great as *Amos 'n' Andy* on the radio. But when they tried to move out into a blackface film, audiences didn't like following the curve to a surprising awareness: The actors were white. And that was twenty years ago.

"But they have a program on *this* year, isn't that so?" he says— meaning *Amos 'n' Andy* on television. And those characters are now played by black actors.

Yes, fine, but that's a comedy. . . .

But even as she said it, she was thinking of a possibility. Could be another *Gone with the Wind,* but a corrective, too—brave, unlikely hero, American soldiers, a Civil War quest. It could be Cecil B. DeMille meets D. W. Griffith. Lucille goes back to reading that now feels like more than reading. Dials have been spun, lightning has struck the cathodes, what had been inanimate now rises off the gurney. I can see this Meriday person, she thinks. As ubiquitous as they are, television screens are small. What if I could make a film myself, direct a film, a *serious* film, she thinks.

"JEWISH," LUCILLE SAYS. She's back in bed a short ninety minutes later, next to Isidore. That after-sex feeling of closeness, of calm sharing. "Is that important to you?" Her head is on his shoulder.

"You mean"—patting her hair—"my being a Jew?" Her non-kinky hair.

"Well, you said your *wife*. When you described her, she was Jewish, you said."

"But why"—How important could it be; I'm here, aren't I? he thinks—"d'you ask now?"

"Your story, the movie, the black fellow is an underdog. Jews always fight City Hall. It's a thing with you people."

"Oh."

Moving her head to look at him. "That's your *I think she's bigoted* response."

"It's, no—it's my *Trying to come up with a good answer* response. I'm finding myself fond of Christians lately."

"Jews think about being Jews, is all I mean. I never think about being Christian. Jeez-o-pete, I was just accused of communism. Now I want to do a movie about a black soldier?"

"And lie with your head on a Semitic shoulder."

Lucille was born (Isidore's read somewhere) a Baptist. And what about him? He has wanted, synagogue attendance or no, to fit his life around at least the general shape of godliness. He has felt the Almighty in his life and, surprising to the sinner he is, never more than he does right now.

"I don't want you to think I'm giving Jews bad press," she says.

"Oh, has the press been good?" he says. "To be a Jew after the Nazis is like being a St. Louis Browns fan." Where is this coming from? he wonders for the tenth time. This quipping is not me. I would usually smile and think too long about what to say.

"The Browns," she says. "Are they good?"

"Haven't won the series even one time."

Why this need to spread his wings, why this need even for wings? he wonders. What makes me think I'm so special?

Could he just go home, that familiar, obsolete place? After these two unthinkable days, how will he again pick up his small-scale concerns? After all this kissing slowly and without fear of interruption? Hold-on and Lucille. Each of them is to the other the first *new* person they'd had sex with, or seen naked, in a decade. At first, they'd felt their own bodies to be spotlighted and magnified—flaws swashing everywhere. But when Lucille noticed Isidore's squirminess (he wasn't an actor and lacked the actor's ability to disguise nerves), she made a joke: "*Extree, extree!* Read all about it! Middle-aged man has middle-aged body!" And then she'd kissed his belly button.

"Let me get myself and my people some good press," he's saying now.

And he slips himself out from under her head; in a deft transposed movement, he is above her again.

They both laugh. But if you look you can see that they're each a little afraid.

HE HAS TO phone Harriet and the boys. That's the only bad part of today. But he has dawdled. In the dawdle there's a temptation that grows with the wait. Isidore's hand hovers above the phone. The temptation pulses in the lull: *Don't phone her.* But . . .

"Har?" he says, after the rigmarole with the long-distance operator. "Hi!" He blushes with guilt—this is not luxuriant, glamorous melancholy, after all; this is the worst guilt. This is self-hate.

He's still in bed, Lucille next to him. She can't allow him privacy; when one is famous, slipping into the hallway and waiting outside a hotel room isn't possible. And getting up to loiter in the bathroom is one pride-killing charade Lucille will not perform.

"Sweetie?" Isidore says to the phone. That word, love made villainous, really opens up in him. The next thing Isidore says—"Miss you, too"—doesn't help.

Harriet is talking about home. She says something about baiting a mousetrap while Lucille curls to the nightstand for a cigarette, and Isidore's helpless gaze floats along her stark torso, the skin, the vigor, the indefinable sorcery of Lucille Ball. Just concentrate on talking to Harriet, he tells himself. You can manage this. But the feeling ("Iz, the exterminator said to use peanut butter; rodents like that better than cheese"), the feeling eats away at the moment. Stretched out here naked under the sheets, he may himself as well be a floorboard infested with chewing rodents, and yet he keeps up the talk.

"I'm not sure the deal is going to happen here. Yeah, no, the, uh, land deal and all that. No. It's, well, the zoning commission . . ." he says.

Lucille, without a word, squints at the match smoke, licks a squiggle of tobacco off her mouth.

He closes his eyes. Maybe he can fix how he feels. Maybe all the guilt-endurer has to do to murder his guilt is to quit doing whatever has caused him that guilt.

So, return home now, he thinks. His real life has pulled up outside the window and is honking its horn.

"Say hi to the boys," he says. "Oh, I can't talk to them now, no. Gotta go."

When he hangs up the phone (". . . bye, love you . . ."), he forgets that he's got the power to commit that guilt-murder, that the gun is in his hand were he only strong enough to pull the trigger. But he experiences guilt as if it were one of the Almighty's mysterious forays against us, like a disease, or a tree fallen on the head, something beyond not only control but comprehension. How could this have happened to me?

And Lucille too seems disgusted with him. That "sweetie" probably didn't help.

Before, without lifting the thought to actual consciousness, he'd actually allowed himself a little righteous indignation. Harriet's not exactly *forcing* me into it, but she's making it very hard not to . . .

and with a father who never respected me, how could I do anything but, etc., etc. But now, in the glaring awfulness of that phone call, he imagines something: Harriet sitting in a theater waiting for some movie to start even though the projectionist has locked up and the screen turned dark as every other patron has up and left.

But now the call is over.

Lucille leans at a kindly angle, lays her hand on his forearm. "I'm sorry," she says. "That was hard." The breasts she is seemingly unmindful of sting his eyes. His body is wild with them.

"Thanks," he says, looking away. "Hard for you, too, listening."

"Yes," she says.

"Well, there you are," he says.

She leans and stubs out the cigarette. He says, "Do you want to maybe call your daughter or something, say hi?"

"No," she says.

Lucille tears the slit to open a new pack of Fatimas. She plucks out a cig, takes a look at it, and lays it on the bedside table without smoking it.

"No," she says, turning back to kiss his chest, and it's not Lucille's bankable magic that relights the candles of fantasy. It's what Isidore sees in her eyes: the defenseless, flagrant intensity of feeling. Harriet doesn't look at him like that, not anymore. "I'm right here," she says, her kisses moving downward.

Just like that, Isidore is in love. He is in lots of it.

IT WOULD BE reckless. There's no way. It's not feasible, she thinks. What, I just drive him to the airport?

"Front desk, please." Isidore sits on the lip of the bed, tying his shoe, the receiver between his shoulder and face. Checking out after two and a half days. "Operator, yes, it's room 317. I'd like to reserve a taxicab. I'm going to—"

"Hang up," Lucille says, breathily. Yes, I *will* drive him.

Being decisive! It's like realizing that you can speak in another voice. Or realizing that your own voice, it so happens, has another register. Desi has been the businessman. The pusher. This new register is her own.

Friends who've driven in Lucille's white Sunliner remember the weirdly caressive sensation of the leather, the mellow clutch, the dashboard flowers thirsting in the sun—the floral scent. Each Monday, a deposit of new white carnations appears on her dash, courtesy of Jess Szilárd, or Szilárd's assistant, who has a key.

It's less conspicuous to have the man at the wheel. She has her hand over his, atop the gearshift. Likewise now, she makes sure her cuddling hand is down low, out of sight. She's wearing the scarf, the hat and sunglasses, the camouflage that will fool nobody. She *never* drives with the convertible's top up; today she is.

"Thank you," Isidore's saying. For letting him drive, the time, the encouraging words about his film idea. Yes. If we make my movie, I will . . . I will *what*? he thinks.

They attempt to keep the talk cheerful and relaxed. The car's qualities. The weather. The duration of a cross-country flight.

But then: "I shouldn't be doing this," she says.

His mind's reaction: *Huh?*

"Driving me to the airport, you mean?" He tries not to take his eyes from the road, its dispassionate particulars. "Or—?"

She extracts her hand from his, she turns away movieishly. Out the window, North Camden Drive is deserted, just hedges, palm trees, and the gawking, buttinsky sun.

"If you want to sell this movie, if you want to do something great with yourself at this late date"—her voice is strident—"why do you strangle yourself to death in the sticks?"

This he hasn't expected, the quick drama, the trapdooring tone.

From the start in the Beverly Hills Hotel, Lucille had smiled, had asked *him* things. As if he'd been the interesting one, as if *his* modest-lawned, two-story life had news appeal. And now, the interest is shown to have been scorn.

So, is your partnership with your brother successful? Yeah, he'd told her, yeah it is, especially lately—not mentioning that a part of the drive to make a success, even in real estate, had been her. He also didn't mention that he believed he'd likely be more successful without Norman; Samuel LeFrak—a seething little genius—had offered him a stake in a huge project. A giant tract of land in Queens, thousands of working-class units, ungodly government subsidies, etc. LeFrak City would be more than a moneymaker; it would be a life changer. But the deal was contingent on Isidore's shutting out Norman. And he couldn't very well abandon—

"Okay, but are your *wives* friends? Yours and Norman's. Do they get together?"

"Wouldn't call them friends, necessarily. Tillie, that's Norman's wife, is—I would say they are respectful of each other."

And then an apology from Isidore: wishing he could lead her to more promising ground. Lucille had kissed him on the hair of his chest. The wives she could picture, their farce of mandatory closeness. She'd absorbed enough. And the brothers—she'd known there was some usable feeling there, some new poignant note of comedy she could sing out in black-and-white, if ever she wanted to change the tenor of the show.

He said, "My life isn't worth plowing through like yours is."

"Ah, except you. You're worth plowing through."

"Well." He laughed. "Here I'm firing on all cylinders. In Long Island, a few of my cylinders conk out. Or, not conk out. They don't exist. Here, I grow new ones."

"I could make a crude joke."

"Another one? I want you to," he said.

"But it's beneath you, all that. It's beneath you."

"Marriage and a family?"

"*That* marriage, *that* existence."

He cleared his throat. "'In the middle of the path of our life, I went astray from the straight road and found myself in a wilderness where the right course was lost.'"

She hadn't known—a confused smile bent her mouth—what he'd been talking about.

"Dante," he'd said. "*The Inferno*. It's the opening."

She'd said that the line—which he'd heard as a howled reproach—

had been beautiful. And soon after that, he'd given her his movie pages. And the rest of the time had passed smoothly. No anger had been presaged; the troubled ending he'd worried over had never materialized—until this ride to the airport.

"Well, okay, Lucille," he says now, squeezing the steering wheel. "I guess not many find success in work *and* at home."

"And you have it in neither." Temper has made her voice flute up.

"Okay, that is not true."

It's not that he worries that her mood will last or that she believes what she's saying. "This anger . . ." he says.

What does worry Isidore: Her last-minute behavior may pollute the memory. For him and for her. Maybe it's a way for her to make it easy on herself to forget him?

She's half-yelling now. "You have to live your life in a way that—"

"That what?"

Lucille pretends to be absorbed in her cigarette. No answer. She cradles her elbow in an upturned palm. The Fatima she holds between two fingers, with her hand bent down like the head of a swan.

"Lucille," Isidore softly says, choosing not to be angry, but flattered. "If this is how you ask me to stay . . ."

She turns from the window to show Hold-on that her eyes have teared.

"I promised myself no scenes, but"—dramatic gulp—"I'm going to miss you." And then to cover the seriousness: "Hold-on, you better promise to stop firing on all cylinders. Keep the charm for me."

As if he could do it all the time!

"Ah, that extra cylinder you found," he says, moved by her tears, "is retired."

They're at a stoplight; he's looking at her and doesn't see the light's now green.

"I can never be alone, is the problem," she says.

Like many teary confessions, none of this costs her much. She's merely repeating something about herself she's often heard and dismissed. She knows it's partially true; she gets lonely. It also feels less than true.

A Lincoln behind them is impatient, *beep beep,* green light, pal.

My hatred of and familiarity with being alone is probably the cause of everything about me people love, she thinks. All that solitary time at her step-grandparents' is the windstorm at the center of who she is.

Isidore chugs ahead. As they pass under the traffic light, he turns—"What are you doing?" Lucille says—off the route. Onto a little street called Lomitas, and another called North Bedford. "One second," he says.

In front of a driveway he would've built out wider, Isidore has shifted the car into park, shifted his glasses from eyes to forehead; he shifts in his seat. A brown Cadillac rolls by. The driver, like all of America, is a *Lucy* fan.

Isidore embraces her. And the passing motorist has no idea that he's driven past his secret love.

Isidore says, "*You're* the wilderness I find myself in," right into the nape of her neck, those smoky little hairs. Trying a little too hard to make a memory. "That's that Dante line," he adds, unnecessarily.

"This is more sad than I want it to be," she says.

Pulling back from her. "Don't feel guilty, Lucille."

"All right," she says. But her expression can't hide its message: *I don't feel guilty. Why would I?*

She tries again:

"If Scarlett O'Hara had married Rhett and then been run over by a bus, think about it," she says. "She would've thought they were meant to be."

"People would've also wondered about how there was a bus."

She waves him off. No jokes; you don't need to impress me now, Hold-on. "That movie is about—Scarlett was meant to be with Ashley Wilkes, not Rhett."

Isidore sighs, not with unhappiness; with informed resignation. "And look at you. You feel guilty," she accuses.

He can't lie. "I mean, it's not Harriet's fault I met you. She doesn't mistreat me the way your husband mis—"

"No, oh, *that's* right." A light in Lucille flares on. "Because I'm the one who takes too much guff from her husband, right? I'm the one who takes it and takes it and is too cowardly to walk away."

"You're Lucille Ball," he says.

"I see." She is angry. "I'm so famous. This isn't real to you," she says. "*You* aren't the one who has to feel guilty. Because this never happened, you're saying."

"You can't think *I* think that. And I thought you didn't feel guilty."

Lucille has about her the attitude of a woman set upon by a million antagonists, more than a million, a hostile audience that doesn't understand her.

"This is the only real thing," he says. He means it.

But what does real mean if he can't, at this moment, recognize himself? When faced with a dramatic moment, his *actual* personality usually shies up its collar and ducks into the alley.

She turns her eyes full on him. "That's what I feel, too," she says—though it's *not* what she feels, not quite.

"I meant, you're *Lucille Ball*," he says. "You're fearless."

She *is* emotional. But Lucille's life *always* feels real to her. This is different.

Everything with Hold-on has been somehow easy and bright, sincere—she's had the feeling there's something crucial she hadn't considered, something now offering itself up to her. It isn't too late. He wouldn't understand that his normality is what excites and frightens her. He's quiet, calm, different. (And sometimes this also repels her.) There's so much he doesn't understand. That being famous is like going to another country, and you only know how lonesome it is in that foreign place once you arrive. That if everyone always concerns themselves with your well-being they're sort of asking you to remain a toddler. That fame is something you rent;

that nobody can occupy that state forever. And that when your lease on celebrity is up—when the public turns against you—it's painful, humbling, inexplicable, and the smirk of the indifferent is lonely in the way of being abandoned by a lover. And they always do turn against you, she thinks. This is America. Do Americans really want idols? Does anyone more than an American hate some-one who thinks he's better than they are? The turn can be giddy and savage. What does that mean for someone like her, and for someone like Hold-on? But even the witty lines Isidore said in the hotel—one was "Every minute you stay here, Frank Capra loses the plot for another movie"—had the bait and the hook of real kind-ness. Or maybe Lucille has just wanted very much to be caught.

He's saying, "I know it's real. Otherwise I would've awakened by now."

"It's real," she says.

They promise, they promise and promise; calls, letters, visits. He has no immediate plans to return, how can he, but she'll be back in New York, maybe even by New Year's. Always some reason to visit the Apple, the sponsors, the network. . . . Isidore realizes he under-stands nothing about the multiple-location, theoretical municipal-ity where she actually resides. California, Madison Avenue, the airwaves. She'll be on television, in Los Angeles, and he'll go back to his family, his business, to the watchful eye of his father. Oh, maybe now and again his hopes will catch fire, but life will come along and pour on them its cold water.

He decides not to mention his movie idea if she doesn't.

"We didn't think this through, Lucille." He's starting up the car and driving again. "You can't take me to the airport. They'll see you—everybody," he says. "I'll get out here at a cabstand or some-thing."

"Oh, to *hell* with everybody." The way she says this doesn't hide her acknowledgment. He's right.

They both picture the impossible TWA scene. Last call an-nounced, travelers wheeling past, bags and goodbyes, and he and

Lucille embracing, kissing, until the cinematographer pans in on the plane flying away out the giant window.

"I'll call you," she says. Desilu was moving offices—a multi-studio space, and her number would soon change. "Anyway, you can't call me, it's too—it's too hard. Everyone watches everything I do."

"All right, Lucille." Gripping the wheel.

"I will call you, I promise," she says. "I will."

In their silence, the tire sounds, the engine, the car humming. At the stoplight, the silence grows louder.

Okay, pull over at North Canon; it's an easy walk back to the hotel, not as trafficked as Rodeo or Sunset, and you can get a cab from there. I'm sorry. . . .

But something happens as Isidore gets out. He has a thought. This is the end of a romantic scene; why aren't these palm trees cheering? And Lucille leans across the seat to look up at Isidore through the rolled-down window. She says: "This is all?" Her smile is an incursion against tears. "Where's the applause for a great finale?"

Then she and the car begin to motor out of his life. I guess my movie idea was silly. Not that he wanted her to think he was *using* her.

Before he's picked up his Samsonite, he sees her brakelights flash, a hopeful red bloom. Lucille has stopped the car. She reverses, slowly, toward him, tires over gravel, that little coughy pop, and he actually feels it in his heart, the almost humid chest warmth, the fullness that's total. Oh, I am happy, happy, happy—and yet this will turn to sadness when I leave, when I have to leave all glamorous this.

His adulthood before now seems like nursery school, like a coloring book. "I almost forgot," Lucille says through the open window. Her eyes are teary. "The movie. Your movie. There's something there. I really think so."

And she gives him her card; on the back, in her handwriting, with its frills and melismas, she'd written her invented endearment, that ridiculous nickname, and, below that, the phone number of Desilu Productions' new offices in Los Angeles: *MU 5-9975—my number, after all.* And, added in a corner: *But let me call you first, okay?*

"When *you* go out to dinner," she says, "and it's a group of builders? I'm guessing the thought never crosses your mind, 'Am I the most successful one here?' Unless you're a jerk. It's a jerk's idea to think like that. When you're famous, that idea is pushed on you all the time. It turns you into a jerk."

How can he answer this? "You? Never."

He wants to add something memorable and true. That thought actually *does* cross his mind whenever he's out with builders. But what he says is an attempt at something more. "You're the juiciest part of the fruit"—and her face is a tangle of the saddest happiness.

Just before she leaves, Lucille blows him a kiss, and the palm trees still don't applaud. What is Lucille without an audience?

CHAPTER NINE

*A*LL THE TCHOTCHKES *inside Suzanne Gluck's cushy William Morris office were of a piece, the plants and framed faces and silver hanging stuff, their display, their alert tones. She frowned reading my grandfather's pages. "You know something?" she said. "Certain publishing houses' tastes aside, there's a difference between a book and a movie."*

"I know there would be interest," I bluffed. "Maybe like a coffee-table thing, with, like—isn't there anyone here who could represent it for a movie?"

She lay the pages facedown on her desk. The unspoken engine here was professionalism.

"There's a man in this office, Wright Torrence is his name, who deals with book-to-film and the rare vice versa," Suzanne said.

Despite her ambivalence to me, despite my knowing she was putting me off, I sort of felt thrilled. Because New York had done its New York thing. My thrill was wrongheaded. But I was a young man and had come to the city for this. Which is to say, New York seemed to be granting what I asked (what everyone asks)—the excitement, discovery, the career and reinvention wishes—but, of course, after the forewarnings that everybody hears but forgets, the city so often shows itself to be one of those genies whose broadchested magic is more trial than reward; who grants and twists the wishes we whisper and who hides in the shadow of our eagerness, waiting to subsist on our bones.

"OH GOD," CRIES the man with the subordinate's face. "I'll never remember!"—the forceful agitation that plays as comedy to all but him.

It's Wednesday, the man hates Wednesdays. He's obliged every Wednesday to begin remembering.

"Oh, again?" says a second man whose wet hair bears a comb's inscription. The two men sit waiting for the others.

"It's hard every time, yeah," the first man says, the inadvertently funny man. This man is lucratively bald.

They are not here to eat, but they will eat. The table is laid, as happens every Wednesday.

"Maybe it's the jokes are bad," the second man, Bob Kargman, says. "Maybe that's why it's hard to remember them."

"Yeah, the jokes. Maybe." This first man, the bald man, has rolled his napkin into a floppy little cone. "The jokes." Brooding now, he unfurls his small project. The man needs someone to write his lines for him. Someone like Bob Kargman. "Yeah," he says. "It's those fuckers."

They start in on the requisite cigarettes. The bald man sparks flame from his Zippo, and this makes him grimace: the burst of glare, his hangover. William Frawley is his name. He plays a supporting role on the most popular entertainment thus far in American history.

"You probably *like* being here, Bob," Frawley says, rubbing his eyes, that timeless gesture of *I'd rather be home relaxing.* "You have a family." A professional beat. "To run away from."

"Bill, I'm not gonna argue with you there, buddy," Kargman says. "Children are, I don't know, it's not easy to say if we are doing right by them."

"Uh-huh," says Frawley. Desi Arnaz told him he had only one more strike before losing this job, but—his headache! His lagging heart!

He rerolls the napkin wearily.

Kargman says, "Just trying to find a decent school for the boy, you know? Anyway, this week won't be so hard to memorize for you, Bill. There are easy lines for—"

"That's what wrecks children," says Frawley, his chin down into his chest. "Mothers."

"Um. *Yes.* Maybe with some, but," says Kargman, shaking his uxorious head *no.* "I mean, with us it's—"

"Why don't you give the boy household chores?"

"Oh, sure. We—"

"Wait a second." Frawley lifts his head in surprised anger, like a brontosaurus who'd stubbed its toe minutes earlier, back at the edge of memory. "You think I have trouble remembering lines if they're not 'easy'?"

"Bill, it was *you* who'd said—"

The door opens, and before anyone enters, a voice calls out: "Hide your liquor—it's a raid!" And Desi Arnaz steps in.

"Here we go!" Frawley says. He's all brightness now.

Behind Desi is Jess Szilárd, with the familiar cravat, the familiar— "Hello, all"—mid-Atlantic voice.

"I'd tell you how long we've been waiting, Dez," says Frawley, "but you wouldn't hear me—your ears are stuffed with money."

Desi sits opposite Bill; rough and friendly joking. Then Desi stops. "Oh, no." He frowns, having smelled the alcohol. "Again, Bill? If *I* can wait . . ."

Frawley, comically dramatic, drops his face to his hands. "Come on, Desi," he says.

Szilárd says, "Well, William."

Frawley, from between the hands he's buried his face in: "Now don't you start, Jess."

Szilárd has been lugging a clutch of papers. These he drops on the middle of the table.

Frawley starts talking about "the girls" being late to this meeting, when a man with a lean, loveless face backs through the door holding a tray. Mealtime! Banana supreme, peach and pear salad, open club sirloin sandwiches. And then a separate little guy, someone unnaturally genteel, pushes in with plates.

No one acknowledges these waiters, let alone eats.

"Where *are* the girls? Seen Lucille, Dez?" asks Kargman. Even the waiters shoot him a look. Wrong question.

Desi is a lot of things, but he is not a convincing dramatic actor. The A/C is rattling from a vent somewhere. Kargman sniffs in a breath and it sounds as if he's got a clogged nose. Desi mumbles, "Oh, her? She's on her way, just, she had to . . ." and doesn't finish. (Evidently not a great dialogue writer, either.)

"Can we start work?" Frawley says, muffled by the hands over his mouth.

"Sorry!" says Lucille, breezing in, a fashionable scarf, a pillbox hat, a dress that whispers after the strong motion of her legs.

"You know us," says Vivian Vance, just a step behind. "Late to the ball."

Frawley groans and collapses onto the table like an old wino paid a dollar to perform Hamlet's death scene.

"Now, now," says Desi. He's sitting with his feet up: a show of confidence and Italianly chic shoes.

Everyone (other than Frawley) grabs a script. This is *Lucy*'s weekly read-through. Desi's confidence is fake. He and Lucille have been fighting; everyone knows it.

"Okay," says Szilárd. "Let's see what we got."

"This is the Wayne episode? Or that's next week?" Vivian says, pulling out her cat-eye reading glasses.

"You can see that it is," says Frawley, the famous crotchety boom of his baritone. "I *think* that's why it's called 'Lucy and John Wayne.'"

"Another charming season under way," Vivian says with fractured bravado; the fracture is there, too, in her expression, her bothered face.

"You know something, Bill?" says Lucille. "Why don't you just—"

Szilárd and Kargman—the horn-rimmed duo—jump over themselves to interrupt.

"Okay! We start—" says Kargman. Kargman with his camel-hair coat and his library complexion resembles a history prof who's chased after the grander lectern of mic and camera.

"The episode opens in the place Lucy and Ricky are renting for their trip to Hollywood," says Szilárd.

"Um, this actually isn't 'Lucy and John Wayne,'" says Kargman, with his odd intonation. His parents escaped Moscow with him when he was a baby; he projects American English through the red filter of his native Russian. "This one, Lucy steals famous footprints from Grauman's Theatre."

"We're doing a two-parter," says Vivian primly. "Wayne's in the follow-up next week."

"Okeydokey, let me take a look." The now-friendly Frawley peruses the script—then looks up, realizing something. "Hey, where's the word girl?"

"Sick," says Kargman.

They're referring to Carol Pugh—the "word girl" being the show's co–head writer.

"Has a dose of the flu."

"My nose is clogged, so I may have some as well. Be warned."

Frawley starts grimacing at the pages. "Ah, hell."

"What is it now?"—he is asked this, all at once, by everyone. Frawley is paid a fortune to look for all America like the friend you love because you feel a little superior to him.

"This line, uh, *here,* this dialogue where I open the show?" Frawley's scratching his head. "So I say, 'I still can't think why we're having this party for Rick.'"

"Right," Lucille says, "and I explain it to Fred. 'It's just something you *do* in Hollywood, Fred. When a person finishes a picture, you give a party.' Simple. Then *you* say, 'Oh.' And then it's, *And Fred returns to hammering up the sign.* What's wrong with that?"

"Is Fred a damn idiot all of a sudden?" The growl of his voice.

"It's exposition," says Kargman.

"Yes, Bill, it's called *exposition*," Lucille says. (Vivian mutters softly, "All of a sudden. *Right.*")

"I know it's *called* that," says Desi, "but it's not called 'good writing.' I have to agree with Bill."

Kargman and Szilárd exchange looks: *Uh-oh.* And Frawley is aiming his wink-like chuckle at Desi.

Lucille is thumbing through the pages. "I see there's a Lana Turner joke in here," she says.

"No one's eating?"—Frawley, reaching for a plate.

Desi says, "Oh, Lana Turner *too* now, Lucille?" His feet come down; he sits curled powerfully over the table. "Her, too?"

"Is there a—problem with Lana Turner?" Kargman says.

"So I'm the writer all of a sudden?" Desi snaps at Lucille. "I choose the jokes? The people in the jokes?"

"Ask Loverboy if there's a problem with Lana, Bob," Lucille says. "*He's* the one who dated her. Is there a Grable joke in here, too?"

"Well, uh," Kargman says, "as a matter of fact—"

"Okay, Lucille, that's enough," Desi says.

"Maybe it's not the writers' fault, dear." Lucille has her nose in the air. "If they want to pick an actress you haven't romanced, Dez, they're limited to dinner theater in Cleveland."

"No, no." Desi smiles, a hint of the pirate captain in the upcurved lips. "I played a show there too, once."

Kargman raises his hands; Szilárd jumps to his feet. "All right, all right. Quick break, everyone."

CUT TO: Just a little while ago "This kind of secret I tell only you, God, and my cleaning lady."

Lucille had said this to Vivian Vance five minutes before the read-through, this conversation being the reason for their lateness.

The ladies' powder room was a fancy one: flowers, a sofa, candlelight.

"Got it," Vivian said. "Tell."

Vivian's stooping shadow climbed the back wall as she bent to splash her cheeks.

Lucille said: "I'm afraid I'm going to come off as ridiculous, Viv."

"You?"

On the show, this would be a laugh-line. In real life, Lucille Ball was far from ridiculous. She was adept at smoothing over the wrinkled parts of life.

Now she blocked the door with her back, eyed the empty room, and talked—and talked—about Hold-on.

Finally Vivian Vance said, "Again?"—then in a whisper, "Again? The guy from New York?"

"I don't know," Lucille said. "Madness, right?"

It'd been eight or nine weeks since she'd seen Hold-on; this talk released him from the privacy of her thoughts and she heard his voice now. *Every minute you stay here, Frank Capra loses the plot for another movie.* It wasn't just that she remembered what he'd said with clarity. *You're the juiciest part of the fruit.* She could also feel what those words had done to her, and this made him burningly present.

She was the first woman with power in television. She was the first person who made televisual power worth having. She would soon come to run an entire studio—the first woman to do so. Power moves through history and presses it into its own image; Lucille would invent the idea of reruns—doubling a network's profits. *You want to air something when I'm pregnant? Just air old episodes.* And so she was a pioneer who was only now beginning to think of herself as one. Yet here she was, with man trouble.

"I feel that I can tell you this, Viv, because you—"

Vivian was on her third unhappy marriage. She would often joke about herself. "My father made me so ashamed of my body that half the time I tried to hide it under men." And because Lucille was both friend and boss to her, Lucille could get away with saying, or almost saying, insulting things.

"Not," said Lucille, with uncharacteristic uncertainty, "that I'm some kind of helpless damsel."

His hands. That was the physical detail she remembered and to her surprise cherished. Desi was a rutting, wild plow in bed. That had its charms. But the touch of Desi's hand had meant nothing to her—it always had been the way station to what they both wanted. But Hold-on's careful, gentle, *aware* fingertips! Yes, that touch was what she relished.

"Why hasn't he called me?"

"Why," Vivian said, "haven't you called him?"

Lucille could be brusque when she wanted. "We should go; they must be waiting," she said.

"Sure, Lucille." Vivian turned to the mirror, her compact open, the powder puff—*whish*—pressed into quick service. "But when has it bothered you to make Bill Frawley wait?" she said.

"I know Desi is my life," Lucille said.

But what this statement brought her now was sadness. Sadness because she had lived her life not knowing that the life might've gone differently. Sadness because she had a husband whose touch was hurried, rough, and perfunctory. Sadness because she thought of a man, often, whom she hadn't phoned after she last saw him.

"I understand that," Vivian was saying. "Desi *is* your life, that's right." She turned to give Lucille her full face.

"But you also know him," Lucille said. "You know how Desi is. And, well—"

Lucille stopped herself. Hold-on wasn't some puppy-love infatuation. She didn't come off as ridiculous, as she'd feared. This was life casting her in the role of a married woman who loved a married man—or who wanted to be able to determine whether she might love him—and she brought to light everything in this role that was gorgeous and grand.

What if she flew Hold-on to L.A.? Her bankrolling the trip would make it more worth it, somehow. She said, "Is it crazy to—"

"You're not cr—"

"—to meet someone and feel maybe as much for them right away as the man you've been with forever?" Lucille would not be interrupted now. "Did you ever fall for someone, and it wasn't that he was beautiful or famous or rich or any reason you can think of?"

"Of course," Vivian said. "Well, I'm not sure."

"When I was with him, the world got smaller." Lucille couldn't describe it in a way that wasn't embarrassing. Couldn't describe the quality of the memory. "I don't know," she said.

The memory that promised to wrap itself around her life, to cover her whole.

"Okay, look." Vivian addressed her without the discomfiture or ass-kissing that afflicted most everybody else in conversation with Lucille:

"Maybe the question is, 'What's in your life that you need to find the opposite of?'"

"Try not to make it about Desi, all right?"

"But listen to yourself, sweetie."

"Sex," Lucille whispered; she hadn't whispered till now. "Don't you think it can be so . . . ?" What was the word. "So everything?"

"Lucille."

She could say what moved her really was the talk, the jokes, the having found someone who understood her. His normalness. And okay—her odd affinity with him, the honesty of their conversation, it was all of a piece. But really, it was the fucking.

Want, again, edged its electric way under her skin, entered her bones.

Vivian didn't dare look at Lucille. "Maybe people who have these magical kind of unrealistic dreams just don't know how an actual relationship is," she said.

Anyone else saying this would've set off Lucille's famous temper. But Lucille knew she felt what she felt. Knowledge, wordless and complete anyway.

"You're wrong," she said. "It's like a—curtain parting."

"All right, sweetie." Vivian dropped her compact without fuss into her handbag. "All right."

"A curtain parts sometimes," Lucille said, failing to explain. It should've been weird when Hold-on watched her take off her robe to go to the shower, just silently watched her, but it wasn't. It was worshipful in every way. They'd both felt it, and that was powerful.

"So," Vivian was saying, "what are you going to do?"

"Who knows if he'd still want to hear from me?"

That skeptical twist Vivian could give to her face was famous for a reason.

"I want him to call *me*."

"But you're going to call him."

"No, no," Lucille said. She finger-swatted the idea, and this made the candlelight wobble.

The man was supposed to call the woman, no matter what. But the reason was more pressing now—for a reason she wasn't telling Vivian, or anyone.

"You're going to be the one who suffers, all I'm going to say," Vivian told her, heading to the door. "You are the woman, and you are famous."

Something in Lucille grew heavy with that. King Midas got his wish, and everyone he loved died when a touch turned them to gold. And it's not as if she doesn't still love Desi, too. Still.

"No, you're right," she said. "I think maybe I will call him." Then a laugh: "*Maybe.*"

And with that, she went to the read-through for the first episode of a two-parter, Grauman's and yet more marital hijinks, the husband and wife never really knowing what the other was doing or thinking. And she never told Vivian Vance that she had just learned she was pregnant, and didn't know whose baby it would be.

· · ·

IF A MAN *could pass through Paradise in a dream, & have a flower presented to him as a pledge that his Soul had really been there, & if he found that flower in his hand when he awoke—yes, what then?*

Books are of only intermittent help. They sting the wound. (The above line comes from Coleridge, that famous salt-pourer.) The worst was recognizing himself among literature's spurned pathetics:

> *While an abstract insight wakes*
> *Among the glaciers and the rocks*
> *The hermit's carnal ecstasy —W. H. Auden*

This isn't to say books *never* provide consolation.

> *There is none righteous, not even one . . .*
> *For there is not a single just man upon earth, who doeth good, and sinneth not. . . .*

"Reading the Bible again, Iz?" Harriet says. "It's a *weekend*. Don't withdraw from the family, please."

She's come this morning across her husband reading scripture in the living room and smiling to himself. *Not even one.* "Mmm," he answers without lifting his head.

> *They are all gone aside, they are all together become filthy: there is none that doeth good, no, not one.*

Yes. Yes! There *is* something holy about his feelings for Lucille. And we're all sinners. His lascivious, his infidelitous, his righteous feelings. It sounds awful to call infidelity holy on this Sabbath morning, but there it is; how can you argue with the Bible? The Beverly Hills Hotel to him revealed the Almighty in the everyday by showing the furthest possibilities for human joy.

And yet, more and more now, guilt comes. It tastes like regret.

His thoughts go back, every so often, to young Harriet leaning into the 1930s threshold, to "Hello, *you*," to the Brandt's Flatbush swooning balcony, to the fur-collared coat thrown open. They had known glamour then. But it had been in 1938 or early '39. That woman, and that young man, no longer exist.

"I can put down the book, sure," he says. "It's the Bible. You can't argue with the Bible."

He's unfulfilled, is that Harriet's fault? Guilt has a way of making him considerate of her. She'd seen very little of the world before him; why would she know how to make and keep—over years and years—another person happy?

Two very long months ago, when he and Lucille had been preparing to leave that lascivious, infidelitous, righteous room, he'd looked at her as she'd slinked out of her hotel robe; looked as she pulled the screaking curtain aside and stepped without a word into the shower; and he reached to check her hand from closing the curtain. "May I watch?" he'd said.

There are some moments in a life that seem more real than others. Examples—cards shuffled randomly from the memory deck: High-school graduation. Or when, with chin held high and in the echo of his own reverent words, he'd gotten bar mitzvahed. Having lost, in his virile twenties, his virginity to Felice Zuckerbrod. And standing poolside at Kutsher's Catskills resort, post-race, the gray umbrellas and cabanas seeming in their restrained presentation to defer to victorious teenaged him. (*Not* the day of his marriage or the birth of his children, each of which, as they happened, felt dreamlike and bizarre and decidedly *un*real.) And then, too, watching her shower. The moment had felt most inarguable. He in Beverly Hills.

He'd half-sat, his backside against the sink, and watched. The showerhead had come wetly to life. The bathroom gave the rococo vibes you get from any high-end place. Swan-necked faucets, lighted cheval glass, blazing white porcelain. Lucille had pretended he wasn't there.

She soaped her torso, hips, her thighs, she soaped her pinkening chest. Oh, oh, oh! In the attitude of a young boy at a brothel window, he watched. Lucille, water-spangled and stepping from the shower, flushed, glittery, daubed off all the little rhinestone shower drops—the slow, loving towel. She didn't say a word; he didn't, either. Lucille made a performance of delighting in the swerves of her own body. She was aware of his watching. Arching her free hand—it reminded Isidore of the arc of the faucets—she traced a finger up her leg. And then the towel again made its happy rounds. The expression Lucille showed the mirror was the same expression she'd worn for her filmed love scenes in *Sorrowful Jones:* Kiss me, you fool!

Everything must end. After the bathroom's chaste burlesque, Lucille walked to the sink. She leaned to the mirror for some lipstick ministrations. Silent, still, close by, Lucille powdered and tweezed. He watched this, too; it was a performance of deeper intimacy. Lucille had been letting him in on a secret. She'd driven her beauty hard, and because of that, it had taken her over farther mountains.

"CAN YOU TELL us what you learned this week in school?" Harriet's saying.

"Aw, it's Sunday," Arthur says.

Isidore's family is at the table—children and parents. Apparently it's evening, dinner already. He's been dipping in and out of time, paying occasional attention to this, his non-Lucille life, his actual life. It hasn't *quite* been unendurable. Just utterly beside the point. Right now is one of the times when everything's dunked in the sticky milk of home life—chatter, schoolwork, chores, suppressed yawns. It's less and less what he thinks of as true existence.

"The Louisiana Purchase," Arthur says finally; he's now in the fourth grade. "We learned it in social studies."

"What is the Louisiana Purchase?" Harriet says.

I will participate, Isidore thinks. "This is quite delicious, Mary," he says to the maid, who is on her way from the kitchen for the night. "No one beats your sweet potatoes."

"Thank you, Mr. Strauss."

"You don't know what the Louisiana Purchase is, Mommy?" Arthur says.

"She knows," Bernie says. "She wants to see if *you* know. Right, Mom?"

"I'm not sure *I* know," Isidore says, his mouth crammed with sweet potato, "and I'm in real estate." After his sons laugh, he decides to keep smiling. But once a smile becomes a decision, it's no longer a smile.

When you suffer from guilt, and when your own actions make you pity someone, you either start really to dislike that person or feel a tender sad beholden fondness for her. Isidore is too decent to blame his wife for his dissatisfaction. That's what he tells himself.

I tried to get Lucille to work on a movie with me, he thinks. How stupid! Dummy! Maybe that's why she hasn't called.

POST-L.A., HE BUYS Harriet stuff. A television, a diamond pendant, each a surprise. Flowers every week. Harriet must be bored. He knows that. Mary handles the cooking and the house cleaning— what does Harriet do with her days? He's offered to pay for lessons if she wants to get more serious about the piano; he's asked her if she'd like to get a job—though he's told her that, of course, she should do so only if she wants to. *No, thanks. I keep busy.* He still takes pleasure in watching her with the children and in going out with her to see friends for cocktails, and soon, they'll head to Miami for the deadest month in winter, living in a hotel, hiring a tutor for the boys. A new affectation. He has begun to spend lavishly, to take glitzy risks at work, and that's all right. Harriet certainly hasn't minded the spending. Over at his brother Norman's house, out to the Copacabana, on a long drive anywhere, he's felt pleased to have her company. Heading (for example) to a party for Sam LeFrak at the Hotel Astor, walking up Broadway, arm in arm, trying not to think about anything other than being here with his wife—Harriet asking if he's all right—"Yes, of course, darling"—and when he turned, her unexpected smile raised a smile on his own face. His marriage was something to which he needn't give himself fully. The edifice of his connection to Harriet was like one of those skyscrapers you see at night where only some of the lights are turned on.

Oddly, he feels furthest from his family when he's with them, on weekends. He can't on those days hover around his office phone, waiting for Lucille to call. She said she would call, she asked that he not call, she promised she would call, and so he waits for her call. Why did I push that stupid movie idea? Well, I cared about it; I wanted to do something creative, Isidore thinks. He resolves never to try to be a creative person again.

"Aah, I'm so wet," Harriet had said recently in a growled and throaty voice. She was being passionate in bed. And her resultant facial expression surprised him—the serious intensity of it. This means something to her!

The sex is rare but not *completely* absent. Mostly he claims to be tired, she has a headache, they're pooped after having gone dancing, or there's been an argument—but most likely, he's just been distant. Ordinarily, having sex doesn't come up. Mostly, he's too busy hiding his sadness. But occasionally, a stray touch or look would lead to a kiss, and that kind of kiss would inevitably lead to the bedroom— the chaste, in-the-dark, missionary-style, non-dirty-talk bedroom. Except for this time. An early showing of How to Marry a Million- aire, Marilyn Monroe, the promise of cinematic romance, and then, when the lights went out, each reached for the other. It was tender in its way. It was like listening to a record playing through a small speaker. (Lucille, of course, was right there, blaring in the orchestra pit of his skull.)

That sex had happened a week ago. And now she teaches their sons to make a hard-boiled egg; Arthur bounces a pot of water on his way to the stove and spills some on Harriet. "Aaaah, I'm so wet," she cries, laughing. And there, right there, is the problem for him.

Infidelity has revealed to Isidore that he is a prude in spirit.

He once read that Jonathan Swift as a newlywed was angry to discover that his bride had to answer the gross calls of the body, belching, farting, the toilet. Isidore knows it's equally ridiculous to deny his wife any carnality simply because she is the mother of his children. But knowing isn't the same as feeling. He can't help it. Harriet saying "I'm so wet" has made him recoil.

He feels bottled-up all the time and has trouble sleeping. There *is* a kind of love with Harriet, he tells himself.

HE'S DIFFERENT ON Tuesdays. Tuesdays, he watches. And that brings a sense of a world to come. The anger he feels at Lucille—why has she not called me?—goes.

The monochromatic show misses the allure of her hair, the complexity of its tones. Isidore remembers one red curl flying at an angle over her forehead, where he made out a reedy black filament, a dark vital principle, like the head of the match burning inside the flame.

"Are you coming with us?" his son Bernie asks. It is a quiet Saturday morning now. "Mommy said we can go get sneakers. Can we buy sneakers, Dad?"

"Look, just—[sigh; lowering the newspaper]—what'd your mother say?"

Isidore neither likes feeling angry at his son nor does he know, precisely, from where the anger really springs.

"Coming with us, Dad?"

He uncreases the *New York Tribune* and lifts it again. "No. No, Bernie"; he tries to read the sports page. He and Bernie are alone in the living room. DIMAGGIO BACK FROM HONEYMOON AFTER MAR-RYING STARLET. No escaping celebrity, even in sports! The telephone rings in the kitchen, and not even trying for tranquility he rushes to answer it. Would Lucille call me at home? Maybe I should've done more work on our movie idea.

"Hello?"—(*Oh please, oh please*)—it's a woman from Temple Beth Shalom, calling about a raffle. Isidore hangs up, shlumps into a chair.

"Just come to buy shoes, Dad. Mom said we could." The boy has followed Isidore into the kitchen.

"I'm not going, okay?" Isidore's voice comes out firing. The boy's face appears stung. A bad father, too! No. Isidore runs a caressing hand up and down Bernie's arm. Entering adolescence, the boy smells the slightest bit sweaty. "I'm sorry. I just can't come now, Bernie. I have things to do at home. You know I *would* if—"

"You're reading the paper."

"Yes, well—"

It's impossible to keep his mind on what he's saying.

He smiles his goodbye to Bernie, yells his goodbye through the wall to Harriet and Arthur, and heads for the bathroom, where he can sit and think. How does the same word stretch over the dissimilar intensities he feels for his sons and for his wife and for his Lucille? He lights a cigarette. Love! He sits there without having lowered his pants. The varieties of the feeling seem like separate elements. Love and love. Someone knocks on the bathroom door. Yes—I'm in here. (It's just Harriet saying goodbye.) Okay, see you all when you get back! Isidore drags on his cigarette and waits for five woebegone minutes. He is restless; his brain is twanging. Finally he opens the door. Finally the family has gone.

He feels a chill. The idea had seemed so easy. It feels now like a risky caper, something almost cat-burglarian. He has a toolbox in his garage. That's where he's heading. Down the porch stairs, out to the front lawn (having barked his knee on the door), over to the garage (whose handle he fumbles with), he looks over his shoulder, preposterously, at each leg of this big little journey, who would be watching, and what's wrong with a man going to his own garage? It is freezing out. Isidore's not wearing a jacket. He thinks of his life. He decides (rubbing that damn knee) that he would have been okay with all of it, had he not met Lucille. Disappointment—and accommodation to disappointment—is a big share of marriage, of normal life itself, and most normal people accept it, and in spite of that, married happiness *is* genuine happiness, or at least a genuine protection from sorrow, as if the fortress that keeps you from the rain and snow and wind needs, in order just to stand upright, a bit of wood rot in its timbers. Or something. But then you see that not *everyone* is normal. And maybe it doesn't have to be that way for some special people. . . .

Yes, here, the toolbox! On the table in the garage! Why wouldn't it be? Some things that appear insignificant in fact matter. Isidore is breathing heavily. The fibs and mistakes; the lucky and unlucky coincidences matter. How thrilling to call her now, he thinks. She *did* give me the number, after all. The decision to go to Fred Trump's beach party; the purchasing of a plane ticket to California; the having told your wife you were actually in Chicago—these turn out to have mattered, he thinks. Lucille saying don't call was maybe a test. He brings his hand up to the toolbox's latch; blinking, he looks off at nothing. She can't be angry if I call. Can she? Why else give me the number? Isidore is not stupid, nor is he morally blind. He understands what having an affair means for people he cares about. It means he's making a choice to be recklessly disrespectful.

The box is filled with his stuff, why wouldn't it be, the number's here somewhere, I put it in the back, but, but, where is the slip of paper, it's not here, where could it have gone? Oh God! Just like that, his heart is a barbell dropping through a stack of wet paper tissues. Oh, wait, here it is! She said don't call but gave me the number, so that means call because she wanted to see if I cared enough to break her orders. Nope, this isn't the number; it's a ticket stub—chills, nausea, thundering palpitations, damn it—just a Broadway souvenir. He pulls the top drawer of the toolbox out as far as it can go without it falling, and then he pulls it farther, the paper is not here. Quaking hands. *Crash.* The paper is not here. The toolbox is on the floor. Spilled from it, there's the face of a bandless watch. Some snapshots of his family. Keys to the lawn mower. Lucille's phone number, the private number, the method by which someone like him can reach someone as famous as she is, is gone. She told me she's harder to reach now. And Harriet knows, she must know, and that means there is nothing I can do. It is gone.

ACT FOUR

"Is there a less poetic word in the English language than 'landlord'?"

—*Richard Brody,* The New Yorker

FLASH-FORWARD TO SEPTEMBER 2000.
TWENTY-NINTH STREET, MANHATTAN

*I*T WASN'T THE unrelenting hours in this shitty bed. Although that was bad. It wasn't the humiliating visitors who saw you wrapped in tissue paper and nausea. Though that too was rough. ("All righty, chow time," a nurse was saying.) It wasn't even your mind's always-present, never-voiced question. No, worst about the whole hospital mise-en-scène—with the ceiling-anchored television, the sham privacy of the curtain ring, with the embarrassment of being laid up, and that awful sickbay mix (disinfectant, plastic, the stink of shit) lingering on the back of your tongue—the very worst was the air of tragic tedium. The spinal ache. Your feet on hard, cold linoleum when and if you managed to make it to the bathroom. The scary phrases delivered in that all-lowercase voice of medical disinterest.

A non-hospitalized person's day is a mountain range. Peak and valley, event, rest. But now, for him—almost ninety and in a shared room off the ICU—waiting for his food tray, and wearing that scratchy frock, eyeing the mound his gut made, time was vast and flat, and gloomy with clouds of defeat.

"Looks scrumptious," the nurse was saying.

Trying now to sit up for her. For Nurse Latavia. Wearing a maroon outfit, this woman—wide torso, powerful legs, sneakers that looked like white bumper cars—brought a meager offering. Tea in a paper cup. A clump of capsules. Some broth or other.

"Uh-oh—one sec; hold on," Nurse Latavia said, turning, and despite himself, he smiled. *Hold-on.*

Pardon me, Mr. Isidore (Nurse Latavia was speaking in a too-sweet voice), I gotta check on your neighbor here. . . . Isidore had been five days in this room and on his third roommate. The first two had been old and ugly and seemed not to want to live. Do *I* come off that way? he wondered. This current roommate (thin, mustached) looked young and fit but complained enough to get tons of care. "Oooh!" he cried. "Aoooo!" Men's tears, like any rare and glittering commodity, get attention.

"Back in a flash, Mr. Isidore."

The nurse moved more solidly than women did when he was young. (Yesterday, Latavia tried and failed to draw blood from his earlobe, and her chummy teasing about it so lacked sexual content that he'd felt unmanned.) When would Mona come? His sweet, brassy Mona. As if she were a woman two decades younger, Mona had pinched his backside yesterday when helping him do his doctor-mandated lap of the NYU Medical Center seventh floor. He was grouchy and responded with no more than a smile. Mona has been the great boon of the second half of his life. It's good that she—who got to know all the nurses, who thought charm made the difference in everything, and who may not have been wrong about this—had yet to see Nurse Latavia lift Isidore and help him to the bathroom; Latavia could wear Isidore like a backpack and tote him around the halls, barely encumbered.

Isidore used to believe about aging that you still felt young in mind while the body changed. Not now. He hadn't slept well here, had nightmares when he did, felt heavily tired, in the middle of the unstructured days. When he lay there not sleeping, he obsessed over a word he wouldn't allow himself to utter or form as a thought.

"Here I come, Mr. Isidore." The tide of professional duty had finally returned Nurse Latavia to his bedside.

"Okay," he said. "I just, ah." He forgot what he'd wanted to tell her.

Now the mind creaks. "Thank you, Nurse," he said. The mind suffers, no doubt, a similar malady to the knee. But I get around, even if it's with a cane sometimes, he thinks. I tremble a bit, but just a bit. So this is not the place where I'm going t— He couldn't finish.

Or, he *had* gotten around with a cane; he *had* only trembled a bit. Having checked in here for a stomach complaint, he'd suffered a heart attack under the hospital's "care."

The nurse, having returned, rested the little tabletop on his gut. Water, broth, a chicken breast whose dry surface showed white lines: scars on the face of a desert. *Wisssht* went the curtain closing around his bed now. Vast and flat time is what he hates here, almost as much as the word he won't even think. Thank goodness for the bulky little TV over his bed.

"You welcome," the nurse said. "Where's your lady friend?"

"That's what I want to know. Mona, she's called."

"She'll come." Latavia had a solemn face and shrewd, half-lowered eyes. "She's not gonna forget you."

The finality of that struck him. *Mmnuh* was the noise he heard himself groan. Death. Death. *That* was the word. Will it come? The never-voiced question.

"You good, Mr. Isidore?"

She smiled at him. Hospital people knew you'd been separated from your dignity, the whole of your dignity. And they were cheerful! And more or less demanded you be cheerful, too.

Isidore felt himself being shoved, manhandled by cheerfulness.

"Well, you can see, Nurse," he said, trying for good-natured sarcasm, ending up at plain sarcasm. "Best day of my goddamn life."

Would he feel, when he got out of here, older still? Would he need more than a cane? Would the fog—the fog in his head, the fog of his aches—thicken over and on and in him? It's ridiculous to—

"No no, none of this self-mockery," the nurse was saying. "You *good*, Mr. Isidore. I can see that."

She looked thirty, though he found it hard to tell. Being his age meant he almost never encountered someone his own age. Society made you embarrassed to be old, he thought. It didn't used to be like that.

Bernie and Arthur thought it vanity that he used a cane instead of a full walker. Easy for them to say! he thought. Ah, but he loved being alive, even this moment is life, even just lying in bed, even an eternity of *this* he'd take, this vast, flat option. Resisting the use of a walker wasn't vanity. It was heroic refusal to acknowledge the coming defeat. That's what no one under eighty can understand.

I've been lucky, he thought.

He asked Latavia: "Can you please"—never knowing the exact time in here, somehow he sensed now was the moment—"turn up the television?"

The satin heart, the string-addled theme song, the elegant cursive, the feeling this all brought him. Or feelings. *I Love Lucy* reruns, 3:30 P.M. weekdays.

I was making illicit love to her one day or so ago in Beverly Hills, and now I'm here. That's the speed of aging, the dirty trick of it. It's a wonder people my age don't all look like roller-coaster riders, hair blown back, eyes goggled in wide terror.

There she was. His Lucille, her regularly scheduled hospital visit. So there were events to his day, there was a peak.

"Oooh!" the man in the other bed cried. "Aaaooo!"

"Is that okay, Mr. Isidore? This station? I've got to check on Hector."

"Yes, thank you. A little louder, please?" Move, you cow! Zip it, Hector!

The episode where Ricky has a gun pulled on him and Lucille (she was never Lucy to Isidore) is sweet to her husband until she wants to sing about the incident in the club. Funny, though Lucille defined the medium, TV never captured her—not her sexiness, her fierce beauty, not her carnality. Not the hair of caught flame, tall on her head.

Hold-on. Of course he'd never been called that again, outside of his cranium. It had been hell to lose her, especially the way he'd lost her. Anyway, now he loved Mona, he did, of course; the great boon and all that. I will love Lucille for as long as my brain works. Not loved, *love.* Lucille—that passion bomb—was the perpetual blast going off in him. That didn't happen with Mona; it hadn't happened with Harriet. He always knew he'd be a little more contented (if he could beat back the sadness) during those half hours he saw Lucille on the TV. Maybe Christians are right and we can be born again. A second, a new self began, when I met her.

"Waa!" Lucy was saying to Ethel.

"Oooh! Aaaooo!" Hector was saying.

Lucille had been dead for more than ten years. Inside him, their communication had and has remained uninterrupted.

I've been lucky, he thought. Blessed.

"You know, I knew her," he said now.

But the nurse had gone. And a curtain isolated him from the man beside him. Ah, who cared. Lucille had been apart from him, and not. She was every watched episode, every image he ever saw of L.A., she was whenever somebody mentioned love at first sight. The years had shuddered by. And the pulse in the wound quieted.

Time is the key to everything. Give a protozoa a billion years and it could make Paris.

You can be in love with two women at once. If one love is conducted entirely in your head, you feel like you're betraying neither woman, neither love. Mona was Mona. Lucille was different. Time and circumstance gave Isidore a Lucille-love that had no expectation or superfluity; he managed (mostly) to avoid feeling sullen about having lost her, about how he lost her.

Blessed. Part of saying the word was the thought that if God heard Isidore, He would reward the gratitude. So, trying to bullshit the Almighty. But also: Isidore *was* thankful. In the cooling, settled depths of who he was, Isidore felt gratitude. He'd been given a second life, one woman who loved him every day in their smallish midtown apartment; and a *different* woman who wore a black-and-white polka-dot dress and took him to the Oscars every year, who held his hand and in a practiced trot led him from the thronging flashbulbs and into a café that the gossip reporters didn't dare enter. One woman gave him daily comfort, steady companionship. With the other he drank champagne and kissed the skin between her breasts (just as he had in reality!). He'd been going through the last portion of his life feeling secretly schizophrenic half the time and in that way found contentment with the woman he hadn't actually seen in decades.

"What are we going to do about this?" Mona had said. And when she'd said it, it had been twenty-nine years before—could it really be that long?—when Isidore had first wooed her and left Harriet. She'd had her head on the hammocky part of his chest, that dip before the rise of the shoulder. The new couple had been having their first sleepover at his new, rented apartment in Manhattan. "We love each other. We do," Mona had said.

A wedding would've suited Mona; her husband had died years before. But Isidore couldn't have married her. "I'm sorry," he'd told her. "Maybe sometime. You *know* Harriet, Mo." Harriet had been her good friend.

This was in 1971, when rules were being reconsidered before they vanished.

He wanted to be happy, on this first night with Mona. No, he had not expected this sadness in his chest at all.

Don't do this to me, Lucille, he thought. Don't make me sad again now.

Back then, Isidore still often directed silent harangues at the Lucille he kept trapped in his head. *Oh, Lucille—shouldn't I move on?* This kind of private broadcast went on all the time.

Besides, he'd thought he was doing the right thing by not marrying Mona. The moral thing. A divorce would've just about killed Harriet, who had by now started drinking. Okay, his not having to divorce would probably save him a lot of money, though that was a train of thought he didn't want to board. Harriet *had* said to him: Whatever you do, please don't divorce me. And when he finally did leave—I can't, I can't, I can't anymore, Harriet, the drinking, the yelling, I'm sorry, I feel like I have no choice—he promised to take care of her financially for the rest of her life; she would receive whatever she needed. He honored his financial promise and at the same time he took up with her best friend. And yet he and Harriet didn't get a legal divorce, and wouldn't. She could still call herself his wife, and would.

"It's okay," said Mona, who was not sentimental. She was shorter than Lucille and thicker than his skinny wife—or ex-wife, or whatever she was—and there was a relaxed sensuality to her body. "No one has to know."

"I'm sorry, Mona."

"No," she said, up off the mattress—a glass of water, she said, be right back—and on her return she said:

"No one has to be sorry. Promise me, here." She handed him the glass for a sip. "This'll be the service, Iz. No one has to know. I have to ask. *I'm* sorry. Don't be sorry."

"This will be the service?" He leaned nightstandward to set down the glass. "We don't rub anybody's nose in it?"

"Why won't you even say her name?"

Whose, he joked grimly to himself. Which name?

The clock ticked twice, a taxi honked outside, and Isidore said, "Harriet. I can say it. Harriet." He kissed Mona's forehead. Harriet had made it impossible to live in their house once she'd started drinking. Such big nastiness from such a small woman.

"Okay, Mo," he said. "Let this be the ceremony."

"Our dirty-little-secret secret," she said, not angry, not happy.

They kissed and without heat took each other's clothes off—he nearing sixty, she at forty-six—and when that was over they came to define and grow comfortable with their decision. They didn't have to tell anybody. A real marriage wouldn't be necessary or possible—and Harriet was the reason. And maybe five percent of it, or two percent, was a separate woman-based reason Mona didn't need to know about. Regardless, he and Mona would live as if they were husband and wife. That was how he'd rolled up that old-world parchment, The Marriage of Isidore and Harriet. But he never shared with her the secret by which, in part, he defined himself, to himself. He was a bigamist of the head.

· · ·

ON THE TV screen now, thirty years later, on the seventh floor of the NYU Medical Center:

Ethel, reading from a textbook: "Here, Lucy! How to win back your husband. If he hunts, take up hunting. If he fishes, take up fishing. If he golfs—"

Lucy: "Mine plays poker. I'll take up poking."

Lucille had accused Isidore of having been with her because—well, because her fame made the risk of their affair unreal to him somehow. Not true! But he wondered. As for her? Maybe it had been his normality. Maybe his normality had been the cure for fame exhaustion.

"Huh?" he said now, in the hospital. "What is this?"

Someone grabbed, was grabbing, his shoulder—hard. The pain grew, digging its nails into his arm; and it clawed through his chest. All down his body it went now and felt very cold. He knew. But this couldn't be the end; he was in a hospital. His own breathing sounded as if it came from within his body and outside his body. Thinking I'm in a hospital, he yelled for help. He yelled what he thought was happening. He screamed, or thought he did, but from his mouth no noise emerged. The unimaginable. That was now really happening. It was sinking onto him from above his bed. His scream of *Nurse!* had come out as "—*!*" A puff of breath, a voiceless cry. Up on the TV, the woman he loved was talking to her husband. Isidore knew he could reach a button, on the bed, by which he might call the nurse. Where, though? The curtain was closed. Oh, Ricky, let me come to the club tonight, I'll be good. Isidore couldn't see the call button. I knew it, he thought. His arm wouldn't move. I just knew it. Through a rift in the curtain: The nurse who recently had been at his bedside was goofing with another nurse, swinging her arms, stomping her chunky sneakers. And she was laughing. Laughing and laughing. *Nurse! Nurse!* ("—*!* —*!*") But the unimaginable, inch by inch, took him, numbing this limb, that muscle, closing the throat; now it infused his face with the oddest sensation, melting the external world. The nurse was laughing, he was dying.

Blessed be the name of the Lord . . . This is what his life had led to. The sadness, the great sadness of it. Trying to believe, to answer the lifelong doubts. *Blessed be the name . . .*

He would lose Lucille for good; even if the afterlife turned out to offer every outlandish, hopeful promise—even if he accepted this, and he didn't, he didn't, it turned out he didn't—what claim would he have on *that* eternity? He and she, impossible anywhere outside his mind, impossible even in heaven. She'd had one husband and another husband and none of them were him. And yet the time he spent haunted by her gave his life, in his eyes, a heroic dimension. Harriet! he thought for the first time in months. Harriet, with her endearingly tough nose. I was selfish with her, he admitted, shivering.

He lay immobile in the bed, and his mind like a man trapped in a dark basement now ran around, looking for a door, frantic. But there was no door, there was no way free. His eyes were burning.

He was dying, he was dying. The bed had a plastic barricade on each side. Surprising to think about Harriet. Amazing to have been so intimately joined, to have your life so close to another that the roots get all tangled, then so wholly to break. Where is she now?

Time had slowed and accelerated in equal measure, it was disorienting. He began to cry for himself. There was fear, but not the fear you'd think.

A trifle, an incident he hadn't thought about in decades, glowed in memory. Isidore's then-young father taking off his hat to say, in his Russian accent: When you die, Izzy, your soul must find someplace to go, and that's why you make friends, have children, build a home that you love, or plant a tree; that's why you leave behind at least one thing you're truly proud of, something to say that you were here. When you die, that's where your soul goes. Judaism says that you live on in those places. Where and when you were proudest. Then I'll live on nowhere, Isidore thought now. My soul will go to a love that died forty years ago and get buried there.

His brain's grasp loosened, and details, starting with color—all around him—the pigment just went. No one ever got to see me at my happiest, he thought. Whole other things went too: bed, television, the moans nearby. No one ever saw me at my best. I was most myself in that hotel and no one I know ever got to see me. Only *she* did.

Really? Cheating in your head? You, Isidore?

Why were you not more like Zusya? Why were you not more like Isidore?

Out Los Angeles airport's giant picture window, his plane flew away once more; and once more the shadows of clouds slid over 1950s California sand toward the Pacific. Dunes as smooth as Lucille's breast. And then those images dissipated.

CHAPTER TEN

I **WAS BORN INTO** *a parade that extended all the way back pretty much to the source of history, and yet the view didn't extend behind my grandparents' shoulders. Many American Jews had no more family knowledge than I did. The facts and even the names got lost in the erasive Atlantic. For a lot of us, that's how it is. My great-great-grandparents were a void; my great-grandfather I never met and couldn't cite his birthplace or even his last name before the mugs on Ellis Island changed it to Strauss; and my beloved grandfather (I was about to learn) was dead.*

In the very slow-moving elevator, leaving the William Morris Agency, I got a call from my father. "I just heard from Uncle Arthur. Poppa Izzy . . ." he said.

Sadness—deep, instant sadness.

The elevator kept descending, and each floor-number lit up and went out, each stood bright and proud for its one meaningless second, like a bad idea in a line of bad ideas, going down.

A LREADY—JUST THE SECOND date—their talk has gone into soft whispers. Words conveying more in the way they're spoken than with their common meaning.

It may already be a romance; it's definitely already a something.

"Okay, I told you about my ex-wife. And everyone knows about *your* ex—"

"Not yet," Lucille says, pensive, and she blows shielding smoke. "He's not *quite* my ex yet." And she looks down at the cigarette she's taking a long time to stub.

They're eating in Danny's Hideaway, the massive four-floor chophouse on Manhattan's steak row. The man had begun the date by joking, "Wait, I'm out on a date with The Big Lady? *Check, please!*"

Okay, not hilarious. But from the first, she'd liked his gravelly voice, his easy-to-decipher voice. She likes that he teases her. ("I'm a nightclub performer, ma'am. What's *your* line?") She likes that Gary's a creative person without being famous. It reminds her of someone. Gary's ego (she decided) won't be huge, nor will he be a drinker. He seems to listen when she talks. She also likes that Gary's Jewish. It reminds her of the same someone.

Which is why it's so coincidental when gravelly-voiced Gary says: "But tell me the truth—we're sharing confidences all of a sudden. How do I know you're over your husband? Is there—ever—I mean—did you love anyone besides him ever?"

To this tangled question, Lucille in 1960 does not have a straight answer.

IT IS A question that has vexed her before. Just about seven years earlier.

It'd been 1953. The Isidore visit had left her feeling plague-hit—knee aching from bursitis and swollen, a bulbous sty, five pounds added in a few weeks—and drenched in gray emotions. And worry. And she'd been pregnant.

She'd said publicly that anxiety from the communism nonsense had caused her bursitis. Regarding Lucille, the conservative press hadn't followed the rest of America round the curve from red traitor to red-headed patriot—not until Eisenhower intervened. An official White House visit. Lucille's hasty heels crunching on the gravel. Some praise in an echoing room from that most potato-headish president. "So you're the gal who keeps elbowing me off the front pages!" Ike rubbing the bristly white hairs on the back of his sunburned neck, then goodbye, good luck, an unspoken *Don't bother the nation with something like this again.*

But really Lucille suspected that fate had punished her. What're plagues for if not to chastise the wanton?

STILL TO HER amazement she wasn't done climbing in 1953. The next year, "Lucy Goes to the Hospital" pulled the show's (and the televisual medium's) highest ratings ever. For much of that season, she'd been pregnant with her second child. The child whose provenance she worried over.

Was Isidore the father?

The very day Lucille delivered her baby in real life, CBS ran "Lucy Goes to the . . ." in which Lucy Ricardo also gives birth to her son. The real child was named Desi Jr., his TV analogue was Little Ricky. And a full third of the country's millions watched. Because Eisenhower had been correct. It wasn't just that Lucille, or

Lucy, consistently out-Nielsenned the president; she knocked all other news out of America's consciousness. TV WAS RIGHT: A BOY FOR LUCILLE (New York *Daily News*); AMERICA SAYS: LUCY'S HAVING OUR BABY (*Los Angeles Examiner*); LUCY STICKS TO THE PLOT! A BOY IT IS! (*New York Daily Mirror*); and WHAT THE SCRIPT ORDERED (*Chicago Sun-Times*). *Newsweek* and *Time* and *Life* gave their covers to the episode, too; the first-ever issue of *TV Guide* had on *its* cover a newborn Desi Arnaz Jr. captioned as "Lucy's $50,000,000 Baby." The dollar figure—by the twenty-first century inflated almost to ten times that number—was by some measures too small. No one was allowed to use the word *pregnant* on TV, but Lucille did. And the country celebrated the birth as a capitalist society celebrates any holiday: People bought shit. That was the $50 million: board games, Little Ricky dolls, books (*Meet the Lucy Baby!*), nursery sets, maternity wear, smoking jackets, bedroom furniture, even a hit single on the pop charts, "There's a Brand New Baby in Our House."

But whose baby was he?

New children are a leading indicator for the stock market of your life. You see what's rising, what's declining. What new children are *not* is a miracle. Their arrival won't turn stones to bread. Desi had viewed a baby optimistically, at least in prospect. He saw babies almost as you would a fancy car. People admire your having a nice one, and it may take you and your wife where you want to go.

"We'll be happy from now on," Desi said in her ear, in the hospital right after she'd given birth to Desi Jr. Her husband bent to kiss her forehead, and she realized he hadn't said what he would do to ensure that.

Please let him look like Desi, Lucille thought. A nurse in pink held the tiny slick crying pruned seraph up for her to see before taking him from the room. Please let him be Desi's. And added to her normal delivery spirits, the love and pain and anxiety and the intense fatigue and exultation and somehow sorrow, the tears that were of joy and also of something else, some changeable emotion that felt kind of like a nothingness, she was afraid to gaze at her baby.

She thought about Hold-on. About his elusive good looks, his wide shoulders, his air of having spent decades helping ladies cross the street. Later, when they brought Lucille her cleaned-up child— his skin, his eyebrows, his nose—she knew he was not Hold-on's. Desi Jr. was Desi's son. And so what now?

Well, for a while, Desi's fatherly solicitude came back. There were quiet nights as a family. There were staged kisses for photographers. There were promises made, and, when Desi placed a new ring on Lucille's finger and sent the staff home early, Lucille felt deliriously wifely. And then, the next headline, the next deposit in the bank where scandal collected interest:

LOWDOWN: DOES DESI REALLY LOVE LUCY? SOURCES SAY 'NO.'

In the months following Desi Jr.'s birth, the family company, Desilu, had grabbed hold of the Nielsen ratings and tickled them at will. And all across the week. It wasn't just the *Lucy* show. It was Jack Benny specials. *Our Miss Brooks. Make Room for Daddy.* It was *Private Secretary*—not to mention commercials they started filming. And they actually purchased and took over the Motion Picture Center on Cahuenga. And so this pair of onetime studio rejects made, owned, and commanded, at last, their own studio. It should've been their time.

More programs came quickly: *December Bride, Those Whiting Girls, Willy, The Jimmy Durante Show, Not in My House, Love Is Grand.* And yet, all this business success was a fault-line rumble underfoot, a readied fist, a curtain yanked back on a deserted stage. And Lucille still would now and then wonder about Hold-on whenever reality became too crowded with argument.

"I hate you," she'd said right after the worst embarrassment came— the scandal. "Doing this to me. And with a six-month-old at home."

"Is it even cheating if people are with people they don't enjoy doing it with?"

"That's your apology? *People?*"

As it turned out, just before this exchange—before the embarrassment—Desi had hired old studio hand Mose Bock to run their expanded day-to-day: the implementing, firing and hiring, scheduling, the below-dreaming stuff needed to keep a dream together. "Ah, here's the man now."

"Dez!" Mose said, marching in on Day One, tall, hands in pockets, a baggy suit. "Let's get to work, eh?"

Mose started in on what he saw as "the problem areas."

The very first: Lucille and Desi's marriage. Mose, a fierce-looking old man who had actually cut Desi from the MGM roster years before, was not shy. "There's just a little something I need you two to *peruse*." Mose's face looked worse when he smiled.

Mose had summoned Lucille and Desi to his office. His smile inflamed his wrinkles. "Here."

Los Angeles burbled under Mose's window. Lucille had a sense of what was coming and turned from Mose. The window looked over some murky hedges and onto Cahuenga, its shops and its lonely palms and—

"Take a gander." Mose slid across the desk to them a reading glass, a contract, two paranoid pens. I am this person's *boss*, Lucille thought. She'd been back at work for three months.

The contract was called a buy-sell agreement: Either spouse could buy the other out. In the event of a divorce. (It was "a way to protect the company.")

There were office girls about now, pretty, slightly less pretty, young, old, colleagues with whom Lucille would never be familiar. She heard two of them whisper their real worry over something—one's boyfriend had insulted her in front of her office manager—and Lucille realized something about fame. I'll never care about that kind of thing again, she thought. Not only that money meant she'd never worry about being fired. But socially, I'm secure. No one will talk badly about me, to me. Fame is the real social security. But must we hire *all* these girls, the expense, the benefits, the office supplies alone! And—it had to be admitted, only to be pushed quickly from the brain—why add the temptation for Desi! There weren't many slightly less pretty office girls, nor many old, come to think on it. Lucille put on shades and looked out again at shimmering Los Angeles. She'd had the baby scare with Hold-on, and—

despite herself—felt bad about having almost deceived Desi so thoroughly. She took the pen and (pretending the contract wasn't a big deal, listening with a nod and even a smile) signed where it said "endorser." Desi had to get up and take a turn around the room; but he didn't speak, signed. (He'd started drinking more.)

Mose with an intentionally bland look on his cheeks reached for the contract. "Moving on . . ." he said.

Desi's eyes held an expression, a glint of reprieve. As if he'd been acquitted from wrongdoing by the mere acknowledgment of having done wrong. He wiped from his lips, with a single finger, a skim of sweat.

Lucille knew the kindly words to say, the wifely words; these kindly, wifely words just sat on her mind. I certainly can't call Hold-on now, she thought. Not for a while, anyway.

Desi cleared his throat. *This contract is about my cheating,* his face said. *And I'm not sorry.* No one got up, and the silence echoed in Lucille's head like a migraine.

Well, it wasn't a secret. Their marriage must have smelled—as a "source close to the couple" would say in that week's *Confidential*—like "hell."

Subhead: AMERICA'S #1 HUSBAND IS ANYTHING BUT?

The article came out the Wednesday after they'd signed. It used the word *prostitutes.* It used the words *Desi makes habitual use of.* The article used the sentence *America's #1 husband isn't what you think.* It used, derogatorily, the word *Latin.*

This news reached Lucille as soon as she'd gotten to her office—alone; as ever, she'd driven the Sunliner in by herself, after Desi, who had tended to arrive late—but she heard about it without having actually seen the article.

"Can you buy a copy and bring it to me?" Lucille asked Bob Kargman with attempted equanimity. "*I* can't be seen buying one." Bob's eyes dimmed. Sure, Lucille, uh, of course. Let me get my hat.

The article came to her as shattering as feared. *Mr. Arnaz has been known to hire two or more at once and . . .*

The magazine's cover, luckily, wasn't taken up with their story; rather, MARILYN MONROE, THE MAKING OF A SUPERSTAR. And yet everyone at Desilu, stagehands, cameramen, secretaries, writers, fellow cast members, and Lucille herself, stole peeks at it, hid it under newspapers, in scripts, behind notebooks. Like elementary students with a *Playboy*. (*"Arnaz's dirty habit is said to threaten America's most cherished . . ."* And why *wasn't* it the cover story? Was Marilyn a bigger star, all of a sudden?)

Where *was* Desi? Would he show today?

He would; he did.

DESI MATERIALIZED AT noon, swept in by shame, borne up into the office like Enoch to heaven. (If there was any consolation, it was that she, years older, now looked younger than ragged, drunken, thirty-eight-year-old he.)

The magazine Desi held high—a track-and-field baton in Los Angeles's most distasteful relay. And he said, in a practiced voice, loud for all to hear: "Can you believe what these SOBs are saying about me now?"

"Believe?" Lucille said. "Of course we do."

Lucille had never before seen him this drunk on a workday. She got up, slumped to her office, closed the door; she had a long and wordless sit behind her desk; a private glass full of scotch; and she had a wrap over her shoulders. Emotion drifted up the flue of the throat—hiccupped grief; gasped anger—and she began, finally, gently, to cry.

THEIR MARRIAGE COULDN·T fail. They *were* American Marriage. Six months back, when Desi Jr. was born, the Associated Press had wired hourly bulletins of Lucille's progress to seventeen hundred newspapers. AMERICA'S GOT A NEWBORN! And now this, she thought. Yes, I cheated, but only after Desi did, and mine *meant* something. And, damn it, the baby was Desi's.

Agreement, schma-greement; how could she divorce Desi when hundreds of employees counted on her?

How could she divorce him and toss out the show and her career?

How much humiliation would this scandal cause, and for how long? (The hurt it caused was, of course, a given.)

Desi now put into practice a kind of wounded pose—slouchy look; sloe-eyed face—as if he had some nebulous back pain. As if he had gotten conked in the head by a shovel. It wasn't just acting, Lucille thought. It was *bad* acting.

Worse, maddeningly worse: The implication was this had hurt *him,* that he was the casualty here. Jesus, the gall of men.

That's when she decided she *would* phone Hold-on. No additional scandal for the Arnazes was possible; no ammunition for Desi to fire back at her now. She needed her anger to be unblemished. So she thought about praying for Hold-on to call her. Honestly—an appeal to the good Lord. But she knew not to push her luck; so many of her prayers had already been answered.

The first night of the scandal, Desi made sure not to be alone with Lucille; the Arnazes and Mose Bock had an appearance at the Beverly Hills Hotel's Hollywood Foreign Press fundraiser. The Beverly Hills Hotel! Desi's infidelities would infect even her memories of this place!

They were seated at a banquet table with Danny Kaye and Kseniya Resnick, the Russian-American light-opera star. Desi drank a scotch slowly and then another quickly. Lucille worried the cheeky Kaye would feel free to make a remark about the odor that had wafted in with Desi from all the earlier scotches.

"What is it we're supposed to *do* at this event?" Lucille asked. "Anyone know?"

"Not I. Oh, Dez?" Kaye said, turning toward Desi with mock admiration. "You made it to the pages of *Confidential!*"

"What is *Confidential?*" Resnick asked in her delicate curlicue voice.

There was a uniqueness to Resnick that you could see imprinted on her very name. The U.S.-suburb sound of "Resnick," the Hitchcock villain Soviet-ness of that lovely "Kseniya."

"My dear Comrade Resnick, you must get to know *Confidential*," Kaye told her with a smile. "It is a magazine about fucking."

Desi leaned forward, jolting the table's edge. Lucille knew this move, this tautness in Desi's body: her drunk husband, readying for a fight. "Desi," she said. And she touched him, a wifely hand to his forearm, a tender gesture, *not here, not now*—tenderness, the very last sentiment she wanted to put out into this air. (On the way over this afternoon: "I hate you." "Is it even cheating if people . . ." *"People?"*)

No talk in the limo ride home. No talk later as Desi skulked off, following some wordless agreement, to sleep in the guest room.

The darkened house. It was very windy around the Desilu Ranch; you could hear it blow at the walls. A desert night.

Seconds after Lucille laid her face to her already teary pillow, Desi opened the door—a small shadow in the lighted threshold, reticent, stuck in uncharacteristic shyness. Not good enough, she thought. He had some 'splainin' to do. Even at this sad hour, she made a grim joke. But it had gone out for the first time—the beam of his splendid confidence had gone out.

"Lucille," he croaked. "Ah, Red."

With his back to the doorjamb, he slid all the way down. Then, on hands and knees, he crawled. He crawled to Lucille. *Is he kidding?* She wouldn't have allowed him to come in with her, under the covers. But he didn't even try to enter the bed. He just knelt beside the mattress, smoothing her hair.

I'll let him do this, she thought. And in the dark, Desi took her hand, bringing it to his cheek, and he gentled her forehead with his knuckles. He could still be a comfort. He could still be a husband. On his knees, in a room pounded by wind, which reached her ears like the approval of a distant crowd.

But it was over, she knew it was over.

· · ·

WHAT COULD BRING her comfort now? Family? Her children could sometimes seem *imposed* on her, even she would admit that. She would say, "Come give Mommy a kiss." And Clara, or somebody—one of the bucket-brigade of foreigners and African Americans she'd contracted to tote the children to the end of the week—somebody would catwalk Lucie and Desi Jr. over to Lucille for a nightly show of affection. "Good night, dears. Mmmm, yes. Kiss." The girl's dry lips on her cheek. And then she would shoo them, subtly. Not with her hands or anything. Her eyes slid doorward and that was that.

Every so often she would feel something more tender, would feel love—the mood would present as a wondrous limpid palm that carried and held her and the children both. It was suitably dramatic. The baby lying on her chest, wearing only a diaper, and Lucille stroking his face and head, kissing an ear at its tiny, pale fuzz. Her daughter's hand in hers as they walked toward the ice cream counter at Woolworth's. That feeling was rare. And the cameramen and crowds at Woolworth's made it hard to focus on the kids. Her heart opened for Lucie and Desi Jr. most when she saw the least of them. Lucie nicknamed Lucille "Fat Chicken"; that's the sort of thing one is obliged to find cute, but I don't, Lucille thought, and the center of her heart would cool, and close a little more.

Certainly, and even here, she was a consummate actress. As with the woman in the Lawrence story, everybody else said of her: "She is such a good mother. She adores her children." Only she herself, and her children themselves, had a sense that this might not be so. Her tapping foot and those doorward glances were indexes of the truth.

Her feelings weren't much different toward her own mother. DeDe lived now on the skirts of Beverly Hills in a house Lucille had bought. They talked nearly every week. DeDe seemed grateful for the home, the car, the allowance, for the life—things Lucille granted her. Everyone thinks they know about fame, but everyone forgets to mention one thing. Becoming a celebrity transforms you; that's what they say. But, more, fame changes people *around* you. Celebrities often end relationships with people they've known forever. That's because it's the loved ones, the friends, who are bent and shifted by groveling. No matter how jam-packed the room or loud the conversation, whenever Lucille opened her mouth, the world as easily as a pool table would tip, and all the attention clacked and rolled her way. Waiters halted mid-stride. Diners quit salting their food, and you could hear the match burn all the way down. I treat everyone the same as I always have, she thought, but no one treats *me* the same. And the fact that DeDe had abandoned her as a girl was there, an always pain. Another valve, another chamber that wouldn't open. Father died, Mother left me, and how *dare* they have? And now Mother's back and kisses my behind!

DeDe liked to say she too had been a woman of ambition and beauty, as if it were a curse that spiraled through the cells of who they were. DeDe didn't get it. For someone like her daughter, "ambition" meant neither talent nor a common want; Lucille Ball's ambition was something like a spiritual power, an added dimension to her character. "Well, I never trusted the Cuban," DeDe liked to say, now.

Oh, Hold-on! is what Lucille thought. It felt like the right time to call Hold-on. Saying "*Mother,* please," is what she did instead, and the voice scraped her throat. "Desi is the father of your grand-children."

"How much is he drinking now?"

"Goodbye, Mother. The man is coming today to install the air conditioner."

"So, Lucille, Miss Hotshot TV Star, is there anyone you ever loved besides your husband?" the gravelly-voiced man says now, again, at Danny's Hideaway.

Yes, I did love a man besides my husband once. I suppose. But I didn't know him well.

ISIDORE PLODDED ON through 1953, confused, dead-hearted, in a private exile. He'd been driving his kids to birthdays, cleaning the gutters; he'd bought an air conditioner. "Wait, let *me* take the boys!" or "No, no, I'll get it!" Errands, duties, meals; he'd managed to square the shoulders of a lot of husbandly stuff. But from it all, he felt cast out. In the kitchen the TV glared steadily over the coffee maker. There was no glamour here.

"So, isn't this stew really good stew, boys? Say 'Thank you' to your mother."

In effect, Isidore was the one who cast *himself* out. Harriet must have known everything. She'd tossed the scribbled number. Or maybe, possibly, nah, but could he maybe have misplaced it? The sort of conundrum that drives you mad. He yawned now.

"Uh, Dad?" said Bernie with a laugh. "Are you falling asleep? What's going on?"

"No no no, I'm fine. Just pooped. I was up there with the guy doing the gutters," Isidore said. "I think also it's the leaves, hay fever."

Yawn. Oh, not again, Isidore thought. He'd found himself yawning a lot. It was kind of a tic.

"Thank you, Isidore," Harriet was saying across the table. She sipped from a glass of table wine. (Harriet had taken to dinnertime drinking whether Isidore was or not.) "It *is* good stew, I think," she said. This was Mary's night off.

Since the loss of the phone number, Harriet struck Isidore as maybe extra-buoyant; here, at its end, her sentence had pirouetted up, a jaunty turn of agreement. Maybe it was the wine. Her hair had gone silver-streaked, and about her face there was a nimbus of stray curls and intelligence—he found himself hating and pitying her, in turn.

"*Yaaaawgff,*" he said, the back of his hand to his open mouth.

"Ho *ho*—again, Iz?" Harriet leaned forward in a sort of clunky way to look at his eyes. Her voice's false cheery note told him it wasn't her first drink of the day. "You've been so tired lately?"

Isidore made his *Don't be anxious, please laugh fondly* with *me rather than be concerned* face; Harriet's answer was her *Well, you may be right* face. Or her *No, actually I'm concerned* face. If a family is a language you learn to speak, Isidore in exile lost the vernacular.

Not that he'd ever leave—unless something forced his hand. She leaned back now. Just making myself happy, that's the thing I lost, Isidore thought. Just that.

It would be such a relief to be able to howl about this.

Bernie kept on. "But, your eyes, Dad. You don't look good."

Isidore's body couldn't make armor against guilt. What it could make is yawns. Yawns and tears. "It's just my eyes are bothering me," he said. All this is what's *actually* real, he thought. "From, you know, the gutters." This family is what's real, if I don't think of the other possible reality.

"What has gotten into you?" his brother Norman had said recently. "Pushing, pushing, pushing these crazy land deals? It's not like you, Iz, the risk."

Isidore could have hired someone to try to reach Lucille again, but it felt too late for that. All the clocks read too late. "I'm fine, Bernie, excuse me," he said now. "There may be eye drops in the bathroom."

Since coming back from Los Angeles, he'd initiated an uncharacteristic deal with Sam LeFrak, and his hands trembled; an uncharacteristic deal with Fred Trump, and his hands trembled; he'd uncharacteristically pushed Norman to be bolder and bolder again; he'd leveraged himself to make a risky deal with Harold J. Kalikow, his hands had trembled, but he'd felt a kind of celebrity by deputation—you're special because someone special liked you once. He felt the infantile need to tell Lucille, *See, I was right; you really didn't like me or think about me anymore because I wasn't famous.*

But look at what I'm doing with real estate! he would tell her. Maybe he, too, could be someone who's always raising a toast to the present?

The image of Lucille crumpling his number (had he even given it to her?) merged in his head with another: Lucille all a-snuggle with Desi on a couch, kissing him, tearing off his shirt so the buttons popped. Was Isidore even entitled to jealousy? Of course he hated these strolls around the felled trees and blighted forest of his understanding. Not a sapling, not a single blossom of comprehension anywhere.

FIVE MINUTES BEFORE tonight's sleep, Harriet takes another drink. None for me, thanks, Isidore says.

HE HAD FOUND himself alone with Harriet a lot—through 1954, into 1955. Arthur and especially Bernie had entered adolescence, that parent-free journey. Hey, Harriet—looks like life recast us into a couple's act, huh? Often, they covered over their paired isolation by spending time with Gary and Mona; but at other times, he was solicitous of his wife, attentive. And sometimes, nowadays, surprisingly, she appeared more solicitous of him, too. Often all day, actually.

Yawn.

Reluctantly and distractedly, he went with her to the movies. Tonight, they were seeing *Cinderfella,* Jerry Lewis playing a Jewish commoner who's after Princess Charming, the 3:30 show. "That was pretty good, eh, Iz?" A week later, on the steep, scuffed steps of Grand Central, he still thought about the film. Cinderfella had feared Princess Charming could never love him because she was "a person" while he was "a people." But the Princess told the Fella that, under the crown, she was "a people," too . . .

Yawn.

Anyway, sometimes, nowadays, surprisingly, he had a sense Harriet wanted to be left alone. But only at very specific times.

Harriet at the edge of the mattress pulled her pale cotton nightshirt on. Unzipping and letting her slacks drop, then pulling back the blankets, she was about to get into bed. Wind shook the window and then lost interest. Isidore hugged her from behind; resting an ear on her, he felt conflicted about it. Maybe in who I am there runs a streak of masochism that others take, at least initially, for kindness, he thought.

He kissed her neck. It must be too late for that, right? All the clocks read too late.

"Come on," Harriet said. Then, turning, she gave him a little crumple of a smile. "No, I'm sorry. Tired." And a shrug he'd never before seen from her. In these past few weeks, she had been solicitous of him all day but never, anymore, at night, in the bedroom.

He said it was fine.

Up close now—even through the fog of lust—he was able clearly to see something. A blush had risen to Harriet's skin. She was, he realized with confusion, nervous. Or upset. The redness spread, her throat, even her ears.

Now came the soft-voiced inevitables. Isidore smiles. A few *Sorry, I just*s (her), at least one *Please, don't apologize* (him). He coughed, looked away from her. If a power station is thrown offline, there's a lot of stalled energy—there's a terrible shuddery fizz. Stunned generator; turbine seething in its coils. A congested potency. He managed to say another nearly affectionate thing at her. "Love you. Good night." But his insides juddered and sadly moaned. What more could he expect from his wife?—he was a low-down cheat, and maybe she knew it. He couldn't in good conscience be annoyed at her for this. But the boss in the control room may have morals that are powerless to keep the reactor from entering meltdown.

She was nearly affectionate at him too, a smile, a brave, somehow self-conscious face. She'd smiled for him sitting on the couch at his father's house as the old man said something Isidore hadn't liked, and she'd smiled for him at milestone synagogues and cemeteries, and in the hospital she had smiled at him as he held each of their children for the first time, and, over a million days and nights, a million million, she'd smiled at him in this house, which he built and that she turned into a home. And all these smiles and moments had accumulated, had mounted. And now, one by one, they made a distance between them that felt like a thousand acres.

CHAPTER ELEVEN

THE WOMAN WHO'D loved my grandfather for his last twenty-five years—the woman whom my family held up as a kind of accessory-grandma—was Mona, his more or less common-law wife, who had always been kind to me, had treated me as if I were one of her own. And yet, after my grandfather's death, when I looked around my life for some terrain on which my sympathy might land, I didn't think of her, the woman who'd lost her companion after decades of common-law togetherness. My sympathy, I realized, was spoken for.

There was a surprise claim on it.

*D*ESI'S HAIR BY the middle 1950s turned fully white under the heavy dye. His gut paunched out, his eye ticced, his brain habitually ached. His personality kind of rolled up and went. Drinking that intensely can do it to anyone. And the drift was hastened by *Confidential* and the article that had cut its malicious path through their lives.

You could see it in the 1957 interview he gave to *Variety* to blunt the *Confidential* debacle—and to show what a clean-living family man he really was. "You both *do* appear happy," said the reporter, sitting in Desilu's lunchroom. Desi said and Lucille said: "We thank you." But when the interviewer turned to his notes, Desi sucked air, wiped sweat from his brow, and generally looked like the first man to have gone into labor. He tried to concentrate. But he kept eyeing his watch—had enough time passed for the exit to be natural?—and then he said, "I have to go to the john." Go, he didn't add, to the bottle of Jack Daniel's he'd hidden behind the toilet.

"Oh," the interviewer said, "I think I'll join you. Hot day today, had lot of water, if you catch my meaning." Trembling, Desi said, "Okay, fine"—his eyes burning with panic.

"I'll hold down the fort," Lucille said. "Not that I'm invited."

When Desi and the interviewer came back to the commissary, Desi managed not to grimace, but he never unclenched his brow.

"I hear you kids are going to be in the next Minnelli picture? What a treat."

Lucille would've answered but Desi groaned. He closed his eyes, offered a queasy smile, and, through clasped teeth, said, "Yes, excited."

The interviewer had some follow-up about *Father of the Bride* and Desi looked at him with uncomprehending eyes, with a face that said, *Has anyone ever suffered as much as I?*

The interviewer was saying, "Don't you find Minnelli to be quite—"

"I have to go," Desi said. "I've got a call with New York."

"It's almost eight P.M. there," said the interviewer. Then, to fill the silence, "A call with an entire city of seven million? I can see why you have to take it."

"I get going so much, sometimes I forget the time," Desi said. "Is it already four now?"

"Working like the devil," the interviewer said. "That's how you get ahead in movies and TV, I suppose. It's nearly five. Who else is in this Minnelli picture, by the way?"

"I'll go get the call sheet for you," Desi said, making to stand.

"Nonsense. I can ring the studio later. I've got you two here now and that's more valuable to me," the interviewer said.

"I'd rather not forget anyone."

"Desi, stay," Lucille said, "and have some coffee. I already poured you a cup."

"But our friend here is right." Desi did stand now, his voice close to a whine. "I'm a professional. I want the world to know the reports are false. Let me go get the call sheet."

"I already poured you a cup when you went to the john," Lucille said. *"Just the way you like it."*

In admiration and hope Desi looked at his wife. Could she have? Was she that thoughtful?

"Thank you," he said and drank the concoction—the only gasoline that could start his motor—faster than anyone could drink hot liquid. "Thank you, Lucille!" And then they finished the interview without any further problem. "Minnelli is a prince, an absolute prince!" Desi said. And how they laughed (except for Lucille)!

"Desilu is a family," Jess Szilárd had taken to saying, "but Daddy's never home anymore."

Well, *I* can run it, Lucille thought. It's my company.

At the end of Season 5, she set about turning herself into an executive. The business had always provided her with a focus, a distraction that now pulled into a calling. But Desi had always handled the business end of the business. She began staying even later. The quiet, dark soundstages she owned; the pencils and pens and staplers and desks she owned; the gated fence with her fancy logo stamped across both opening halves; the talent assembled in all the shows, on all the stages, in front of all the audiences—she owned them, too; the plaster smell over the new backlot; the dark gray carpets of the offices she owned; the coffee steaming in the countless paper cups she owned; the chill of the newfangled air conditioners, the goose-pimpled skin of aspiration. She owned it all.

This new kind of achievement was rejuvenating. Desi, by the end of Season 6, did almost nothing.

Learning a new trade can be a sort of amnesia. You can almost forget your marriage is shit. When you decide—in the face of your close relationship with CBS—to develop programming for other networks; when you sign a clutch of weekly checks for more dough than your father earned in a year; when you beget from nothing a lunchroom, a conference room, an office; when you buy and renovate the old Guion-Handelman theater to establish an in-house training program for Desilu actors; when you find a new calling, your mind can sort of fly above all that earthbound stuff. It can for a while, anyway. After Mose Bock had approved a quick-failing show for the gossip columnist Walter Winchell—a double insult (such a reward for someone who tried to ruin her with Red Scare hearsay; such an uncommercial idea)—she'd said, Screw it. I've been in more movies than Technicolor. I can see what audiences like. I can make sure I'm the only decider.

It wasn't easy. The slow steps forward, the managerial notknowing—and so being made to feel young again, for good and ill—and, finally, the edging from shadows into this new and warm waiting success. Over about two years she approved:

The Life and Legend of Wyatt Earp

Meet McGraw

Whirlybirds

The Real McCoys

Those Twins!

The Ann Sothern Show

San Francisco Beat

Sheriff of Cochise

. . . and other such televisual nuggets you haven't seen or even heard of but that were very successful in the late fifties, along with:

The Untouchables

and

The Andy Griffith Show

. . . those big fat hits you *have* heard of. She bounded from one task to another, and with each new jump her pride was fully realized. A window by the stage in the Guion-Handelman often caught the sun; when she stood there telling the prospective teenage comedian Joe DiPietro that surprise was key, because "ha" and "aha!" were related industries, her face looked warm in the fierce glare—and warm with the personal flush of deep satisfaction. She didn't have the time to think of her marriage, or of Hold-on—except when she did.

"And what are these?" she asked Mose one office morning early in her self-education.

"These?" Mose shambled over. "These are official show presentations. Writers propose, in a formalized way, ideas for television shows." While he spoke, her shoulder had to contend with the meat of his hand, his drumming fingers.

"And we can revise them? I mean, make changes?" Lucille said.

"That would, in theory, be acceptable, yes. But." Out the window, sunny Cahuenga was already trafficked. "Depends on the extent, and the manner," Mose said. "We, generally, as executives, steer clear of the creative side of things."

And then Mose hoped to be asked a follow-up question. But Lucille had gotten all she needed. She was thinking that she'd rewrite the character of the hotel's assistant manager for a woman; and she'd make the boss's wife an overbearing bully, maybe played by Reta Shaw; and the bellboy would now have a crush on the heroine; and, for laughs, the clerk should be French and have a Pepe Le Pew accent. . . .

In her eyes, there was again the gleam of joy.

Business took ascendancy now. Not just over home but over acting. Around Desilu, people had the feeling that Executive Lucille had drawn into the business all her stores of creativity and vision and left *I Love Lucy* Lucille more than a bit drained. But if the show suffered, only the critics—only the few best of the critics—noticed. She walked from one of her lots to another, one of her sets to another and, in her mind, she stood hands on hips, thin-muscled and caped atop the Hollywood sign, looking down at Beachwood Canyon. She owned more studios than MGM did when in 1949 it had fired her. It may have been the first time she felt truly independent, truly unreliant on Desi. On any man. She had climbed above her humiliation, her subservience, and her heart was reinflating in the kicked places.

A setback came when Lucille tried to pitch a movie to Paramount about a freeman named Meriday Edgefield, who had to march with fellow black soldiers through the Civil War South. ("Good idea. But no one is going to let you make a movie about *blacks.*")

And—and—and . . . the time, early in 1958, when Desi, at the ranch in Chatsworth, had just for an instant smiled when she'd walked in on him with another woman—a prostitute, it turned out—and she realized that maybe it brought Desi joy to hurt her.

The prostitute more or less ran out of the house, and the whole time Desi refused to award Lucille a pause in his cold stare. "Despite what some people think," he said, "I'm still part of this family."

Oh! Lucille marveled at him. You had to tip your hat. The masterful self-righteousness.

"Why do you despise me?" he said. "That's why I do this."

"Despise you?" she said. "No, I just like to picture you falling off the Capitol Records building and landing on your head." She stubbed out her cigarette. "But not the head that people care about. I mean the one on your neck."

Desi took a step to her. "I look at you here, and I don't see a wife. I don't see a woman."

She stood. "Why are you—"

"I don't."

"—so goddamn cruel?"

"I look at you sometimes. I *never* see a woman."

"The only reason for your success." Her voice was shaking, her hand, her leg. "That's what you see when you look at me. Your success."

"If you were a woman, I'd take you right here," he said. "Too bad."

The fierce bright thrilled look in his smile. Desi was trying to make her act cruel too; he was trying to make it so they were both wrong, to ease his guilt.

"That's no surprise, Dez," she said, trying to steady her hand as she lighted a new cigarette. "You'd take anyone in a skirt."

The composure was a giveaway. It was too blatant. Her heart was Sugar Ray Robinson, jabbing *whomp whomp whomp* into the ribs.

"Not *everyone*." Desi gestured at her. "I draw the line somewhere."

"Well, somebody has to. Maybe it should be me." But her gaze faltered.

Desi leaned both hands against the table. "I draw the line too." He knew he was being a shit and this made him more cruel, more angry, more thrilled. "I draw the line at aging nags," he said.

She stared at Desi and his face looked perplexingly new to her. Maybe that's just what happens to something familiar that you think you're going to leave forever.

"In a way, it's my fault. I wasn't strong enough," she said. "I am now."

I asked for so little. That's the shock, Lucille thought. I asked him to keep his cheating quiet. From me and from everyone else. That's it.

LUCILLE'S HOME, SCARCELY calm before, stood nervously waiting for the resolution, the big finish. But there wasn't a big finish.

Even with its wounds the marriage had staggered and wobbled ahead. The late-period Arnazes even starred together in a non-*Lucy* movie, and in another, but no one wanted to see Lucy and Ricky as bigger than life. Or Lucy and Ricky with different names. Friends like the Ricardos you would rather get together with informally, in the lax comfort of your home. But they weren't visiting as often now.

The weekly *I Love Lucy* became a few specials a year, each named *The Lucy–Desi Comedy Hour*. By the penultimate episode (aka *The Ricardos Go to Japan*), Lucille and Desi were hardly speaking except on camera. Each show did well, and each was less good than the last. She had performed red-eyed after yet another crying scream-ing embarrassing belittling demoralizing argument. That struck her as a sign.

Lucille would now find a new home; she would file the sad paperwork.

"Will we see you more now?" Desi Jr. said, his eyes blinking fast. The now almost six-year-old boy was fighting tears, was about to cry; now he had a wet face. "Will you work less if you're divorced?"

And Lucille thought merely, *This couch*. The kissing, the sex that she and Desi had enjoyed on this very couch, the kids and Clara having gone upstairs to bed. It is possible, it turns out, to be re-lieved and bereft at once.

Desi had held himself above her there, his arms flexed. "Mommy has to work to give us all this, sweetie," she said.

Sometimes the natural light in her next home, the Beverly Hills house that she would soon come to live in, was very bright, and this would infuse it with a Chatsworth-like warmth that ushered in some nostalgia.

In memory she'd only had three days with Desi, and each one lasted years: a day of sex, a day of fighting, a day of work. These had (she felt) run in succession. No commonplace days in between, or days otherwise good or bad.

"Do you like your new house?"

I do, thanks, she wrote in response to this question posed by her fan club. *I picked it out. ~~It's hard to be here without a husband.~~*

In the animation studio behind her eyes, she would draw various scenes of reconciliation or triumphantly bitter reunion. A fateful rendezvous on Fifty-second Street and Broadway. Oh, is that *you*, Desi? So wrinkled and out of shape! Sometimes her memories or fantasies would mix, it was Desi *and* Hold-on merging, the men, the beds, the hotel and the home.

Ah, beautiful Desi. Now that was over.

And yet Desi had one more humiliation for her, one last awful surprise.

WHEN THE MARRIAGE ended—when the glass of the façade of perfection broke—the American people worried for her. Or the people nestled worry for themselves in worry for her. If you learn that the ideal of perfection is fake, the disappointment can feel like a national hex. But Lucille didn't worry. To be a famous woman after a divorce took an odd mix of skills that she had a talent for. Guile, camouflage, and poise. (She had less aptitude for happiness.)

And, of course, it hadn't helped to get Desi's weaponized letter. "One last fuck you on the way out," she told Vivian.

This was 1960. The TV show had gone. Her winning streak too. On stage, starring in a Broadway production of *Wildcat*—something to keep her busy—she realized that her new life had begun. A life that now looked like a question mark. "Oh, this is my life now!" she thought, standing amid the applause. Cheering, another cloud of faces, another curtsy, but this curtsy performed alone. Lucille was still "a looker, a knockout, a doll" (*The New York Times*), though the thickening in her face and hips was emphasized by cameras. And there was a sadness too. Or maybe it was the lines around the mouth. Age, the reverse sculptor, slowly marring, slowly unchiseling.

"What's your idea of fun and happiness offstage?" asked the *New York Daily Mirror*'s theater critic after her first *Wildcat* performance. The answer was there was no answer. "Well, you know," she said. The critic seemed rudely young. He smiled and stared, stared and smiled. Lucille felt her jowls thicken and her wrinkles deepen and that made her blush. She could have answered, *My kids are my idea of happiness,* but Lucie and Desi Jr. were back in Los Angeles, so that might not've come off well. She could've answered, *When other people aren't exactly all that real to you, there's a limit to how much something like this can hurt.* Though Lucille hadn't believed she had that particular flaw. That line had just been something mean someone told her about herself once. She could've answered, *You know what's not much fun? When everything in your life is shown to be made of shit. Get out of my dressing room, you little turd.* Sometimes, not always, or even often, but sometimes she thought fun and happiness had been Desi, and her relationship with Desi, her show with Desi, the studio she ran with Desi, the house and plans she'd shared with Desi. Not counting that momentary escape with Hold-on, Desi had been life to me. Hadn't he? Maybe that was more dramatic bullshit. Why else did I need Hold-on?

Hold-on. Isidore Strauss. Why can't I just call Isidore now? she thought. I'm in New York. I'm not married. What am I afraid of? I'll find him and call him. Why not?

But she knew why. Recently, life had given her a reason.

THE DIVORCE HAD been handled by a mediator—to avoid the press; to make the awfulness end quickly; and because neither party had any material wants. And so the for-the-last-time Arnazes appeared before Thurman I. Shepherd (Retired Judge and Certified Family Law Specialist), of Palm Springs Mediation Services, Palm Springs, California. Cozy little chambers, a sofa, no black robe—the exes sitting across from each other. And just before Shepherd uncorked the proceedings, Desi walked over (the heels of his shoes went *tsk-tsk*) pulling a letter from a hesitant briefcase. He stopped, thought better of it, then pulled it out again. *To my wife, while she still is,* the envelope read. And for Lucille a tidal push of quiet washed away all sound.

Typed up, on Desilu stationery, his difficulties with the language making him seem less brilliant than he, in fact, truly was:

> You act all hi and mighty. Making me feel bad.
>
> I hired a private "eye." And he tells me that you were up to no good yourself. I have been aware for awhile. It's the man from New York. I know about the one time but may be there were others. I may be was right about Archer too.
>
> The point is, I am not going to let you make me sub-conscious about my own actions. <u>You don't care because no one is real to you but yourself.</u>

And as she read, Lucille felt a hot sickly feeling in her chest. She crumpled the letter. Closing her eyes, she rubbed the lids. For a while. At last she turned at Desi and saw he throbbed with satisfaction.

No one is real to you but yourself. He could be a shrewd character; she would cite the accusation often, in the cozy little chambers of her head. It's a lonely life when you don't really trust in the reality of anyone but yourself.

That was Day One of the mediation. On the third and final day, when lunch break was announced, Desi asked if he could talk to Lucille for a secon', jus' me and you. (Don't mock the voice of the father of your children, especially not in a bigoted fashion, she admonished herself.) Can we, Red, just the two of us, get away from these moochers for a second? "Lucille," said her lawyer, Lew Got-kin, snapping shut his briefcase, "as your counsel, I can't in good faith advise this."

"Lew, as your client," she said, "I *can* in good faith mention who's paying who."

There were no reporters in front of Palm Springs Mediation Services, just desert trees, the asphalt parking lot, six boatish cars, endless sky.

"Okay, Dez," said Lucille; her face added, *What now?*

She didn't want to be talking alone with Desi and yet was in some way glad, for the first time in weeks, to return to the comfortable pang of him. She hadn't told Gotkin about Desi's note, and she wondered if his own lawyers knew. Likely not; they would've cleaned up the spelling.

"What are we doing here, huh?" he said. "I mean, really." Anger and longing were behind them both, and over them; anger and longing and even forgiveness.

"It's pretty plain." She said it as if it were an endearment, soft, with a breath of friendliness. "We're set to right a twenty-year wrong, is why *I* am here. You're here, I'd say, because you bedded too many whores. Though you didn't always use a bed, did you?"

"You wouldn't talk like that if I was still young. Twenty-*one* years it was, actually, we were together."

He was a little unsteady on his feet. With a backward step he leaned his big tobacco-stained hand on the wall: sweat-ruined underarms on his white shirt.

"Jesus, you think this is that you're not *young* anymore, Dez? You're younger than I am and—no." She waved him off. "Don't come near me. You're just talking to talk."

"Ah, Christ, Red." The words came out kind of fuzzy and wet. "What are we doing?"

Palm Springs Mediation Services had a big front window, and Lucille saw both parties' lawyers standing there, peeping out through the uncurtained glass.

Desi hadn't always looked like this. Someone may as well have plugged a tire pump into the back of his skull and inflated his head. "Let's call it off," he said, then stared off at nothing. He was drunk. Worse, he was thirsting, hard, for another drink.

"Don't look at me like that, Red." He said, "Let's call it off." And he looked right at her and asked her again.

"Oh, come now." She turned away, surprised at all she was feeling. "Desi."

He was a lush and halfway to fat and still Lucille thought of him as hers. He still calls me "Red." That was the pull of him, the feeling of marriage in each part of her—the feeling in the nose that smelled his familiar smell and in the eyes that took in that known face and in the fingertips that itched to go to his. It was a whole-body inclination. The pushpins jabbing behind her nose were a cry, a good long cry that wouldn't come out. Oh, she wanted to say yes, yes, let's call it off. You say tomato, I say tomahto.

Desi took a drag on his cigarette so deeply that the orange end flared bright. How can anyone walk away from twenty years with a man like him? How could anyone stay twenty years with a man like him?

"No, Desi, no."—that's how you walk away. "No," she said. "No."

But what about Isidore? The Desi letter, which made it clear she couldn't call Isidore, immediately exalted Isidore. Why hadn't she called him? Worse, why hadn't Isidore disregarded her request and called her?

Desi raised his thick eyebrows a little; he didn't even frown or shake his head. "Do you want to go inside?" he asked politely. He stood taller, almost stately in his lamenting. She managed a tender look as she headed back to Gotkin.

Desi put a hand on her arm to check her forward progress. He held a second, looking up, as if hoping the sky would swallow him in its wide blue mouth. And then, "I do have one demand," he said.

A THREAT! AFTER all the nameless women Desi had been with!

More of that unfairness at which 1950s men did fairly excel.

"If it's that Jewish guy, that New York guy," Desi told her in the Palm Springs Mediation Services parking lot, "I take it to your public."

"Why? Why do you care who—"

"Not him," Desi said. "Just not him." His one demand.

She drove the next day to the studio early in the morning, the sunshine brightening the lot. Earlier than she'd ever arrived, hoping to be there alone. *He thinks he can tell me what to do?* She felt the sunshine kind of emblaze the warm light of her ambition.

The phone on her desk at Desilu was chunky and black, with thick rubbery wires. Lucille never accepted ultimatums. Especially not from Desi. And inside the vast desk, hidden in a drawer, lay a slip of paper with Isidore's number on it. Even as she picked up the receiver and fingered its curlicue wire she felt—even before she called—she felt as you feel when landing at the airport and nobody's there to greet you.

The truth is, she had never been going to call Isidore. Or probably hadn't ever been. She couldn't have said why. Lord knows she wanted to. It felt like a matter of propriety. If the marriage failed, then maybe Isidore seemed bound up with that failure. In a way, the decision not to call amounted to Lucille's punishing herself. Or maybe she didn't want the normal life she thought she wanted.

No. Now she realized why. *I Love Lucy* fans had made her marriage into the Washington Monument of wedlock, and she'd always felt something sacred in that, something true, something like the most genuine and deep relationship she'd had—the one between her and the public. They stood with her when she'd been an avowed member of the Commie Party. And they stood with her when *I Love Lucy* slipped. And if she got committedly romantic with someone whom she'd had sex with before the divorce, even if the romance's timeline wouldn't go public, something about that would feel, to her, like a violation of the trust the entire country had put in her. And, of course, it would possibly go public; Desi would tell.

Lucille's anxiety for Isidore had loitered for years like a ball in her chest, but now it rolled out from her and vanished. How could she admire a man who would listen to an injunction (no matter if she'd made it herself) not to call her? She sighed. What was *wrong* with that guy? If you're worshipped by millions it's sad not to have someone you can worship back. It's not a fate known by mortals. And Zeus and his famed siblings had eventually to quit Olympus and live among us.

That was that.

"YES, THERE WAS someone I loved besides my husband," she says in Danny's Hideaway, on steak row, at the end of 1960, in the beginning of her date with Gary Morton, the second man she would marry, and the last.

"Tell me," says Morton.

Lucille forks a slice of rib eye around her plate, into a lake of brown sauce.

"Maybe next time I'll tell," she says. "Let's talk about you."

CHAPTER TWELVE

NEVER IN HIS later life of windfall and loss did my grandfather divorce my grandmother. Who can say why? When he died, I didn't feel sad, as I said, for Mona, the woman he loved and lived with and who acted as my surrogate grandmother for almost thirty years. No, I felt sad for the woman who hadn't lived with him since before I'd been born.

Grandma Harriet was a mean, isolated drunk for most of the time I'd known her. Around my grandmother I didn't feel comfortable as a kid. She was unpleasant to spend time with and wasn't traditionally grandmotherly toward me. It didn't matter. Compassion is a clear, open stream. It flows where it will.

Maybe it was that my grandfather wanted to avoid the three icy winds of a trial—claims, judgment, expense. Not that he skimped on what he thought was his duty. The Great Neck home; the housekeeper; a monthly allowance for the wife he'd abandoned. He'd kept all this up well past when he could afford it. But he managed to skip receiving someone else's verdict on his life. "No," he often said with perhaps a little martyrdom, "I'm going to do what's best for Harriet." She hadn't wanted a court's finality, either. She wanted still—forever—to call herself his wife. And, again, even as he lost all his money, he paid generously. But leaving room for hope where there is no hope is not generous. Because she would have returned to him, no matter what. She spent the last forty years of her life a recluse.

CLOSING NUMBER

1977, 1932, 2000

*T*HE PATH SQUIRTS between the Sheraton's pool and some palms and leads to the foot-torture of hot sand. But *how* hot on the tootsies; *how* humid is it today? These questions now mark the only stress this generally stressed-out woman feels. In front of her, the glistening Atlantic. Jacketed waiters, drinks on their trays, scoot across the beach. The cool sea air, like a reassuring memory, blows in. Isidore would kiss me. And I would let him do more. And that was how we started, Harriet thinks.

At bedtime, if it's breezy out her window, the palm fronds rake their fingers over the night sky, poking holes in the black. Stars, trees, the sound of the ocean. And people say I can't be happy, she thinks. Here I can be happy, still. At least here.

Now it's morning. A man and woman cross Harriet's line of sight, young marrieds probably, mid-twenties, the man's ankle cuffs rolled. The woman's fingers possessive on her husband's neck. Harriet watches her. The woman yelps. The ocean must be cold. "Ahh!"—the woman starts laughingly to flee the waterline; the man laughingly reaches back to the woman's elbow, they fall into each other; and Harriet has to look away. The air is warm.

Even from the beginning, Isidore and I slept on far shores on the bed, my grandmother thinks.

HARRIET TAKES HALF a month in Puerto Rico every January on her husband's dime. Not-quite-husband. She's here alone now. Harriet hasn't seen Isidore in three years and hasn't lived with him for six. She takes two weeks on this warm island every winter. It's more or less the only time she sets foot outside—the one sortie flown away from base—and these trips seem, to the rest of the family, not just an anomaly, but inexplicable. *A person can un-hermit herself? Just like that?* Her "husband" pays for everything—the husband who's lived with her onetime best friend for more than half a decade. It's 1977, and Harriet is sixty-something and an alcoholic.

What she feels when recollecting her marriage is the pushing hand on her back, the tripping foot across her shin. Her outrage doesn't lessen.

If she still has friends at home, they've slipped her mind. Her best buddy here is the gay man who rents her this hacienda (or rents it to her absent "husband," *for* her)—the guy's name is Reed, and he's the manager of the U.N. hotel in New York. His brother died four years ago in a plane crash. And so now Reed has this extra hacienda, next to the one that he already owned with *his* companion, Steve. And every night on this trip she's seen Reed and Steve for cocktails, and nothing is as it is in Great Neck. Maybe because she's not chugging beers ashamedly, she can drink with self-control here. "Are they called cocktails because they lead to such *raunchy* stories?" she, who never before said the word *cock* in vain, said last night.

"Hi, Reed," she calls now—Reed has come out to his porch, greeting the sun with mock-Hestonian enthusiasm, hands raised and arms stretched, *Egyptian or Hebrew, I am still Moses!* Meanwhile, she is unsteady on her feet. It is four P.M., and Harriet is plastered. She laughs. Forget that self-control stuff. Her tiredness from having swum—a contented fatigue—comes out as a little sigh.

How often has she laughed since Isidore? Five times a year, each in January, she thinks. Harriet looks at her face in the window. Can people see what she sees in the skin? The fleck of disbelief still there in her expression.

Abandoned? says her face. *Me?*

Ask her when it all went wrong. She'll say that damn party the

Kramers threw for the graduating students of Arthur's elementary school. Well, you can't really isolate a thing like this so exactly, she tells herself. But that party was really when it got—

But why think of *that* now?

He would kiss me, and I would let him do more, and that was how we started. ("Isaac, right?" she had said once. "Is it Isaac?" "Isidore," he'd answered. "It's Isidore.")

HER MARRIAGE IS a tall city she's sailing away from. Harriet can still see the whole skyline, the uptown and the downtown; the faces in the windows. But it shrinks as it gets farther from her. So now her mind—often—reaches back for it.

A young dark-haired man had come up Brooklyn's Fifty-third Street, near Avenue D. A Great Depression springtime, early 1930s. The afternoon had started like any other in East Flatbush that April—bleakly uneventful. Brooklyn was green, brown, and gray. That neighborhood's desperation was obvious, in those sidewalks, in the doors boarded with pinewood. The streets, this far from Prospect Park, had been sealed into the cement of the sky. Young Harriet lived there. Grass like whiskers had nudged up from cracks in the sidewalk.

On this afternoon, she sat alone out on her stoop, where it was pleasant—to get away from her mother, if you must know.

"Why, hi there," the young, dark-haired man said coming up to her. "It's you?"

She's now forgotten how or where, but they'd met once before this.

"Isaac, right?" she said. "Is it Isaac?"

"Isidore," he said, and you couldn't help but notice his soft lips. And it was no longer a bleak two P.M out in East Flatbush; it was suddenly the smiles and loosened-tie hour.

"Nice car you've got there, Isidore," she said.

Isidore hadn't had a car with him. He was walking a 1932 Schwinn up the sidewalk. (The Depression found its second wind, and you'd often see grown men riding bicycles down the street.) Isidore then was a tall strong thing, early twenties, with a witty look in his long black eyes.

"Busted cylinder head on my Packard," he told her. "So all week I've got this two-wheeled hot rod"—he kicked his tire in affectionate derision.

"A Packard, huh?"

The rest is all elusive. Isidore wore a broad-shouldered sport jacket, was Gable-haired and -browed; in fact, his eyes looked ringed by eyeliner. He was in the neighborhood doing a work errand for his father, he said—looking for a building they might buy. She felt her polite smile loosen into something authentic.

They'd been introduced—it comes back now, so many years later—weeks before at a Lionel Hampton show and had chatted. He'd been there with Mabel Schwartz. Harriet had known Mabel from Kutsher's, kind of a motormouth girl, not the kind of person she would've thought Isidore would like. Not that she knew him at all yet. But with his shy charm he'd seemed—

Friday night? Friday night would be, gosh, Friday night would be swell.

Isidore stood admiring her slim, elegant figure, the rigid shoulders, the thin, pale wrists, the eyes that were the sad part of her.

"Great," he said. "We can recapture the times we haven't quite had yet."

AND THEN IT was that giddy, appointed night; she let him take her to the Roseland Ballroom, where they heard Jerry Wall and His Famous Orchestra. Oh, just a club soda, thanks—I get tipsy. And then two hours of restrained swing. And next, Sunday afternoon—protocol be damned—just two days after the Roseland, she joined Isidore and his five-year-old brother, Phil, at the Prospect Park Carousel, the parade grounds elated with sunlight. Five-cent rides; laughs. 1932, '33, something like that. An old-world polka blaring as the horses spun. Harriet feeling every 1930s unmarried woman's urgencies around a single man. Yet she wasn't shy with this one. At some point the sky clouded and stormed. She felt nervous and glad. As it thundered she moved close to Isidore, under a canopy and the heavy wing of attraction. Standing intimately. Fists of rain punching the slate roof. The bodily awareness of his hand almost touching hers. Isidore giving her the sort of aimed look that demands a response. And the rain ended, just when she wished it would. That almost hushed park, that sparkly grass, that dreamy complicit winking world.

Little Philip rode the wooden horse, and she and Isidore disappeared behind a column. "Oh, now?" Harriet said, after Isidore told her it was getting late. "You want to—end the afternoon?"

She felt her cheeks go warm and herself about to do something. This wasn't like her. She took Isidore's jaw in her thin fingers. As if surprised by her actions she swallowed, then raised her parted lips voluptuously.

The snips of her teeth hinted against his mouth. She kept her eyes open the whole kiss.

"How do you like them apples?" she said after. It sounded fake, a foreign idiom she'd picked up. What am I doing? she thought. This isn't me. But she could see her forwardness intrigued him. Isidore looked in her eyes, squeezed her close to him. She opened her mouth to his, again.

Harriet had gone out with other men, been romanced. The telephone at Neergaard Pharmacy on Fifty-third Street (her family didn't have a phone) often would ring for her. The cry would toll down the block: "Harriet! Another caller!" But there was something about this Isidore Strauss fellow—sure, he had money, and maybe that was part of it, a class thing that looked like loftiness— but mostly it was the intelligence, the gravity, the decency. She didn't find that in other Brooklyn boys. It made her feel relaxed around another person, maybe for the first time.

She was not a complete innocent about getting boys; no woman in that prelapsarian era could be. Harriet held a wide expertise— what women then had instead of men's baseball stats and carburetor

fluency. How best to use light to accent shadow. That was something she knew. How posture could play up what you had to play
up and just where, in relation to the door, a woman might stand to
catch a man's eye. How lipstick can draw attention from the nose.
Applied cosmetics, instilled behavior. But with him, she was bold.
Back at that Lionel Hampton show, for example, Harriet had noticed Mabel Schwartz sitting beside this handsome man who filled
out his well-cut sport coat. *Well, hi, Mabel. Hello.* And then what
choice did Mabel have but, grimly, to say: Isidore Strauss, this is
Harriet Joseph.

"Lionel Hampton fan, are you, Miss Joseph?"

And she'd responded, "Not many people enjoy the vibraphone,
and I think it's perfectly worthwhile as an instrument—expressive,
if the right person is playing."

And Isidore noticed.

"Oh, well thanks, but they're just my opinions." A blush. Then
she added, "I play the piano. A little."

Then she'd caught Mabel trying not to frown. I'm usually so
shy! Harriet thought. Finally, a man who makes me feel myself!

Her first boyfriend—a kiss, a hand sweaty on her breast—was
one of her father's Irish friends' sons. Danny Baker wouldn't marry
a Jew (and who thought about marrying *him*?). He was so intent on
never drinking that he'd been no fun to go steady with, anyway.
Harriet could seem serious at times, but she loved to dance, loved
wearing big quirky hats.

She lived with her grandfather, her siblings (seventeen-year-old
Lottie and seven-year-old Melvy), and her parents. "Not true,
Mother," she said. "I *am* looking for a husband. Tell me where to
look."

Her father was a nonreligious man who had ears like handles on
a loving-cup trophy—old-world ears; Franz Kafka ears—and he
often got called a chronic dawdler. He looked for real work. He did!
But was he to take something beneath what he thought a Joseph was
worth? Eventually his wife gave up smiling, even at her husband's
best tries. Also, he was having trouble breathing—emphysema. He

finally got a job as a janitor, "the ambitionless dummy's trade," he called it. That's when *his* father, flat broke too, moved in. And Harriet, the oldest child, got her first job. And her father's breathing grew worse. And Harriet's love life became the family avocation.

After Danny Baker, Harriet had gone with Saul Renman, her milkman beau, whom her family often confused with David Shondman, her beau of the month before, who'd been a *postman*. The two *mans* with their -man jobs. She didn't know how precisely to define husband material, per se. But she did know that Saul Renman and David Shondman were men, or *mans,* whose lives she'd skim across at the edges, or who would skim across hers. A kiss. An inconsequential walk through the unchaperoned park.

The 1930s in middle-class Brooklyn was a time of negligible intimacy between daters. Not just *sexual* intimacy. Intimacy of any sort was rare. A few clever statements or even a single revealing discussion pushed lovers to the altar. It seemed enough; birds made their homes out of straw and twigs.

Other callers were still ringing Harriet on the Neergaard drugstore phone when she and Isidore planned their third date. "You have some tomato or something under your lip," she said, pointing at schmutz. "Not tomato. Blood," he said, smiling. "I helped my father negotiate today and we took no prisoners."

There was something about this Isidore fellow. He had a handsome chest and even if he was shy sometimes, his dark brown eyes told the whole story. (It *had* been tomato on his chin, not blood.)

Harriet's personality could arch its back and toss its hair for him. "I think Hemingway," Harriet said, "is better in his short stories"— having brought up books, a subject she knew he liked. It was a point of pride for her to appear more thoughtful than other neighborhood girls—not that she didn't know at least some other thoughtful girls; but unlike them, Harriet allowed herself to come off as thoughtful— and she could tell this meant something to Isidore.

Without great talent or extreme beauty, she had to be strategic like an admiral facing a blockade, looking for a way in.

"I think so about Hemingway too," Isidore said. "I'm not even a fan of Hemingway, you want the truth."

"Ah," she said. "Who then do you like?"

Still, it wasn't merely that she enjoyed being smart around him; she began to enjoy being smart, period. Like putting aside a little extra food for yourself. The world in that era and her family gave her little practice and opportunity to act smart. Still, Isidore and she had some real things to say to each other.

She shared her enthusiasms: Sinatra and Goodman and the mourned Bix Beiderbecke. Once, in a taxi, they talked about the social atmosphere—Jewish, middle class—in which they both felt constrained. On this narrow pole of confidence they raised the courtship a bit higher.

Almost midnight, Saturday at the soda counter: *"Harun Omar and Master Hafiz, keep your dead beautiful ladies. Mine is a little lovelier than any of your ladies were,"* Isidore recited, softly, with a little self-conscious look over his shoulder. He didn't know any more by heart. It had been enough. She hadn't thought for that second about where she was, the grime on the counter, the shadows out the late window.

She told him it reminded her of Walt Whitman, is it "I Wandered Like a Cloud"? Some Whitman poem, anyway.

"Who're you calling a cloud?" he said. That Strauss mix of shy and blabbing.

There were men whom (unbeknownst to the men themselves) she'd lined up behind Isidore in a notional chain. Very quickly now the chain was cut, and these men fell away. Bye, Saul Renman. Marriage in the 1930s had to be—six dates into a courtship—seriously considered. Bye, David Shondman. It was the golden age of the insouciant cigarette, and many women just as casually plucked a fiancé out of the pack.

Also, why wouldn't Harriet feel discontent? That little apartment; father's throat of woofs and howls; mother's anger; those sad, short curtains. She had the feeling that everything in her life was kind of cramped.

"I heard he's rich," Harriet's cousin Esther said at Rosh Hashanah dinner. The family had a complicated attitude about money. The proud Josephs, progeny of scholars, thought cash would sprout in their pockets because they were beyond digging for it.

"A rich boyfriend?" said another of Harriet's cousins. "Tell."

Harriet's mother, from the far side of the table—her hearing was only good when her daughter was being discussed—cut in. "Money doesn't care who has it."

"I suppose Isidore *is* rich," Harriet said.

"Who?" Esther said. "We still on Harriet's beau?"

And a hail of coughs came from her parents' bedroom, repeated bronchospasms, heaves, roars.

"Oh, she *supposes* he's rich," said the other cousin.

"I'll go check on Pop," said Harriet.

She did like, in an abstract way, that Isidore's family had money. But that was beside the point. He was tall and handsome, and even when you left him, his dark eyes held your hand all the way down the street.

That's why I'm not shy around him, she thought—and only him.

Her friends and cousins were all either looking for a man or had just been discarded by a man, and this gave her romance the texture of something fated—an arbitrary happenstance she rendered as *It's meant to be.*

"He's already taking you to his parents, my *word,*" said Esther on Yom Kippur.

She kissed Isidore later that night with gratefulness. Isidore said, "What I want is, if I could take you to my family's house for dinner every week." He smiled. "I like to see them seeing how nice you are."

"And then later in the week, we can see a movie?" she asked.

"And maybe this time"—his fingertips touched her face—"we actually *watch* the movie?"

With this, she'd blushed, said in a whisper, "I hope not."

"I'll sign up for a double feature of not watching," he said. And it had been like there were windows in her mind, and every one of them had gotten thrown open all at once.

He will kiss me, and I will let him go on without stopping him, she'd thought.

HARRIET HAS TO stop remembering these moments from her youth. It makes her feel slathered in embarrassment.

Isidore had asked her to marry him at Coney Island. The sun, the whoops and screams, the salt air. I do.

In the beginning of her marriage, Harriet found that—entering that invisible structure, the airy beams and girders of matrimony—everything was sunlit and warm. "How about the Copa this evening, Harriet?" "That's just what *I* was going to suggest, Iz." She was aware of this invisible structure without thinking much about it, as you're aware of the sun even when you don't see the light it casts. There also came the knowledge that what you were doing—even the prison-break sensation of leaving your mother; even the sex—was somehow not wicked but endorsed by society. (The first laundry she did as a housewife involved cleaning the blood-dotted sheet on which she'd lost her virginity.) She'd passed on details to her sister after the honeymoon, a blushed half-story—a kitchen secret, over dishwater bubbles.

"That was, wow, that was nice," Isidore'd said, a few grains from the sand of sleep having already entered his voice.

What should I say? she'd thought. *It* was *nice?* The fan purred and kneaded the warm air. *I never knew I'd enjoy it so much?* This was late on a Friday night. *That I feel wicked and virtuous when I'm naked with you?* "Thank you," she said.

There *was* something between them. And maybe, had they met in a later, more patient generation, they would have grown really to love each other before they'd gotten married. Or realized it wasn't going to happen. Or maybe they had, in fact, grown to love each other.

.   .   .

AROUND THE TIME of Harriet's wedding, Isidore and his brother Norman were straightening their ties, shooting their cuffs, and trying on their careers. She knew he also hoped—or, it was more pipe dream, almost never discussed—to become a writer. His father wouldn't have it. The Strausses were a real estate family. But exciting things were happening; he and Norman were leaving their father to open an office on Court Street.

She hoped that when he got home from the office, she'd be able to share his optimism, his energy. She'd opened a bottle of wine. And, waiting for him, she had had some before he'd arrived. This felt a tad decadent. It was the end of his first week, and it had been her idea to celebrate. But now he came home tired. She swallowed the sentence she was going to ask (*Why are you so late?*). "Tell me about your day," she said, putting his dinner on the table. "You're a little late," she apologized for him.

Her shrug posed a question. Do you hold a grudge if you stub your own toe? Isidore was she; Harriet was he—wasn't that out-and-out unification what marriage was?

Sometimes before bed she surprised him, and herself, by wanting to be intimate more than he did, and, when it happened, enjoying it more. And sometimes—though she didn't have the words for it—if an encounter didn't end as satisfyingly as she had wanted, she would lie staring up in the dark toward the ceiling.

Some days, she'd sit alone at the kitchen table while he was at work, pondering unanswerable questions. The differences between men and women—or husbands and wives, more precisely—and about the fairness of marriage compared to the fairness of love. And she wondered about the distance between a real estate contract and a novel. She had a hard, flashing thought: Isidore's being married to me is keeping him back.

It's that wine, she told herself. It makes depressing thoughts. He would've been a good writer, she thought, without having read a word. Or having asked to.

The bottle was already opened. May as well have a glass so it won't go to waste, she thought. Another glass.

Isidore when he came home smiled at her, and took her hand. "Sorry. Just tired. What do you want to know?"

And she smiled and caressed the hand that had taken hers.

ONE NIGHT, ISIDORE didn't follow Harriet to the bedroom. When she in her usual, gently leading way yawned and told him she was tired, he proffered up a good-night but stayed downstairs to watch the late rebroadcast of a show he'd once said he didn't like but now seemed captivated by. "Okay," she said, hoping to have been kissed good night or touched by him. "Night."

The wordless theme song filtered through her bedroom wall— not loud enough to keep her up, but she did, for some reason, find herself staying awake, listening.

I'm being silly, she thought. It was that TV music, its upbeat and somehow longing melody, that floated her into sleep. She knew why the I Love Lucy theme felt like longing to her, and she didn't begrudge her husband his time alone with that popular TV show; it must have been a kind of lamenting way for Isidore to remain connected to his lost dream of writing something that would entertain people.

AND THEN CAME the party where things changed. It was the 1950s, almost twenty-five years after Harriet first met Isidore, and a time when a hostess greeted you by the open door wearing her knee-length dress.

The Kramers in their 3,700-square-foot, three-story Dutch colonial were hosting a party for eighth-graders and their families. Autumn in the suburbs, one big nap of get-togethers, cocktails, jazz on the phonograph.

"Ah, the Strausses are here!" said Mrs. Kramer in the entrance hall with its overflow of coats. "Minus one, I guess."

The living room was a snooper's chance to see people you hadn't for a while—children and adults, talking, laughing, tipsy. Isidore wasn't here. He was out of town working for a few sudden days—he said some project in Chicago or somewhere—and now, as Arthur went off to orbit the prettier of his classmates, Harriet was left alone.

These are not my friends. They're just people I know, Harriet thought, as she always did, with a few rays of self-pity. She didn't like the country club people of University Gardens, the chintz dynamism.

Two strides into that packed room, and she decided first to veer to the kitchen for a glass of water.

"Oh," she said, "no, sorry," upon seeing youngish Ron Naraniss kiss his wife by the kitchen door. Harriet saw the mouths open, saw the eyes close. Harriet said, "Excuse me—"

Ron Naraniss's kitchen-door kiss she could almost feel—still. As if he had kissed her, were kissing her. Why does it affect me so? I'm not a newlywed, she thought.

Over Harold Kramer's shoulder, in a corner: the neighborhood's averting, blushing adolescents. By the bar—living rooms in University Gardens had bars—by the wrists, adults grabbed one another, or leaned too close, talking low and huskily.

Harriet found herself listening to Renata Corman, Arthur's best friend's mother. "Isidore isn't here," Renata asked, no question in the sentence.

"Building something out of town," Harriet said.

"Ah."

Harriet chewed on her mouth to rid it of the ghostly kiss she felt. She had no special attraction toward that Naraniss guy, in fact, she barely knew him. Why did she—this was the question scalding up her throat; she wanted to say it aloud—why did she imagine sucking the oyster of Naraniss's tongue in the shell of his mouth?

It had been a while. But Harriet still expected gently to disturb the atoms of a room. At least *some* man at a party would note her entrance. (She knew how to make her lipstick do a lot of work for her.) But she hadn't realized until now how much she'd relied on that silent approval. Was that past? She was just about middle-aged.

"On business, you say?" Renata Corman asked. That forthright tone of interest.

Some people take whatever script life hands them and make it a fancy production. Harriet's brother-in-law and neighbor Norman now arrived at the party. He came in like Sinatra tramping through the Sands. With his short dumpy imbecilic wife, his receding hairline, even with his shirt untucked in the back—and a big stride that conveyed appealing recklessness—Norman busted into the midday murk of Jewish suburbia, lit by imminent adventure. "Harriet," he said, and on seeing her the light went out. "Oh, uh, hey, doll," he said. Norman was the type who always grabbed your arm excitedly. But now he made an effort to keep his eyes from scudding down.

Harriet said hi. Norman lowered his chin. "Um, okay, Har!" And he was off. He shouldn't have done that. Harriet spanned the living room to the bar. No, a brother-in-law really shouldn't do that. She poured herself a very tall scotch. A brother-in-law shouldn't look away like that, with his chin at that guilty angle, having set her heart galloping, confirming something she didn't know she feared. She poured herself another. She thought: Isidore had said he'd been on the phone with Norman that time, but I knew he wasn't, or almost knew, or didn't let myself know. It's because I'm shy around other people, and Iz hates when I'm awkward, she thought—and so I overcompensate and am afraid to seem awkward about *anything*. Another realization in the Kramers' living room.

Then she was outside. After saying her goodbyes, and, in a dying blaze of late sun, with the boys walking two feet in front of her—down this street of lawns where she and her husband sometimes took strolls—Harriet thought, Being a mother is the last and only real job I will ever have. And how much of that work is left?

She'd made her family her world. Which is something you notice only when you think your husband is unfaithful and your boys are growing up and you ask what there would be of you if they all left. She had no real friends in Great Neck. And no career. Or the skills to start one.

Harriet thought of Naraniss's kiss, and the image stirred her in the lower half of her body. She might have liked the feeling, the possibility—even if merely in fantasy—of kissing someone else herself. But it just frightened her.

THE STANDARD METAPHORS about marriage were not right. She felt like someone on a calm and flat river who realizes the uselessness of what she'd been told to do when the weather got rough—to row to a safe harbor; to scoop water from the boat. No, that stuff doesn't work. The oars didn't catch, she had no control, there was only air underneath. There never had been a river.

After Isidore got back from his trip to who-knew-where, Harriet greeted him with her mouth clinched shut, as if her suspicion was a little bird behind her teeth that she couldn't let escape. Looking, she found a phone number in a woman's hand. After many raids on many parts of the house. A card from Desilu Productions. A card that read *Lucille Ball*. Incredible. Impossible.

That night in bed, she rolled away from Isidore.

He took this for the indicator that it was and said, "Is everything okay?" He poked his finger onto the page he was reading, as if to pin down attention that was otherwise likely to wriggle away. "I've been away a lot," he said. "I only—"

Harriet spun back toward him. He looked at her with a broad smile. He might say something vaguely apologetic. He might say she'd been right to worry, but he was going to stay home from now on.

"I only wish I knew why you were so irritable about this," Isidore said. He opened his book wider and stared into it, and as he read his lips stiffened into a long glum derisive line.

They'd once promised not to be like other couples. They wouldn't mark every error. They wouldn't like gem appraisers lift every last detail to the bright lamp of faultfinding. They wouldn't look to devalue. They hadn't realized this basically meant promising to avoid frank and candid talk.

Harriet decided to give it a last try, to be even more attentive to Isidore. She had to lean on forgetfulness, smiles, and on acquiescence. A wife's three pillars.

HARRIET STRAUSS, NÉE Joseph, was my grandmother.

Look at her. Memories glimpsed through cigarette smoke. What's there to see? Potential, and love, and the failure of love. Maybe you just see an alcoholic old housewife.

I'd wanted this book to chronicle my grandfather's secret love affair with Lucille Ball, and end with my efforts to get the movie they conceived of together made. But my grandmother kept pulling the story to her. And stories have multiple strands.

CHAPTER THIRTEEN

CODA
1987, 1989, 2000

WHEN I WALKED up to the guy at his favorite restaurant, he was scratching a finger along his dark beard, through its sprinkling of salt. "You're asking for something that is generally," the guy said, "*not* done." Scratch, scratch. "Even if everyone knows I *do* have a thing for Lucille."

He was tall even sitting and dressed in the T-shirt/blazer uniform of the generation of douchey men just older than mine (Bad Brains; Brooks Brothers). His date was very feminine, thin-mouthed, and she—flashing the tip of her tongue as she reached for her wine—ignored me. I was interrupting an after-hours date, an eleven P.M. meal amid the coq au vin, leather banquettes, and grand opera vibrations of the Dahlberg Café, a restaurant downtown I'd heard about via Suzanne Gluck at the William Morris Agency. The year, if I haven't said so before, was 2000. There were candles all around.

"We haven't been introduced, I don't think?" I said with a smile to the douchey guy.

"Haven't been introduced. Okay," the douchey guy said. He had a funhouse-mirror skill, picking up and reflecting back your words, slightly altering their tone—distorting them into caricature.

"What's your name?"

I said, "Darin?"

"As long as you're sure," he said. "Ask me anyhow, I guess. *Quick.*"

Saying my unsteady thanks I stepped closer. First surprise: His handshake was slack and damp, your pillow on a sweaty night.

I was unused to the cockeyed sprockets of a showbiz conversation—that is, I was unused to having to play the dual role of myself and Greek chorus for myself.

"Kid, speak up. No one respects a mumbler." His voice had the confidence of money.

The guy's name was P. N. Defoe. Wright Torrence's assistant said he'd be here. ("This guy Defoe's a Lucille Ball nut. . . . You didn't hear it from me, but he has a late dinner almost every night at the Dahlberg.") Torrence was the guy Suzanne Gluck had told me to contact.

P. N. Defoe was a producer. I almost hadn't made it here. First, a traffic jam and its cramped taxicab frustrations, and then—when I'd had enough of *that*—the lurid sigh of a listless subway. And the whole trip, slanting forty or so blocks southeast, I ruminated about how Ms. Gluck had told me no one would care about my grandfather's movie, or my trying to make it.

I gave Defoe my spiel; he watched me along his nose. Then he said, "Talk a little more about the love affair. Between your grandfather and Lucille Ball?"

My mouth opened in throttled complaint. "There *wasn't* a love affair," I said. "I don't think there was anything like that. Let me tell you a little more about the story of Meriday, the slave who, well, okay. First, it's based on Xenophon . . ."

I lost Defoe—and his date, too. Their looks dropped.

"Uh, kid," Defoe said. "You want to make a movie about, you know, black men of color?"

Then he looked up to give me a dry little frowning nod. "Tell me about your grandfather's affair."

Defoe filled the lengthening silence by looking at me in protest as if to say: "You want to come in here and bother my meal and then hold out on me, well then it's your loss."

I had the strong sensation that I'd seen him (aloof, tenuous, his fat lower lip a bit menacing) somewhere before. I knew this person. I often had this hunch, but this time, I felt positive.

But then his demeanor changed. "No one's going to let *you*

make a movie about, uh, African Americans," Defoe said. "There's *something* you could write, though. We're talking about Lucille Ball."

APRIL 1989. LUCILLE had lain in her bed in Cedars-Sinai Medical Center, sighing under the cautionary luck of a close medical call. Twenty-four hours earlier, she'd had gray skin and turbulent hair and been near death. A grab in the chest, ambulance; lying flat on a gurney; the bumping rush to the ER.

But it was not her time, not the end yet at seventy-seven. The head nurse—Jolene? She must try to memorize it—asked Lucille, Did she see the Hard Rock Cafe out the window?

Beside Jolene, Lucille shuffled across the cardiac wing; she wore a hospital "gown"—a real gown was Oscar de la Renta, blue crushed velvet, simple lines that turned heads on the red carpet. No, this was a sheaf of crepe paper, yawning at the back and chilly. Gary wasn't here; it was 5:30 A.M. She felt alone in this white hospital world.

Nice man, Gary, but a putz, Lucille thought.

Jolene was very fat, you could hear the fabric *shuff shuff* on her brushing thighs, even at this pace.

Lucille had just had surgery, eight hours of it, to heal a dissecting aortic aneurysm; but she'd survived, the Ball luck again coming through. There was a twenty-seven-year-old's aorta in her chest; her old heart was spitting blood to her organs through a greased, young tube. But I'm not lucky, Lucille thought. Jolene would likely tell people for the rest of her life about this walk around the hall. Fame like that's not luck, Lucille thought; I worked my whole life for it. She would never think to ask the donor's name, or gender, or cause of death (Eric, male, motorcycle accident).

Lung cancer had taken Desi two years before. She hadn't spoken to him in four.

"The Hard Rock Cafe?" Lucille said. "My taste." A rasp. "Runs more to." Eyes closing, and determinedly opening. "Frank Sinatra."

Jolene said, "They have you on their awning, though. See?"

I shouldn't call Gary a putz, Lucille thought. He's a good man. At least. To me. It seemed to her even her thoughts were panting.

"THE HARD ROCK LOVES LUCY." Jolene's eyes shone with the romance of it. "Right out there."

On her biceps Lucille felt Jolene's hand shift for a moment into a near-caress.

"It's hard for the mind to conceive," Jolene said. "Being like so famous."

"You want to be. Famous so that in the future. Someone you don't know will say. 'Did you hear Jolene so-and-so died?'—and then immediately get on. With their life."

She'd meant it as a joke—or, kinder than a joke; as a blessing on this woman's not-special existence. But her words came out sounding snappy and distancing. I'm out of practice talking to normal people, she thought. Vivian Vance was always good at that. Oh, well. Think of something else. Screw it, she felt lighter, better, having insulted Jolene. (Vivian Vance, ten years dead.)

Jolene's hair was cut short in the front, like a boy's; but in the back, a little Niagara of ringlets ran to her shoulders.

"That's it, Lucille," Jolene said. "Walking good now." But Lucille was back in the yard at Chatsworth with Desi.

"You are doing great," said Desi in Jolene's voice. "Lucille?"

His strong thick hand squeezing her biceps right before the reporters asked their questions about communism—the incredible team she and he made—and the destruction of that team. It wasn't her, she loved Desi and would always love Desi. But she wasn't innocent, either.

She felt the nurse's hands slide up her spine. Lucille found Jolene's half-boy/half-girl hair not unpleasant, just odd. These aren't my times, she thought. Jolene's hair made her look like the Apache wife in a John Ford picture. I almost did a western once, Lucille thought.

"Okay," Jolene said, "that's a good walk, right?"

"Oh God, Nurse," Lucille said. "I'm so tired."

The empty hallway was a bit ridiculous—lonely, like a movie set of a hospital. Abstruse machines here and there. Lucille stopped walking, took a huge breath, and thought: It wasn't a western I almost did. It was a Civil War picture, with a black lead.

"You're doing fine, Lucille," Jolene said, the *l*'s getting twirled around some accent Lucille was too tired to place. "The doctor says if you're feeling well at this stage, the operation was a success."

Lucille nodded; fatigue had taken away her words. Okay, she thought. But who says I'm feeling well?

Back to her own room now and its view. THE HARD ROCK LOVES LUCY. GET WELL! Jolene was arranging her own hair behind her big pink ear, having shouldered (and hipped and buttocked) the slack Lucille into bed.

Lying down, Lucille eyed a spot on the ceiling. She could feel herself gathering directly beneath that spot, at the root of the skull. I'm going to be all right, she thought. Her son popped into her head (she was thinking about the hospitalizations of a drug addiction like his) as she'd had the thought that the very old were addicted to living no matter what—were life-junkies. My son's a dopehead, I'm a lifehead, she thought. She hadn't seen either of her children that much lately.

Once, she'd had this vacation with Desi in Florida. She didn't remember exactly why, but they'd driven a rented Chevy Bel Air into the Everglades. Windows rolled down. They'd sung Bing Crosby and "Babalu"; the roads lost their shape. Swamps crowding onto asphalt. Songs sung about love. The Chevy bumping through the thick air. "Down here is where you find the real me!" Desi claimed. Orange groves. Crayon-pink skies. This happened in one of the frazzled weeks before they'd sold *I Love Lucy;* she was living with the rumor of renewed fame but not the brass tacks of it. "A swamp? Who are you kidding, city boy," she said. "I would fin' *you* in the city of Miami, Dez." When they neared the town called Chokoloskee, Lucille had to go to the toilet. (This far in, the Glades had begun to edge into pinewoods.) Can you wait, sweetheart? No—she couldn't. There was a hotel up on the left. The Beau Meadows, a tin roof, a veranda scattered with potted trees, and all boarded up. The Glades themselves felt boarded up too; deserted. Okay then: off into the woods. (Desi waited in the car, humming.) Frogs' ribbits and a shaggy curtain of mosquitoes. Lucille (who squatted behind a bald cypress with her slacks pulled down) saw something. It took her a second. There was an alligator, that Sherman tank on short legs—armored brow, tire-tread skin, jammed with menace. No more than fifteen feet from her. *Desi! Come quick!*—but she breathed the words out, a wheeze no one could hear. What a monster it was! If I run now, Lucille thought. The beast made a noise like a very throaty snore. Its egg-sized teeth were pointed at rude angles. Now the beast took a baby step forward, with its baby feet. Her bump-a-bump pulse, the flutter in her thighs. Up close, its eyes contained not pupils but flecks of gold leaf. Lucille crawled stiffly to stand.

She tried to hurry; poking into the soft earth, her ankles crumpling—she tried to hurry. Pants down at her shins. "Help!" Both hands on her hat so that it wouldn't blow off. "Help! Help!"

Desi (opening the passenger-side door, leaning sideways within the car) would eventually be credited with the invention of the rerun and of multiple-camera programs—and with the very idea of a live TV audience for taped shows. What Lucille sought here (falling into the car now, slamming the door after her) was just husbandly concern. Or a little sympathy. What he said was, " 'Help, help,' she says!"—and that was it. He was weak with laughter. Ha ha ha! You looked so funny!

Even in those days Lucille had taken him for what he was, no more or less. She'd gotten married in a delirium of twilight pleasures and an impoverishment of empathy. Oh, you should of seen yourself, Red!

"I almost got killed, Desi!" And her poor heart, exhausted from having thrown uppercut after uppercut.

" 'Help, help,' the hat—you are so funny," he said. "Oh, we are going to make a million dollars."

People often don't notice, when the beginning of the end comes. "Drive, will you?" she'd said. The beginning of the end may seem, to those who live through it, just like another beginning. This had been 1943.

Now, out the predawn 1989 hospital window, the blue wiped away the last star, and then the blue went pale. Lucille felt the course of her blood. She felt it with such certainty and precision that she could say where in her the dead man's aorta was, just by closing her eyes. She had no doubt. She felt the buzzing telephone-wire hum of it. All through her, the brilliant shimmering of life. When would her husband and her children come? Her new husband. New as of twenty-eight years ago. She lay there winded, still a little scared. But it was a fake scared. She was positive it was: she felt life, didn't she? Desi had mocked her terror, Gary and her children wanted comfort from her. All she needed, even now, was someone who cared for her as *her*. She found herself thinking of Hold-on Strauss.

TWO YEARS EARLIER, Isidore, poking his face into the Riverside-Nassau North Chapel, could still hear—couldn't stop hearing—his brother's voice, its joviality and its naughtiness. "Well," Norman's voice somehow said, "this is not my idea of a weekend." Oh, Norman. Norman, Norman, Norman, how could you?

Norman had died. And this—death for Isidore's longtime business partner and forever brother—wasn't even the most upsetting Norman-related news of these past days.

"You okay, Iz?"

Mona, his girlfriend (strange how puny the word felt, but what else?), stepped in beside, her hand on his back.

From a clear plastic bowl by the entrance, Isidore plucked a scratchy, black, faux-silk yarmulke. He covered his head unthinkingly. Today he felt old.

"Yup, sure," he said. "I'm all right."

A planned milling-about period; a murmury gathering—some fifty people in all. Everyone's voices going out on tiptoe. Would Harriet come? Abruptly woozy, Isidore felt something kick—

hard—one side of his heart, then the other. Harriet showing up would be all I need, he thought.

Then came the memory-blow of what Norman did. How could I be so stupid? Well, he thought, because he is your brother. Was your brother.

"You okay, sweetie? Seriously." Mona's hair was dyed an unnatural red, meant to represent nothing but itself. Her cheery sweetness in the face of everything often had its benefits but didn't today.

"No," he said.

All around, the exchange of muted condolence. How people love to come out and do a support act and gloat inwardly it's not their turn. And there was the suddenly scary matter of Isidore's heart. More fists, more shoves, coming from more sides. This wasn't nerves, he thought. His heart was getting worked over.

"Dad?" Bernie had evidently come up and put his hand on Isidore's arm. "It's true?" Bernie said.

Bernie was forty-seven. Isidore was seventy-four. No, seventy-six! He couldn't even keep track. And Norman was dead. Also, evidently, Norman was the kind of man who embezzled from the company he shared with his brother. Isidore felt his jaw tighten. No, don't let your anger—

"Hi, Dad." This was Arthur, having come up next to Bernie.

"Your mother here, boys?" Isidore asked. He said this with, for some reason, a radiant look.

His sons' gazes veered like scrambling jets to the neutral space of the floor.

All right, Isidore almost told Bernie and Arthur, what your mother told you is true. Your uncle screwed me. But now his sons' wives (hesitantly) walked up and offered the whispered unavoidables. The prattle of sympathy, the pats and strokes of comfort. They wouldn't look him in the face; they knew, they knew.

Arthur and Bernie each had a family with two adolescent children. But Isidore had seen none of his grandkids, though they were probably here, too.

"What a day," Isidore said.

Every old man's life is a bullet train picking up speed. But standing here at his brother's funeral—twelve hours after learning that Norman had embezzled a fortune from their shared pile—Isidore couldn't help feeling his life had derailed.

Now Isidore's youngest brother (now only brother) approached. Phil tried to give Isidore a smile. "Iz, Mo," he said, hugging his brother, kissing his brother's girlfriend.

Philip in 1960 had married an Episcopalian; their father as a result had disowned him. Now Philip was middle-aging out in Oakland with a wife and kids the rest of his family barely knew.

Isidore tried to smile and Phil tried to smile but their chins had trouble.

And then, questions no one needed the answer to. The flight was good—got in an hour ago. She's good, Bernie, thanks. Yeah, Phil, Darin's sixteen now—he's over there somewhere. (Isidore's oldest grandson hoped, as Isidore himself had hoped, to become a writer.) "—so, are you?" Phil was asking Isidore.

And Isidore realized the microphone in the center of his brain had registered that Phil had asked him a question.

"Am I what? Going to speak?" Isidore said. He rubbed his hands. "Um, I—"

Mona buoyed him with her look, head tilted. "Do what you want, sweetie," she said. "Don't feel any pressure."

Men of his social class and generation didn't know how to live without a woman. By 1987, he and Mona had been married/not-married for closing on twenty years. "Oh, there's Aunt Tillie," Bernie said. "She doesn't see us."

Yes, she does, Isidore thought. She's just embarrassed.

Norman's wife, Matilda, short, nervous, stupid, walked beside a bleak little rabbi, past the gathered mourners and into some antechamber, some green room for the celebrities of this death.

Don't be nasty. Not her fault, Isidore thought.

His sense of himself and his brother had changed in short order. Norman collapsed, massive heart attack, seventy-four. Matilda happened to have called Harriet first, soon as she'd found Norman dead. Harriet, the shut-in, the abandoned, the forever neighbor. Next, Harriet called Isidore; they still spoke occasionally over the phone, very occasionally, even in those days, because Isidore paid for the house and the bills, for everything except her freedom. *Your brother is dead.* Just like that. Then Matilda called Harriet again the next morning. *Har, I found something in my sewing closet, what is it?* Dumb, sweet Tillie. She'd come across a suitcase full of money. Cash, in high-denomination bills. Harriet had called Isidore right away. *Did Norman do something bad to us, Iz?* Harriet said. Us, as if they were still married. Isidore did some poking though Chase Manhattan statements; Norman had cleaned out much of the business. So yes, something bad. If I'd walked away from him; if I'd joined LeFrak! he thought. *You, Isidore, I want to work with. But that Norman I don't trust.* And now Isidore's future was in doubt. How broke was he? He didn't know. Norman had managed the books.

It was time to head over to the service, to cross a little hallway and its little fjord of carpet. Time to say some words over the lacquered box that held his brother. Poor Norman. In the ground in an hour.

Isidore took Mona by the pronounced ball of her elbow—an older person's elbow. But I *feel* young; brain's the same as ever, though my knees and neck hurt, he thought, and I'm out of breath and I look like my father in any photograph or reflection. But that's not me. Where I'm *really* me, I feel I'm still young. Hey, don't say *Poor Norman.* Isidore got angry that he felt sad, and then sad that he'd gotten angry. Poor, assholic Norman.

Isidore changed his angle of vision just enough to see Harriet enter, wearing a neon-blue knit cap. Immediately he lowered his gaze. Oh, no, he thought.

One of our earliest beliefs is that if you don't see someone, they don't see you.

Having spoken to her on the phone every five–six months made it feel as if they still saw each other often. Well, that and the vividness of memory. Images of a lapsed life. But seeing her in person was another matter. Could Harriet look that old? Could he? He had to lift his chin to swallow, like someone struggling with a large pill. There was no mistaking Harriet, her dark poking eyes, her frailty and lipstick. The sharp nose. It was her. He'd know his own wife.

"Condolences to you"; people who passed him, "Hi, Isidore," offering eloquent smiles or saying these ready-mades, sad bouquets offered in the air, sorry, sorry, sorry for your loss. You have no *idea* what I've lost, he thought.

Harriet stood holding shut the collar of her long, cream-colored coat; its fur-trimmed sleeves were very stylish twenty years earlier.

"Wait," Mona said, pulling her elbow from Isidore's touch, as if caught doing something shameful. "There's Harriet. *Wait.*"

She always adopted what she thought of as a magnanimous attitude toward her former best friend: *Why aren't we all more sociable?* Mona's good cheer was the box she'd made to house the black pellet of her remorse.

Isidore said, "I have to, I know."

Walking over to Harriet alone felt like walking back into guilty days and insomniac nights. She stood next to an easel that held a spray of pink carnations.

Harriet said, too wifelily, "Oh, hello, you." The past wobbled the air between them, a shiver on his skin.

Isidore saw Harriet's young self rise inside her old face. It was like someone coming up from quicksand, or a sheet of pink plastic taking, on an assembly line, a mask's shape.

"Iz," she said. "Iz, Iz, Iz."

This ended the special effect of memory. Harriet was a drunken old woman. But, oh, the ashed cigarette of that snuffed love—it still gave off a little of its particular smoke.

"Hi," he said.

"I'm truly sorry about Norman"—too formal, as though it hadn't been her who had broken the news to him on the phone.

He said, "Nice you came."

"Are you *joking*?" she said. Her hand twisted one of the carnations into a pinwheel. *I'm your wife,* she didn't say.

I'm going to apologize to her now, he thought. For everything.

She was looking at him with shining, matrimonial eyes. She considered herself his eternal spouse.

"So I take it you've been thinking about it" is what he said. "The money Norman took. And you told the boys."

"Well," Harriet said, straightening her hat that didn't need straightening.

She seemed irked for his not understanding that such knowledge was part of being a wife—a family.

That was it; too much. Isidore had to excuse himself, find Mona. Thank you for coming, Harriet.

He'd never been able to figure out *exactly* what had happened to him at Coney Island, on that sandy celebrity night, back when Lucille Ball had first given him a kiss.

"You okay, sweetie?" Mona said, placing her possessive hand on his back. "You're not, because look at that frown. I can tell. Was Harriet nasty?"

Isidore's memory scampered off and for some reason this is what it brought back in its jaws: going on a picnic with the family at some land he'd bought. He felt returned to 1951 or '52 now, to holding his two little boys' hands, to walking through a grassy lot— a blue and green and bright contentment, his wife dutifully at his side. He didn't know why, but those little hands in his, under the wide sky of God's abundance, hadn't been enough.

WHO MR. P. N. Defoe at the Dahlberg Café reminded me of, ironically enough, was my grandfather. Not Isidore as he had been these last few weeks in the hospital—bent, docile, paper-gowned in moderate eyeglasses, and picking through his memories. No. Defoe reminded me of Poppa Izzy fifteen or so years before, when he stood straight and had confident black eyebrows and may have still believed he might see Lucille one last time.

"What are you asking me to do, Mr. Defoe?" I said.

. . .

HARRIET'S DISTRUST HAD begun on the corner of Sixth and West Fifty-first, outside the Havana-Madrid. And back home from the theater, later on, sleeping next to her husband, or *not* sleeping in that vale of snores and blanket hogging, Harriet lay there and told herself, No, you're being silly. Sometimes, in their house, Isidore didn't make himself fully at home. He'd kind of wander from room to room, as if he were trying to find something that was his.

But I must have done something wrong! she thought after the Kramers' party. Even before she'd found Lucille's note, she put questions to him ("Chicago is where you and Norman were planning to do *what* again?"); she told fibs to uncover possible lies ("Matilda said Norman was excited about that possible project in Chicago?" "She *did*?"). But at the same time Harriet became a detective; in her head she donned the tweed cap, picked up the magnifying glass, and scoured every corner.

"Just going to the garage for a sec, kids," she said one day. And then she stumbled upon the folded-up end of her innocence.

"For Hold-on." He had gone so far as inventing another life for himself. What was the story behind *"Hold-on"*? It's because I'm shy around other people, and this woman is the opposite of me, she thought. Isidore has stories (and this is what was unbelievable) that didn't involve me? *All* she had were stories about him and her. And yet she said nothing. And the weeks kept coming.

When with Gary and Mona they'd watched *I Love Lucy,* Isidore had looked rapt. For Harriet, this was one of those odd things you notice without quite registering, until later.

She'd crumpled the note—and then decided that wasn't enough, fished it out an hour later, tore it up, and dropped it in a garbage can at the Gristedes. A few weeks later, she came home from some errand and saw Isidore emerge from the garage pale and shaken. "Hello, hi everyone," Isidore said, with wet and quivering vocal cords, vines out in a rainstorm.

And she kept her grief a private misfortune; she would not lose her family that easily. She unlisted their number. And when, under a fake calm, Isidore asked why she did, Harriet—rather than admit to what she'd done with his note—told him, with fake composure, about the physical ailments she'd been keeping to herself these last weeks and months, an acid catalog. "Have you noticed I haven't been feeling well?"—loss of appetite, nausea, decreased weight, waking at two in the morning. The decipherable effects of the cause she wouldn't name. This is when she began *really* to drink.

Sometimes at dinner; or when getting ready for bed; or behind the sound-compliant laundry room door, Harriet couldn't hold back a cry. Or turning from the kids as they walked to the bus stop. She tried to picture herself as a body of water—tranquil, no matter what churned on the bottom, a placid surface. Her sons would wrap a parentish arm around her. Her husband would, too. Some lake she was. Waves slapped in her and foamed. But she had held Isidore in check. For the next decade, from his first coffee sip in the morning to his last sock removed at bedtime, Isidore was home, and didn't stray.

But she'd become a lady with a handy drink and thin wrists who began to pull down the shades on her life. And Isidore changed, too. Once his kids were grown, and once Harriet's alcoholism became too difficult—and his father's death removed the barricade—Isidore left his wife for her best friend.

"MY GRANDFATHER WASN'T the type to have an affair with Lucille Ball, Mr. Defoe," I said.

"All I'm saying," he answered, raking his fingers across his forehead, "you're being naïve."

"My grandfather did kind of abandon my grandmother. But not for Lucy."

"Mmm." A scowl overcast his face. Then a smile came. "How many people you know cheat, they only cheated once?"

"I don't think my grandfather ever cheated." I lifted my chin primly, a grandson. "He left my grandmother, but *then* went to Mona."

Defoe's date's face lowered; her brows lifted. "Really now," she said.

. . .

LUCILLE JUST WOKE from a short hospital sleep that felt like a snuggle. That man had been kind. The memory of his hands kind on her cheeks, breasts, his lips kind on her waist. At a hotel in Beverly Hills. But now she's here, on a bed that's the opposite of a snuggle.

One long ago night at Danny's Hideaway on steak row, Lucille had looked upon her new boyfriend, Gary, his heavy head peaceful over his fillet—his unimpeachable eyes, his weariness—and it hit her. You could not only survive companionship without love, but find yourself happier in the bargain.

It's when we're young that we cobble together our ambitions, and later have to deface them to fit our adult lives. People like Lucille can leave their ambitions intact until their very last hour. Fame, lonely independence, those had been hers—had it been worth it?

Daydreams are all the art most people ever make. Lucille's daydreams have helped other people—they say art helps us live—but Lucille's art has not helped her.

Hold-on probably would never have left his wife anyway, she thinks.

HARRIET DRANK at dinner, and not the demure single glass that was common in that time, when so many housewives were melancholics. Isidore would say nothing. By the time Bernie left for college, Harriet was drinking in the morning, in front of Arthur. By the time Arthur had graduated from college, Isidore was gone. And people, when they encountered her, would pretend not to smell the truth.

Once it became known that Harriet's husband had abandoned her, "How are you?" came as a cruel mockery. Luckily, the party and lunch invites stopped coming. By the time her grandchildren knew her, she had become a glassy-eyed and snapping presence, disheveled in her robe at the kitchen table, a cigarette held between two fingers with misplaced elegance.

What she wanted was the finality of anger. But when something came up that she wanted to tell her husband—"The toilet is backed up" or "Norman and Matilda were fighting last night; you could hear from next door"—she would talk to him. Just start chatting.

At first, this meant phoning him at the apartment he shared with Mona; more often—and more comfortably—it meant talking as if he were next to her, as if he'd never left. "Remember that time we went to see *Judgment at Nuremberg* in Manhasset?" she'd say to the air. Then, even more to herself, "That may have been the last time we were happy." It became less strange, this feeling of eating with, sleeping next to, asking questions of someone who wasn't present—at least not present in a way you could measure. She stopped phoning Isidore altogether and talked to him much more often in the more comfortable living room of her mind.

She didn't remove the framed wedding shot from the dresser.

She stopped going outside altogether.

When her need grew its loudest, she would hear his answers, she would *see* him answering. With him not around, physically, the marriage was better than it had been in years.

There were drawbacks, of course. "I'm lonely; did you ever think of that?" she'd said once to Air-Isidore. This was February 1977.

"I'm sorry," Harriet heard Isidore say. He shrugged, inside Harriet's brain. "I did this for us, Harriet. My leaving was the only way we could stay together."

And then she blinked away her husband and thought of Lucille Ball. "I know why that hussy did it," Harriet thought.

"I don't know why I did it," Lucille thought, once, in her hospital bed. She realized what had begun happening to her, but to some extent she felt outside the bleak scene. Her time with Isidore, of all things, took her attention now.

"You *did* do it—you fell for me, Lucille," Isidore said, silently. He'd said it in his head one foggy night, not long after Norman's funeral, when he was out near the Havana-Madrid after a late dinner with Arthur. "I know you fell for me." Walking among the crowds of 1980s New York, Isidore for a moment failed to see Arthur, the unkempt hair and sunglasses in his periphery. Instead, when Isidore noticed which marquee's lights were piercing the haze, he left the Times Square tableau of beer cans and crumpled papers; he addressed Lucille, as he had been doing more since Norman's funeral. "You *did* fall for me."

"Well, come to think of it, there *may* have been something there between them, Mr. Defoe," I said.

"The hussy did it because she never knew a thing about love," Harriet told her absent husband. "People like that never love anyone but themselves."

"That's not true, Harriet," Isidore said. (Or imagined telling her.) "Not true. She loved me."

As for Lucille, she thought, "I did love Desi." She had trouble breathing now, her cold skin bothered by tingles. "So much. But I was in love with that other man, too. I was. And then he changed his number." He changed his number on her; she was convinced she'd actually tried calling. He changed his number on me! Anyway, the memory vanished; it was like waking from a dream that within seconds you can't recall.

She thought about what was beginning to happen to her— *thought* more than felt the physicality of it, although she did feel that, too. This calm empty brightening hospital room seemed cruelly undramatic for such an occasion, for such a woman.

Lucille! is what Isidore thought, standing at his brother's casket.

Oh, how long ago it all was! he thought. (Even here, even now, he thought this. And of the little space in the calendar they'd clawed out for themselves—having found the Almighty in the everyday. The juddering heart and sighed breath; sunlight in the windows; that too-soft bed; that indolent, warm, kind of slithery bed.) I'd fallen helplessly in—collapsed into, been lifted high toward—love, he thought. Oh, stop bullshitting yourself. A car horn was blaring somewhere close to ruin the effect of funereal drama. Norman's wiglike hair lay across his dead brow. My brother was an asshole. But he had the advantage of having lived his life without bullshitting himself, Isidore thought. Look at Norman—the dead chin resting so gentle on the dead upper body, amid all the dead satin. Norman was a shrewd man. He cheated on his wife. He cheated me, Isidore thought. But you couldn't say Norman hadn't seen what was what. He knew what the things in his life meant to him; he died with that, at least.

What will I die with? Isidore thought. The dunes at the beach. The way Lucille raised an eyebrow in pleasure . . . How much had Isidore asked those few memories to do for him? He'd asked them to embrace him. In front of his brother's casket, images of Lucille now hit. He'd asked them to see him through wind and rain. Even here, they flashed into view—flashed across his inner sky like white streaking wings.

I pined, he thought. But for what? I pined over what I'd had for a few days. A weekend I made into a magnet that pulled my life toward it.

Christ, what glamour was there in sitting on a Long Island sofa, watching Lucille, watching *Lucy,* sipping Coca-Cola as your kids and life played at the side of your vision?

I believed a weekend had not been a weekend. A weekend had been a ladder to the could-be. I beat myself up that I'd never climbed it. There was no glamour in that, he thought.

And so now he quickly excused himself and told his sons and Mona that he was sorry, he had to go; he asked them all (on his way out of the funeral home) to offer Matilda his regrets, and he jumped into a cab; and the driver sped down the Long Island Expressway to LaGuardia, where Isidore went to catch the next plane to L.A.; and next, when Isidore's flight arrived—ten hours and twenty-seven minutes later—when he emerged without baggage onto the lighted, slick, midnight taxi line, and got into his second hired car of this very long day, Isidore decided to spring for a room at the Beverly Hills Hotel, where he could plan his search in comfort, and begin lavishing some of his recently abbreviated savings on a P.I., a professional searcher, who would probably determine in five minutes where Lucille Ball lived; this would mean he'd get to see her widemouthed indulgent warm smile the next day; he'd get to say hi to her again; and when that happened, when he arrived at her surprisingly modest little mansion, and when in a new-bought shirt he walked across her porch and futzed with the bell, it was Lucille who opened the door for him; and it was Lucille who, after a stunned moment, took him into her hug (Lucille was always partial to a good hug, he remembered that detail, or maybe he'd invented it, but it seemed right)—and now she exclaimed *Hold-on!* as a kind of hubba-hubba welcome, the verbal equivalent of a kiss. And in a minute he and she were sitting together on her couch, holding hands—each finding the other's hand skeletal and sandpapery and yet somehow the perfect hello—and they began talking freely about the last few decades, about their new significant others, and, as they spoke about finding a way to begin enjoying time together, Lucille caught his eye (her own big blue eyes biggening), and, even at her advanced age, there was some excited bounce to her legs, a bounce that revealed so much about her life's final act, the act whose surprise ending would costar him: he who would live out his days seeing her, being in her presence, as much as possible.

Wouldn't it be a perfect gift to my grandfather if I could write that and have it be true?

No one, Isidore thought as Norman's funeral continued apace, can tell I'm not really here.

EPILOGUE

*I*T'S THE OLD STORY.

In every life you get what effectively are two passports made of circumstance. The first passport you receive at birth. This one has been stamped: genetics, surroundings, all the influencing factors, the stuff that establishes who you're meant to be. And this passport sets you on your early way. The second passport is one you hand to yourself. As your life firms into its shape, the reach of your imagination and of your tenacity determines just how like the first this second passport will be. How many of the old limitations will it have? How much will you let it govern where you can't go? You start off cleared to travel a certain distance, and, if you're strong enough, you might advance to worlds beyond what you once knew.

It's a function, above all, of bravery.

If you have been stamped as a poor girl in a time of men, if you're from a cold upstate nowhere in an age when distances were not easily spanned, if your father died young, if your mother dumped you with distant relatives, if you are deemed plain and inept, if you don't fit in, if you feel unloved, if you showed no early talent, how do you travel all the way to your own giant room in the temple of fame?

Lucille Ball traveled, by some measures, further than any American woman before her; she was astonishing, exalted, six hundred and fifty feet tall, she glowed, and on April 26, 1989, in Cedars-

Sinai Medical Center, at 5:47 A.M., she died, convalescing from surgery.

THE TRAIN PUNCHED through the dark. This was the F line, those miles of swerve and whoosh, ridden all the way to the end. I sat in the front of the first car; the glass showed a TV program of speeding tunnels. The whole point of America was to believe that anything was possible. I felt a kind of full-body palpitation while, on the crossing to Brooklyn, the train lights went dead. This American belief that anything was possible wasn't necessarily beneficial—not on any kind of large scale—or morally right. It had helped people like Lucille, and it may have helped P. N. Defoe, but I didn't feel helped by it. After my midnight at the Dahlberg Café, I'd had nowhere to go. I'd boarded the F train, riding for no reason but an urge to ride. I wanted to commune with the dark, with the lonesomeness, with the bumps of the trip. The F had pulled into a station called Bay Parkway. Stand clear of the closing doors, please. If you see something, say something. And the coming end of the line meant Coney Island.

Out on the boardwalk, it was cold. The amusement park in off-season; that giant empty roller-coaster, with its branched look of belligerence. A couple feet ahead of me, a crowd of European tourists stood at a fence: just staring at this famous, impassive thing. (I thought of my grandfather—had that American belief in the possible helped him? Had it helped my grandmother?) Up ahead, one of the tourists bent her blond head to her camera, a stubby 35 mm, in motionless concentration. I approached. She snapped a Cyclone photo and, unfolding her posture, stood just in time to ignore anonymous me as I passed.

The realization of what I had to do came slowly. But it did come.

Off the Atlantic there came a current of refrigerated air. I hardly noticed. What had for a long time been a burden to me no longer had weight. The wind, meanwhile, kept performing the usual wind tricks, flinging newspapers, gusting the sky free of clouds. Anyway, I knew what I had to write.

My imagination began clearing its throat. But, no. Defoe was wrong. The story didn't call for any imagination. I began to walk toward the tide line, the first pleats of brown sand. A few beach birds nearby took off to flicker softly, in formation, overhead. A work of imagination wasn't the book I needed to write. This was.

INSTEAD OF AN AFTERWORD

*I*N FAMILIES, AT least in families like mine, a fact is interesting or useful only if it's been encrusted into myth.

Strauss family memories are dunked in legend; my relatives make fanciful splashes. And I do too. We're left with a kind of minikin *Iliad*—the collective inheritance of a bunch of would-be singer-poets. And the truth sinks into the wine-dark sea.

Of course, another word for legend is *bullshit*.

MY GRANDMOTHER'S FATHER played baseball for the Brooklyn Kings before the team found the name by which you know them: the Dodgers. First base, quick bat, glove like flypaper. That was the legend I grew up on, anyway.

I have a copy of the carefree team photo. A memento from the crack of the twentieth century. Manny Joseph, the Jewish King—the *only* Jewish King, the one not in uniform—had escaped shul to join the picture. (It'd been taken on Yom Kippur, 1901.) Clean in his straw hat, and in intricate necktie, Manny Joseph doesn't exactly look handsome among his scruffier teammates; all of them wear the old-fashioned mitt that's like a cartoon-swollen hand. But my grandfather's black-and-white face is lighted by one of those rakish smiles so beneficial to a good boy's looks when he's acting naughty, or thinks he is. Holidays he never cared for. His wife he didn't like. But pro baseball was my great-grandfather's delight.

Or so the story goes.

I drove recently to the library at Cooperstown's Baseball Hall of Fame. And this is where the bullshit comes in.

"There is no Manny Joseph here," said the reluctant librarian, her snail-like gaze creeping over a book of all those who've ever played professional baseball in America. It was as impressively bound as you'd imagine, this Saint Peter's roll of all who'd passed the exalted gates and gone into the majors. "And," this woman said, with a voice practiced at killing the already slain, "the Brooklyn Dodgers came out of a team called the Superbas, not the Kings. The Kings were maybe a semipro team, or like an adult Little League. You've been steered wrong."

So that's the kind of family I have.

THERE'S A BUNCH I don't know about my grandfather Isidore Strauss, the man you just read about. I could say I wrote the book you hold in your hand to suss out the truth. Fact is, I wrote the book in your hand because I had an innocent dream. Or what I thought was an innocent dream.

I woke one three A.M. with a start: An idea had materialized. On my nightstand (inherited from my grandmother), I jotted some words, then popped back to sleep. These would be the seeds of my next novel! By morning, I'd forgotten the idea; *Lucille Ball* and *Poppa Izzy* were scribbled next to the bed. Huh? That's all. What book is *that*? I began doing research—yeah, what the hell, why not—and not only did I find Lucille Ball fascinating and intricate and a surprise, but there was a coincidence, too. The sort of coincidence that argued, as Norman Mailer put it, that coincidences are just omens magnetized into lines of force. (Look, I'm a guy who wrote about identical twins and, years later, *had* real-life identical twins. So I do kind of wonder if writing, in certain instances, calls up hidden energies.)

The coincidence here was a bit of family lore I had missed: that my grandfather had in fact attended a party with Lucille Ball—a party thrown, it turns out, by Donald Trump's piggish father. A party where Trump Sr., in the name of modernization, destroyed a tiny piece of what was dignified and special about old-time America. And it emerged, too, that there had been rumors about my grandfather, rumors of infidelity. (Though not, in real life, with Lucille.) I started writing that day.

I LOVE MY grandfather and don't know what's true about him and what's not. He was the head of the family and so a big recipient of the trite acclamations of patriarchy. Our family told ourselves that he *needed* to leave his wife, having landed in an impossible situation. She drank, he was a kind man, and so he ended up with her best friend—what are you gonna do?

The myth always seemed unfair to my grandmother.

By the time I popped into the world, Grandma Harriet was a recluse who wouldn't quit referring to my grandfather as her husband, though by then he'd already taken up with the woman who'd become his wife in every sense but the legal one. She lived alone for the next three musty decades in the big Long Island house that my grandfather had built for her and then abandoned her to.

Grandma was a proud lady, even in her hermit years. She had fine china, a maid she couldn't afford, and myth. She lost the china and the maid, but the myth she kept until her death.

She talked about her past with the glassy face of someone watching a favorite movie. The stickball games that neighborhood boys played; the schoolgirls watching and giggling, their long skirts flapping as they ran from the greasy boys who asked for kisses. And, of course, the night pilgrimages into Manhattan to see Sinatra, to see Benny Goodman. Bygone scenes, dissolve cuts, fade-outs. She died talking about her husband—who, eighteen months earlier, near his Manhattan apartment, had himself died in the arms of her erstwhile best friend Mona—his live-in girlfriend of almost thirty years.

SHAKESPEARE SAYS: BY indirections find directions out. The only way I could tell this story, could disentangle the mysteries, was to write it at a slant. This book is a hybrid: half memoir and half make-believe. The true story of this celebrity everyone adores, the true story of my own people, and the passionate and fictionalized sexual affair they reveled in and suffered from.

That isn't to say I wrote a book involved only with private matters or that followed the story of my family at all its twists. I used the facts of the family only as the firm ground on which I could find my feet. The steps I took from there were my own.

This book is a novel, at bottom, because—for those of us who love literature—it's fiction that best addresses difficult realities; it's fiction where individual concerns can be made to feel universal. When you write nonfiction, especially about your family, sometimes you have to withdraw from the thorniest parts of a story. Maybe feelings need to be spared; maybe some of the truth can't be known. But a novel can elbow the facts toward literature's own idea of truth, which is something else entirely.

I have to admit I fell in love, a little, with Lucille Ball in writing this novel. The woman in these pages is *my* Lucille Ball, however—an imagined Lucille who makes no claims to the Lucille who thrived outside of these hard covers. Again, I do think fiction is the best way to write someone like her. You stand in the shadow on the low bench of your imagination, looking up at the towering and sun-dappled peaks of Mt. Lucille, just glad you can see up to the top. Still, as you return to your writing desk, you keep sneaking a glance over your shoulder at the heights of that soaring, real-life woman.

Lucille was so charismatic, she took over the novel.

Lucille Ball has become so ubiquitous, it's hard to get a clear view of her—not to mention that our country is now so fragmented, you can't imagine anyone ever again reaching from the screen and into each American living room. I hope the book will help remind people that Lucille Ball starred in America's first big-time interracial love story; was the first powerful woman in Hollywood; that she owned more movie sets at one point than did any movie studio. It was an honor to be in her presence for a few years. A number of nonfiction books helped me build my version of her: *I Loved Lucy: My Friendship with Lucille Ball* by Lee Tannen; *Lucy & Ricky & Fred & Ethel: The Story of I Love Lucy* by

Bart Andrews; *Ball of Fire: The Tumultuous Life and Comic Art of Lucille Ball* by Stefan Kanfer; *Desilu: The Story of Lucille Ball and Desi Arnaz* by Coyne Steven Sanders and Tom Gilbert; *Lucille* by Kathleen Brady, which provided the basis for the interaction among Lucille, Desi, Danny Kaye, and the fictional Kseniya Resnick; *Laughs, Luck . . . and Lucy* by Jess Oppenheimer; and *Love, Lucy* by Lucille Ball herself.

I am aware that there are some anomalies here. I know, for instance, that G.I. Joe dolls did not exist in 1951. But—as my mentor and eventual colleague E. L. Doctorow once told a woman who complained that one of his novels featured a genus of cactus thriving in Arizona, even though that particular genus couldn't be found in Arizona—"And yet it is there in *my* Arizona, madam." Similarly, *I Love Lucy* ran on Monday nights everywhere but my 1950s.

Oh, and Lucille never knew John Archer or Nanette Fabray, as far as I can tell.

Regarding my grandfather, I wanted to try to learn more about this man who was rich before I was born and who died with very little. Who radiated kindness and was a beloved figure in my family— even after having done some questionable things.

My first novel, though its subject matter was much less personal to me, had also been a fiction based—in some part—on truth. In talking with the descendants of the heroes of *that* book, I was reminded that the differences between biography and novel can seem esoteric, and while I hold them precious, a book is merely a book; a family is sacred. And so, some clarifications.

My uncle Arthur is not "duller" than my father. In fact, he's charming and kind and a brilliant lawyer. Moreover, my grandparents, IRL, had two more children—my uncle Emanuel and aunt Fran. Both of them are wonderful people, but my editor thought they were superfluous to this narrative. Sorry, guys. I love you.

Still, I will likely piss off some relatives with this one, and maybe Lucille's relatives, too. But though I changed a lot of facts—down to the year of Fred Trump's Coney Island party, even the birth year for Desi Arnaz Jr.—it is my profound hope that I haven't done the memory of any of these people anything that approaches dishonor.

ACKNOWLEDGMENTS

WRITING BOOKS IS hard; writing an acknowledgment page is easy. At least in theory it is. You know who helped you, and therefore whom to thank. What's impossible is doing justice to those helping people. But here goes.

First, Susan Kamil—the late Susan Kamil, unbearable as that is to say. Susan died, suddenly, as we were finishing up the final work on this book. She was a legendary editor and champion, and this novel is the last to bear her stamp. I'm very proud of this book, but that's an honor of which I don't feel worthy. Thanks, too, to the truly great Andrea Walker, who stepped into a difficult situation and was magnificent, advocative, and just plain cool. I really hope she and I work together for a long time, on a lot of books.

Thanks of course and forever to my wife, Susannah Meadows. For the multiple reads, the nights of enduring my bellyaching, for being my ambassador to the world outside our house, just for being yourself—thanks. Susannah both keeps our family running and is a brilliant writer/editor/journalist in her own right. This book—no joke—was originally twice as long, and had a second plotline, which now lives nowhere but my memory. That's thanks to Susannah and Susan.

Thank you to my agent, Suzanne Gluck, who is the toughest tiny person you'll ever meet, and is nice to boot. (And who never-theless allowed me to write her into this novel.) Thank you, too, to her assistant, Andrea Blatt, who is very hands-on and probably won't be assistant to anyone by the time you read this.

(Of note, perhaps, to coincidence buffs: the names of these women who helped the book so much: two Andreas, a Susan, a Suzanne, and a Susannah. There is a maxim: "Coincidences mean you're on the right path." Sounds cool, though I'm likelier to believe G. K. Chesterton: "Coincidences are just spiritual puns." Either way: odd.)

I want to thank friends who have done one of the kindest things anyone can do for someone else—read the early drafts of a person you're not related to, and not for money. Jeff Giles, Adam Dalva, Matt Thomas, Joshua Ferris, thank you very much. Thank you to the rest of the team at Random House, all of whom have been kind and smart and great: the hardworking and creative Rachel Rokicki, Avideh Bashirrad, Jessica Bonet, Claire Strickland (who was once my student, and is now a trusted colleague), and Emma Caruso. Thanks to Andy Ward for being a part of it as well—attending meetings, overseeing the endeavor, and acting as a benign presence over everything. Thanks to Deborah Landau, at NYU, for running the writing department in such a way that allowed me the time to work on this book.

Also, thanks to Hunter College's Hertog program, and its administrator, Gabriel Packard, who pairs established writers with researchers, free of charge. Those wonderful helpers were Leilani Zee, Kim Lester, Jeannie Venasco, Christopher Fox, and Clare Needham. These are all not just researchers—each of them is a great young writer, and has my eternal gratitude.

Thanks of course to my family: my parents, Ellen and Bernie Strauss—my mom for reading and offering (surprisingly harsh) notes, and my dad for allowing me to write about his father, and for supplying me with stories to help me do it. Thank you to my grandparents, Isidore and Harriet Strauss, two complex and interesting and, in their own way, kind and superb people whose lives I tried to honor here. (I was also going to thank Lucille Ball, but that seems presumptuous—she doesn't need my thanks, or anything, really.)

And to my sons, Beau and Shepherd, great people and friends, who say they don't want to read this, but who, I have a feeling, will change their minds one day.

Photo: © Robert Birnbaum

ABOUT THE AUTHOR

DARIN STRAUSS is the bestselling author of the novels *Chang & Eng, The Real McCoy, More Than It Hurts You,* and *The Queen of Tuesday,* the memoir *Half a Life,* and (with Adam Dalva) a graphic novel and comic book series centered on the character Olivia Twist. He is the winner of numerous prizes, including most recently a National Book Critics Circle Award, and his work has appeared in fourteen languages and nineteen countries. He is a clinical professor at New York University.

Facebook.com/darin.strauss
Twitter: @darinstrauss

To inquire about booking Darin Strauss for a speaking engagement, please contact the Penguin Random House Speakers Bureau at speakers@penguinrandomhouse.com.

ABOUT THE TYPE

This book was set in Bembo, a typeface based on an old-style Roman face that was used for Cardinal Pietro Bembo's tract *De Aetna* in 1495. Bembo was cut by Francesco Griffo (1450–1518) in the early sixteenth century for Italian Renaissance printer and publisher Aldus Manutius (1449–1515). The Lanston Monotype Company of Philadelphia brought the well-proportioned letterforms of Bembo to the United States in the 1930s.